Desert

HEARTS

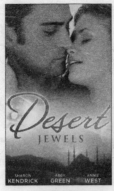

April 2014

May 2014

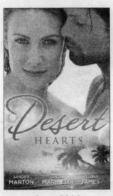

June 2014

July 2014

Desert
HEARTS

SANDRA MARTON
CAROL MARINELLI
MELISSA JAMES

MILLS & BOON

Published in Great Britain 2014
by Mills & Boon, an imprint of Harlequin (UK) Limited,
Eton House, 18-24 Paradise Road, Richmond, Surrey, TW9 1SR

DESERT HEARTS © 2014 Harlequin Books S.A.

Sheikh Without a Heart © 2012 Sandra Marton
Heart of the Desert © 2011 Carol Marinelli
The Sheikh's Destiny © 2010 Lisa Chaplin

ISBN: 978 0 263 24651 3

011-0614

Harlequin (UK) Limited's policy is to use papers that are natural, renewable and recyclable products and made from wood grown in sustainable forests. The logging and manufacturing processes conform to the legal environmental regulations of the country of origin.

Printed and bound in Spain
by Blackprint CPI, Barcelona

Sheikh Without a Heart

SANDRA MARTON

Sandra Marton wrote her first novel while she was still in infant school. Her doting parents told her she'd be a writer someday and Sandra believed them. In senior school and college, she wrote dark poetry nobody but her boyfriend understood, though looking back she suspects he was just being kind. As a wife and mother, she wrote murky short stories in what little spare time she could manage, but not even her boyfriend-turned-husband could pretend to understand those. Sandra tried her hand at other things, among them teaching and serving on the board of education in her home town, but the dream of becoming a writer was always in her heart.

At last Sandra realised she wanted to write books about what all women hope to find: love with that one special man, love that's rich with fire and passion, love that lasts forever. She wrote a novel, her very first, and sold it to Mills & Boon. Since then, she's written more than seventy books, all of them featuring sexy, gorgeous, larger-than-life heroes. A four-time RITA® Award finalist, she has also received an *RT Book Reviews* Career Achievement Award for Series Romance. Sandra lives with her very own sexy, gorgeous, larger-than-life hero in a sun-filled house on a quiet country lane in the north-eastern United States.

Sandra loves to hear from her readers. You can contact her through her website www.sandramarton.com or at PO Box 295, Storrs, CT 06268, USA.

CHAPTER ONE

IT WAS the kind of night that made a man long to ride his favorite stallion across a sea of desert sand.

Black silk sky. Stars as brilliant as bonfires. An ivory moon that cast a milky glow over the endless sea of sand.

But there was no horse beneath Sheikh Karim al Safir. Not on this night. His Royal Highness the Prince of Alcantar, heir to its Ancient and Honorable throne, was twenty-five thousand feet above the desert, soaring through the darkness in the cabin of his private jet. A rapidly-cooling cup of coffee stood on a small glass-topped table beside him; his leather attaché case lay open on the next seat.

Minutes ago he'd started to go through its contents until he'd suddenly thought, what the hell was the point?

He knew what was in the case.

He'd gone through the contents endlessly during the last two weeks and then again tonight, flying from the British West Indies toward his final destination, as if doing so would somehow make more sense of things when he knew damned well that was not going to happen.

Karim reached for the cup of coffee and brought it to his lips. The black liquid had gone from cool to chilly.

He drank it anyway.

He needed it. The bitterness, the punch of caffeine. He

needed something, God knew, to keep him going. He was exhausted. In body. In mind.

In spirit.

If only he could walk to the cockpit, tell his pilot to put the plane down. Here. Right now. On the desert below.

Crazy, of course.

It was just that he ached for the few moments of tranquility he might find if he could take only one long, deep breath of desert air.

Karim snorted. His head was full of crazy thoughts tonight.

For all he knew, there would never be a sense of peace to be drawn from this land.

This was not the desert of his childhood. Alcantar was thousands of miles away and its endless miles of gently undulating sand ended at the turquoise waters of the Persian Sea.

The desert over which his plane was flying ended at the eye-popping neon lights of Las Vegas.

Karim drank more cold coffee.

Las Vegas.

He had been there once. An acquaintance had tried to convince him to invest in a hotel being built there. He'd flown to McCarran field early in the morning—

And flown back to New York that same night.

He had not put his money into the hotel—or, rather, his fund's money. And he'd never returned to Vegas.

He'd found the city tawdry. Seedy. Even its much-hyped glamour had struck him as false, like a whore trying to pass herself off as a courtesan by applying garish layers of make-up.

So, no. Las Vegas was not a city for him—but it had been one for his brother.

Rami had spent almost three months there, longer than

he'd spent anywhere else the past few years. He'd have been drawn to it like a moth to flame.

Karim sat back in his leather seat.

Knowing all he now knew about his brother, that came as no surprise.

He'd finally had to face the truth about him. Tying up the loose ends of his dead brother's life had torn away the final illusions.

Tying up loose ends, Karim thought.

His mouth twisted.

That was his father's phrase. What he was really doing was cleaning up the messes Rami had left behind, but then, his father didn't know about those. The King believed his younger son had simply been unable or unwilling to settle down, that he'd traveled from place to place in an endless search to find himself.

The first time his father had said those words Karim had almost pointed out that finding oneself was a luxury denied princes. They had duties to assume, obligations to keep from childhood on.

Except Rami had been exempted from such things. He'd always had a wild streak, always found ways to evade responsibility.

"You're the heir, brother," he used to tell Karim, a grin on his handsome face. "I'm only the spare."

Perhaps adherence to a code of duty and honor would have kept Rami from such an early and ugly death, but it was too late for speculation. He was gone, his throat slit on a frigid Moscow street.

When the news had come, Karim had felt an almost unbearable grief. He'd hoped that "tying up the loose ends" of his brother's life would provide some kind of meaning to it and, thus, closure.

He drew a long breath, then let it out.

Now, the best he could do was hope that he had somehow removed the stain from his brother's name, that those Rami had cheated would no longer speak that name with disgust…

Cheated?

Karim almost laughed.

His brother had gambled. Whored. He'd ingested a pharmacopoeia's worth of illicit drugs. He'd borrowed money and never repaid it. He'd given chits to casinos around the world, walked out on huge hotel bills.

The bottom line was that he'd left behind staggering debts in half a dozen cities. Singapore. Moscow. Paris. Rio. Jamaica. Las Vegas.

All those debts had to be settled—if not for legal reasons then for moral ones.

Duty. Obligation. Responsibility.

All the things Rami had scoffed at were now Karim's burden.

So he had embarked on a pilgrimage, if you could use such a word to describe this unholy journey. He had handed over checks to bankers, to casino managers, to boutique owners. He'd paid out obscene amounts of cash to oily men in grimy rooms. He'd heard things about his brother, seen things that he suspected he would never forget, no matter how he tried.

Now, with most of the "loose ends" gone, his ugly journey through Rami's life was almost over.

Two days in Vegas. Three at the most. It was why he was flying in at night. Why waste part of tomorrow on travel when he could, instead, spend it doing the remaining clean-up chores?

After that he would return to Alcantar, assure his father that Rami's affairs were all in order without ever divulging the details. Then, at last, he could go back to his own life, to New York, to his responsibilities as head of the Alcantar Foundation.

He could put all this behind him, the reminders of a brother he'd once loved, a brother who'd lost his way—

"Your Highness?"

Karim bit back a groan. His flight crew was small and efficient. Two pilots, one flight attendant—but this attendant was new and still visibly thrilled to be on the royal staff.

She knew only what everyone else knew: that the duty of settling his brother's affairs had fallen to him. He assumed she misread his tight-lipped silence for grief when the truth was that his pain warred with rage.

It was difficult to know which emotion had the upper hand.

"Sir?"

As if all that weren't enough, she couldn't seem to absorb the fact that he hated being hovered over.

"Yes, Miss Sterling?"

"It's Moira, sir, and we'll be landing within the hour."

"Thank you," he said politely.

"Is there anything I can do for you before then?"

Could she turn back the calendar and return his brother to life so he could shake some sense into him?

Better still, could she bring back the carefree, laughing Rami from their childhood?

"Thank you, I'm fine."

"Yes, Your Highness—but if you should change your mind—"

"I'll ring."

The girl did a little knee-bob that was not quite the curtsy he was sure his chief of staff had warned her against.

"Most certainly, Your Highness."

Another dip of the knee and then, mercifully, she walked back up the aisle and disappeared into the galley.

He'd have to remember to have his chief of staff remind

her that the world was long past the time when people bowed to royalty.

Hell.

Karim laid his head back against the head-rest.

The girl was only doing what she saw as her duty. He, better than anyone, understood that.

He had been raised to honor his obligations. His father and mother had instilled that in him from childhood on.

His father had been and still was a stern man, a king first and a father second.

His mother had been a sometime movie-star-*cum*-Boston-debutante with great beauty, impeccable manners and, ultimately, a burning need to spend her life as far from her husband and sons as possible.

She'd hated Alcantar. The hot days, the cool nights, the wind that could whip the sea of sand into a blinding froth...

She'd despised it all.

In some of his earliest memories of her he stood clutching a nanny's hand, holding back tears because a prince was not permitted to cry, watching as his beautiful mother drove off in a limousine.

Rami had looked just like her. Tall. Fair-haired. Intense blue eyes.

Karim, on the other hand, was an amalgam of both his parents.

In him, his mother's blue eyes and his father's brown ones had somehow morphed into ice-gray. He had her high cheekbones and firmly-sculpted mouth, but his build—broad shoulders, long legs, hard, leanly muscled body—he owed to his father.

Rami had favored her in other ways. He hadn't hated Alcantar but he'd always preferred places of sybaritic comfort.

Karim, on the other hand, could not remember a time he had not loved his desert homeland.

He'd grown up in his father's palace, built on a huge oasis at the foot of the Great Wilderness Mountains. His companions were Rami and the sons of his father's ministers and advisors.

By the age of seven he'd been able to ride a horse bareback, start a fire with kindling and flint, sleep as contentedly under the cold fire of the stars as if he were in the elaborate palace nursery.

Even then, twenty-six years ago, only a handful of Alcantaran tribesmen had still lived that kind of life, but the King had deemed it vital to understand and respect it.

"One day," he would say to Karim, "you will rule our people and they must know that you understand the old ways." Always there would be a pause, and then he would look at Rami and say, not unkindly, "You must respect the people and the old ways as well, my son, even though you will not sit on the throne."

Had that been the turning point for his brother? Karim wondered. Or had it come when their mother died and their father, mourning her even though she had spent most of her time far from him and her children, had thrown himself ever deeper into the business of governance and sent his sons away?

He sent them to the United States, to be educated, he said, as their mother would have wished.

With terrifying suddenness the brothers had found themselves in what seemed an alien culture. They'd both been brutally homesick, though for different reasons.

Rami had longed for the luxuries of the palace.

Karim had longed for the endless sky of the desert.

Rami had coped by cutting classes and taking up with a bunch of kids who went from one scrape to another. He'd barely made it through prep school and had been admitted to a small college in California where he'd majored in women and cards, and in promises that he never kept.

Karin had coped by burying himself in his studies. He'd finished preparatory school with honors and had been admitted to Yale, where he'd majored in finance and law. At twenty-six he'd created a private investment fund for the benefit of his people and managed it himself instead of turning it over to a slick-talking Wall Street wizard.

Rami had taken a job in Hollywood. Assistant to a B-list producer, assistant to this and assistant that—all of it dependent upon his looks, his glib line of patter and his title.

At thirty, when he'd come into a trust left him by their mother, he'd given up any pretense at work and instead had done what she had done.

He'd traveled the world.

Karim had tried to talk to him. Not once. Not twice. Many, many times. He'd spoken of responsibility. Of duty. Of honor.

Rami's reply had always been the same, and always delivered with a grin.

"Not me," he'd say. "I'm just the spare, not the heir."

After a while they hadn't seen much of each other. And now—

Now Rami was dead.

Dead, Karim thought.

His belly knotted.

His brother's body had been flown home from Moscow and laid to rest with all the panoply befitting a prince.

Their father had stood stiffly at his grave.

"How did he die?" he'd asked Karim.

And Karim, seeing how fragile the older man had become, had lied.

"An automobile accident," he'd told him.

It was almost true.

All he'd left out was that Rami had evidently met with his cocaine dealer, something had gone wrong, the man had slit his throat and a dying Rami had wandered into the path of an oncoming car.

And why go over it again? The death was old news. Soon "tying up loose ends" would be old news, too.

One last stop. A handful of things to sort out—

A dull rumble vibrated through the plane. The landing gear was being deployed. As if on signal, the flight attendant materialized at the front of the cabin.

Karim waved her off. He wasn't in the mood for her misplaced look of compassion. All he wanted was to put this mess behind him.

Moments later, they landed.

He rose to his feet and reached for his attaché case. Inside it was what he thought of as the final folder. It held letters from three hotels, expressing sympathy on Rami's death and reminders that he had run up considerable bills in their casinos and shops.

There was also a small envelope that contained a key and a slip of paper with an address scrawled on it in Rami's hand.

Had he considered putting down some kind of roots here?

Not that it mattered, Karim thought grimly. It was too late for roots or anything else that might have resembled a normal life.

He'd get an early start tomorrow, pay his brother's bills, then locate the place that went with the key, pay whatever was due—because surely the rent was in arrears despite the lack of a dunning letter.

And then all this would be behind him.

His chief of staff had arranged for a rental car and for a suite at one of the city's big hotels.

The car had a GPS; Karim selected the name of the hotel from a long list and drove toward the city.

It was close to one in the morning, but when he reached the Las Vegas Strip it blazed with light. Shops were open; people were everywhere. There was a frenzy to the place, a kind of circus atmosphere of gaiety Karim didn't quite buy into.

At the hotel, a valet took his car. Karim handed the kid a twenty-dollar bill, said he was fine with carrying his own things, and headed into the lobby.

The metallic sounds of slot machines assaulted his ears.

He made his way to the reception desk through a crowd of shrieking and laughing revelers. The clerk who greeted him was pleasant and efficient, and soon Karim was in an elevator, on his way to the tenth floor along with two women and a man. The man stood with an arm around each of the women; one had her hand on his chest, the other had her tongue in his ear.

The elevator doors whisked open. Karim stepped out.

The sooner he finished his business here, the better.

His suite, at least, was big and surprisingly attractive.

Within minutes he'd stripped off his clothes and stepped into the shower. He let the hot water beat down on his neck and shoulders, hoping that would drive away some of the weariness.

It didn't.

Okay. What he needed was sleep.

But sleep didn't come. No surprise. After two weeks of coming into cities he knew would hold yet additional ugly truths about his brother, sleep had become more and more elusive.

After a while, he gave up.

He had to do something. Take a walk. A drive. Check out the hotels where Rami had run up enormous bills—this place, he had made certain, was not one of them. Maybe he'd drive by the flat his brother had leased. He could even stop, go inside, take a quick look around.

Not that he expected to find anything worth keeping, but if there was something personal, a memento that said something good about Rami's wasted life, their father might want it.

Karim put on jeans, a black T-shirt, sneakers and a soft black leather bomber jacket. Deserts were cold at night, even ones that arrowed into the heart of a city whose glow could be seen for miles.

He opened his attaché case, grabbed the key and noted the scribbled address. A tag that read "4B" hung from the key itself. An apartment number, obviously.

The valet brought him his car. Karim handed him another twenty. Then he entered the address into the GPS and followed its directions.

Fifteen minutes later, he reached his destination.

It was a nondescript building in a part of the city that was as different from the Las Vegas he'd so far seen as night from day.

The area was bleak and shabby, as was the building itself…

Karim frowned. He'd connected to global positioning satellites often enough to know that when they worked they were great and when they didn't you could end up in the middle of nowhere.

Yes, but this was the correct address.

Had Rami run out of the ability to talk himself into the best hotels at some point during his time here?

There was only one way to find out.

Karim got out of the car, locked it, and headed toward the building.

The outside door was unlocked. The vestibule stank. The

stairs creaked; he stepped in something sticky and tried not to think about what it might be.

One flight. Two. Three, and there it was, straight ahead. Apartment 4B, even though the "4" hung drunkenly to the side and the "B" was upside down.

Karim hesitated.

Did he really want to do this tonight? Was he up to what was surely going to be a dirty hovel? He remembered the time he'd flown out to the coast to visit Rami when he was in school. Dirty dishes in the sink and all over the counters. Spoiled food in the refrigerator. Clothes spilling out of the hamper.

"Goddammit," he said, under his breath.

The truth was, he didn't give a crap about the apartment being dirty. What mattered was that it would be filled with Rami's things. The hotel rooms had not been; the hotels had all removed his brother's clothes, his toiletries, and put them in storage.

This would be different.

And he was a coward.

"A damned coward," he said, and he stepped purposefully forward, stabbed the key into the lock, turned it—

The door swung open.

The first thing he noticed was the smell—not of dirt but of something pleasant. Sugar? Cookies?

Milk?

The second thing was that he wasn't alone. There was someone standing maybe ten feet away…

Not someone.

A woman. She stood with her back to him, tall and slender and—

And naked.

His eyes swept over her. Her hair was a spill of pale gold down her shoulders; her spine was long and graceful. She had a narrow waist that emphasized the curve of her hips and incredibly long legs.

Legs as long as sin.

Hell. Wrong building. Wrong apartment. Wrong—

The woman spun around. She wasn't naked. She wore a thing that was barely a bra, covered in spangles. And a thong—a tiny triangle of glittery silver.

It was a cheap outfit that made the most of a beautiful body, though her face was even more beautiful…

And what did that matter at moment like this, when he had obviously wandered into the wrong place…and, dammit, her eyes were wide with terror?

Karim held up his hands.

"It's all right," he said quickly. "I made a mistake. I thought—"

"I know precisely what you thought, you—you pervert," the woman said, and before he could react she flew at him, a blur of motion with something in her hand.

It was a shoe. A shoe with a heel as long and sharp as a stiletto.

"Hey!" Karim danced back. "Listen to me. I'm trying to tell you some—"

She slammed the shoe against him, aiming for his face, but he moved fast; the blow caught him in the shoulder. He grabbed her wrist and dragged her hand to her side.

"Will you wait a minute? Just one damned minute—"

"Wait?" Rachel Donnelly said. "*Wait?*" The perv from the lounge wanted her to wait? Wait so he could rape her? "The hell I will," she snarled, and she wrenched her hand free of his, swung hard…

This time, the heel of the shoe flashed by his face.

That was the good news.

The bad was that he muttered something and now he wasn't defending himself; he was coming straight for her.

Panting, she reacted with all her strength, but he was too big, too strong, too determined. A second later he had both her wrists in his hands and she was pinned against the wall.

"Dammit, woman! Will you listen to me?"

"There's nothing to listen to. I know what you want. You were in the lounge tonight. I brought you drink after drink and I knew you were going to be trouble and I was right, here you are, and—and—"

Her breath caught.

Wrong.

This wasn't the guy who'd undressed her with his eyes.

That perv had been bald with squinty eyes behind Coke-bottle lenses.

This guy had a full head of dark hair and eyes the cool gray of winter ice.

Not that it mattered. He'd broken into her apartment. He was male. She was female. After three years in Vegas she knew what that—

"You're wrong."

She blinked. Either she'd spoken aloud or he was a mind-reader.

"I'm not here to hurt you."

"Then turn around and go away. Right now. I won't scream, I won't call the cops—"

"Will you listen? One of us is in the wrong apartment."

Despite everything, she choked out a laugh. The man scowled and tightened his hold on her wrists.

"What I'm trying to tell you is that I didn't expect anyone to be here. I thought this was my brother's apartment."

"Well, it isn't. This apartment is—is—" She stared at him. "What brother?"

"My brother. Rami."

The floor seemed to shift under Rachel's feet. She felt the

blood drain from her face. The man saw it; those cold gray eyes narrowed.

"You know of him?"

She knew. Of course she knew. And if this was Rami's brother—if this was Karim of Alcantar, the all-powerful, stone-hearted, ruthless prince…

"I'm going to let go of you," he said. "If you scream, you will regret it. Is that clear?"

Rachel swallowed hard. "Yes."

Slowly, carefully, his eyes locked to hers, he took his hands from her.

"Obviously," he said, "I was correct. This place *is* my brother's."

"I—I—"

"You—you, what?" he growled with imperial impatience. "What are you doing here? This apartment belongs to Rami."

It didn't. It never had. It was hers and always had been—though that hadn't stopped first Suki and then Suki's lover from moving in.

Now, thank goodness, they were both gone. She lived alone…

Oh, God!

Her heart, already racing, went into overdrive.

She didn't. She didn't live here alone—

"Who are you?" the man growled.

Who, indeed? Her head was spinning. She should have known this would happen, that, sooner or later someone would come.

His hand shot out and manacled her wrist.

"Answer the question! Who are you? What are you doing here?"

"I—I'm a friend," Rachel said. And then, because she

had no idea what this man knew or didn't know or, most of all, what he wanted, she said, "I'm Rami's friend. His very good friend."

CHAPTER TWO

KARIM'S mouth thinned.

Friend, hell.

She'd been Rami's woman.

His mistress. His girlfriend. Whatever she'd been, for once in his life Rami had apparently fallen for a woman who wasn't his usual type.

He'd been into flash. This woman's costume, whatever you called it, was flashy, and yet somehow or other she was not. There was something removed about her, something in those dark blue eyes that said, *Be careful how you deal with me.*

Perhaps that had appealed to Rami. The challenge of getting past the invisible barricade around her. Maybe that had made up for the fact that she didn't speak in breathy little sentences or flutter her lashes.

Rami had been a sucker for nonsense like that.

Karim couldn't imagine this woman doing either.

She was tough. Hell, she was fearless.

Any other woman would have screamed for help. Run shrieking into the night. Or, at the very least, begged an intruder for mercy.

She'd come at him with a weapon.

A rather unusual weapon, he thought with wry amusement. The stiletto-heeled shoe lay on the floor next to him; its mate lay a few feet away. The thing could have done real damage, considering that the heels had to be four or five inches high.

"Stilettos are torture," a mistress had once admitted, but she'd worn them anyway.

He knew the reason.

Women wore them because they knew damned well that men loved the look those high, thin heels gave to a female body: the slight forward tilt of the pelvis, the added length of leg.

Not that Rami's woman needed anything to make her legs look longer.

Even now, they seemed endless.

She had stockings on. Hose. Whatever you called sheer black mesh that drew his eyes up and up to where the mesh disappeared beneath that thong.

With stilettos or without them she was a fantastic sight. Sleek. Sexy. All woman.

Why deny it?

She was beautiful, and he was sure it was natural. He'd seen enough women who'd been surgically and chemically enhanced until they were little more than mannequins.

Cheekbones implanted. Lips injected. Foreheads all but immobilized and, worst of all, breasts that looked and felt like balloons instead of soft, warm flesh.

This woman's breasts would feel just right in a man's hands. The nipples would taste sweet on his tongue…

Karim felt his body stir.

Hell. He'd been too long without sex. Why else would he react to her? She was beautiful, but she was—she had been Rami's.

Besides, he liked his women to be…well, at least somewhat demure.

He was a sheikh from an ancient kingdom, a culture still

learning to accept some modern concepts about women, but he was also a man of the twenty-first century. He had been educated in the west.

He believed in male-female equality, yes, but some degree of diffidence was still a good thing in a woman. He doubted if this particular woman would even understand the concept.

Karim frowned.

What did any of that matter? Rami was dead. And it was time to get down to business. Tell her that her lover was gone—and that she had until the end of the month to vacate the flat.

She'd said it was hers, but surely only by default. She was here; Rami wasn't.

Still, he'd write her a generous check. It was the right thing to do. Then, tomorrow—today, he thought, glancing at his watch and seeing that it was past six in the morning—he'd make good on the rest of his brother's Las Vegas debts.

With luck, he'd be in Alcantar by the weekend. Then he'd return to Manhattan and get on with his life—

"Well?" the woman said sharply. "Say something. If you're really Rami's brother, what's your name? And what are you doing here?"

Karim blinked.

Indeed, that was the big question.

Did she know about her lover's death? He didn't think so. She spoke of him in the present tense.

Then what was the best way to tell her? Break it to her gently? Or just state the facts?

That might be the best way. Be direct. Get it over with.

For all her feminine looks—the mouth that reminded him of a rose petal, the up-thrust breasts, the gently curved hips—for all that, he couldn't imagine there was anything fragile about her.

She was still the picture of defiance, dark blue eyes flashing, chin raised, ready to fight.

He could change that in a heartbeat.

All he had to do was remind her that he held the upper hand.

And there was an easy way to do that.

He'd pull her into his arms, plunge one hand deep into that mass of silky gold hair, lift her face to his and take her mouth. She'd fight him, but only for a few seconds.

Then her skin would flush with desire. Her lips would part. She'd moan and surrender to him, and it wouldn't matter if her surrender was real or if she was playing a part because he'd carry her to the sofa, strip away the bra, the thong, the spiderweb stockings, and by then her moans would be not a lie because he would make her want him, open for him, move under him...

Dammit!

Karim turned away, pretended to study the wall, the floor, anything at all while he got his traitorous body under control.

No wonder Rami had kept this one, he thought as he swung toward her again.

"What is your name?" he said sharply.

"I asked first."

He almost laughed. She sounded like a kid squaring off for a schoolyard fight.

"Is it really that difficult to tell me who you are?"

He could almost hear her considering his request. Then she tossed her head.

"Rachel. Rachel Donnelly."

"Well, Rachel Donnelly, I am Karim." He folded his arms over his chest. "Perhaps Rami mentioned me."

Rachel struggled to hide her distress.

Her unwanted visitor had confirmed her worst fear.

Rami had, indeed, mentioned Karim. Not to her. He'd never said more than "hello" and "goodbye" to her—unless you counted the times he'd brushed past her and whispered how much he wanted to take her to bed.

Suki had told her all about Rami's brother.

Her sister had hated him, sight unseen.

Karim, Suki said, was the reason Rami had no money, the reason he would never be treated properly by their father, the King.

It was all because of him.

Karim.

Karim the Greedy. Karim the Arrogant. Karim the Prince, who had deliberately driven a wedge between Rami and his father. Karim the Prince, with no concern for anyone but himself, no greater wish than to stop anyone else from possibly inheriting even a piece of their father's fortune.

Karim, the Sheikh with no heart.

Rachel had not paid much attention to any of it until Rami and then Suki had taken off.

Rami had left first. No warning, no goodbye. One day he was here and the next he and his things were gone.

Suki, no surprise, had hung in as long as she had to. And when it had been okay for her to take off, she had.

All she'd left behind was a stack of unwashed clothes, a wisp of cheap perfume—

And the one thing that had never mattered to Rami or even Suki but only to Rachel.

After that, Rachel had begun to think about the man she'd never laid eyes on.

About what he knew. Or didn't know. About how he'd react if he ever learned of what Suki had left behind.

Still, she'd never expected him to turn up on her doorstep without warning.

From all Rami had told Suki, his brother traveled with a staff of sycophants and bodyguards…but here he was.

Alone.

And treating her with barely concealed contempt when he wasn't looking at her with lust in his wintry eyes.

Rachel knew that look.

A woman who wore an outfit like this, who served drinks in a casino, was fair game.

She hated everything about her job. The customers. The atmosphere. The clink of the chips.

This awful costume.

She'd balked at wearing it until her boss said, "You want the job? Do what you're told and stop bitching."

The girls she worked with were even more direct.

"You wanna be Miss High and Mighty," one of them told her, "go pick up dirty dishes at the all-the-pigs-can-eat buffet."

Rachel had already done a turn like that. You couldn't pay the rent and support Suki—because Suki certainly hadn't supported herself—you couldn't pay the rent or anything else with what she'd earned clearing tables.

So each day she gritted her teeth, hid herself inside this sleazy costume and went to work where men pretty much figured she was available for lots more than taking their drink orders.

She hated it, but then, that was how men were. No big surprise there.

Then Rami had moved in. After a few months, when she couldn't stand living with either him or Suki anymore, Rachel had confronted her sister and demanded she and her boyfriend find a place of their own.

Suki had burst into tears and said she couldn't do that. She was in trouble…

That "trouble" had changed everything.

Rachel could no more have tossed Suki out than she could have flown to the moon, and—and—

"Have you lost the ability to speak, Rachel Donnelly? I have no time to waste."

No time, Rachel thought, no time...

Oh, God!

She'd been so caught up in what was happening that she'd almost forgotten the hour.

The wall clock read six-fifteen.

She'd gotten off work two hours ago, same as always. Which meant that the reason she'd stayed in Vegas was going to turn up at the door in forty-five minutes.

She'd never been sure what she was going to do if and when this moment came.

She was sure now.

She was sure of something else, too.

Rami's brother knew nothing.

If he had, he'd have already demanded his rights to that which he surely would have seen as his.

"Such a fuss over wanting to know my name."

Rachel looked up. The Sheikh stood with his arms folded, a big, hard-faced, hard-bodied, cold-as-ice piece of work who just happened to look like a god.

Unfortunately for him she knew the truth: that he was a cold-hearted SOB who was an expert at manipulating people to see him as he wanted to be seen.

"Such a fuss," he said, his tone ripe with sarcasm, "and now you have nothing to say."

She squared her shoulders.

The thing to do was face him down and get him out of here.

"Actually, I just wanted to be sure. I'd already figured it out myself."

"Really?" he purred.

"Rami described you pretty accurately. Self-important. Arrogant. A despot. Yes, he got it right."

A hit. She saw a flush rise over those high cheekbones.

"You're a sheikh, aren't you? From Alashazam. Or Alcatraz. Something like that."

The imprints of color deepened. He took a step forward. Rachel fought the desire to retreat.

"Something like that," he said coldly.

"Well, Rami isn't here."

That brought a thin smile to his lips. Had she said something amusing?

"But I'll be sure and tell him you called. Now, Sheikh-Whatever-You're-Called, I'm busy. And—"

"I am called Prince Karim," Karim said stiffly. "Or Your Highness. Or I am addressed as Sheikh."

Damn. Was he actually saying this stuff? If there was anything he despised, it was the use of these outmoded titles, but this Rachel Donnelly brought out the worst in him.

"Yes, well, your Sheikhiness, I'll give Rami your message. Anything else?"

The way she'd combined his titles was an obviously deliberate insult. He wanted to grab her and shake her—

Or grab her and wipe that little smirk off her lips in a very different way—one that would change her demeanor altogether.

For all he knew, that was the reason she'd taunted him. A woman who looked like this would surely use sex to gain the upper hand.

He wasn't fool enough to let it happen.

"No?" she said brightly. "Is that it? Well, in that case, goodbye, good luck, and on your way out don't let the door slam you in the—"

"Rami is dead."

He had not intended to give her the news that abruptly but,

dammit, she'd driven him to it. Well, it was too late to call back his brusque words. He could only hope he'd assessed her correctly: that she was too tough to faint or—

"Dead?"

He'd guessed right. She wasn't the fainting type. Evidently she wasn't the weepy type, either. Her only reaction, as far as he could tell, was a slight widening of her eyes.

He was willing to be generous.

Perhaps she was in shock.

Karim nodded. "Yes. He died last month. An accident in—"

"Then why are you here?"

He had not really had the time to consider all her possible reactions to his news, but if he had, this—this removed curiosity would not have been on the list.

"That's it? I tell you your lover is dead and all you can say is, 'Why are you here?'"

"My lover?"

"The man who kept you," he said coldly. "Is that a better way to put it?"

"But Rami..."

Her voice trailed away. He could see her reassessing. Of course. She was trying to process the situation, determine what would do her the most good now that Rami was gone.

And he had been gone for a while.

She hadn't known he was dead but it had happened weeks ago, making that casual "I'll be sure and tell him you called" remark an obvious lie.

Why?

"But Rami...what?" Karim said coldly.

She shook her head. "Nothing. I mean, I just— I just—"

"He left you."

Rachel's mind was whirling and that blunt statement of fact only added to her confusion.

Rami was dead.

Did that make things worse? Did it make them better?

No. It changed nothing except to give her all the more reason to stay the course until she heard from Suki.

She gasped as Karim's hands closed on her arms.

"Why lie to me, Ms. Donnelly? We both know that my brother left you weeks ago."

Rachel looked up. She had never seen eyes more filled with contempt.

"Why ask me a question if you already know the answer?"

"What I know," Karim said, his mouth twisting, 'is that you don't give a damn that he's dead."

"You're hurting me!"

"How long did it take you to find his successor?"

She stared at him. "His—?"

"Another fool who'd keep you. Pay your bills. Buy what you're selling."

Her eyes flashed.

"Get out of my home!"

"Your home?" Karim raised her to her toes. "Rami paid the bills here. All you did was have the good fortune to warm his bed."

"If warming your brother's bed was an example of good fortune, heaven help us all!"

God, he wanted to shake her until she was dizzy!

Once, a very long time ago, he had loved his brother with all his heart.

They'd played together, told each other the secrets boys tell; they'd wept together at the news of their mother's death, bolstered each other's spirits the first weeks at boarding school in a strange new land.

That boy was only a memory… A memory that suddenly raised a storm of emotion Karim had kept hidden even from himself.

Now that emotion flooded through him, set loose by the coldness of a woman his brother had once cared for.

Karim had seen people show more sorrow at the sight of a deer dead on the road than Rachel Donnelly was showing now.

"Damn you," he growled. "Have you no feelings?"

Her eyes glittered with a burst of blue light.

"What a question, coming from a man like you!"

There was a red haze in front of his eyes. Karim cursed; his hands tightened on her.

"Let go of me!"

She slammed a fist against his shoulder. He caught both hands in one of his, immobilized them against his chest.

"Is that how you dealt with Rami?" he growled. "Did you drive him crazy, too?"

Mercilessly, he dragged her closer. Clasped her face in one big hand. Lowered his head toward hers…

And stopped.

What was he doing?

This was not him.

He was not the kind of man who'd force himself on a woman. Sex had nothing to do with anger.

No matter that she'd brought him to this, or that she was a grasping, heartless schemer. It didn't give him the right to treat her this way.

He let go of her. Took a step back. Cleared his throat.

"Miss Donnelly," he said carefully, "Rachel—"

"Get out!" Her voice shook; her eyes were enormous. "Did you hear me? Get out, get out, get—"

"Rachel?"

Karim swung toward the door. A woman, middle-aged, plump, pleasant-faced, looked from Rachel to him, then at Rachel again.

"Honey, is everything all right?"

Rachel didn't answer. Karim turned toward her. She'd
gone pale; he could see the swift rise and fall of her breasts.

"Mrs. Grey." Her voice was a hoarse whisper. She looked
at Karim, then at the woman in the doorway. "Mrs. Grey. If
you could just—if you could just come back a little later—"

"I thought it was him at first," Mrs. Grey said, frowning.
"Wrong hair color but same height, same way of standin'.
You know who I mean? That foreigner. Randy. Raymond.
Rasi. Whatever his name is."

"No." Rachel shook her head. "It isn't. Look, I hate to ask,
but if you would—"

"Just as well, if you ask me. Good-lookin' man, but any
fool could see right through him."

"Mrs. Grey." Rachel's voice was unnaturally high. "This—
this gentleman and I have some business to conclude and then
I'll—"

"Sorry, honey, but I'm runnin' late. Brought my daughter
along today. She's gonna work the mornin' shift and I have
to drop her off after I leave here. Save her takin' the bus, you
know, and…" Her eyes over to Karim again. "This a new
friend?"

"No," Karim said coldly, "I am not Miss Donnelly's
friend."

"Too bad. You look a nice sort. Not like that Rasi." The
woman shook her head. "Still, you'd think he'd come back,
do the right thing by—"

"Momma? Honestly, you move too fast for me. You was
up these stairs before I was half-started," a woman's voice
said with a little laugh.

A younger version of Mrs. Grey appeared beside her.

She had something in her arms.

A blanket? A bundle?

Karim's breath caught.

It was a child. An infant—and it reminded him of some-one. Someone from long, long ago.

"You'd think a man would want to do right for his very own son and his mama, wouldn't you?" Mrs. Grey said to Karim.

Rachel Donnelly, who had shown no emotion at all at the news of Rami's death, made a little sound. Karim tore his eyes from the baby and looked at her.

She was trembling.

Carefully, he reached for the child. Thanked the two women. Said something polite. Closed the door.

Stared down at the baby in his arms.

And saw perfectly miniaturized replicas of his brother's eyes. His brother's nose.

And Rachel Donnelly's mouth.

CHAPTER THREE

THE world stood still.

Such a trite phrase, Karim knew, but it took a conscious effort to draw air into his lungs.

What he was thinking was impossible.

This child had nothing to do with his brother.

Eye color. The shape of a nose. So what? There were only so many shades of blue in the world and only so many kinds of noses.

He took a deep breath.

Okay.

He'd been at this too long. That was the problem. He had certain routines. Rami had teased him unmercifully about how boring his life must be, but a routine was what kept a man grounded.

Up at six, half an hour in his private gym, shower, dress, coffee and toast at seven, at his desk by eight.

He'd been away from that schedule for too long, flying almost non-stop from city to city, seeing all the unpleasant details of his brother's life unfold.

It was having an effect.

If Rami had fathered a child, he'd have known.

They were brothers. Out of touch, but surely a man would not keep something like that to himself...

"Blaa," the baby said, "blaa-blaa-blaa."

Karim stared down at the child.

Blah, indeed.

Of course Rami would have kept it to himself—the same as he'd never mentioned his gambling debts.

You didn't talk about your mistakes—and the birth of a child out of wedlock was a mistake.

Rami had scoffed at convention, but under it all he'd known he was the son of a king and, after Karim, next in line to the throne.

There were certain rules of behavior that applied, even to him.

News of an illegitimate child would have resulted in a scandal back home. Their father might have completely cut off his younger son, even banished him from the kingdom.

So, yes. The child was Rami's, and it was illegitimate. There had not been a marriage certificate among his brother's papers. There'd been lots of other stuff. Expired drivers' licenses. Outdated checkbooks. Scribbled notes and, of course, endless bills and IOUs.

Nothing that even hinted at a wife.

Rachel Donnelly stood before him, as frozen as a marble statue, her eyes locked on the child in his arms.

No. Rami had not married her. Drunk or not, he surely would have known better than to tie himself permanently to a woman like this.

She was a woman a man bedded, not wedded, Karim thought, without even a hint of humor.

Beautiful.

Fiery.

Tough as nails.

His brother might have found all that spirit and defiance sexy.

He did not and would not. But this wasn't about him.

"Give me the baby."

Her voice was low, a little thready, but the color had come back into her face. She was regaining her composure.

Why had she reacted with such distress?

If this was Rami's child, this could be a golden opportunity. Her lover's child and her lover's brother, coming face to face…

"Give me the baby!"

He wondered why she hadn't tried to contact him before this. Well, that was obvious. She'd thought Rami would come back to her.

Was this the reason he'd left her? Because she'd become pregnant?

It was an ugly thought, that his brother would have abandoned his own child, but nothing about Rami surprised him anymore.

Assuming, of course, the child was his.

How had his brother let this happen? Drunk or sober, how could he have forgotten to use a condom?

Had the woman seduced him into forgetting? That was always a possibility.

Karim wasn't naïve. A man who was born to a title and a fortune learned early how things went.

Women set snares; his own mother had been pregnant with him before his father had married her.

He wasn't supposed to know that, but any fool could count. And once he'd figured it out he'd had a better idea of why his parents' marriage had failed.

You chose a wife—especially if you had the responsibilities of a prince—because she met certain criteria. Common interests and backgrounds. Common goals and expectations.

You *chose* her; you didn't put yourself in a position where fate or expediency or, even worse, a foolish night of passion became the deciding factor—

A small fist hit his shoulder. Karim blinked in surprise.

The woman had moved right up to him. Her eyes flashed with anger.

"Are you deaf? Give—me—the—baby!"

The child made an unhappy sound. Its mouth, that mouth that was the image of hers, began to tremble.

Karim narrowed his eyes.

"Whose child is this?"

"What is this? An interrogation? Give Ethan to me and then get the hell out!"

"Ethan?"

Dammit, Rachel thought, she hadn't intended to give him anything—not even the baby's name.

"Yes. And he's wary of strangers."

Karim's mouth twisted. "Was he wary of my brother?"

"I'd tell you that you've overstayed your welcome, Your Sheikhiness, but you were not welcome here in the first place."

"Do not," Karim said grimly, "call me that."

He regretted the words even as he said them. It was a mistake to let her know she was annoying him because that was damned well what she wanted to do.

"I'll ask you again," he said, struggling to control his temper. "Who does this child belong to?"

"He belongs to himself. Unlike you and your countrymen, Americans don't believe people can be owned like property."

"A charming speech. I'm sure it will win applause on your Fourth of July holiday. But it hasn't got a damned thing to do with my question. Once again, then. Whose child is this?"

Rachel chewed on her lip.

Whose, indeed?

Suki and Rami had created Ethan.

But from the very beginning he'd been hers.

For Suki, the bump in her belly had been a nine-month

annoyance, especially once she'd realized she couldn't use her pregnancy to convince Rami to marry her.

He'd packed his things and taken off well before Ethan's birth.

It had been Rachel who'd held Suki's hand during labor, Rachel who'd cut the baby's umbilical cord.

When Suki and her son had come home from the hospital, the baby had cried endlessly. He'd been hungry; Suki had refused to nurse him.

"What," she'd said in horror, "and ruin my boobs?"

The formula hadn't agreed with him. He'd kept spitting up; his tiny diaper had always been full and foul-smelling. Suki had shuddered, and left his care to Rachel.

Rachel had been fine with that.

She'd changed his formula. Changed his diapers. The baby thrived.

And Rachel adored him.

She'd loved him even before he was born. It was she who'd come up with a name, who'd bought a crib and baby clothes. He was hers, not Suki's. And when Suki had finally left, Rachel was almost ashamed to admit she'd been happy to see her go.

Now everything was falling apart.

She had never worried that Rami might return and claim his son—even if he had, she'd sensed that he was a coward underneath the charm and good looks.

She could have faced him down.

But if this arrogant bully wanted Ethan...

"Ms. Donnelly. I asked a simple question."

The baby began to whimper.

"That's it," Rachel said. "Raise your voice. Terrify the baby. Is that your specialty? Walking into places you aren't welcome? Scaring small children?"

"I asked you a simple question, and you will answer it! Whose child is he?"

"You," Rachel said, stalling for time, "you are an awful man!"

His teeth showed in a wolfish grin.

"I'm heartbroken to hear it."

"What will it take to get you out of here?"

"The truth," he snapped. "Whose baby is this?"

Rachel looked straight into his cold eyes.

"Mine," she said, without hesitation, forcing the lie through a suddenly constricted throat, because Ethan *was* hers.

It was just that she hadn't given birth to him.

"Don't play games with me, madam. You know what I'm asking. Who is the father?"

There.

They'd reached the impasse she'd been dreading. Now what? She should have known he wouldn't be satisfied with her answer.

The Sheikh, the Prince, whatever you were supposed to call him, was not a fool.

Ethan looked like his parents. He had Rami's coloring and eyes, Suki's chin and mouth. Well, hers, too, because she and Suki resembled each other, but the Sheikh wouldn't know that.

He didn't even know Suki existed.

And she had to keep it that way.

"Answer me!"

"Lower your voice. You keep yelling—"

"You think I'm yelling?" the Sheikh yelled.

Predictably, Ethan began to cry.

The mighty Prince looked stunned. Evidently not even infants were permitted to interrupt a royal tirade.

"Now see what you've done," Rachel snapped, and scooped Ethan into her arms.

His cries became wails; his little body shook with outrage. The look on the Sheikh's face was priceless.

Under other circumstances she'd have laughed, but there was nothing to laugh at in this situation.

Instead, she walked slowly around the small living room, cooing to the baby, stroking his back, pressing kisses to his forehead.

His cries lessened, became soft sobs.

"Good baby," she whispered.

She felt Karim's eyes following her.

No way was he going to stop peppering her with questions. With *one* question.

Was Rami her baby's father?

And, yes, Ethan was hers. He always would be. She'd made the baby that promise the day Suki left.

Now that could change in a heartbeat.

Once she acknowledged what the Sheikh surely already suspected, her life, and Ethan's, would be in his hands.

He would surely decide to claim his brother's son. He was cold, yes. Heartless, absolutely. Rami had said so, and the last hour had proved it, and she could not imagine he'd feel anything for anyone, not even a baby.

Nevertheless, he'd never leave Ethan with her.

There was that whole royal bloodlines thing. Rachel had heard Rami whine about it to Suki. The fact that you were a royal was what set the path of your existence.

The Sheikh would demand custody and he'd get it.

He had money. Power. Access to lawyers and politicians and judges—people she couldn't even envision.

She had nothing.

This dark little apartment. Maybe four hundred dollars in the bank. A job she despised and, yes, she could just see how

"Occupation: half-dressed cocktail waitress" would stack up against "Occupation: powerful prince who spends the days counting his money."

The answer was inevitable.

He'd take Ethan from her.

Raise him as Rami had told Suki he'd been raised.

No love. No affection. Nothing but discipline and criticism and the harsh words and impossible demands of an imperious father and now, for Ethan, the demands of a heartless uncle.

A lump rose in Rachel's throat.

She couldn't let that happen. She *wouldn't* let it happen.

She'd do whatever was necessary to keep her baby—and there was only one way to accomplish that.

Show the Sheikh that he couldn't intimidate her, get him out the door—then pack a suitcase and run.

The baby's cries had faded to wet snuffles. Rachel took a breath and turned toward the Sheikh.

"He needs a new diaper."

"And I need answers."

"Fine. You'll get them when I have time. I'll meet you later. Say, four o'clock in front of the Dancing Waters at the... What's so amusing?"

"Did you really think I'd fall for such a stupidly transparent lie?" His smile vanished. "Change the child's diaper. I'll wait."

"Don't try to give me orders in my own home."

"It was my brother's home, not yours. You lived here with him. You were his mistress."

"Wrong on both counts. This apartment is mine."

"And my brother just happened to have the key."

His tone was snide and self-confident, and if it weren't for Ethan, she'd have slapped it off his all-too-handsome face.

"My mistake for giving him one. He moved in with me, not me with him. And, for the record, I've never been any-

body's mistress. I've always supported myself and I damned
well always will."

There it was again. Fire. Spirit. Absolute defiance. Her
eyes were snapping with anger even as she kept her voice
low for the baby's sake, kept stroking her hand gently down
his back.

Karim watched that slow-moving hand.

The feel of it would soothe anyone. A child. A beast.

A man.

Without thinking, he reached out and touched the baby.
His fingers brushed accidentally against the curve of the
Donnelly woman's breast.

She caught her breath. Their eyes met. Color rushed into
her face.

"The boy is asleep," Karim said softly.

"Yes. He is." She swallowed hard. He could see her throat
arch. "I—I'm going to take him into the bedroom, change
his diaper and put him down for a nap."

"Fine," he said briskly.

He watched her walk away with the dignity of a queen,
back straight, only the slightest sway of her hips.

He wanted to laugh.

What an act! The personification of dignity in a cheap
costume.

It was an act, wasn't it? The way she held herself. The love
she seemed to show the baby. Her adamant refusal to name
Rami as the child's father, as if she suspected what Karim's
next move would be.

She wasn't stupid; far from it. Surely, she knew he would
demand custody of the boy.

And he would get it. A DNA test, quickly performed,
would settle things.

She was—whatever she was. A dancer. A stripper. She
was broke or close to it, judging by where she lived.

And he was a prince.

There was no doubt which of them would win in a court of law—if this ever got that far.

But there was no need for that to happen.

Rachel Donnelly would not give up the child without a fuss. If he were generous, he'd say it was because she cared for the boy but he was not feeling generous. He was feeling deceived. By Rami. By fate. And now, for all he knew, by a woman who was an excellent actress, making a show of being a caring mother.

Whatever her motive, she could not be permitted to keep the boy.

That was out of the question.

He would not leave the child to be raised in squalid surroundings by a woman who, at best, might euphemistically be called a dancer.

With him, the boy—Ethan—would have everything Rami could have given him. A comfortable home. The best possible education. The knowledge of his ancient and honorable past.

He would not have a mother but Rami had not had one, either. For that matter, neither had he, and he was none the worse for it today.

Karim looked at the closed bedroom door and frowned. What was taking her so long? Changing a diaper could not be a complicated procedure.

Did she expect him to stand here, cooling his heels?

He had things to do. Settling Rami's debts, of course. And now he'd have to make arrangements for taking the child to Alcantar. What would he need? Clothes? Formula? The boy's birth certificate?

Not really.

He had diplomatic status. Only the State department had the authority to question him, and they would not do so.

What else would he require?

Of course.

A nanny.

That was the primary requirement. A woman who'd be capable of knowing a baby's needs. She could care for the boy from now until Karim had him back home, where he could make more permanent arrangements.

Relatively simple, all of it.

Assuming Rachel Donnelly didn't cause trouble—but why would she? He would write her a handsome check and if she balked he'd make her see how much better off her son would be in his new life as a prince in his father's kingdom.

He might even agree to permitting her to visit a couple of times a year—

And, dammit, he was wasting time!

Karim strode to the closed door and rapped his knuckles against it.

"Miss Donnelly?"

Nothing.

"Miss Donnelly, I cannot spend the entire morning waiting for you. I have other business to conduct."

Still nothing.

Hell.

Was it possible there was another exit from the apartment? A window that opened on an outside stairway?

Karim flung the door open.

The furnishings were spare.

A chest of drawers. A chair. A crib, Ethan sound asleep in it, his backside in the air.

And a bed.

Narrow. Covered in white. The only color came from the bra, the thong, the dark mesh stockings that lay in a tiny heap in its center.

His belly knotted.

His gaze flew to a half-open door, wisps of steam curling from it.

The sound of running water drummed in his ears, or was it the beat of his pulse?

Get out of this room, a voice within him whispered. *She's in the shower, naked. You don't belong here.*

Instead, he took a step forward. Then another.

Ah, God.

He could see into the bathroom. Into the small stall shower. Condensation clouded the glass but he could see her. See her as Matisse or Degas might have painted her—just the hint of that lovely face, that exquisite body.

The water stopped.

Get out, he thought again, but his feet seemed rooted to the floor.

She slid the shower door open.

And he saw her without the glass.

Her hair, wet and streaming over her shoulders, almost hiding the rounded perfection of her breasts.

Her waist, surely narrow enough for his hands to span.

Her hips, ripely curved.

Her legs, long enough so he could almost feel them wrapped around him.

And the golden curls at the juncture of her thighs, guarding the female heart of her.

She didn't see him. Wet strands of her hair hung over her eyes.

He watched as she reached toward the towel rack, her hand fumbling for a white bath sheet.

That was when he moved.

Grabbed the terrycloth bath sheet before she found it.

His fingers brushed hers. She cried out, swiped the hair from her eyes.

"No," she said, "don't—"

Karim threaded his hands in the rich, wet gold of her hair. Lifted her face to his and took her mouth in a hard, hungry kiss.

It was what he'd wanted to do that first time.

Then, he'd been able to stop.

No way could he stop now.

She struggled.

He persisted.

And the kiss changed.

It took all his determination to gentle it into something soft and seductive.

His lips moved gently over hers; he whispered her name, whispered how much he wanted her, first in his own language and then in hers.

Everything within him slowed. He wanted the kiss to last forever…

She stopped struggling. She sighed. Her lips clung to his. Her hands rose, touched his chest.

He could feel her trembling, but not with fear.

He felt his blood roar. Felt the earth tilt.

Now, everything in him said, *take her now*…

Karim shuddered.

Then he lifted his head, wrapped the towel around her and got the hell out of the bathroom, out of the apartment, out of the honeyed trap that had surely been set by his brother's clever, beautiful mistress.

CHAPTER FOUR

RACHEL stood where he'd left her, clutching the bath sheet as if it could shield her from him.

Too late, her body hummed, *much too late*.

He'd already done what he'd wanted. Touched her. Kissed her. Taken her on an emotional rollercoaster ride that had taken her from terror to—to—

She jumped at the sound of the front door slamming.

He was gone.

Gasping for air, trembling, she sank down on the closed toilet.

Her brain seemed to be in free-fall. She couldn't think, couldn't make sense of anything.

What had just happened?

Maybe the better question was, what hadn't happened?

The Sheikh had forced himself on her.

He'd walked in while she was naked, drawn her against him, kissed her...

And then he'd let her go.

Why?

Rachel shuddered.

He could have done anything he'd wanted. There'd been nobody to stop him. Certainly not her. He was too big, too strong, that hard body, those sculpted muscles hidden beneath the expensive suit.

She'd have fought him but he'd easily have overpowered her...

A moan broke from her throat.

He *had* overpowered her.

Not just physically.

Mentally.

How else to explain that infinitesimal moment when his mouth had gentled on hers, when his touch had eased and she—and she—

Rachel swallowed dryly.

Never mind that.

His actions had all been deliberate. Terrifying her with a display of strength, the old I-am-Tarzan-you-are-Jane thing.

She knew how that went.

It was a typical male ploy.

The men she dealt with when she waited tables. The ones who were her bosses now in the casino. The players. They were the worst of all. They tossed around their money, showed off their power, stank of cologne...

He hadn't.

Karim.

The Sheikh. The Prince. Whatever he liked to call himself.

No cologne on him. Just the clean scent of himself. The hot scent of a man who wanted a woman

And yet he'd let her go.

Rami would not have done that.

She'd always sensed it in him, the need to dominate, to take what he wanted and to hell with anyone else...

Rachel thrust her fingers into her wet hair and drove it back from her face.

She wasn't dealing with Rami; she was dealing with his brother—and now that she'd had a minute to think, she could see that the brother was a much more wily adversary.

She understood what he'd done. Taken her in a deep, hard kiss and then suddenly turned it into something that was soft, seductive and almost tender.

He'd wanted to confuse her. And he had. That last instant when he'd been kissing her, when she—when she'd had some kind of response to the feel of his mouth on hers…

No. *No!*

Rachel took a deep breath.

She hadn't responded. Not the way he'd wanted. Her reaction had been intuitive. Instinctive. Whatever you wanted to call it.

The I-can-survive-anything woman who lived inside her had taken her straight to automatic pilot.

Let the kiss happen. Stop struggling. That was all she'd done.

She wasn't like Suki.

Money, power, good looks didn't turn her on.

Rachel rose to her feet. She felt better. In fact, she felt fine. Strong. In control.

She even had a plan. Well, a plan of sorts.

And she was wasting precious time, dissecting the ugly little scene as if it mattered when she knew that it didn't.

Karim, the Sheikh of All he Surveyed, would be back.

She didn't have any doubt about it.

Her make-up bag was on a shelf over the sink. Quickly, she opened it, opened the tiny medicine cabinet, swept lipsticks, mascara, eyeliner, aspirin, everything that was there straight inside.

Of course he'd be back, she thought as she pulled a comb through her hair, then secured it in a ponytail.

The man was a lot of things but he was far from stupid.

She knew that he'd seen straight through her lies. Not the one she'd acted out, as if she'd kissed him back when she damned well hadn't.

The other lie. The bigger one.

Not admitting that Ethan was his brother's child.

He knew that he was.

She'd seen it in his cold-as-ice eyes. He didn't have proof yet. That was the only reason he hadn't pushed the conversation further—but he knew.

What he didn't know, couldn't possibly know and absolutely must never know, was that Ethan was not hers.

On the face of it—with Suki gone who knew where and Rami dead—she had as much of a claim to the baby as the Sheikh.

She was his aunt.

He was his uncle.

It should have been a draw—but it wasn't. He had unimaginable wealth. She worried about next month's rent. He had power over a kingdom. She had the power to choose which shift she worked at the casino.

Rachel hurried into the bedroom, pulled open dresser drawers, yanked on a bra and panties, T-shirt, jeans, socks and sneakers.

She had to get out of town, and fast.

The baby was still sleeping. Thank God for small favors. She'd let him sleep until she was ready to leave...

Her breath caught.

The door. The front door. Maybe the Sheikh had only slammed it shut to fool her. Maybe he was still here. And even if he'd left, so what?

He had that damned key.

She flew through the tiny apartment, breathed a sigh of relief when she saw that the living room was empty, secured the lock, grabbed a wooden chair from beside a rickety table and jammed it under the knob.

Let him try and get past that.

A sheikh. A prince. An egotistical anachronism who

thought the world had stood still for the last few hundred years and that he could do anything he wanted.

Anything.

Like take her baby.

"Wrong," Rachel said aloud as she went back to Ethan. "Wrong, wrong, wrong. Dead wrong."

The baby was hers.

Nobody was going to take him from her.

By now, Ethan was awake and fretful. He'd been out of sorts lately; there was a tiny pale spot visible in his pink gums where he was cutting his very first tooth.

Ordinarily she'd have taken him in her arms, settled into the old rocker she'd bought at a Goodwill thrift shop and talked to him—he liked being talked to—but time was a priority now.

"Hey, little man," she cooed as she leaned over the crib, "guess what we're going to do?"

The look he gave her—mouth down-curved, eyes scrunched—said that he didn't much care. Rachel plucked a soft plastic teething ring from the foot of the crib and held it out. The baby's plump fingers closed around the ring and brought it to his mouth.

Good.

She'd bought a few minutes of peace. That was all she needed.

Her suitcase was in the rear of the closet. She took the case out, tossed it on the bed and unzipped it.

Okay.

She packed another pair of jeans. A handful of Ts. Bras. Panties. Socks. A sweater. A zippered hoodie. It all went into the suitcase.

"Ta-da," she told Ethan, still chomping on the brightly colored teething ring. "See how quick that was? Now it's your turn. Any thoughts about what you feel like wearing for our trip? You mean I didn't tell you the surprise? We're going traveling. Doesn't that sound exciting?"

The baby made a rude sound.

"Okay. Maybe not." Rachel pulled open the drawers that held Ethan's clothes. Sleepers. Onesies. Socks. Tiny shirts and sweaters, a pair of grown-up-looking overalls she hadn't been able to resist. "I admit I used to hate it when Mama told me we were going on a trip. She'd take us out of school, Suki and me, just when we'd finally settled in." What else? Diapers, of course. A couple of crib blankets. "Well, I'll never do that to you, little guy. I promise." What was she forgetting? Ah. Formula. Bottles. Little jars of strained fruits and veggies. A quick detour to the kitchen, then back to the bedroom. "I'll find us a place where we can settle down and have a garden and maybe even a kitten."

Rachel paused.

Was that even anywhere near true?

Her mother had run from bill collectors and scandal, but somehow or other those things had always managed to find her anyway.

This was different.

She was running from a prince with the resources of the world at his fingertips.

Rachel shuddered. She wasn't going to think about that now.

Other things were more vital.

Should she head for the airport and blow a stack of cash on a plane ticket, or head for the bus terminal and the first bus out of town?

No contest.

The airport.

She could get away faster and farther, and speed and distance were of paramount importance.

She'd put half her money on a ticket to wherever, half in

reserve for when she and Ethan got there. She had a credit card, too. It was pristine; she'd kept it for emergencies and if this wasn't an emergency, what was?

She'd go as far from Vegas and Rami's brother as that combination of cash and credit would take her. San Francisco, maybe. Or Biloxi, where there were riverboat casinos.

Then she'd get a room, a cheap one, and give herself a couple of days to figure out her next step.

"Ffft," Ethan said.

It made her laugh. Her baby could always do that; he was the one bit of joy she could count on.

"Well, maybe," she said, "but at least it's a plan."

Not much of a plan, but it was a start.

Suki had always teased her about what she'd called "Rachel's obsession with planning" but without some kind of blueprint you could end up like Mama or Suki or half the women in this town.

And that—being kept, living on a man's largesse, being a...a possession—was never, ever going to happen to her.

As for leaving Las Vegas...

She was ready. More than ready.

Vegas had never been more than a stop on the road to something better. She'd only come here after Suki had called, babbling with excitement as she told her that two of the casinos were hiring new dealers.

"It's a great job," Suki had said. "They'll train you and then you can make a lot of money."

Maybe once. Not anymore. The economy was in the toilet. The need for new dealers had gone with it. Rachel had ended up waiting tables, then working the room at the casino—and wondering how she could have been so stupid as to have listened to her sister.

For one thing, if anybody had been hiring dealers why hadn't Suki applied?

For another, Suki hadn't bothered mentioning that she was living week-to-week in a furnished room.

The real reason she'd wanted Rachel to come west was because she'd known Rachel would be resourceful, find a job and an apartment, and she could move in.

She hadn't even asked if her boyfriend, Rami al Safir, could move in, too. He'd just strolled out of Suki's room one morning and after that he had become pretty much a permanent fixture.

A non-bill-paying fixture.

"Fool," Rachel muttered.

But then, she reminded herself as she stuffed a few diapers, a box of baby wipes and some plastic Baggies into a tote, if she hadn't come to Las Vegas she wouldn't have Ethan.

The baby gave a pathetic little sob. He'd lost his teething ring through the bars of the crib. Rachel picked it up, wiped it off and gave it back to him.

He flashed a happy smile.

"Yes," Rachel said, "you're right. This is a fresh start for us both."

A new town. A new place to live. A job that wouldn't put her in costumes that made men see her as an item they could purchase.

A fresh start. Definitely. And all because of a man who thought his money, his titles, his gorgeous good looks—because, yes, he was good-looking, if you liked the type and she certainly didn't—all because of his Sheikhiness, the Prince.

The baby blew a loud, wet bubble. Rachel grinned.

"My very thought," she said.

Okay. Diapers? Check. Formula? Check. A few tiny jars of baby food? A bottle in a small insulted bag? Double check.

And that was it.

Goodbye, Sheikh Karim.

Hello, brand-new life.

Rachel scooped Ethan up and bundled him in a crib blanket printed with prancing blue giraffes. Then, the baby in the curve of one arm, her purse over that shoulder, the diaper bag over the other, she hoisted the suitcase from the bed and walked briskly through the apartment to the front door, shoved the chair out from under the knob, undid the locks and without a single backward glance headed down the stairs.

She was happy to be leaving Las Vegas. She'd been planning on it, only waiting to save a little more money, but what had happened this morning made that irrelevant.

Rachel paused on the ground floor landing.

Dammit. The taxi. She'd neglected to phone for one. And she hadn't called Mrs. Grey to say she wouldn't be needing her to babysit anymore.

No problem.

She could do both things as soon as she got outside and dug her cell phone from her purse.

Wrong.

She couldn't dig out her phone, or call Mrs. Grey, or phone for a taxi.

She couldn't do anything because when she opened the door to the street the first thing she saw was a shiny black car at the curb, its rear door open.

The second thing was the Sheikh, leaning against the fender, arms folded, eyes narrowed, mouth set in a thin line.

Rachel stopped dead. "You," she said.

It was a painfully clichéd reaction and she knew it.

He seemed to think so, too, because a smile knifed across his lips.

"Me," he said, in a voice that reminded her of steel swathed in silk. His gaze dropped to her suitcase. "Going somewhere?"

She felt her face heat. "Get out of my way."

He smiled again, moved toward her, took the suitcase

from her suddenly nerveless fingers, the diaper bag from
her shoulder, and dumped them into the back of the car.

That was when she saw the baby seat.

Her stomach dropped.

"If you think—"

"Put the boy in the seat, Rachel."

"How did you—?"

He gave a negligent shrug. "A cell phone and a title can
do wonders," he said dryly. "Go on. Put him in the seat."

"You're crazy if you think you're going to take him from
me!"

"He is Rami's," Karim said coldly

"He is mine!"

"And that is the only reason I've decided to take you with
me."

She blinked. "Take me with you where?"

"There are details to arrange." A faint look of distaste
passed over his face. "And I have no intention of dealing
with them in this place."

"I don't—I don't know what you're talking ab—"

"Oh, for God's sake, woman." Karim stalked toward her.
He stopped inches away, towering over her, his face stern,
hard as granite. "Don't play dumb. It doesn't become you.
I want my brother's child. You'll want recompense." He
paused. "Unless you're willing to give him to me right now."

Rachel stood as straight and tall as she could. For the first
time in her life she wished she were wearing those damned
stiletto heels.

"If you think I'd ever do that—"

"No. I didn't think it, but then, anything is possible."

"What's possible," she said, "is that I'll scream for help.
There are laws in this country—"

"Laws against an uncle wishing to see to the welfare of
his dead brother's child? I think not."

"You don't give a damn for Ethan's welfare! You just want to steal my baby, take him far away and bring him up to be— to be a clone of you!"

Karim laughed. She felt a rush of fury sweep through her.

"You're a despicable person!"

"Shall we deal with this in a civilized manner or not?"

Rachel stared up into that beautiful, emotionless face. Then she brushed past him, buckled Ethan into the baby seat and started to get into the car beside him.

The Sheikh closed his hand tightly around her elbow and drew her onto the sidewalk.

"You will sit in the passenger seat," he snapped, "next to me. I am not your chauffeur."

Rachel glared at him.

"You are not anything honest or decent," she said.

It wasn't much of a line, but at the moment it was all she had.

CHAPTER FIVE

WHERE was Karim taking her?

When she'd asked, he'd avoided a direct answer.

Why ask again and give him the pleasure of acknowledging that he was in charge? Maybe thinking that way was foolish but it was the way Rachel felt.

He'd done everything he could to humiliate her. The way he looked at her, talked to her, snapped orders at her…

The way he'd kissed her.

No. She wasn't going to add to it by pleading for information.

She looked back at Ethan and came as close to a smile as she could. Her boy was content; he loved car rides. She had a beat-up old Ford. It wasn't much to look at but it was fairly reliable.

Early on, when Ethan was colicky and crying, and Suki would cover her ears and say, *"Can't that baby ever be quiet?"* Rachel had discovered that taking him for a ride into the desert, sometimes as far as Red Rock Canyon, almost always turned those heartbreaking sobs to gurgles of contentment.

If only she and her baby were alone and heading for the peaceful canyon now, she thought, folding her hands tightly in her lap and staring out the window.

Rachel glanced at the Sheikh.

He drove quickly and competently, his left hand on the steering wheel, his right resting lightly on the gear shifter. His profile was unalterably stern.

The logical destination would be a lawyer's office, but she dismissed that as soon as she thought of it.

Snapping his fingers and making a car seat materialize in the middle of the desert was one thing.

Conjuring up an attorney he'd trust to sort out all the legalese of Ethan's custody was another.

Was he heading for a lab for a DNA test?

No. She doubted that, too.

The Sheikh was accustomed to using his power and money to get what he wanted, but even he had to know that he'd need her consent to get a sample of Ethan's DNA.

After all, she was his mother.

Rachel swallowed hard.

He'd accepted her in that role without hesitation; clearly he didn't know a thing about Suki or the months his brother had spent with her.

And she had every intention of keeping it that way.

Then, where were they going?

To the Strip. That had to be the answer.

It was not terribly far from the grimy building she lived in to the glitzy hotels on the Strip, but you measured the distance in money, not in miles.

That had to be where he was taking her. A restaurant. A coffee shop. Or his suite.

A man like him, a sheikh, would surely have a suite, an enormous, glamorous set of rooms reserved for the rich and famous.

She'd demand they stay in the suite's sitting room and that he leave the door open, though she suspected he would not repeat that kiss.

She was certain she'd figured right, that the kiss had been

a mark of male dominance. Like an alpha wolf marking the boundaries of his turf by peeing on rocks and trees, she thought.

The image made her want to laugh.

But she didn't.

There was nothing funny in being dragged off by a man who thought he owned the world and everyone in it.

The car flew past Circus Circus, past the Venetian, past the Flamingo.

Rachel swung toward her abductor. To hell with not asking him where they were going. He was using mental and emotional muscle to get what he wanted. It was what he excelled at.

The thing she had to do was fight it.

"I want to know where you're taking me."

"I told you," he said calmly. "Somewhere quiet, where we can discuss our situation."

"Our situation?" Rachel snorted. "We have no situation."

Ahead, a traffic light glowed crimson. Karim slowed the car, brought it to a stop.

"You would be wise," he said softly, "not to take me for a fool."

"I asked you a simple question. Surely you can give me a simple answer. Where are we—?"

The light turned green. He made a turn. They were heading away from the Strip, away from the hotels.

A lump of fear lodged in her throat.

The only thing that could possibly draw a visitor to this part of town was the airport.

"Either you tell me where you're going or—"

"We're going to my plane."

Full-blown panic flooded through her.

"I am not getting on a plane!"

"Yes," he said in a quiet voice that resonated with command, "you are."

"No!"

"We're flying to New York."

"*You're* flying to New York! I'm going home."

"Home?" His tone changed, became hard. "Really? Is that why you came out the door with a suitcase?" There was a gate ahead; he slowed the car as they approached it. "I told you not to take me for a fool, Rachel. When you came down those steps your only thought was to run. I'd bet you didn't even have a destination. Well, now you do."

"Get this through your head, Your Highness. There's not a way in hell I'm flying to New York or anyplace else with you. If you think you can—you can pick up where you left off in my apartment—"

He looked at her, his eyes cold. Then he swung the wheel to the right and pulled onto the shoulder of the road.

"I assure you, Ms. Donnelly, I'm not the least bit interested in you sexually."

"If that's your idea of an apology—"

"It's a statement of fact. What happened earlier was a mistake."

"You're damned right it was. And if you think it could ever happen again—"

"I'm taking you to New York so we can move to the end of this little drama as quickly as possible."

"We can do that right here."

"No, we cannot. I have a home in Manhattan. Commitments to keep."

"I have commitments, too."

He laughed. She felt her face heat.

"I'm sure my life doesn't seem anywhere near as important as yours," she said coldly, "but it is to my baby and me."

"I'll have the DNA of the child tested."

His tone was flat. Matter-of-fact, as if the issue had been decided.

That frightened her more than anything else. His certainty that there would be a test. That whatever he demanded would happen.

She knew she had to sound decisive, even in the face of his determination.

"The name of the person who fathered my child is my affair."

"Not if that person was my brother."

His answer was so logical that for a couple of seconds her mind went blank. What could she say to that?

"Why, Rachel," he said softly, "don't tell me you've run out of arguments."

"Here's the bottom line, Your Highness. There won't be a test. I won't grant permission. And there's not a thing you can do about it."

"You're correct," he said quietly. "I can't force you."

Rachel wanted to cheer. Instead, she folded her arms and waited. She knew it couldn't be this easy.

"You may, indeed, refuse my request. You have that right." He smiled. It was a terrible smile; it chilled her to the bone. "But I, too, have rights. Don't bother telling me I don't. I've already spoken with my attorney."

"You've had a busy morning," she said, trying to sound glib despite the race of her heart.

"I have reasonable grounds to think Rami is the child's father."

"So you say."

"So my lawyer will say. If you refuse to have him tested, I'll put this in the hands of the judicial system." He paused. "It is, my attorney says, a very slow-moving system. Who knows how long Ethan will be in foster care?"

Rachel blanched. "No! You can't—"

"Certainly I can," he said calmly. "I have one of the best legal firms in the United States on retainer. Six full partners. Endless associates from the nation's top law schools. Paralegals. Clerks. Offices on both coasts. And who will represent you? A fresh-out-of-law-school kid from Legal Aid? A lawyer with a closet for an office?" Another cool smile touched his lips. "The contest should prove interesting."

It was a direct hit.

Karim knew it; the proof was in the sudden tremor of Rachel Donnelly's mouth, the glitter of unshed tears in her eyes.

He wanted to feel triumphant.

But he didn't.

She was an easy opponent and he'd never been a man who enjoyed easy victories. The power was all his; she had nothing but possession of Rami's son—because, without question, this *was* Rami's son.

Why wouldn't she admit it?

She had everything to gain. She had to know he'd pay whatever price she set for the child.

Unless the child really mattered to her.

He supposed that was possible. Not likely, in his experience. His mother, whenever she'd been around, had shown more affection for her poodles than for him or Rami; he had female employees, executives on the fast track, whose kids were virtually being raised by nannies.

Nothing wrong with that.

It did children good to grow up with a sense of independence.

Wasn't he living proof of that?

Still, he knew there were other kinds of mothers.

He saw them on weekends when he ran in Central Park, playing and laughing with their children

Maybe Rachel had that kind of thing in her.

Maybe not.

Maybe it was all an act.

Either way, he didn't give a damn.

Whatever her reason for making this so complicated, he would be the victor. How much she gained from the battle— six figures, seven, the right to visit with the boy from time to time if she wished—depended on how many obstacles she put in his way.

He really didn't want a court fight.

He knew damned well it would end up splashed in the tabloids, on the cable talk shows, on internet blogs. And both he and Alcantar were better off without that kind of publicity.

Rachel would acquiesce before things went public. He was certain of it. And this, her silence, was the first proof.

So he waited, watching her without saying a word, until at last she blinked back those unshed tears.

"Why are you doing this to me?"

Her voice was whisper-thin. It almost made him feel guilty—until he thought about his duty to his brother.

"This isn't about you," he said, not unkindly. "It's about Rami."

Rachel shook her head. "I don't believe that."

Karim narrowed his eyes.

"No one calls me a liar."

"Not even when you lie to yourself?"

"I have no idea what you're talking about."

"I'm talking about too little, too late." Her voice took on strength; she folded her arms in what was fast-becoming a familiar indication of defiance. "Because, Your Highness, if you'd really cared about your brother you'd have been there for him. You'd have made him see that he couldn't go on drinking and gambling and living the kind of life people like you live, neck-deep in self-indulgence and money and to hell with decency and honor and—"

She gasped as he reached for her, ignoring the pull of his seat belt and hers, digging his hands into her shoulders as he pulled her toward him.

"You don't know a damned thing about what you call 'people like me,' and you sure as hell don't know anything about my brother except what he showed you when he took you to bed."

"I know that you're heartless. To do what you're doing to Ethan and me and, yes, even to your brother's memory—"

"I'm doing this *for* his memory. For the honor of our people—an honor he never understood."

His hands bit into her shoulders. Then he said something under his breath in a language that sounded as hard and unyielding as he was, and flung her from him.

"Agree to the testing or find yourself a way to fight me in court," he growled as he started the car. "Those are your choices. The flight east is a long one. I suggest you use the time to come to a decision."

They stopped at the security gate. Karim produced his ID; the guard waved them through. Rachel waited until he'd parked. Then she turned toward him.

"I just want to get one thing straight." Her voice shook; she cleared her throat, sat straighter, reminded herself that her enemy would surely make the most of any sign of weakness. "You remember that—that moment in the bathroom when—when I seemed to stop fighting you?"

"No," he said coldly, "not in any detail. Did you think I would?"

She felt her face heat but she'd gone too far to back off now.

"You'd have remembered my knee where it would have done the most good if you hadn't let go of me."

"So that was... What shall I call it? Misdirection?"

"It was doing whatever I had to do to get you off me!"

He nodded, his expression suddenly grave. "I'll keep that in mind for next time."

"Believe me, Your Highness, there won't be a next time."

He gave her a long, steady look. Was he laughing at her? Did he think this was a joke?

Rachel didn't wait to find out.

Instead, she undid her seat belt, got out of the car and took Ethan from the baby seat. Karim reached past her, grabbed her suitcase and the diaper bag, then clasped her elbow with his free hand and began walking toward a silver jet with the emblem of a falcon on its fuselage.

Steps led up to the open cabin door where two men and a woman, all in dark gray suits, stood watching them.

"My crew," Karim said.

His crew.

His plane.

His life.

The sudden reality of what was happening hit Rachel with breath-stealing force. She stumbled; Karim dropped the bags and swept his arm around her waist.

"Dammit," he growled.

The woman rushed down the steps and hurried toward them. She reached for the suitcase and diaper bag but Karim shook his head.

"Take the child."

Rachel pulled back. The woman smiled reassuringly.

"He'll be fine with me, ma'am. I'll take him to the galley. I have diapers ready, food, a little carrier… His Highness saw to everything."

Rachel blinked. "He did?"

"He did," Karim said briskly. "Go on. Give the baby to Moira, or would you rather run the risk of dropping him?"

Rachel handed Ethan over. Then she stared at the Sheikh.

"When did you order all those things?"

"I had plenty of time to make phone calls while you were packing. There isn't a woman alive who doesn't take forever to pack."

"I didn't take forever. And are you always so sure of how things will work out? That I was packing at all? Just because you want something doesn't mean it—" She gasped as he swung her up in his arms. "I can walk!"

"Yes. So you just demonstrated."

He strode to the steps and climbed them. The two men— his pilots, she assumed—snapped to attention.

Rachel could feel her face burning. Maybe the Sheikh's crew was accustomed to seeing their lord and master board his plane with a woman in his arms but this kind of dramatic entrance was new to her.

"I'll see to those bags, sir," one of the men said.

The Sheikh nodded.

"Fine. I want to get airborne ASAP."

"Yes sir."

One man went for the bags. The other made his way to the cockpit. Karim carried Rachel through what might easily have passed as someone's handsome living room.

"Don't they click their heels?" she said.

He raised an eyebrow. "Excuse me?"

She pulled back as far as she could in his hard, encircling arms.

"I said, don't they click their heels?"

"They do," he said, "but only on state occasions."

Her eyes went to his. Okay. It was a joke; she could tell by the look on his face. At least there was something human about him.

"You can put me down now."

"Can I?"

"Put-me-down!"

His mouth twitched. "I heard you."

"Then, dammit, put me—"

"That isn't a very ladylike way of speaking."

"I'm not a very ladylike lady. And I want you to—"

His arms tightened around her as the plane lifted into the sky.

"I know what you want," he said gruffly, and he bent his head and kissed her.

She made a little sound of protest and he asked himself what in hell he was doing.

And then she made another little sound that had nothing to do with protest.

Karim traced the outline of her lips with the tip of his tongue. He sank onto a leather loveseat, Rachel still in his arms. One hand swept into her hair; the other found the sweet swell of her breast. Her taut nipple pressed into his palm through her cotton T-shirt, and he shuddered.

"Rachel," he whispered.

She moaned and her lips parted, giving him access to the honeyed sweetness of her mouth.

He drew her closer. Swept his hand under her shirt. Cupped her breast.

She put her arms around his neck.

He brought his hand to her face, cupped her jaw, rested his thumb in the delicate hollow of her throat. Her pulse leaped under his touch.

What in hell was he doing?

It was wrong. It was madness. And yet he wanted this, wanted her—

The plane hit an air pocket. It jumped, and so did Rachel. She jerked back in his arms, face pale, eyes wide and blurred. He blinked and let go of her.

She sprang to her feet.

"Do not," she breathed, "do not ever touch me again you—"

you vile, arrogant, heartless, manipulative bastard! Do you always ignore the truth of what other people feel?"

She didn't wait for an answer. A good thing, he thought as she stumbled to a seat far from his, because he didn't have one.

Was she right?

Had he ignored what might have been Rami's unspoken cries for help? Could he have saved him from his path of self-destruction? Could he have somehow turned his brother's wasted life around?

And this.

What he'd just done.

Kissing Rachel. Forcing his kisses on her. An ugly way to describe it, but wasn't that what he'd done? Kissed her until she'd kissed him back, until her sighs, the sweetness of her mouth were proof that she was in danger of succumbing to the same hot darkness that threatened him?

Only one thing was certain.

It was too late to do anything about Rami.

But he could do something about the child. Raise him to be the man Rami might have been.

And he could do something about Rami's woman.

He could never touch her again.

Never, Karim told himself, and he turned his face to the window as the plane gained speed and altitude until, at last, the glittering lights far below were no more substantial than a mirage.

CHAPTER SIX

RACHEL was shaking with anger.

Bad enough the Sheikh had walked into her life and seized control of it.

Ordering her around. Making assumptions.

And this. Man-handling her as if—as if she existed for his pleasure.

She knew what he thought of her.

Rami had treated Suki like a slave. *Bring me this, hand me that, don't argue when I say something...*

He'd tried that with her, too, but it hadn't worked.

"Maybe that's how men deal with women where you come from," she'd told him, "but this is America."

America. Where a woman like her wore a costume that made her look like a whore because management said she had to. Where a man judged her by the damned costume, or maybe by the belief that she'd been his brother's mistress.

She'd told him she hadn't been Rami's mistress. He hadn't believed her. Now she wanted to tell him she hadn't been his lover, either.

She wanted to say, *I'd sooner have lived on the streets than have slept with your horrible brother.*

But she couldn't say it. She had to play out this charade because all that mattered was Ethan.

Okay. She had to calm down. Take a deep breath. Let it out slowly. Take another…

"Goddammit," she said.

How could she calm down? How?

"You gotta go with the flow," Mama had always said.

Mama hadn't just gone with the flow, she'd ridden it like a surfer on a wave.

Rachel snorted.

Mama used to say a lot of things. Folksy crap. Stupid nonsense.

Not so stupid anymore.

Go with the flow. And that other old bromide.

"First impressions count."

That had always made Rachel cringe, because Mama had probably said it a hundred times, always in a cheery voice, always as she stood in front of a mirror primping for her first date with the latest jowly, sweaty-faced fool who'd come sniffing at her heels.

Turned out Mama had been right about that, too. First impressions did count. The Sheikh had judged her on how she'd looked. And she'd hadn't helped the situation, letting him bark out commands—

Letting him kiss her in the bathroom and kiss her again, here on his plane. Sure, she'd fought back, but then—but then—

Come on, Rachel. Be honest, at least with yourself.

She'd fought about as hard as a poker player fought against ending up with a Royal Flush.

He'd kissed her.

And after a token kind of resistance she'd kissed him back.

That was the awful truth.

He was every miserable thing a man could be. Too rich, too good-looking, too egotistical to tolerate. Dammit, he was a man, and that was enough.

Until he'd kissed her and her brain had turned to mush.

How could such a thing have happened?

Yes, he was good-looking. Hell, what he was, was sexy.

But she wasn't into sexy.

She wasn't into sex.

She wasn't into anything that might interfere with the life she wanted, the life she'd been planning ever since she woke up in a lumpy bed in a cheap room in Pocatello, Idaho, the morning of her seventeenth birthday. Sixteen-year-old Suki had been asleep next to her, mouth hanging open, each exhalation stinking of beer.

"Mama?" Rachel remembered saying, with a kind of awful premonition.

She'd sat up, pushed away the thin blanket—and had seen the birthday card propped on the table near the bed. A big, garish thing with purple and yellow balloons drawn all over it.

Happy Birthday! it said.

Inside were two crisp twenty dollar bills. And a note.

Gone for a little vacation with Lou! You girls be good until I send for you!
   Luv you!

Lou had been Mama's latest "beau." That was what she always called her men-friends. She'd gone on "little vacations" before. A weekend. A few days. One scary time, when Rachel was ten and Suki was nine, she'd gone off for an entire week.

That morning in Pocatello Rachel had told herself that Mama would be back.

It never happened.

After three weeks she'd found a night job at Walmart but it hadn't been enough to pay for their miserable room and put food in their bellies.

So she'd quit school.

One more year until she'd have had her diploma. It had killed her to walk away, but what choice had there been? She'd had to work to support herself and her sister.

"You stay in school, Suki," she'd told her. "You hear me? One of us in going to graduate!"

In August, Rachel had moved the two of them to a bigger furnished room in a safer neighborhood. She'd used her Walmart discount for Suki's school supplies and bought their clothes at Goodwill.

Suki wouldn't wear them.

"Holy crap, how can you wear somebody's old stuff?" she'd demanded. "And you're wasting your money, buying me school stuff. I'm not going to go no more."

When the first snow fell they got a card from Mama. She was in Hollywood. She knew someone who knew someone who was making a movie. She was going to get a part in it.

And then I'll send for my girls!

More exclamation marks. More lies. They'd never heard from her again.

Or maybe they had. There was no way to know because by January Idaho was nothing but a memory.

Suki had taken off. No goodbyes, no explanations. Just a note.

See you, it said.

Just like Mama, except Mama had left those twenties. Suki had emptied the sugar bowl of the fifty bucks Rachel had kept in it.

Rachel moved to Bismarck, North Dakota. Took a job as a waitress. Moved to Minneapolis. Took another job waitressing. A couple more stops and she'd ended up in a Little Rock, Arkansas, diner.

Bad food, grungy customers, lousy tips.

"There's got to be somewhere better than this," she'd muttered one night, after a guy walked out without paying his bill, much less leaving a tip.

"Dallas is lots better," the other girl working the night shift had said.

Right, Rachel thought now, swallowing a bitter laugh. And after Dallas came Albuquerque, and after that Phoenix.

Rachel had seen more than her share of the West.

Then Suki had called. Told her about Las Vegas.

In some ways Vegas had been an improvement. When customers were happy because they'd won at the slots they left decent tips. And once she'd swallowed her pride and taken the job she had now the tips had got even better.

She'd started taking classes at the university, planned a better life for herself, and then for herself and Ethan...

What time was it, anyway?

She wasn't sure what time they'd left Las Vegas. Ten, eleven o'clock—something around there. They were moving fast but there was no feeling of motion, no sense that they were miles above the earth, going from one time zone to another.

Could that be disorienting? Could it explain...

No. There'd been no plane, no soaring through the sky that first time the Sheikh had kissed her.

Nothing but the man himself. The taste of him. The feel of him. The heat and hardness of his body.

It didn't make sense. She wasn't like that. She wasn't into what Suki called "hooking up."

It drove Suki crazy

"My sister, the saint," she'd sneered when Rachel had caught her drinking Southern Comfort after she knew she was pregnant. "Such a good girl. Always flosses. Always eats her veggies. Never gets laid."

Rachel had snatched the bottle from Suki's hand and dumped the whiskey into the sink.

"A little screwing would make you more human," Suki had yelled after her.

No, Rachel had thought, it wouldn't. It would just mark her as her mother's daughter.

Sex had been her mother's addiction. Her sister's.

Not hers.

Sex was a trap. It robbed you of common sense, and for what? A few minutes of pleasure, or so she'd heard women say. She had no idea if that was true or not. She'd tried being with a man once or twice and all she'd ended up feeling was even more alone.

She didn't need men, didn't need sex, didn't need anything or anyone. Well, except for Ethan. Other than the baby, she was content to be alone.

She was a cool-headed woman who thought things through. A pragmatist. A survivor.

And that was why she'd defeat the Sheikh at this game.

She was not handing control of her life to him.

She was not giving up her baby.

Rachel rose to her feet.

Half a dozen steps took her to the alcove where Ethan slept in his carrier. The flight attendant was sleeping, too; she sensed Rachel's presence and jerked awake.

"What can I get you, miss?" she said quickly. "Something to eat, perhaps? There are sandwiches, fruit, coffee—"

"Nothing, thank you. I just wanted to see how my baby's doing."

"Oh. He's fine. I changed him a while ago, fed him—"

"Yes. That's great. I'm just going to take him back to my seat with me."

Rachel picked up the carrier, took it down the aisle. It was impossible not to see Karim but her gaze swept over him without their eyes making contact.

He didn't even know she was there.

He was talking on his cell phone. She heard a couple of words. "Suite." "Accommodations for an infant." Nothing more than that.

She sat down, put Ethan's carrier on the seat next to hers, took a soft throw blanket from another seat and draped it over her lap.

She was cold. And, yes, she was hungry. But she didn't want the Sheikh's food.

What she wanted was to know his next move.

A stop at a law office or a laboratory, at this hour of the night?

She didn't think so.

She thought about what she'd heard him say. "Suite." "Accommodations for an infant."

He was making hotel arrangements.

A suite for Ethan and her. A gilded cage where he could keep them prisoner while he arranged for that damned DNA test.

Until this minute she hadn't had time to think about the test. Or tests. What would testing involve?

Some of Rami's DNA, obviously. Easy enough to come by a strand of hair, she supposed, for a brother.

What if he wanted a DNA sample from her? She couldn't imagine why he would. He'd never questioned whether or not she was Ethan's mother, but what if he did? She knew little about DNA tests, only what she'd picked up from television and movies. Was her DNA the same as Suki's? Was it at least similar enough to establish the baby as hers?

What if it wasn't?

Bad enough that the test would confirm Rami as his father, but if it didn't confirm her as his mother—

She couldn't wait to find out.

She had to run. She'd failed the first time. But she wouldn't fail again.

She'd be as devious as her enemy.

He was putting her in a hotel. He wouldn't leave her on her own; he'd leave her with watchers. Flunkies to make sure she stayed put like an obedient dog.

Oh, she could read him like a book. But she had the one thing he didn't.

Street-smarts.

If he left a guy in her suite, she'd put on an act of desperation.

I need diapers right away, she'd say. *The baby's made an awful mess!*

That would get her watcher out the door.

And she'd take Ethan and run. Not to the lobby, because the Sheikh might have somebody there, too.

No problem. She'd worked in enough hotels to know there were other ways out. Fire exits. Delivery entrances. Basements.

When the Sheikh came for Ethan and her in the morning, all he'd find was an empty suite. And a note.

For the first time in hours Rachel almost smiled.

Goodbye notes were a Donnelly family tradition.

Several rows back, Karim watched Rachel through narrowed eyes.

He was good at reading body language. Years in the stuffy formality of the palace, followed by years of negotiating multi-million-dollar deals with some of the world's toughest opponents, had given him that ability.

For the past hour he'd been reading hers.

For a long time she'd sat stiffly in her seat, her body almost quivering with anger.

She hated him for that kiss.

At first he'd been a heartbeat away from marching up the aisle, hauling her into his arms and carrying her to the small private bedroom in the rear of the cabin.

Two minutes alone and he'd damned well show her that he had not forced that kiss on her, that whatever dark and dangerous thing was happening between them involved her as much as him.

Thank God, sanity had prevailed.

He'd calmed down. So had she. Her shoulders had relaxed, if only a little, and then she'd gone to collect the child.

He'd watched her come down the aisle again, head up, eyes cold as they raked over his face.

Do not even think of touching me, that look had said, but he wouldn't have anyway.

The sight of the baby had reminded him of what this was about—that taking her to New York had nothing to do with her or him; it had to do with Rami.

If the child was his brother's, then it was also his.

He owed it to the boy.

Maybe he owed it to Rami, too.

What he'd thought about earlier, that maybe, just maybe, he'd missed the opportunity to help his brother turn his life around, had set him thinking.

Doing right by Rami's son would go a long way toward doing right by Rami. It would leave a far better legacy than all those bills and chits.

That it would also strip the Donnelly woman of her son was secondary. The boy would obviously be better off in a new life. He could explain that to her.

If she truly loved the child…

He was a second away from heading up the aisle to try and explain that to her when he noticed that she no longer looked tense.

That was when he knew she was planning something.

So much for explaining anything.

He'd kept her from making a break for freedom. And she was going to try again. Not that her trying to get away made any more sense now than before.

What did she have to gain by running?

And yet, had he not been waiting outside that miserable building in which she lived, she'd have disappeared by now.

Did she figure she could get more money out of him if he had to waste time searching for her?

The truth was, he didn't give a damn what it would cost to gain custody of the boy. He'd threatened her with legal proceedings but going to court would be a last resort. Most of his clients abhorred publicity.

As for the effect back home...

The eyes of the world would fix on the scandal. His father would be devastated.

Karim shut his eyes.

He didn't want to think about it. Not yet. Not until he absolutely had the test results in hand.

Which he would, tomorrow.

He'd made the necessary calls. First he'd phoned the Vegas hotels where Rami had owed money and arranged for payment to them all. With that out of the way, he'd contacted his attorney. His physician. His chief of staff. They were the only people he could trust right now. He'd given instructions to each of them and now all he had to do was make sure the woman didn't slip away with the child.

He still couldn't imagine why she would want to. That was a puzzle, but then, so was she.

She seemed to really care about the boy. That, alone, was hard to comprehend. She was clearly broke, and having a baby to worry about surely only made her financial situation more difficult.

And then there were her other traits.

She was stubborn. Defiant. Outspoken. The worst qualities of modern women, all in one package.

Women, modern or not, should not be like that.

Women were supposed to be…perhaps *compliant* was too strong a word.

He had never dealt with a woman like this before.

"Of course you're right, sir," they'd say in business, because he was, after all, not only a sheikh but head of a multi-billion-dollar investment fund.

If the relationship was intimate, a woman would leave off the "sir", but both he and she knew who was in charge.

His last mistress had been spectacularly beautiful and, supposedly, incredibly intelligent—but she'd never argued with him over anything.

He liked it that way…

Then how come, after a while, he'd had the grim feeling that if he'd said something like, *Alanna, how about walking on coals to amuse me?* she'd have smiled prettily and said, *Just let me get a match.*

He scowled, pushed aside the papers he'd been pretending to read, and folded his arms.

He knew how Rachel would react if he said something like that to her.

Angry as he was—at his brother, at her, at the situation the two of them had left for him to deal with—he wanted to laugh.

She'd begin with *You can go to hell* and work up exponentially from there.

He knew, too, what his response would be.

He'd pull her into his arms, whisper what she could do to please him, and that look of indignation would be replaced by one of hot desire.

She'd rise on her toes and bring her mouth to his and he

would ease her down on his bed, undress her, bare her to his mouth, his hands...

Dammit!

He was hard as a rock.

An intelligent man didn't mix business with pleasure, and this was strictly business.

Yes, she was attractive.

All right.

She was beautiful.

And she surely would know how to pleasure a man.

That was a given.

For one thing, Rami had never been interested in innocence. And then a man had only to see her in that costume to know that, whatever her work might be, she was a sexual sophisticate.

Still, when you came down to it, she was just a woman. Not that he held women in low esteem or anything, but she wasn't special—not to a man who'd always had his pick of them.

His mother's genes, his father's royal lineage, his own success... Add all that together and he'd always had his share of desirable lovers.

More than his share, to be brutally honest.

Then why all this schoolboy nonsense?

Karim frowned.

Because he'd been living like a monk, that was why. He'd been so busy cleaning up after Rami instead of living his own life that he had not been with a woman in weeks.

Well, he'd remedy that soon enough.

Karim glanced at his watch.

They'd be in New York in a couple of hours. His driver would meet them at the airport. It would be early evening by the time they reached his penthouse; he'd given orders to ready one of the guest suites for the woman and the child.

A hot shower. A night's sleep. Then, in the morning, a meeting with his attorney, a stop at the lab his doctor had recommended, a bit of serious negotiating with the woman, and custody would be his.

With any luck at all, this would be settled in a couple of days, after which he'd take out his BlackBerry, choose a name and number, and put an end to these weeks of celibacy.

Talk about tying up loose ends, Karim thought with a tight smile.

That would surely do it.

CHAPTER SEVEN

"Miss?"

Rachel's eyes flew open. The flight attendant smiled at her.

"We'll be landing within the hour. I thought you might have changed your mind about eating something, or that you'd like some coffee or juice while we still have time."

"Coffee would be—" Rachel cleared her throat. "Coffee would be fine, thank you."

"I'll bring it right away."

Rachel nodded. Her throat wasn't the only thing needed clearing. Her brain did, too. She was groggier than before she'd fallen asleep...

Where was Ethan?

Her heart thudded.

He'd been in his carrier, right next to her.

"Moira?"

"Yes, miss?"

"Where's my baby?"

"Oh, I brought him up front with me. He woke up and he seemed hungry—"

Rachel sighed with relief. "Thank you."

"No problem, miss. He's a very sweet little boy."

Rachel smiled. "He's teething, you know, and—"

"I figured as much. I remember my own children at that

age. I chilled one of the teething rings you had in the diaper bag and gave it to him. It seemed to make him happy. He's sound asleep now, though. Why don't I keep him with me? That way, we won't risk waking him and he might sleep through the landing. Descents, the change in pressure, can make some babies uncomfortable."

"Yes. That's fine. Thanks again."

"My pleasure, miss. I'll get that coffee now."

"Black, please."

"Black it is."

Rachel brought her seat upright and looked out the window. Were they as high over the earth as they'd been before? It was hard to tell. The long flight, the change in time zones…all of it was disorienting—though not as disorienting as being plucked out of your own life at the command of a prince.

Was he still seated in the middle of the plane? She wanted to turn around and look but she wouldn't give him the satisfaction.

What was he doing? Was he asleep? Was he working on those papers he'd taken from his attaché case? Was he staring out the window the way she was while he planned his next move?

She could find out.

She didn't have to make a point of looking at him. All she had to do was rise from her seat and walk to the lavatory in the rear of the plane.

She needed to do that, anyway, sheikh or no sheikh.

Quickly, before she could change her mind, Rachel rose to her feet.

He was still seated where he'd been all along. His seat was halfway reclined; he looked completely relaxed, long legs stretched out, big shoulders pressed against the leather seat-back, hands folded loosely in his lap.

And his face…

Her breath caught.

It was an incredible face.

His eyes were shut; his lashes, so thick and dark a woman would kill for them, lay arced against his chiseled cheek-bones. Stubble smudged his jaw.

He was—there was no other word for it—beautiful.

Dark. Sleek. A magnificent predatory animal.

A panther.

His eyes flew open and met hers. His pupils contracted; she saw his mouth thin.

Heat flared in her belly.

She stared at his mouth, remembered the silken feel of it against hers…

Stop it!

She wanted to run, but you didn't try to escape from a panther. You stood your ground.

Head up, eyes straight ahead, she walked briskly past him to the lavatory, shut the door—

And fell back against it, heart at full gallop.

This had to stop.

He was the enemy. He was a very dangerous enemy. There was no reason for her to be attracted to him. She'd never been drawn to bad boys at the age some girls were, and she'd certainly never been drawn to the grown-up version.

Bad boys were Suki territory, not hers.

Okay. A couple of deep breaths. A couple of slow exhalations. Then she stepped away from the door.

The bathroom held a marble sink and vanity, a glass-enclosed shower, a toilet and glass-fronted cabinets neatly stocked with folded towels, packaged soaps, toothbrushes and pretty much everything anyone could want.

Rachel gave the shower a look of longing but, no, she wasn't going to use it. The thought of stripping naked with only the door between the Sheikh and her brought back the memory of what had happened this morning. Or yesterday morning. Or, dammit, whatever day this was and that had been…

What did the day matter?

It was what had happened that counted.

Karim, his eyes going dark as he looked at her naked body. His hands cupping her breasts, his fingers feathering over her suddenly erect nipples, the liquid heat gathering low in her belly…

A moan rose in her throat.

She bit it back and stared at herself in the mirror.

"He caught you by surprise," she said.

Her reflection returned the stare. *Really?* it said in a sly voice. *So what are you saying, hmm? That you've never been caught by surprise before?*

Rachel blinked.

Why was she wasting time and energy over this? What happened next was all that mattered. She had to be prepared to deal with it.

But not looking like this.

Looks were important. Another Mama-ism, like the one about first impressions and, again, true enough. Look weak, people saw you as weak. Look tough, they figured that you were.

Right now, she looked pitiful.

Red-rimmed eyes. The pallor that came of exhaustion. Hair that was half in, half out of a ponytail.

"You," she told her reflection, "look worn and defeated. Is that how you want his Imperial Sheikhiness to see you?"

The answer was obvious.

So she got busy. Used the toilet. Ran water into the sink. Washed her hands and face with a soapy liquid that smelled like lemons. Brushed her teeth. Yanked her hair free of the band that constrained it and then combed it again and again until it was tangle-free.

Then she stood tall and looked into the mirror again.

"Better," she said.

Not much, but anything was an improvement.

A deep breath. A toss of her head. Then she unlocked the door, started up the aisle...

The plane hit an air pocket. Not much of an air pocket, just enough to make her stumble. The problem was that it happened just as she reached the seat where he was sitting.

Not again, she thought as his hand shot out and closed around her wrist.

The panther was wide awake.

His fingers were warm and hard against her skin. Rachel looked at him. He looked at her. *Say something,* she told herself, and she forced a polite smile.

"Thank you."

"Amazing."

"What?"

"That 'thank you.' Surely that's a phrase I never thought to hear you say, *habibi.*"

He was smiling. It wasn't much of a smile, only a tilt of his lips, but it was so private and sexy that, just for an instant, she wanted to smile back.

She didn't, of course. All the sexy smiles in his no doubt considerable repertoire wouldn't be enough to lull her into forgetting who he was and what he wanted.

"I am polite when politeness is appropriate," she said coolly.

This time, he grinned.

"Nicely done. It takes talent to deliver a remark that sounds polite but is really an insult." He tugged on her hand. "Sit down."

"Thank you, but I'm fine."

"Two thank-yous—only one with real validity. Sit down, *please*. Is that better?"

What now? If she refused, would he let go of her, or would he force her to take the seat next to his? Finding out might not be worth what it would cost in terms of losing face over such a stupid game.

Rachel shrugged and slipped into the seat nearest to him.

"Good," he said, and let go of her wrist. "Moira's bringing us coffee. And something to eat."

"She's bringing *me* coffee at my seat. And I'm not hungry."

"Don't be foolish, Rachel. Of course you're hungry. Besides, in my country, refusing to break bread with someone is a discourtesy."

"We're not in your country."

"But we are." The flight attendant came down the aisle, pushing a small wheeled cart laden with trays of fruit, cheese and small sandwiches as well as a silver coffee service.

To her horror, Rachel's belly growled. Karim grinned.

"So much for not being hungry." He waved the attendant away, poured two cups of coffee, then picked up a plate and filled it with tiny sandwiches and fruit. "And so much for not being in my country." He looked at her as he handed her the plate, silverware and an enormous linen napkin. "I am a prince."

"So you've made clear."

"I am my country's diplomat."

"How nice for you," Rachel said sweetly.

"It means that wherever I live is a part of Alcantar." Karim sipped his coffee. "My home in New York. My weekend place in Connecticut." He paused. "This aircraft. When you are in those locations you are subject to the laws of my people. Do you understand?"

"I'm an American citizen. You can't simply—"

"This is not subject to debate. It is fact. When you are on what you Americans would call my turf, the laws of Alcantar apply."

Rachel's hand shook. Carefully, she put down the coffee cup.

"Stop talking in circles," she said flatly. "And stop telling me you can do whatever you wish about Ethan. I'm a citizen. So is he. End of story."

"Perhaps you'd let me finish speaking before you start lecturing me." Karim waited. Then he cleared his throat. "I have been thinking…"

"Am I supposed to be impressed?"

He wanted to laugh. So determined to show no weakness—but he'd noticed how her hand had trembled. She was, indeed, an interesting woman. Tough and tender at the same time. Loving, at least to the child.

Would she be like that in bed?

Dammit, he had to stop his thoughts from wandering.

"We are adults," he said calmly. "And we both want what is best for the boy."

"Ethan, you mean."

"Yes. We want the right thing for him. There's no reason we should be enemies."

"And what is it you see as the right thing, Your Highness?"

"Please. Call me Karim."

What kind of game was this?

Rachel sipped her coffee, hid her confusion in the cup. This was a new approach but she wasn't buying it, not for a second.

Maybe he'd spent the flight reviewing the situation and he'd decided it would be simpler to have her cooperation than to fight for it.

And maybe it took one liar to see through the falsehoods

told by another, because it was painfully obvious that they didn't want the same thing for Ethan at all.

She wanted her baby to be raised with love and warmth.

He wanted him to be raised as Rami's son. And just look at how well that had turned out for Rami, she thought coldly.

"I'm glad we agree on the importance of Ethan's welfare," she said politely. "But—"

"Why did my brother abandon you?"

The question took her by surprise.

"You know, I really don't want to talk about—"

"Why not? I should think you'd have a lot to say about a man who was your lover, who made a child with you and then left you both."

"That's in the past. And—"

"Did he not make any financial arrangements for you and the baby?"

Rachel put down her cup.

"I appreciate your concern, Your Highness, but as I said, that's in the past."

"And this is the future with which my brother should have been concerned. He made no provisions for you or the boy, did he?"

She stared at him. His face was taut with anger. At Rami, she realized, not at her.

It made her feel guilty about the lies she'd told him, the one enormous lie, and wasn't that ridiculous?

"Did he walk out? Did he at least tell you he was leaving?"

Rachel shook her head.

"No," she said softly. That, at least, was true.

There was a silence.

"But he cared for you," Karim finally said.

Rachel didn't answer. A couple of seconds went by. Then he cleared his throat.

"I know it won't change things but you should know that he was not always so—so uncaring. Our childhoods were—difficult. The things we experienced changed him."

"And they didn't change you?"

"I am sure they did, but we chose different ways of dealing with those experiences." A shrug of those wide, masculine shoulders. "Who can explain why one sibling takes one approach to life and the other—"

"No one can explain it," Rachel heard herself say.

"That's kind of you, but—"

"It isn't kind at all. It's just a fact. I have—I have a sister. And—and I have better memories of her when we were little than I do of the years after."

Karim nodded. "She is not like you," he said quietly.

"No. We've always been very different."

"And she would not fight me to keep her child, as you surely will, even though I will raise him as a prince."

"No," Rachel said quickly, "I don't care that he's a prince. He's—he's—"

She clamped her lips together, but it was too late.

Karim's eyes were dark and unreadable, but there was a harshness in his voice that hadn't been there a moment ago.

"It is too late to deny it, Rachel. The boy is Rami's."

She stared at him. That was what this had been about. It hadn't been a peace offering. It had been a clever way of getting her to confess that Rami had fathered her baby.

What a fool she'd been to think this man might truly have a heart, or to forget that he was the enemy.

Rachel put her cup and plate on the cart.

"You keep missing the one thing that matters," she said coldly. "Ethan is mine."

"He is a prince."

"He is a little boy. And he has a name."

"What has that to do with anything?"

"You never use his name. You speak of him as if he were a—a thing. A commodity."

Karim dumped his plate on the cart and shoved the cart away.

"This is ridiculous! Will it make you happy if I call him by the name my brother chose for him? Fine. I'll do that. I'll call him—"

Rachel shot to her feet.

"Your brother didn't name Ethan. I did."

Karim rose, too. If only he didn't tower over her. She hated having to look up at him, to give him that seeming authority over her.

"In that case," Karim said stiffly, "I apologize for him yet again. Apparently, he ignored all his responsibilities."

"Dammit, stop apologizing for him!"

"It is my duty. I understand that he hurt you, but—"

"Hurt me?" Rachel slapped her hands on her hips. "I hated your brother!"

"And yet," Karim said coldly, "you slept with him."

Her cheeks heated.

"You let him put a child in your womb."

She turned away from him and started up the aisle. Karim went after her, caught her by the shoulder and swung her toward him.

"What kind of woman are you? You hated him. But you slept with him. You let him give you a child."

Her mouth trembled. If ever she'd wanted to tell the truth, it was now. But she couldn't, couldn't, couldn't—

"Things—things happen," she said, knowing just how ugly the answer sounded.

Karim's mouth twisted with distaste.

"Is that what you say when you give yourself to a man? That *things happen*?"

"It wasn't—it wasn't the way you make it sound."

"I'll bet it wasn't." He caught her chin, forced her to look into his eyes. "Was he flush with winnings when he first bedded you?"

Rachel's hand shot up. He caught it, caught both her wrists and imprisoned them against his chest.

"How much did you cost him? How much did it take to overcome your hatred, *habibi*?"

"You bastard! You miserable bastard! You don't know anything about me. Not a damned thing—do you understand? Not one single damned—"

His mouth closed over hers.

She fought him. Struggled. And then, as before, the earth tilted beneath her feet and her mind emptied of everything but the taste of him, the feel of him, the way his arms closed around her.

He lifted her off the floor, his mouth angling over hers, plundering hers, and she tunneled her fingers into his hair as he drew her hard against him.

"I hate you," she whispered against his mouth even as she kissed him, even as she gasped at the feel of his hands cupping her bottom. "I hate you, Karim, I hate you..."

A bell rang. It rang again, and then the pilot's disembodied voice announced that they'd be landing in five minutes.

Karim set her on her feet. His face was all planes and angles; his eyes were dark.

Her own eyes stung with tears.

"If you ever do anything like that again..." she said, and then she clamped her lips together.

She was as much to blame as he. He'd started the kiss but she had fallen into it.

Tears of rage stung her eyes. At him? At herself? It didn't matter. This wouldn't happen again.

She wouldn't let it.

She spun away, took a seat and belted herself in. The

wheels kissed the runway. As soon as the plane came to a stop she undid her seat belt and got to her feet, but not in time to prevent the Sheikh from clasping her shoulder and pulling her to him.

"Welcome to New York, *habibi*," he growled. "And do not make promises you won't be able to keep."

He bent his head to hers. Captured her mouth. She groaned, felt her body flush with heat...

And she bit him.

Bit his bottom lip hard enough to make him jerk back and let her go.

A spot of crimson bloomed against his flesh. He touched his finger to it, looked at her, and then his eyes narrowed.

"If you want to play games," he said softly, "I'll be happy to accommodate you."

She wanted to respond, to make some clever remark, but her brain refused to function.

Karim kept his eyes on hers as he lowered his head again, kissed her again, a slow, lingering kiss. She tasted the salt of his blood, the heat of his hunger. She wanted to tear her lips from his but she didn't, she didn't—

He raised his head, looked into her flushed face with a hot glint of triumph in his eyes.

Then he brushed past her on his way to the exit door.

A chauffeured black Mercedes was waiting for them.

The driver held the door open.

The interior of the car was handsome and urbane—except for the baby seat.

The man had thought of everything.

How far was it to the hotel?

Rachel was exhausted, as desperate for sleep as she'd ever been in her life. She needed a long, hot shower, some sleep and then—

Then, freedom.

The Mercedes merged onto a multi-lane highway. What time was it, anyway? It was too dim in the car to read her watch properly. Did it say four p.m.? That was the time in Nevada, and this was New York, which meant it was—

"It's seven," Karim said. "In the evening."

Rachel looked at him. "Thank you," she said coolly, "but I didn't ask."

"You didn't have to. I know you're probably feeling disoriented."

"Sorry to disappoint you, Your Highness, but I'm not."

"Of course you are."

What would she gain by arguing? Instead, she stared out the window. The ride into the city seemed endless, but finally they were on a wide street, tall buildings on one side, what seemed to be a dense park on the other.

Where was the hotel?

She turned toward him. "How much further to the hotel?"

"What hotel?"

"The one where you're stashing Ethan and me."

He laughed. God, she wanted to slap his face!

The Mercedes pulled to the curb. The door swung open. The hotel, Rachel thought. But the man who bent down and peered into the car wasn't a hotel doorman because what hotel doorman would all but click his heels and say, "Welcome home, Your Highness. I trust you had a good trip."

"Home?" Rachel said. Her voice rose. "Home?"

"My home," Karim said coldly. "My little piece of Alcantar."

Ethan began to wail. Karim reached for him. Rachel tried to stop him. Ethan screamed louder.

"Let go of the boy," Karim said quietly, and, really, what choice was there?

She let go, watched her baby all but disappear in the arms

of the only man she'd ever hated more than she'd hated Rami, more than she'd hated the endless chain of men who had tromped through her mother's life.

The doorman stared at her. Then he held out his hand.

"Miss?"

She slid across the soft leather seat, ignored the extended hand and marched to the lobby door. The doorman rushed by her and managed to open it just as she reached it. She breezed past him, past a high desk with another uniformed flunky seated behind it.

"Miss," he said, as politely as if this kind of circus took place here every day.

Karim was waiting for her, standing beside an elevator with Ethan in his arms.

A smiling, gurgling Ethan.

Traitor, Rachel thought, as she stepped inside the elevator car.

Unless she was willing to walk away from her baby—and that would never happen—she was now, to all intents and purposes, the Sheikh's prisoner.

CHAPTER EIGHT

SOMEWHERE around three in the morning, even New York City finally slept.

Not Karim.

He stood at one of the floor-to-ceiling windows in his darkened bedroom, bare-chested, wearing only gray sweatpants that were a leftover from his days at Yale. Behind him, the rumpled bed offered mute testimony to the hours he'd spent tossing and turning.

Ridiculous.

He should have been exhausted.

He hadn't slept at all last night, and his day had started with the discovery that his brother had a child. Add in his confrontations with Rachel, the five-hour flight from Nevada to New York, the hours spent in his study, trying to catch up with the messages and emails on his cell phone and his computer...

He'd fallen into bed somewhere after midnight. Sleep should have come quickly.

It hadn't.

Instead, he'd envisioned Rachel in a guest suite down the corridor. What was she thinking? What was she doing? Had her anger at him eased or was she still breathing fire as she had hours earlier, when she'd found out he wasn't taking her to a hotel but to his home?

The memory almost made him laugh.

He'd never seen a woman so furious. And she hadn't been shy about letting him know it.

He couldn't think of another woman in his life who'd have objected to spending the night with him—but, of course, she wasn't really spending it with him.

If she were, he wouldn't be asleep now, either. He'd be in his bed with her in his arms...

"Hell!"

Karim strode into his bathroom, turned on the sink faucet, bent his head under the flow of cold water and took a long drink while the water cooled his face. He toweled off with impatient strokes and then went back to the window again.

He was not a man given to erotic imaginings. Why would he be, when there was always a woman eager to offer the real thing?

He wasn't given to insomnia, either, no matter how long or difficult his day had been.

And yet he was standing here, wide awake.

Eighteen stories below, Fifth Avenue was deserted save for an occasional taxi or some unlucky dog owner being pulled along at the end of a leash. Central Park was a hushed dark green jungle on the opposite side of the street. Beyond the park, even the glittering lights of the Manhattan skyline seemed dim.

Wonderful, Karim thought grimly. The entire world was asleep except for him.

He'd never needed much sleep, four or five hours was more than enough, but he wasn't fool enough to think he could get through a day of decision-making without some kind of rest, and tomorrow was going to be a day filled with decision-making.

After speaking with his P.A. he'd set up two meetings: breakfast with a Tokyo banker at the Regency, then midmorning coffee downtown, at Balthazar, with an official from India. At noon, he'd have lunch in the boardroom with his own staff.

He'd been away from his office far too long. He had business to conduct and he also needed to touch base with his people.

And then there was the rest.

Karim's mouth thinned.

At two o'clock he'd meet with his attorney.

He and Rachel.

He knew it would not be easy to negotiate a custodial arrangement with her. She was going to be difficult.

What would it take to get her to give up her rights to the boy? She'd said she never would but that was talk. People always had a price. Women, especially.

Yes, they liked his looks. They liked his virility. But he knew damned well they liked his title and his wealth even more.

That was surely how Rami had caught Rachel's attention. Money, a title…

But Rami hadn't had money. The proof was in that desolate little apartment where he'd lived with her. As for the title… Rachel found titles laughable.

He found that amusing, because he wasn't impressed by them, either. He had, at least, earned his own fortune, but he'd been born to the silly string of honorifics. He hadn't done a thing to earn them but he'd grown accustomed to others not seeing things that same way.

Most people, especially women, heard who he was and began to act as if this was pre-revolutionary France and he was the Sun King. They gushed. They fluttered their lashes. He'd been on the receiving end of more than one curtsy and it always embarrassed the hell out of him when it happened.

The thought of Rachel gushing or fluttering or curtsying was laughable.

She'd made it clear that she was disdainful of his being a prince, a sheikh, heir to the throne of Alcantar. That he was almost embarrassingly rich didn't win any points from her, either.

She treated him the way he suspected she'd treat anybody else. Anybody else she didn't like, he thought, and he smiled.

Rachel was a very interesting woman.

She was a woman making it on her own, with a child to raise. That couldn't be easy. His mother—his and Rami's—had been a woman with all possible means and resources at her fingertips, yet her sons had been amusing at best and at worst an inconvenience.

He could not imagine Rachel ever feeling inconvenienced by the child.

So what?

Good mother or not, the baby would be better off with him. Being a prince was the child's destiny. Rachel would get over losing him…

Dammit, why was he thinking about her at all?

His mouth thinned.

He knew why.

Sex.

He wanted Rachel in his bed.

He wanted her naked and moaning beneath him, wanted the taste of her on his tongue. He wanted her scent on him, her wet heat on him, he wanted to sink into her and watch her eyes blur as he made her come and come and come…

Karim cursed and rubbed his hands over his face. He was being a damned fool.

He'd kissed her but that would not happen again. Absolutely it would not. He certainly would not sleep with her—and standing here, thinking about it, was pointless.

He strode through his rooms, yanked open the door and headed for the stairs.

A brandy. Two brandies. Then he'd stop this nonsense, go back to his rooms, fall into bed—

What was that? A faint sound. The wind?

The sound came again.

It was the baby.

Rachel had said something about teething. Babies cried when they teethed; he'd heard that or read it somewhere.

Dammit, that was all he needed. A crying child…

The sound stopped.

Karim waited but it didn't come again. Either the child had gone back to sleep or Rachel was soothing him…

Enough thinking about Rachel tonight.

Moonlight dappled the living room, lost itself high in the shadowy darkness of the fourteen-foot ceilings. He went straight to his study, to the teak shelves and a Steuben decanter of—

Hell.

The child was crying again.

He must have been wrong. Rachel wasn't dealing with the boy, but that was her responsibility.

His was to gain custody, see to it the child was raised properly.

As he had been raised.

By tutors and nannies and governesses, so Rami's son would learn to be responsible and not waste his life on frivolity or anything but meeting his obligations…

The crying was annoying.

"Dammit," Karim growled, and he put down the glass, left the study, went quickly up the stairs and down a long corridor to the suite where Rachel and the boy slept.

The sitting room door was shut. He tapped his knuckles against it.

"Rachel?"

No answer.

Great.

She was fast asleep while he paced the floor.

He tried again. Knocked harder, said her name more loudly. Still nothing.

A muscle in his jaw knotted.

"Dammit," he muttered again, and he opened the door and stepped into the sitting room. She had to be in one of the two bedrooms that opened off it.

The noise had stopped but he knew it would start again. There was only one way to deal with it. He'd find Rachel and tell her to keep the child quiet.

He had a full schedule ahead and needed his rest.

He moved briskly through the sitting room. The first door was ajar. He hesitated, then pushed it open.

No crib. No stacks of baby gear—all the stuff he'd arranged to have delivered. He saw only a bed in the same condition as his own, blankets twisted and pushed aside as if the occupant had had difficulty sleeping.

It was Rachel's room. Rachel's bed.

There was the faint scent of lemon in the air. Rachel smelled of lemon. It suited her, that fresh, sweet-sharp tang. It was clean. Delicate.

Honest.

Who but an honest woman would have looked him in the eye when she admitted she'd hated the man who had been her lover?

Then, how had it happened? How could a woman like her have gone to the bed of a man she didn't love?

Karim cursed under his breath.

He was here to deal with a crying baby. Nothing more, nothing less. That his thoughts were wandering was proof that he had to get some sleep if he was going to be able to function well enough tomorrow—actually, today—and put this mess behind him.

He strode back through the sitting room, went straight to the second door.

It, too, was ajar. He stepped inside.

Yes, this was the boy's room. There was the crib. Boxes of baby stuff. The soft illumination of a lamp—what was that, anyway?

A lamp shaped like a carousel.

The work of his assistant?

He'd have to remember to thank her for her creativity, Karim thought wryly...

And then he saw Rachel.

She was asleep in a big wing chair, the baby in her arms. Her hair was loose, falling like a glossy rain over the shoulders of a high-necked white cotton nightgown long enough to cover her feet, which were tucked up under her.

Karim's throat constricted.

He had seen this woman in glitter. In denim. He had seen her naked. She had been beautiful each time, but this, the way she sat now, so unselfconsciously lovely, so perfect and vulnerable, was almost enough to stop his heart.

Whatever the reason she'd been with Rami it didn't matter.

What did matter was that he wanted her more than he'd ever wanted any other woman.

He drew a long, shuddering breath.

But wanting was not the same as having. And he could not have her.

It would only complicate something that was already far too complicated. He had a responsibility. A duty. To his father, his people, his dead brother's memory.

The boy.

That was what this was all about.

His mother had been focused on herself. So had Rami. But he was not like that. He never would be. He—

"Babababa."

The baby was awake, looking at him through his brother's long-lashed blue eyes. Karim shook his head and put his finger to his lips.

"Shh."

Wrong comment. The child's mouth trembled. He made a little sound, not quite a cry but very close. Karim shook his head again.

"No," he whispered. "Don't. You must let Rachel sleep."

The child's mouth turned down. His small face darkened. Karim moved fast, lifted him carefully from the curve of Rachel's arm and walked quickly into the sitting room.

Now what?

What did you do with a crying child? For that matter, what did you do with one that was not crying?

The boy blew a noisy bubble. Karim looked at him. What the hell did a bubble mean?

"Bzzzt," the kid said.

Karim cleared his throat. He needed a translator.

Little hands waved. Small feet kicked. The round face screwed up.

"Okay," Karim said quickly. "How about we, ah, we go downstairs for a while?"

Down the stairs they went.

The baby began to make little noises. Not happy ones.

"I don't know what you want," Karim said desperately.

God help him if it was a bottle of formula or, worse still, a diaper change.

The living room was lighter now; dawn was touching the soaring towers of the city. Karim went to one of the big, arched windows.

"Look," he said. "It's going to be a sunny day."

More little noises. Karim had a yacht that sounded like that when it started up. Well, no. Not the yacht. The motor-boat that could be launched from it—

"Naaah. Naaah. Naaah."

"Shh," Karim said frantically...

Hell.

The kid was crying. Hard. Genuine tears were rolling down his plump cheeks. Karim looked for something to use to wipe them away. Dammit, how come he hadn't thought to put on a T-shirt?

"Don't cry," he said. Carefully, he swiped a finger along the baby's cheeks. A little hand grabbed his finger, dragged it to the rosebud mouth.

The noise stopped.

The tears stopped.

Teething. The kid was teething on his finger.

Karim smiled. He sat down in the corner of one of the curved living room sofas. Put his feet up on the teak and glass coffee table. Carefully arranged himself so there was a throw pillow behind him.

The kid was chomping away. And—*thank you, God*—this time the sounds he made were obviously ones of satisfaction.

"Good, huh?" Karim said softly.

That won him a bubbly smile. Karim smiled back. The kid was cute, if you liked kids. He didn't. Well, no. That wasn't true. He didn't dislike them.

He'd just never spent any time around one.

The kid smelled good, too. Something soft. Not lemony, like Rachel; this was a smell even a man who knew zero about children would automatically associate with babies.

The baby cooed. Smiled around Karim's finger. Karim grinned. And yawned.

The baby yawned, too.

The curving lashes drooped.

"That's it, kid," Karim said softly. "Time to call it a night. You doze off; I'll take you back to Rachel…"

Ethan's lashes fell against his cheeks and didn't lift again.

Karim's did the same.

A moment later, man and baby were sound asleep.

Karim woke abruptly, the baby still in his arms.

Asleep.

An excellent idea. Karim was desperate to do the same thing. Sleep for another couple of hours, then phone his P.A. and tell her to cancel his appointments for the day.

Why not? The guy from Tokyo, the one from India, both could wait until he'd finished dealing with Rami's affairs and had a clear head.

Rami's affairs, he thought, his mouth thinning. That was certainly what Vegas had been all about—his dead brother's affair with a dancer, a stripper, whatever Rachel Donnelly was.

She was also a mother.

A good mother. Hell, an excellent one, from what he'd seen. Responsible. Caring. Determined.

It was surprising that Rami would have been attracted to such a woman. Party girls with boobs bigger than their brains had always been his type.

Not that Rachel lacked anything in that department.

Her breasts, all of her that he'd seen in that quick encounter in her bathroom, were lush and female…

And how many times had he told himself to stop thinking such things, dammit? Because what Rachel was or was not had nothing to do with him or what he had to do next.

Karim got to his feet, carried the baby back to the guest suite. Rachel was still curled in the big chair, asleep.

She looked incredibly beautiful. And innocent.

Amazing how deceiving looks could be.

Amazing how he hungered for her.

He turned away, carefully lowered the baby into the crib, pulled up the blanket, started from the room...

A muscle knotted in his jaw.

He went back to the crib, leaned into it and lightly stroked the boy's soft fair curls.

"Sleep well, little one," he whispered, and then, before he could succumb to the insane desire to go to Rachel and do the same thing, he strode out of the suite, down the corridor to his own rooms, phoned his P.A.—but not to cancel his appointments.

To make more of them.

He'd neglected business for far too long.

Besides, work would clear his head, he told himself as he made a second call, this one to his lawyer, and a third, to the testing laboratory, and cancelled both meetings.

Then he stripped off his sweatpants, got into the shower and let the water beat down on him,

Those things could wait. A day, two—even three.

Putting them off had nothing to do with Rachel.

Nothing at all.

Down the hall, in the guest suite, Rachel, who had awakened as Karim entered the room, opened her eyes only when she was sure he'd gone.

Nothing made sense.

Not the fact that the stern Sheikh had apparently been caring for Ethan while she slept, or that he'd handled the baby with something that could only be defined as tenderness.

And it certainly didn't make sense that as she'd watched him from under her lashes she'd thought what it would be like if he came to her, touched her with those big, gentle hands...

"Fool," she whispered, and she rose to her feet.

It was time to start the day.

And to start planning her escape.

Except escape wasn't possible. There were always eyes on her.

Karim had a household staff.

Rachel knew that he'd told them something about her.

She had no idea what he'd said, but when she appeared in the kitchen that first morning, Ethan in her arms, a bosomy woman with flour-dusted hands had turned from the stove, a polite smile on her lips.

"Good morning, ma'am. I'm Mrs. Jensen, the Sheikh's cook."

And I'm the Sheikh's prisoner, Rachel wanted to say, but she didn't of course, she simply kept her expression neutral.

Karim was the enemy. So, then, was anyone he employed.

"And this is little Ethan. Oh, His Highness was right! He's a beautiful child."

Rachel was surprised.

"Is that what he said?"

"Oh, yes, ma'am. He told us the baby was—"

"Us?"

"Ah." Mrs. Jensen wiped her hands on her apron and pressed a button on the wall phone. "Sorry, ma'am. Prince Karim asked me to be sure and introduce you to the others."

"What others?"

"Why, the rest of the household staff. There's me. And the housekeeper, Mrs. Lopez. The prince's driver—well, you met him at the airport last night. And we've an addition. My granddaughter Roberta. She'll be here within the hour. To help with the baby," the cook added, when she saw the puzzled look on Rachel's face.

"I don't need any help with my baby," Rachel said quickly, drawing Ethan closer.

"You'll like Roberta, ma'am. She's a professional nanny and she adores babies."

"I'm perfectly capable of taking care of Ethan myself."

"Of course you are, Ms. Donnelly. But His Highness asked if my Roberta was available—just, you know, just to help you."

"To keep an eye on me, you mean," Rachel said coldly.

"No, ma'am. Certainly not. To help you, is all." The cook's tone was indignant. "He knows my Roberta's an excellent nanny."

Rachel's voice turned frigid. "Oh, yes," she said, the words heavy with sarcasm. "He'd surely know that."

Mrs. Jensen eyed her with distaste.

"His Highness put Roberta through school, Ms. Donnelly. She'd floundered a bit and he paid for her to have a tutor, and then for her college tuition, until she decided she wanted to work with little ones, so he sent her to a school for nannies."

"Because?"

"I don't understand your question, ma'am."

"Why would he do all that?"

"Because that's how he is," the cook said, her voice almost as chilly as Rachel's. "He honors what he sees as his responsibilities."

"He meddles in people's lives, you mean."

The cook's expression hardened.

"You won't find anyone here who would agree with that, ma'am," she said stiffly.

Fortunately for both Rachel and the cook, the others had chosen that moment to enter the kitchen.

Rachel had been prepared to dislike the entire staff.

She couldn't. How could she dislike people who adored Ethan?

After a couple of days Ethan, the sweet little traitor, adored them right back.

Roberta, in particular.

It was hard to resent her. She didn't interfere at all, and simply gave Rachel a hand when permitted. Finally, Rachel decided it was foolish to take her anger out on a girl only a few years her junior who was a wonder with babies.

Her relationship with the others remained cool.

Surely it was because of whatever Karim had told them about her...

But it wasn't.

One morning, coming down the stairs, she heard Mrs. Lopez and Mrs. Jensen talking in low voices.

"The Prince said she was a nice young woman," Mrs. Jensen was saying, "and that she's had some difficulty lately, but honestly, Miriam, I hate to say it, but I don't think she's nice at all."

"Well," Mrs. Lopez said, "she's wonderful with her baby—anyone can see that. But it's impossible to get a smile from her, isn't it? If I didn't know better, Amelia, I'd think she dislikes us—but why would she, when she hardly know us?"

Damn! Damn! Double damn!

Rachel eased back up the stairs.

Was it possible she'd been wrong about Karim's staff?

Little by little, her dealings with them changed. She smiled; so did they. She said nice things; so did they. She had to admit it made life more pleasant.

As for Karim... She never saw him. What had happened to the meetings with his lawyers? Lab tests?

Rachel didn't ask. Why rush the things she dreaded? Apparently His Sheikhiness was too busy with work to deal with anything else.

She wasn't really surprised. Ethan's welfare would always take second place.

Karim left for his office early in the morning. Not by car. When she asked the reason, strictly as a matter of curiosity—because why would a prince with a Mercedes and a man to drive it leave both behind—John, his driver, said that His Highness generally took the subway.

"Or he walks," he added, and Rachel could almost hear the *tsk-tsk* in the words. "His Highness says it's the best way to beat the traffic."

Big deal, she thought. The mighty Sheikh joins the commoners.

He could travel by broomstick, for all she cared.

And he didn't return until late at night. Very late, never in time for dinner. Their paths never crossed. Fine with her. Excellent, in fact...

And then, one morning, after another night spent walking the floor with Ethan, Rachel finally put him down for a nap. She was too tired to sleep, so went quietly downstairs for coffee.

It was very early. No one would be up and about yet. It meant, she thought, yawning as she stepped into the silent kitchen, that she could show up just as she was, in a long flannel nightgown, her hair loose and her feet bare, put up a pot of coffee and—

The kitchen lights came on.

Rachel gasped, whirled toward the door—

And saw Karim.

He was wearing gray sweatpants, a gray T-shirt with the sleeves cut off, and sneakers that had clearly seen better days. His face and muscled arms glistened with sweat; his hair was in his eyes; his jaw was dark with early-morning stubble...

He was absolutely beautiful.

"I'm sorry—"

"I'm sorry—"

They spoke at the same time. Flustered, Rachel started again.

"I didn't think—"

"I had no idea—"

Their words collided.

Karim grinned, took the towel looped around his neck and dried his face and arms.

Rachel bit her lip, then offered a hesitant smile.

"You first," he said.

She swallowed hard.

"I was going to say that I didn't think I'd be disturbing anyone if—"

"You're not. Disturbing anyone. Disturbing me, I mean," he said. "I just finished working out and I thought—"

"Working out?" she repeated foolishly, because she couldn't seem to think straight. Well, who would? She hadn't expected to see him...

To see him looking so male, so gorgeous, in such a non-princely outfit.

The thought made her laugh. She tried to swallow the laugh, but she wasn't quick enough.

"What?" he said, with a little smile.

"Nothing. It's just—I don't know. I never imagined..."

"What?" he said again, his smile broadening as he looked at her. God, she was easy on the eyes. No make-up. Her hair a golden cloud. Her body hidden beneath the old-fashioned nightgown, just the sweet hint of breasts and hips...

"I, uh, I never thought of you working out."

He grinned. Slapped his incredibly flat belly.

"Have to. Otherwise I'd weigh five hundred pounds."

Rachel laughed. "Somehow, I doubt that."

He moved past her, opened the fridge, took out a container of orange juice.

"Yeah. Well, the truth is, I spend a lot of time behind a desk lately. Not much chance to play sports. And I always did, you know? I still run a little, but when I was in college I played football—"

"Football? Or soccer?"

He looked at her.

"Football. American-style." He smiled. "So, you know they call soccer football everywhere but here in the States, huh?"

She nodded. "When Ethan had colic I used to take him for long drives to soothe him. He loved the motion of the car. Then I'd head home, but I learned, fast that he might wake up if I put him straight into his crib so I'd plop down on the sofa, turn on the TV, and if it was the middle of the night—" she smiled "—which, of course, it almost always was—well, at two and three in the morning there's nothing much on except soccer re-runs—"

"Goooal!" Karim said solemnly.

Rachel laughed. "Right. Oh, and infomercials."

"Infomercials?"

"Yes. You know—men shouting as they try to sell you things you never heard of and never dreamed you needed."

Karim took two glasses from a cabinet, filled them with juice and handed one to Rachel.

"Oh," she said quickly, "no. No, thanks. I, ah, I should get out of your way—"

"You're not in my way. Besides," he said, his expression dead-pan, "if you order this glass of OJ right now, we'll include a cup of coffee at no extra charge. You'll just pay separate shipping and handling."

She burst out laughing. It was as perfect an infomercial as any she'd ever seen.

Karim smiled. "Seriously, I make one heck of a cup of coffee. No shipping or handling charge at all. Okay?"

Not okay, her head told her…

"Okay," she said, because, after all, what harm could there be in something so simple?

He made coffee.

She made toast.

He took his with strawberry jam. She took hers with cream cheese.

"Jam's better," he said.

She shook her head. "Too sweet first thing in the morning."

"I like sweet tastes first thing in the morning," he said, and though he hadn't meant it as a *double entendre* she flushed, and he thought, just for a second, about leaning across the counter and kissing her...

But he didn't.

Somehow this moment, this brief *détente*, was important.

So he cleared his throat, said the weather was unseasonably cool, and then they talked about this and that, the traffic, the newest plans for Central Park...

And then they fell silent.

What if he kisses me? Rachel thought.

I want to kiss her, Karim thought.

Her heartbeat quickened. So did his.

Their eyes met.

"Well..." he said.

"Well..." she said.

They got to their feet.

And moved in opposite directions.

"Got to get moving," he said briskly.

Rachel nodded. "Me, too," she said, just as briskly.

He told himself he was glad he hadn't touched her.

She told herself the same thing.

But those easy moments in the quiet early-morning hours were all either of them thought of that entire day.

The early-morning meeting didn't happen again.

Rachel made sure of that. She didn't leave her room until she was certain Karim was gone.

Yes, she'd discovered her captor had a human side.

So what?

Days passed, and though he didn't mention DNA tests or legal appointments eventually he would.

What would she do then?

Clearly she'd been wrong, thinking she'd be able to take Ethan and fade into the crowd.

She decided she had to confront him.

At the end of a long day—Ethan's first tooth had come in, and he was cutting another—Rachel showered, put on a nightgown, tucked the baby into his crib and settled into the wing chair, pen and notepad in hand.

Time to get organized, she told herself, and began writing.

Contact Legal Aid. Or look up names of attorneys?
Qualifications? General law? Family law?
How to know if a lawyer is a good one?
Would a lawyer work on a payment plan?

Rachel yawned. She was exhausted. A nap. A brief one. And then—and then—

The pad and pen fell to the floor and she dropped into sleep.

CHAPTER NINE

Hours later, Karim stepped from his private elevator.

The penthouse was silent; lamps glowed discreetly, just enough to chase away the gloom.

Rachel was always in her rooms by now.

And they hadn't run into each other in the morning again.

They couldn't; he'd taken to skipping his workouts. He left even earlier than before.

It was safer that way.

Otherwise, he thought grimly as he loosened his tie and went quietly up the stairs, otherwise he'd—

What?

Take Rachel in his arms? No way. That could only lead to disaster. He was going to take custody of the child. The last thing he needed was sleep with that child's mother.

Right.

Then, why hadn't he started the ball rolling? Why had he not yet called his lawyer or the DNA lab?

A better question was, why did he walk quietly down the corridor each night, pause outside Rachel's always-closed door, feel his pulse quicken as he imagined himself opening that door, going to her, waking her by taking her in his arms…?

Dammit.

He'd been over this ground before. Hadn't he just thought

the same thing again? The complications if he did such a crazy thing? Even the nasty possibility that her responses to him had been deliberate because she figured she could divert him from his plan?

His body tightened.

Or maybe, like him, she needed to get this impossible hunger out of her system.

Maybe this was the night to do it. Maybe—

What was that?

A sound. A whimper.

It was the baby.

Karim hesitated. He thought of the last time he'd heard the child crying, how he'd found him awake and Rachel asleep...

He stepped forward and opened the door.

It was the same. The dark sitting room. The soft light glowing through the partly open door of the nursery. And Rachel, asleep in the big wing chair, her hair loose and shining against the ivory fabric of one of those old-fashioned nightgowns he'd never known any other woman to wear.

His mistresses wore silk. Or lace. Sexy stuff, meant to turn up the heat...

And never getting it half as high as Rachel did in throat-to-toe cotton.

He wanted to kneel beside her, take her in his arms, draw her down to the floor with him. Kiss her, taste her, make her moan with hunger.

The baby. Concentrate on the baby.

Ethan was in the crib, wide awake, kicking those little arms and legs like a marathon runner and smiling from ear to ear.

Karim smiled back.

"Hey, pal," he whispered.

He moved forward. Stepped on something. A pen and, under it, a notebook. He picked it up, glanced at the page.

Rachel had scrawled a "To Do" list. None of his business what it was…

Except he could see it was about keeping Ethan.

He felt a quick tug of guilt. Which was ridiculous.

He had no reason to feel guilty. The baby was a prince's son. He owed it to his brother's memory, his king and his people, to see to it he was raised as a prince.

"Gaa gaa?"

Karim put the pad and pen on a table, scooped the baby into his arms and tiptoed from the room.

It was close to dawn when something drew Rachel from sleep.

A noise. A stir of sound somewhere in the vast apartment.

"Mmm," she murmured, stretching her arms high over her head.

Falling asleep in this big chair had become something of a habit. It was surprisingly comfortable; she awoke feeling rested and—

"Ethan?"

The crib was empty.

Rachel shot to her feet.

Had he awakened and started to cry and she'd slept through it?

She told herself to calm down.

Ethan was fine. He was somewhere in the apartment and he was fine. But when she found the person who'd taken him instead of waking her—

Barefoot, she made her way down the silent corridor, down the stairs, through the dark rooms…

And ended her search by following the pale flow of light into the big living room, where she found her little boy and her captor.

They were fast asleep.

Rachel's throat constricted.

The room reflected the life and wealth of its owner. White walls. White furniture highlighted by touches of deepest black. It was a sophisticated setting for a sophisticated man...

A man who lay sprawled on one of the long white sofas, shoes, suit coat and tie tossed aside, with Ethan lying spread-eagled against his chest—Ethan so small and sweet in the powerful arms of the powerful man who, except for that first night, behaved as if he didn't exist.

The baby sighed into the tiny damp spot his sore gums had left on what was surely a hand-made white shirt.

Karim drew him closer and, in his sleep, stroked a big hand down Ethan's back.

The baby snuggled in.

Something hot and dangerous flooded Rachel's heart.

No. No, she was not going to let this scene affect her. She knew better, knew what men were, knew what this man was...

Knew that he could be hard as well as tender, not just when he held a baby but when he held her.

She must have made a sound, perhaps a sigh like the baby's, because Karim's dark, thick lashes fluttered, then rose.

His eyes, still blurry with sleep, met hers.

"Ethan was crying." His voice was late-night hoarse. "You were sleeping. I didn't want him to wake you." He paused. Why was she looking at him as if she'd never seen him before? Karim cleared his throat. "So I brought him down here with me."

He fell silent. His heart was racing.

How could she be so beautiful? Such an insignificant word to describe her but it was the only one he had.

She was beautiful.

Her soft, rosy mouth. Her sleep-tousled hair.

And all the rest.

Her breasts, pressing against the thin cotton of her gown. Her long legs, outlined by the soft fabric.

Only the weight of the child against his chest kept him sane, enabled him to raise his eyes to Rachel's without embarrassing them both.

"I'll…" He cleared his throat. "I'll take him upstairs."

"Thank you. For taking care of him."

Karim smiled. "He's a nice little boy."

"Yes. Yes, he is." She swallowed dryly. "I'll take him up."

"That's liable to wake him. Let me."

She nodded. Karim got to his feet and she fell in behind him, followed him up the stairs to the nursery.

She watched him bend over the crib, carefully place the sleeping baby in it. There was a light blanket at the foot; he drew it up, tucked it around the child, touched his pale curls lightly with his hand as he had done that first time.

"Sleep well," he whispered.

Rachel felt a tightness in her chest.

How many times had she held the baby and thought, *If only you were truly mine…*?

Impossible, of course.

Karim's brother and her sister had created this little boy.

But what if fate had written a different story? What if Ethan were not Rami's and Suki's but hers and—and—

She spun away, went into the sitting room and out to the hall.

Karim came after her. "Rachel?"

She was trembling. God, she was—

"Rachel," he said again, "what is it?"

Walk away, she told herself. *Don't be a fool…don't, don't, don't—*

His hand fell on her shoulder. She could feel his hard body behind hers, could feel the heat emanating from him.

He said her name again, his voice low and rough, and she turned and faced him.

What she saw in his eyes told her that tonight, at least, anything was possible.

"Karim," she whispered, and when he reached for her she went straight into his arms.

He told himself there were endless reasons to let go of her. To step back from this while he still could.

He had always done the right thing, the logical thing, the dutiful thing...

Karim groaned, and gathered her close.

This, only this, was the right thing. This was where Rachel belonged.

"Karim."

His name was a sigh on her lips. He looked down into her face, her lovely face, and knew she was feeling the same emotions. Desire. Confusion. The realization that what they were doing could be dangerous, that there would be no going back...

"We can't," she said in a thready whisper, and he said she was right, they couldn't...

She moaned. Rose on her toes. Pressed against him.

He bent to her and captured her mouth.

She tasted of the night, of honey, of herself. She tasted like cream and vanilla, and he shuddered, took the kiss deep, deeper still.

"You are so beautiful," he whispered, and she trembled and wrapped her arms around his neck, and he knew they were both lost.

He slid his hands down her back, cupped her bottom, lifted her into him.

Another groan came from his throat.

He could feel all of her against him now. Her breasts. Her belly. Her hips.

Her body was hot. So was her mouth as he drank from it.

Half the buttons of his shirt were undone and she slid her hands inside, stroked them over his naked shoulders, and he shuddered under that feather-soft, tantalizing touch.

He drew her closer, holding her as if his arms were bands of steel, but it wasn't enough, it couldn't be enough—not when the need to make her his pounded through him with every beat of his heart.

He wanted to sweep her into his arms. Carry her to his bed.

But first—first just a taste of her skin. Here, behind her ear. Here, in the tender hollow of her throat. Here, at the delicate juncture of neck and shoulder.

She cried out.

The sound raced through him like a river of flame.

"Do you want this?' he whispered. "Tell me, *habibi*. Tell me what you want."

She cupped his face, dragged it down to hers and kissed him.

"This," she whispered. "You. But we can't. We can't—"

His kiss was hot and hard. Her knees buckled; he swung her up into his arms, his mouth never leaving hers, and carried her to his bedroom.

Moonlight poured in through the windows, spilling over them in a pool of ivory iridescence. He put her on her feet beside his bed and his eyes locked on her face.

"Tell me to stop," he said thickly, "and I will. But tell me now, before it's too late. Do you understand, Rachel? Once I start to touch you—once I start there's no going back."

The room filled with silence broken only by the rasp of his breath. Then, slowly, she brought her hands to the top button of her nightgown.

Karim's hand closed on hers.

"Let me undress you."

He heard the catch of her breath. Her hands fell to her sides. He reached for the first of what were surely a thousand buttons, none made for male fingers as big and suddenly clumsy as his, but he wanted to be the one who bared her to his eyes.

One button gave way.

Two.

Three.

And finally he could see—ah, God—he could see the slope of her breasts.

"Karim," she whispered.

He tore his gaze from her breasts, fixed his eyes on her face. Saw her parted lips, the flush of desire that streaked her cheeks, the darkness of her pupils.

His throat constricted. He leaned forward, kissed her mouth.

And undid the next button.

And the one after that.

Undid them, button by button, until there were none left.

Slowly, the gown parted.

And he saw her.

Saw all of her. Naked and incredibly lovely.

Her breasts were small and round, and he knew instantly that they were meant to fit perfectly in his cupped palms.

Her nipples were elegant buds, their color the dusty pink of the early-summer roses that grew wild in the valleys of the Great Wilderness Mountains.

Her hips were lushly feminine curves, the perfect framework for the soft curls at the junction of her thighs.

God, he needed to touch her.

Cup her breasts with his hands. Brush his fingers over her erect nipples. Put his mouth to the heart of her, let her feel the heat of his tongue between her thighs.

He looked up. Watched her face. Reached out slowly,

brushed his fingers over her nipples. She gasped, and he
bent his head, kissed her mouth, her throat, her breasts...

Drew one rosy bud between his lips.

She sobbed his name, shuddered. Her head fell back and
she cried out with pleasure.

It almost undid him.

He drew her down with him onto the bed. Go slow, he told
himself. Go slow...

Her body was hot against his.

Her mouth was soft.

And his erection was so hard it was almost painful.

"Rachel," he said unsteadily, and she wound her arms
around his neck, and somehow, somehow, her nightgown
was ruched around her hips and somehow, somehow, his
hand was between her thighs and she was wet and hot and
slick, and he found that sweet nub that was the essence of
her, and when he did she arched against his hand and gave
a cry that made him rear back, tear off his clothes and pull
open the drawer of the nightstand.

He found a condom. Fumbled with it. And then—

Then he was inside her.

A groan tore from his throat.

Rachel was tight around him, so tight he was afraid he'd
hurt her, and he went still, his body trembling with the effort, holding back, letting her stretch to accommodate him.
But she wouldn't let that happen. She was sobbing, moving
against him, moving, moving, moving...

She said his name. He could feel her trembling; she was
on that razor-thin edge of eternity with him.

Could a man's entire life have been meant to bring him
to this one moment?

He thrust forward, harder, deeper, faster. She whispered
his name again and then she screamed in ecstasy.

And Karim let go of everything—the pain of the last

weeks, the rigidity of his life—and flew with her along the moonlit path into the heart of the night sky.

He collapsed over her, his body slick with sweat.

His face was buried in the curve of her shoulder, her hair was a silken tangle and he loved the feel of it against his lips. His heart was pounding; so was hers. He could feel it beating hard against his.

He knew he was too heavy for her but he didn't want to move—not if it meant giving up this moment. Rachel's skin against his skin, her arms around him, her legs wrapped around his hips...

She gave a little sigh.

He sighed, too, rolled to his side and drew her into his arms.

"Are you all right?" he said softly.

She nodded. "I'm fine."

"Very fine?" he said, and smiled. He used one hand to tilt her face to his. "Incredibly fine?" he whispered, and kissed her.

Her lips were soft. They clung to his but only for a heartbeat. Then she drew back.

"I—I have to get up," she whispered.

"Not yet," he said in a sexy, rough voice as he stroked a lock of hair from her temple and tucked it behind her ear. "Stay with me a little longer."

"No. Really. I have to—I have to get up."

A simple request, Karim told himself. She wanted to use the bathroom. A simple, normal request.

But her voice was strained and her eyes darted away from his.

"Rachel?"

She didn't answer.

"Rachel. Sweetheart—"

"Let me up!"

For a horrible few seconds she was afraid he was going to keep his arms where they were, one around her shoulders, the other draped over her waist, but finally he let her go.

Now the trick was to sit up and not let him see her, because she was naked and, yes, he'd already seen her, he'd more than seen her…

Somehow, she managed to struggle upright and drag the edges of her nightgown together. Then she got to her feet, her back to him.

"Where are you going?"

He didn't sound sexy anymore. No matter. She would sound brisk and bright.

"To the bathroom."

Karim sat up. "The bathroom's behind you."

"The bathroom in the guest suite."

"What's going on, Rachel? You have regrets?"

"Honestly, Karim, I'd think you would know that there's nothing less appealing than a—a post-sex analysis. So if you don't mind—"

She turned away from him and started for the door, her posture stiff and unyielding. He grabbed his discarded trousers, pulled them on, got to the door before she did, stood with his back to it, arms folded over his chest, legs slightly apart, face without expression.

"Please," she said. "Get out of my way."

"Not until you talk to me."

"I told you, I have to go to the—"

"You're running away."

Her head came up. "The hell I am," she snapped.

So much for brisk and bright.

"A minute ago you were in my arms. And now—"

"And now it's over. You got what you wanted."

She cried out as his hands closed on her shoulders.

"Don't," he growled.

"Don't what? Tell the truth? Dammit, let go of me!"

"We made love. Don't try to turn it into something ugly."

"We went to bed." Her eyes flashed. "Don't try to turn it into something pretty."

His mouth twisted.

"Next thing I know," he said, very softly, "you're going to claim I forced you."

"No." Her chin lifted; color striped her cheekbones. "I'm not. There are already too many—too many lies between us!"

"For instance."

"For instance— For instance—"

Rachel fell silent. It was one lie, one huge lie, that lay between them, but she couldn't tell him that. If he knew the truth he'd have all the ammunition he needed to take Ethan from her.

"I'm waiting," he said coldly. "Exactly what lies are you talking about?"

She looked up. Moistened her lips with the tip of her tongue.

"There's really no point to this," she said wearily. "We did—what we did. And now—"

"And now you want to forget it ever happened."

Yes, she wanted to say, but that would be an even greater lie. She knew she'd never forget being with Karim. Never.

"I just—I just want to move on."

Karim's eyes darkened.

"Move on?"

"Yes. You know, this was—it was nice, but—"

He cupped her face, cut off her words with a kiss. She fought it, but only for a second. Then she gave a soft little cry, put her arms around his neck and gave herself up to him.

When he finally took his mouth from hers she was shaking.

"We can't," she whispered.

"We already did," he said. "And I wouldn't change it for all the riches of the world, sweetheart." He paused. "And neither would you." His voice softened. "Tell me that isn't true and I'll let you walk away."

Here was her chance.

He was a man of honor. She knew that already. If she said, *What just happened means nothing to me,* he would let her turn her back on this—whatever "this" was.

But she couldn't say those words—couldn't turn what had been so beautiful into something ugly.

"Karim—"

"I like the way you say my name."

"You don't know anything about me."

He smiled. "I know that you're hell on my ego. And that's a lot, coming from a man who's— What was it you called me? Arrogant. Self-centered. A despot." Another smile. "Did I leave anything out?"

"We'd just met. And—and I know you won't believe me, but I don't do—I don't do—"

"Do what?" he said solemnly.

Color swept into her face.

"I'm not the woman you think I am." That, at least, was true. "And I don't go to bed with—with strange men."

"I'm strange, huh?"

"No! I didn't mean—"

"That's okay," he said, even more solemnly. "Don't hold back. Just say what you think."

There was laughter in his eyes. She could feel a smile trying to form on her lips but there was nothing to smile about—certainly not to laugh about.

"You're impossible," she said. "I'm trying to be serious."

"So am I." He bent to her, kissed her with a tenderness

she knew she didn't deserve. "You think this is wrong be-cause—because of Rami."

The weight of her deception made it hard to breathe. She nodded; how could she trust herself to speak?

"Because," he said gruffly, "you slept with him."

"Karim, please. I don't want to—"

"No. Neither do I. Hell, Rami's the last thing I want to talk about right now."

"You think—you think I cared for him. But—"

"No. I don't. You said you hated him, remember?" His dark eyes narrowed. "But we can't pretend you and he…" He took a long, harsh breath. "You slept with him. You bore his child."

A sob burst from Rachel's throat. She spun away, but Karim caught her, turned her toward him.

"You think I need to hear the reasons?" His eyes met hers. "I don't. What happened is in the past. Now, today, tomor-row…that's what matters." His voice turned husky. "Besides, if there is one thing I know with all my heart it is that you may have slept with Rami—but you and I just made love."

Tears rose in her eyes.

"We made love," he said fiercely. "You know it. I know it. Why won't you admit it?"

"Because—because—"

She gave a muffled sob. Karim cursed and gathered her in his arms. She buried her face against him and her hot tears fell on his bare chest.

"I don't give a damn about anything that happened be-fore we met," he said, his voice raw. "This. Us. That's all that matters."

"There is no 'us.' There can't be. I told you—you don't know anything about me…"

He bent his head, took her mouth in a hard, quick kiss.

"I know everything I need to know," he said roughly.

"You're brave. And strong. You face life with dignity and courage."

Guilt was sharp as the thrust of a knife into her heart.

Tell him, a voice within her whispered. *You must tell him. You have to...you have to—*

"I was wrong to say I'd take your son from you."

Oh, God! "Karim," she said quickly. "Karim. About—about the baby—"

"No. You don't have to say anything, *habibi*. You are a good mother. A wonderful mother. We'll find a way around this." His expression softened; he smiled and ran his thumb gently over her mouth. "And you're beautiful," he said softly. "Not just your face and your body. Inside, where it counts, you're the most beautiful woman in the world. So you see? I know all I need to know about you." His smile broadened. "Except, perhaps, what you would like for a midnight snack."

Rachel looked into the eyes of this man who had turned out to be nothing like his brother, nothing like any man she'd ever known.

Despite herself, her lips curved in an answering smile.

"You're changing the subject, Your Highness."

"Aha. Progress." His tone was solemn, but his eyes were filled with laughter. "That's the first time you've used those words without making me cringe."

Her smile broadened. "Don't let it go to your head, but you can be a very nice man."

He grinned.

"For an arrogant, self-centered despot, you mean?"

Rachel laid her hand against Karim's jaw. It was rough with end-of-day stubble. It made him look dangerous and incredibly sexy.

"Maybe I was wrong about that."

"You were right, *habibi*. I am all those things—but not when I am with you." He caught her hand, pressed a kiss into her palm. "On second thought…" His voice turned as rough as that stubble. "On second thought…" His teeth sank lightly into the flesh at the base of her thumb. "Are you hungry, too, sweetheart?"

Rachel looked up into her lover's dark eyes and answered the question she saw there.

"Yes," she whispered. "I'm hungry for you."

Karim groaned, brought her hard against him and kissed her.

The world, and the web of lies she had created, spun away.

CHAPTER TEN

Now they could make love more slowly.

There was time to learn each other's most intimate secrets, to explore with slow hands and deep kisses, to speak in a lovers' language of soft whispers and softer sighs.

"I love the taste of you," Karim said as he lay back with Rachel in his arms.

God, he did.

Her skin was silk against his lips, her nipples honey-tipped buds. Her scent was intoxicating, pure and female. Everything about her heightened his desire: the way she moaned when he caressed her, the curve of her mouth against his, the blurring of her eyes when he entered her.

He enjoyed sex, and there was no sense in not admitting he was an accomplished lover. Still, a part of him always remained a little removed during the act, and if he'd given it any thought he'd have said that was a good thing; it meant he could hold on to his self-control until the last possible second.

Not with Rachel.

He couldn't tell where her pleasure began and his ended.

It was an incredible sensation.

And when she grew bolder and began to explore him— touching the tip of her tongue to his salty skin, lightly biting his lip, running her hands over his muscled shoulders and arms—

He almost went crazy.

He wanted to tumble her on her back, drive into her until the earth trembled.

Somehow he forced himself to keep from doing it—

Like now, when her hand moved lower.

And stilled.

Karim whispered her name. She looked up. Her eyes were pools of hot darkness; *I could drown in those eyes,* he thought, *and die happy.*

"Touch me," he said thickly.

Rachel had never wanted to touch a man so intimately, never really looked at a man's hard, erect flesh.

Now she wanted to do both.

It took less courage to look. She did, and caught her breath.

This part of her lover that gave her such pleasure was beautiful, a symbol not only of his virility but of his desire for her.

"Rachel."

Karim's voice was low. Strained. Gently, he clasped her wrist and brought her hand closer.

And waited, barely breathing.

Slowly, slowly enough so he could feel the sweat gathering on his forehead, he watched her reach out.

Her fingers brushed his taut flesh.

He groaned.

She jerked back.

"I don't—I don't want to hurt you…"

Did a man laugh or cry at such a moment?

"You won't hurt me," he said, his voice gruff. He made a sound he hoped was a laugh. "You may kill me, *habibi,* but you won't hurt me."

Rachel slicked the tip of her tongue over her bottom lip.

Karim bit back another groan—and then she closed her hand around him.

He shuddered.

"Yes," he whispered, "yes, sweetheart. That's it. Touch me like that. Like that…"

His hand closed over hers; he taught her how to make that soft groan rise in his throat again, but now she understood that it wasn't a sound of pain.

It was pleasure.

Pleasure only she could bring him.

She saw it in his face, the way his golden skin seemed to tighten over the bones, the way his nostrils flared…

Until he caught her wrist again and stopped her.

"Wait," he said thickly.

He took a long, deep breath. Expelled it. Another breath. Then he leaned toward her.

"My turn," he whispered.

He eased her onto her back. Knelt between her thighs. Kissed her mouth. Her throat. Her breasts.

It was she who groaned this time, and moved restlessly under his caresses.

"I love watching you," he said softly. "The rise of color in your face. The way your lashes veil your eyes. I love seeing what happens to you when I touch you. When I kiss you. When I do this…"

She gasped as he parted her with his fingers. Stroked her, then bent to her, licked her, sucked on her. She came on a dizzying wave of release.

But there was more.

First, another condom.

Then he brought the head of his erect penis against her silken folds.

"Look," he said. "Watch me enter you, *habibi*."

His words made her tremble with anticipation.

She raised her head, looked at the place where their bodies met in the most intimate of kisses.

"Watch," he said again, his voice rough as gravel.

She watched. Cried out at the sweet, sweet torture of seeing him penetrate her, feeling him claim her.

"Rachel..."

He thrust hard, thrust deep, and she gave a long, wild sob of joy, fingers clenched around his biceps, her legs wrapped high around his hips.

Karim's body glistened with sweat. His heart was racing. He wanted to follow her into oblivion...

Teeth gritted, he fought against it.

And took her to the brink again.

It was too much.

She could feel herself starting to come apart.

"Please," she sobbed, "please, Karim, please..."

He drove deep one final time.

And as she screamed he let go, spent himself within her silken walls, then collapsed in her arms.

The moments slipped by.

Then Karim lifted his head, brushed his lips gently over hers and rolled to his side with Rachel safe in his arms.

She gave him a slow, sweet kiss. And she smiled.

It was the kind of smile a man dreamt of seeing on the face of the woman he'd just made love with, and he smiled back.

Hell, he grinned.

"I take it," he said, trying to sound solemn but not succeeding, "that smile signifies satisfaction."

"In triplicate," she said softly.

He gave a soft, delighted laugh. She smiled again.

"No pretensions at modesty, Your Highness?"

"None whatsoever," he said, "because you're the reason this was so wonderful, *habibi*. So incredibly perfect."

He brought his mouth to hers for a tender, lingering kiss, and when she sighed against his lips he felt his heart swell.

"Perfect," he murmured.

Rachel closed her eyes, put her head on his shoulder, her hand over his heart.

"What does that mean? *Habibi*?"

"It means sweetheart," he said, pressing a kiss into her hair.

"In Arabic, yes?"

He nodded. "Yes. It was my first language."

She raised her head, moved her hand just enough so she could prop her chin on it.

God, she was beautiful!

Her hair was a tangle of soft waves around her face. Their lovemaking had turned her eyes bright and given her skin a pink glow.

He wanted to rise over her and make love to her again.

"Your first language? You mean, before English?"

"Before French. Then I learned English. And Spanish. And German. And… What?"

"Five languages?"

"Six. Well, almost six. I'm still having trouble with Japanese."

She laughed.

"I'm still having trouble with Spanish," she said, "which is pretty sad, considering that I took a year of it in high school. Of course that was a long time back."

"I'll bet it was," Karim said as seriously as possible. "What was it? Twenty years ago? Twenty-five?"

Rachel balled her fist and punched him lightly in the belly.

"Oof! Okay, not twenty-five."

"I was in high school seven years ago, Sir Sheikh," she said, trying to sound indignant.

"Sir Sheikh, huh?" He smiled, brushed a strand of glossy hair back from her cheek. "I'll bet you were an honors student."

A cloud seemed to darken her eyes.

"I wasn't."

"Too busy being the homecoming queen to study?"

She stared at him for what seemed a long time. Then she rolled away, sat up, grabbed the comforter and wrapped it around herself like an oversized cloak.

"Rachel." Karim moved fast, caught her hand before she could get to her feet. "Sweetheart, what did I say?"

"Nothing."

"Don't do this. If I said something that hurt you, tell me."

The tension in her damned near radiated through his hand.

"Remember what I told you? That there are lots of things you don't know about me? Well, here's one of them. I didn't graduate from high school. I finally qualified for an equivalency diploma a couple of years ago and that's how come I'm still struggling with Spanish—because I only began taking it again in night classes at college. So, no, I don't speak six languages, and, no, I don't have a university degree, and, no—"

Karim swung her toward him and stopped the flow of angry, pained words with a kiss.

"I couldn't stay in school," Rachel said in a low voice when he lifted his lips from hers. "I had to take care of my sister and me."

"Your parents?" Karim said, trying to sound calm.

She shook her head. "My father died when Suki and I were little. My mother—my mother liked to have fun. She went away one day and we never saw her again."

"You see?" he said, trying to conceal the rage he felt at a

woman he had never laid eyes on. "We have something in common. My mother left Rami and me, too."

"It's hard—it's hard to know how a mother could—could—"

Karim cursed, pulled her into his lap and kissed her.

"*Habibi,*" he whispered. "*Habibi. Ana behibek—*"

"What does that mean?"

He swallowed hard.

"It means—it means you are very brave, sweetheart. It means I love holding you in my arms."

"I'm not brave at all," she said in a wobbly voice, and Karim tumbled back on the bed with her because the only safe way to show her that she was everything he'd just said was to make love to her again.

There was nothing at all safe in telling her the truth—

That what he'd really said was that he loved her.

They slept locked in each other's arms.

Sunlight woke them.

Karim looked into Rachel's eyes.

"Good morning," he said softly.

Rachel smiled. "Good morning."

"Did you sleep well?"

"Wonderfully well. In fact…" She rose on her elbow and looked past him to the iPod docked on the nightstand. "Oh! It's past seven. Ethan—"

"Ethan is fine."

"But—"

"Really. I checked a little while ago. Roberta has him downstairs. She's feeding him some unidentifiable yellow slop mixed with some equally unidentifiable white slop."

Rachel laughed at her lover's excellent description of strained peaches combined with rice cereal.

"He loves that slop," she said

"Which only proves Ethan's a baby. She says she's going to take him to the park when he's finished eating."

"Then I'd better hurry and get showered and—"

"I'm a man of the desert, *habibi*."

"Meaning…?"

"Meaning," he said, looking very serious, "I understand things you do not."

"Such as?"

"Water is a precious commodity. So saving water is an imperative." His mouth twitched. "Therefore we must make the sacrifice of showering together."

Rachel smiled. "And a lovely sacrifice it would be," she said softly, "but if Roberta's taking Ethan to Central Park…"

"She loves the boy, Rachel."

"I know. She's wonderful with him, and—"

"And she has a very impressive certificate from a very fancy school."

Rachel nodded.

"Yes. And you paid her tuition."

"Mrs. Jensen told you about that?"

"She certainly— Karim! You're blushing!"

"I am not blushing," he said, blushing harder.

"First tutoring. Then college. Then nanny school." She kissed his chin. "You really are a very nice man."

Karim smiled.

"What I am," he said, "is a man in desperate need of food."

"That's it. Change the subject." She sighed. "Ethan will have a fine time with Roberta. And you do need food. We both do."

"I love knowing I've given you an appetite."

It was Rachel's turn to blush. She put her palms against his chest and gave him a gentle shove.

"I'll make us some breakfast."

"And force Mrs. Jensen out of her own kitchen?"

"Oh. I didn't think of—"

"I'd love to have you make breakfast, sweetheart."

"But Mrs. Jensen—"

Karim gathered her to him. "I'll send her to the market."

Rachel batted her lashes.

"Such a wise man, Your Highness!"

"Training," he said loftily. "When a man is destined to be king, he knows how to keep the peace."

Her teasing smile faded.

"For a little while," she whispered, "I almost forgot that."

Yes. So had he. But now there it was. Reality. The commitment to duty. Honor. Responsibility. The very things that had brought this woman into his life.

There was only one problem.

He had never expected to fall in love with her.

But he had. She was everything to him.

How could that be?

She had been Rami's.

No. She had said it herself. No one was anyone's property. Besides, he had told her that the past didn't matter.

And he meant it.

It didn't.

What mattered was that he loved Rachel. She was good and kind and honest; he had never let himself even imagine finding a woman like her to complete him, and that was what she did.

She completed him…

The breath caught in his throat.

Suddenly he saw a path ahead of him—one that would enable him to fulfill his duties, maintain his honor, meet his responsibilities to his father, his country, his dead brother and his brother's child.

In one simple step he could do all those things and keep

the promise he'd made to Rachel about finding a way she could keep Ethan…

Be truthful, Karim.

Those things were all important…but they were not the real reason for what he was about to do.

Duty was important.

But love was everything. Everything—

"Karim?"

He blinked, looked into the face of the woman he loved. She looked worried. For him. And wasn't that amazing? Had he ever thought a woman would care for him, the man, and not for him, the Sheikh?

"Karim. Please, talk to me. What's wrong?"

"Nothing," he said—and then he gave a whoop of laughter, tugged her to her feet, whirled her around the room to music only he could hear and, when she was breathless and laughing with him, brought them to a halt and took her in his arms.

"Remember when I promised you I'd find a solution for our problem?"

Their problem.

Ah, God!

In her joy these last hours Rachel had managed to tuck reality aside. Now it had returned.

"Yes," she said slowly. "I remember. You want Ethan."

He nodded and drew her closer.

"At first he was all I wanted."

"You said—you said you wouldn't take him from me…"

"Sweetheart." Karim cleared his throat. Framed her face with his hands, lifted it to his. "The answer to our problem is to see that it isn't a problem at all."

"But it is. I wish it weren't, but—"

"I love you, *habibi.*"

His voice was gruff; his words were the most beautiful

she'd ever heard. Tears stung her eyes. He kissed them away, then kissed her mouth, gently and tenderly.

"Rachel." He took a deep breath. "I've lived my life alone. By choice. I—I don't want to sound like one of those TV shows where people put their emotions on display." He gave a small laugh. "Hell, there've been times I've been told I don't have emotions."

Rachel shook her head. "You're a wonderful man," she said fiercely, "with a heart as big as the world."

"A heart you have awakened, *habibi*." He kissed her again, his mouth soft against hers. "What I said…that I love you…I've never said those words before. Not to anyone." He paused. "And I've never trusted anyone fully. Never—not since I was a little boy." He smiled. "And then—and then I found you."

Tears rose in Rachel's eyes. This was it. She had to tell him the truth, no matter what the cost…

"Rachel." Karim looked deep into her eyes. "Marry me. Become my wife. The mother to the children we will have together as you already are to Ethan, who I've come to love as my own, who I will adopt and give my name."

Rachel began weeping.

"Rachel? Sweetheart, I adore you. I thought—I thought you felt the same—"

She flung her arms around his neck. Lifted herself to him. Kissed his mouth with all the love he had brought to her lonely heart.

"I love you," she whispered, between kisses. "I love you, love you, love you—"

"Marry me," Karim said.

No, a voice inside her whispered. *Rachel, you mustn't…*

"Rachel?"

Rachel threw caution to the wind and said, "Yes."

CHAPTER ELEVEN

Who would have thought that busy, crowded, shark-eat-shark Manhattan could be a paradise for lovers?

Not Karim.

He knew the city the way he knew London and Paris and Istanbul, knew its hotels, its restaurants, its business centers.

And, though he wasn't given to musing about romance, if pressed, he'd have said those cities were probably romantic.

Paris had a unique beauty and charm. Istanbul had a mystery that came of the blended cultures of east and west. London had crooked streets layered in history.

But New York? Frenetic. Impatient. Crowded. Rude. Boisterous.

And yet magnificent.

Those were the words that described his adopted home.

But romantic? No. That was what he would have said, had anyone asked. Had he even thought about such things. Which he didn't, because, after all, what did *he* know of romance? What place did it have in his life?

Not a thing—until ten days ago.

Rachel had changed his life.

He had lived in New York for a decade. And yet he knew he'd never really seen it before.

Central Park was no longer just a place for an early-morning run. It was, instead, a stretch of green as beautiful as the forested slopes that rose above his desert home. The cobbled streets of SoHo and Greenwich Village weren't places to avoid because of the traffic; they were as delightful to stroll as Montmartre.

Hand in hand, they explored the city together. They discovered quite cafés, pretty little parks, places where a man and woman could be alone despite the crowds all around them.

He managed a small miracle, too, when he finally convinced his bride-to-be that there was nothing wrong in letting him take her into half a dozen elegant boutiques and buying her soft, summery dresses, delicate lingerie and pairs of shoes that made her ooh and ahh with delight.

Heels? Yes.

"But no stilettos," she said, with a mock shudder.

That was when he learned she hadn't been a dancer, that she'd been a waitress, that she'd hated the shoes and the spangles and the thong, and her expression had turned so grave that right there, at the crowded intersection of Spring and Mercer, he'd taken her in his arms and kissed her.

In all the ways that mattered, the city was almost as new to Karim as it was to Rachel.

Even the restaurants he took her to were places he'd never seen before…except he had. He'd taken clients to the Four Seasons, to Daniel, to La Grenouille, but they were different places when he went to them with the woman he loved.

The woman he loved, he thought as he and Rachel sat at an intimate table for two in the River Café, the lights of Manhattan reflected in the dark, deep waters of the East River visible through the wall of windows beside them.

Karim's mouth curved in a very private smile.

He loved Rachel. And she loved him. He was still trying to get used to the idea.

There was so much to get his head around—starting with

coming awake each morning with her in his arms and ending with falling asleep that same way each night.

He'd gone to his office only twice. Even he found that unbelievable. He knew his staff damned well did.

He'd had good intentions the first time he'd gone to work, but he'd left before hardly anyone had known he was there. He'd thought about phoning John for his car, thought of flagging a taxi, but the streets had been clogged with vehicles, as always, and the fastest way home was to jog.

Which was what he'd done.

One hell of a sight, he was sure, a guy running up Madison Avenue in a Brioni suit and Gucci loafers, then rushing from the elevator into the foyer of his penthouse.

"Rachel?" he'd shouted. "Rachel?"

"Karim?" she'd said, from the top of the stairs. "What's the matter?"

"Nothing," he'd replied, taking the stairs two at a time. "Everything," he'd added, scooping her into his arms and kissing her. "I missed you," he whispered, and her face had lit with such joy that he'd carried her straight back to bed.

The second time he'd gone to his office he'd stayed just long enough to go through his calendar, assign whatever had to be dealt with to members of his administrative staff, and instruct his P.A. to cancel his appointments and to tell anyone trying to reach him that he was unavailable.

His P.A. had looked at him as if he'd lost his sanity.

"Unavailable, sir?"

"Unavailable," Karim had said firmly.

Because he was. Unavailable. Unreachable. Incommunicado to anyone but Rachel.

Or Ethan.

The baby was, without doubt, the smartest, most adorable kid in the world.

He giggled with delight when Karim introduced him to

the wonders of "I See." Belly-laughed when Karim lifted him high in the air. Adored having Karim blow bubbles against his tummy.

Laughter, and the love that accompanied it, was not something Karim or Rami had experienced much in their childhoods.

Which had turned him into a man with a heart so well disguised it had been all but non-existent, and Rami into a man who'd frittered his life away.

In some small measure, Karim hoped he could make up for the emptiness of Rami's existence by raising his son with all the love possible.

The best part was that it was easy to do.

Who'd have thought that he, the all-powerful Sheikh of Wall Street—a laughable title dumped on him in some foolish internet blog—would change diapers, do feedings, walk the floor with a crying child in his arms, sit in the park with Rachel and a baby carriage and be so content that half the time he suspected he had a goofy grin on his face?

God, he was happy.

Though sometimes he caught a look in Rachel's eyes that worried him.

A darkness.

Maybe he only imagined it.

He had to be imagining it—except there it was again, right now, as she looked out the window of the restaurant into the night: a sudden shift from smiling to something that wasn't quite a smile, as if a thought, a memory, had surfaced and brought her pain.

"Sweetheart?" he said softly. He saw her throat constrict as she swallowed. When she turned to him her smile was a smile again. Karim brought her hand to his lips. "Are you okay?"

"Yes."

"You sure? You looked—I don't know. Sad."

She shook her head, brought their joined hands to her own lips and kissed his knuckles.

"How could I be sad when I'm with you? I was just—I was just thinking how beautiful it is here."

"You're what's beautiful," Karim said.

And Rachel thought, as she had thought just a moment ago, *If only lies could be untold. If only time would stand still.*

Growing up, she'd loathed the slow passage of time.

Of course she knew time moved at only one speed. Sure, she'd bounced from school to school, but she'd read a lot. She'd read everything she could get her hands on.

"Pay half as much attention to how you look as you do to those books," Mama would say, "you'll be a happier girl."

But knowing time could move like molasses dripping from a cold jug had nothing to do with book-learning.

It had to do with…well, with her life.

Mama meeting a new man. Weeks or months taking on a snail's pace while she lavished all her attention on him until the new man became old news. Then Mama would haul their suitcases from under the bed. A day later they'd be on the Greyhound again, heading for a new town.

That was the only time things moved fast. After that…

A new town. New school. New kids. Rachel not fitting in. Suki running wild. And, always, a new man for Mama.

And time would once again grind to a halt, until Mama would get that look on her face, make her usual little speech about being tired of Jim or Bill or Art, or whatever man had just dumped her, and the entire sad pattern would start over.

So, no.

Rachel had never hoped time would stand still. She'd wanted it to rush on by…

Because she'd never been happy.

It had taken her twenty-four years to figure it out. When you were happy, time standing still was exactly what you wanted.

The first time she'd felt that way was the day Suki had handed Ethan to her.

And now there was this.

There was Karim.

She loved him. She adored him. There were moments she could hardly breathe for the joy in her heart.

Sitting here tonight, her lover across from her, his big hand clasping hers, seeing him smile, having him feed her bits of his lobster, hearing his rough whisper of warning about what he was liable to do if she parted her lips and showed him the tip of her tongue one more time...

If he'd grabbed her from her chair and carried her from the restaurant she'd have let him do it.

Over dinner, he'd talked about his childhood. Like the time he'd sneaked into the palace stables, selected his father's favorite stallion, put on the bit, bridle and reins and ridden bareback over the desert until his father's men caught up to him hours later and brought him back.

"My father was furious."

"I'll bet. What if the horse had thrown you?"

"He cared about the horse, *habibi*. He'd paid hundreds of thousands of dollars for it. And I was only seven. Not really big enough to control the animal."

"He wasn't worried about you? Oh, that's terrible!"

"And that's very nice."

"What is?"

"The way that tempting mouth of yours just dropped open, as if it needs me to kiss it." He brought her hand to his lips and bit lightly into it. "Perhaps other parts of you need kissing, too."

"Hush," she whispered. "What if someone hears you?"

But she was smiling, and he could tell by the pink blush on her face that what he'd said had pleased her.

Which was excellent, considering that all he wanted was to please her...

Especially tonight. With dessert.

A very special dessert, he thought, as their waiter approached the table.

"Your Highness. Miss." The waiter grinned. Karim gave him a warning look and the guy quickly cleared his throat. "The chef sends his compliments and says he's prepared a special dessert." He shot Rachel a big smile. "In the lady's honor."

"For me?" she said with delight.

"Yes, ma'am. If you're ready, sir...?

Karim nodded. He was ready. Nervous, but ready.

After almost two weeks together, he still couldn't believe his luck.

That he'd gone to Las Vegas to try to put right the problems his brother had left and had, instead, met this wonderful woman.

What a fool you were, Rami, he thought.

And yet he had Rami to thank for this miracle. Rachel. Her little boy.

He'd have liked to be able to tell him that.

They had been close, once upon a time. Now, in some strange way, he felt close to Rami again.

The only thing that troubled him was trying to accept that Rachel had—had been with Rami.

It wasn't about sex.

Okay.

Maybe it was, a little.

But he wasn't a male chauvinist. He came from a culture where women had, until relatively recently, been denied the rights to which men were born, but he'd never considered virginity something he'd demand in a wife.

The problem went beyond that.

He could not imagine Rami and Rachel having a conversation together, much less sleeping together. Rami had been all about the way a woman looked. Rachel was beautiful, but she was much more than that.

She was bright. Articulate. Opinionated.

Definitely opinionated.

He'd been reading a political blog on his laptop this morning; she'd been reading the same blog on his iPad. He hadn't known she was reading it and he'd mumbled something about it to himself. She'd mumbled back, and the next thing he knew she'd been debating with him for all she was worth.

Rami wouldn't have given a damn.

He loved it.

Loved her—which brought him back to the beginning. How could there have been anything between two such different people?

He wanted to ask.

But he didn't.

For one thing, Rachel had made it clear she didn't want to talk about the time she'd spent with Rami.

For another, he wasn't sure he'd be comfortable with the answers.

As he'd told her at the beginning, it was best to leave the past in the past and concentrate on today. On right now— because the waiter was coming with dessert.

A fanciful, miniature chocolate Brooklyn Bridge for him…

A scoop of vanilla ice cream for her.

The waiter put the dishes in front of them, shot a conspiratorial grin at Karim, said, "Enjoy!" and almost skipped away.

Karim watched Rachel look from his little bridge replica

to her scoop of vanilla ice cream. Her eyes flashed to his and he had to work at not laughing.

She looked like a kid who'd been promised cotton candy and instead was handed a lollypop.

"Mmm," he said cheerfully. "Looks good."

"Uh—uh, yes, it looks delicious."

How he loved her! What other woman would smile as if she was really thrilled to pass up a chocolate sculpture for what appeared to be a scoop of plain vanilla?

Karim picked up his dessert fork and sliced into his dessert.

"Fantastic," he said. And then, politely, "How's yours?"

Rachel cleared her throat.

"I'm sure it's wonderful," she said, picking up her dessert spoon, dipping it into the ice cream… "Oh." She smiled with surprise. "There's a chocolate shell under the—under the—"

"Something wrong?"

"No. Well, maybe. There's something inside the shell. It's—it's—"

She went very still.

Karim put down his fork. His heart was racing.

"Cake?" he said, trying to sound calm. "Strawberries?"

She shook her head. "It's—it's…" She looked up again.

Why couldn't he read the expression on her face?

"It's a box," she whispered. "A little blue box."

Suddenly his carefully crafted, oh-so-romantic plan seemed full of holes. Hell, what did he know about what a woman would or wouldn't find romantic?

"Rachel," he said. "Rachel, sweetheart, look, if you want to leave—"

Rachel swallowed hard.

She put down her spoon. Lifted the little blue box from its chocolate shell. Opened it…

A burst of blue-white light seemed to leap from the box to her eyes.

"Karim," she said. "Oh, Karim!"

It was a diamond ring—but that was like saying that the sun was just another star.

The diamond was huge. It looked as if all the fire that had created the universe had been captured within its blazing heart. It was set in white gold, flanked by sapphires that were the exact shade of the sky on a perfect June morning...

Karim watched Rachel's face. He waited for her to say something.

She didn't.

The silence grew.

He wanted to die.

He'd been so careful, selecting the ring when he'd supposedly made a third trip to his office. He knew his Rachel. She would not want anything ostentatious but he wanted something special.

He loved her, and he wanted the world to know it.

He'd spent most of the morning choosing this ring.

Didn't she like it? Didn't she want it? Had she thought things over, changed her mind about him? About becoming his wife?

Calm down, he told himself. Relax. Give her another minute, then say something casual. Say, *I hope you like it.* Or say, *If it's not what you'd have chosen we'll get something else.* Or tell her, *I thought this was kind of nice, but it you don't—*

"Dammit, Rachel," he said in a hoarse whisper, "say something!"

She held the ring in the palm of her hand, looked from it to him.

"It's—it's the most beautiful thing in the world!"

Thank God. "I love you," he said.

"Karim." Tears filled her eyes. "I don't—I don't deserve—"

He took the ring from her, slipped it on her finger. Yes. It was right. It was perfect. It was beautiful—but not as beautiful as she.

"I love you," he said again, and he pushed back his chair, held her hand, brought her to her feet and took her mouth in a kiss that said, as clearly as words, what he was feeling.

He'd waited all his life for this one woman.

Fate, destiny, karma had meant them to find each other, and to be together for all eternity.

"Rachel," he whispered, and she gave a soft, sweet cry, wrapped her arms around his neck and kissed him back.

"I love you with all my heart," she said through her tears. "I'll always love you. Remember that. Remember that I'll always, always love you."

"*Enti hayati, habibi.* You are my life."

Somebody in the room whistled, somebody else applauded, and Rachel blushed the brightest pink he'd ever seen her blush.

And dazzled him with her smile.

He dropped a handful of bills on the table, led her out into the night and took her home, to their bed, to the private little world that belonged only to them.

They slept in each other's arms.

He woke her during the night and made love to her again. Woke her at dawn to claim her once more.

The next time he woke the room was golden with sunlight. When he saw her lashes flutter, then lift, he smiled.

"Morning, sleepyhead," he murmured.

Rachel smiled. She put her hand against his cheek, rubbing her palm lightly over that deliciously sexy stubble.

"What time is it?" she said sleepily.

He gave her a soft, lingering kiss.

"Time to get showered and dressed, *habibi*. My plane is waiting."

A feeling of dread washed over her. She sat up, the bedclothes clutched to her breast.

"Your plane?"

Karim tugged the bedclothes away. Bent his head, kissed her breasts.

"We're going home," he said softly. "To Alcantar."

The plane ride seemed endless—far longer than the one from Vegas to New York.

Roberta had come with them. She and Ethan settled comfortably in the bedroom in the rear of the cabin.

Rachel was full of questions.

"Why didn't you tell me we were flying to Alcantar today?"

Karim laced his fingers through hers.

"I was going to. Then I thought it would only make you nervous."

True enough. She wasn't just nervous, she was terrified. The realization that she was about to meet Karim's father was daunting.

"But what if he doesn't like me?"

Karim put his arm around her and drew her head to his shoulder.

"Sweetheart, he will." He smiled. "Besides, he's been after me for years to find a proper wife."

"Am I a proper wife for you?" Rachel said in a small voice.

He laughed and dropped a kiss on her temple.

"You are a proper wife for any man, but especially for one who loves you as I do." He paused. "I told him about Ethan."

Rachel looked at him.

"And—and what did he say?"

What, indeed? Karim cleared his throat.

"He was surprised, of course. But my father, for all his— what shall I call it?—for all his imperial attitude, my father is a practical man. He is glad he has a grandson."

"But—but he thinks—I mean, he knows that Rami—that I—"

"Yes."

"And?"

Karim hesitated. This was a time for absolute honesty. That was one of the most remarkable things about his relationship with his beautiful fiancée.

They could always speak the truth to each other.

"And," he said slowly, "he will love you as a daughter— once he gets to know you."

She nodded.

"But not yet."

A muscle flickered in Karim's jaw. His conversation with his father had been a difficult one.

"A woman who would bear a son to a man who has not married her," his father had said coldly, "is a woman of questionable morality."

Karim had fought back a hot rush of anger.

"The world has changed, Father."

"Not our world here in Alcantar."

Wrong, Karim had thought.

The world *had* changed, even in Alcantar, and it would change again when he ascended the throne. But there was no sense in arguing the point.

What mattered was making it clear that he would not tolerate any interference in his decision to marry Rachel, or any show of disrespect to her.

"But *my* world has changed," he'd said. "Rachel changed it. I love her and I am proud to take her as my wife."

His father must have heard the steel in his voice because he'd ended the conversation by saying he would see Karim soon.

Very soon, Karim thought, as the plane touched the runway.

The pilot's disembodied voice floated through the cabin. "We have arrived, Your Highness."

Karim undid his seat belt and Rachel's; he drew her to her feet. Her face was pale and his heart went out to her. Her world was about to change, too.

Alcantar was a beautiful, proud country, but it was surely different from any place she had been before.

And he, once he stepped from the plane, would be different, too.

Perhaps he should have warned her of that, he thought as they reached the door and the steps that led down from the jet.

Too late.

He heard her whispered "Oh!" when she saw the convoy of white Bentleys flying the falcon flag of Alcantar, the uniformed honor guard standing at attention, the pomp and circumstance that awaited them.

"Karim," she whispered, "I don't know if I—if I—"

He put his arm around her. It was a breach of protocol, but to hell with protocol. Rachel was what mattered.

"You can," he said softly.

She leaned against him as if to draw on his strength for one brief second. Then she stood erect.

He was right.

She could do this.

I can do this, Rachel thought.

She could do anything for Karim. It was only that his titles—sheikh, prince, heir to the throne—had, until now, been nothing but words—and that she could not possibly be the perfect wife he wanted because she was a world-class liar.

Okay.

That was over.

If she could do anything for the man she loved, then she could tell him the truth.

He loved her. He understood her.

He'd understand that lying had been her only option.

The decision gave her the last bit of courage she needed.

She forced a smile as he led her down the steps, kept smiling when he paused and saluted the captain of the honor guard. She kept her hand on his arm and wondered if he could feel her trembling.

"All right, sweetheart?" he said softly once they were in the lead car, Roberta and the baby in the second.

"Yes," she whispered.

And thought what a really fine liar she was.

They drove along a palm-fringed road, through a town that looked modern and prosperous, toward an ivory and gold palace that rose against a cloudless blue sky, then made their way through a golden gate, down another tree-lined road and stopped in an enormous courtyard, with the dome of the palace looming above them.

A man in a white *keffiyeh* opened the door of their car and snapped to attention.

Karim stepped out, offered his hand to Rachel. She put her icy fingers in his.

"Everything will be fine," he told her softly. "You'll see."

Everything *was* fine as they walked up the palace steps, Roberta just behind them with Ethan in her arms.

Everything was still fine as they went through its massive gold doors, down a long marble corridor that led not to the throne room but to the King's private chambers.

That surprised Karim. Was it a good sign that his father chose to receive them here, or was it a bad one?

He stopped wondering once they were ushered into his father's enormous sitting room.

The drapes had been drawn against the afternoon sun; the King sat in an elaborate ivory and ebony chair, dark shadows clustered behind him.

Karim could feel the tension in the air.

He kept his arm around Rachel's waist.

"Father," he said.

The King rose to his feet.

"We are not to be disturbed," he snapped to the servant who'd escorted them.

The servant bowed. The door swung shut.

"Father," Karim said, "this is—"

His father held up his hand, looked from him to Rachel. There was icy fire in his eyes.

"This is a woman who saw the perfect way to lure a fool into her bed."

Karim's eyes narrowed. "Listen to me, old man—"

"No, my son. You will do the listening."

As if it were a signal, a woman with long blond hair and bright blue eyes stepped out from the shadows behind him.

Rachel's hand flew to her throat.

"Suki?"

"Damned right," Suki said sharply. "Did you really think you could get away with this, Rachel?"

Karim looked from one woman to the other.

"Rachel? Is this your sister?"

Rachel swung toward him.

"Karim." Her voice shook. "Karim, please… I tried to tell you. I tried so hard—"

Karim felt as if a dark pit were opening at his feet.

"Tell me what?"

"Really?" Suki said, her hands on her hips. "You tried to tell him? I don't think so. I don't think you had any intention of telling the truth, ever. I mean, you couldn't take Rami away from me. Snagging his brother was the next best thing."

Karim stared at Rachel.

"What is she talking about?"

Rachel shook her head.

He clasped her shoulders and drew her to her toes. "Dammit, what does she mean?"

"What I mean," Suki said, "is that my beloved sister worked her ass off, trying to land a guy with money. First at the casino. Then right under my nose."

"Suki," Rachel whispered, "don't—"

"But she couldn't. See, Rami loved me. And then he and I had a silly quarrel." Suki pulled a tissue from the neckline of her tight pink top and dabbed her eyes. "He left me. And I was frantic. I loved him, you know? And he was the father of my baby—"

"What?"

"I asked her if she'd take care of Ethan while I went looking for Rami, but—"

"Is this true?" Karim's voice was hoarse; his eyes blazed into Rachel's. "Ethan is your sister's child?"

Rachel was numb. "Karim," she whispered. "Karim, please—"

"Of course he's mine," Suki said sharply. "And you stole him."

Even in her despair, Rachel wondered why only she could see the glint of malice in her sister's eyes.

"I didn't steal him. You know that. You abandoned him—"

"You mean I trusted you to take care of him while I tried to find work." Suki looked at Karim. "See, after your brother left me—well, I was broke. I couldn't find a job in Vegas. Man, I was desperate. I asked Rachel to take care of Ethan for a while, just for a while, and I went to Los Angeles and finally got hired—"

"It wasn't like that," Rachel said desperately.

"I sent her money each week but she always wanted more. And then she saw her chance. Rami's brother—you, Prince Karim—turned up, and you was rich—even richer than Rami—"

"No," Rachel said in a thin voice. "Suki, don't do this! I beg you—"

Karim's hands tightened on Rachel's shoulders.

"Tell me she's lying," he said in a low voice. "Tell me none of this is true, that the last weeks were not a lie—"

"Karim," Rachel pleaded. "Ethan is hers. But nothing else was the way she makes it sound…"

Karim's eyes filled with pain. He lifted his hands from her shoulders, turned on his heel and walked out of the room.

Suki smiled in triumph. She brushed past Rachel and reached for the baby.

"Precious boy," she cooed, "come to your mommy."

Ethan gave an unhappy cry and Rachel sank to the floor, weeping.

CHAPTER TWELVE

ROBERTA hurried to Rachel and threw her arms around her.

"Please," she said as she helped her to her feet, "Rachel, don't cry! Those things that woman said—"

"What she said about Ethan is the truth," Rachel sobbed. "She gave birth to him… But I'm the one who loves him."

"But the rest was lies. Anybody who knows you would know that." The girl's tone was bitter. "Prince Karim should have known it, too. How could he have believed those things she said?"

It was the question that was breaking Rachel's heart.

Karim had said he loved her, but he'd accepted all Suki's horrible lies. How could he?

The answer was simple.

He'd accepted Suki's story because the core of it was true.

She, Rachel, had lied to him from the minute he'd entered her life. She'd lied about Ethan, about Rami, and now those lies had cost her everything.

The child she loved as if he were her own.

The man she adored.

She'd lost them both, forever.

Oh, she could blame Suki for it. For abandoning Ethan, for telling a twisted story to Karim and his father. She could blame Karim for turning back into the heartless man he had always been.

But the terrible truth was that she had only herself to blame. Not just for lying. For giving in to emotions she had always known were dangerous.

Love was the greatest lie of all.

Lust was what drew men and women together. If only she'd remembered that instead of trying to dress it up…

And after a lifetime of knowing.

"Miss?"

Rachel looked up. It was the servant who'd escorted them to this room, but he was speaking to Roberta, not to her.

"The child…" The man cast a furtive glance at Rachel. "The child's mother needs your help."

"Let her get it from someone else," Roberta said angrily.

Rachel touched her arm.

"Please," she said, "go with him. Help her."

"Help your sister? Are you crazy? She's a—"

"I know what she is," Rachel said bitterly. "But you won't be doing it for her. It's for—for my baby." Her voice broke. "He must be terrified. He's in a strange place with a person he doesn't—he doesn't—" Tears flooded her eyes. She put her hand out and Roberta clasped it in hers. "Please, Roberta," Rachel whispered. "My little boy needs you."

Roberta began to weep.

"Yes. You're right. Don't worry. I'll stay with him as long as they'll let me."

The women hugged. Then Roberta hurried after the servant, and Rachel was alone.

Even the King was gone.

The huge room filled with silence.

Rachel wiped her hands over her wet eyes, uncertain of what to do next. She had to leave this terrible place, but how?

"Rachel."

That deep, familiar voice. She whirled toward the door

and saw her lover. His face was cold with anger but it didn't matter.

She knew that she had just added one lie to another, telling herself what she'd felt for him was only lust.

She loved him.

And she had lost him.

A yawning emptiness stretched ahead. Years alone, without her baby. Without the man she adored.

He stood looking at her, arms folded, eyes narrowed. Still, hope rose within her breast, as bright as the mythical phoenix would surely have been as it rose from the flames.

"Karim," she said unsteadily, "Karim, please, if you'd just listen—"

"That was my first mistake. I *did* listen—to you, and your lies."

"I shouldn't have lied. I know that. But I never lied about us."

His mouth thinned.

"There is no 'us.' There never was."

"I love you, Karim. You have to—"

He held out his hand.

She stared at the piece of paper in it. "What is that?"

"A check."

"A check?" She looked at him blankly. "For what?"

"For a masterful performance. Go on. Take it."

Rachel raised her hands in front of her, as if she were warding off something evil.

"It's for fifty thousand dollars. Not enough?" He shrugged. "How much, then? One hundred thousand? I warn you, Rachel, there's a limit to my generosity."

"Do you really think I'd take your money?" She gave a sad, disbelieving laugh. "I don't want money. I want—"

"You want what you almost had," he said coldly. "My fortune. My title. A child who is not yours."

Each accusation was like a blow.

"That isn't true!"

"You are not a woman to speak of what is and is not true."

"You never loved me at all," Rachel whispered. "If you had, you'd know I don't want money. You'd know Suki made up that entire story. She gave birth to Ethan, yes, but she didn't leave him with me so she could find a job. She left him because she didn't want him. She took off without a word, and I never heard from her again."

"You're fast on your feet," Karim said tonelessly. "As I said, you give an excellent performance."

"Dammit, will you listen? Suki made it all up! I never tried to seduce Rami. I barely spoke to him. Yes. I lied about Ethan. But if I hadn't you'd have taken him from me. Don't you see that?"

"What I see is that you're incapable of speaking the truth."

Rachel stared at Karim. Before her eyes he'd become all the things she'd called him when they'd met: an egotistical, arrogant despot.

How could she have thought she loved him?

Losing Ethan would hurt forever.

Losing Karim was the best thing that could have happened to her.

"And you," she said, "are incapable of being a man. The only thing you're suited for is being what you are. A cold, heartless sheikh!"

She took a deep breath. Then, head high, she brushed past him.

"Rachel!" She didn't answer. He cursed and went after her, dropped a heavy hand on her shoulder and swung her toward him. "No one walks away from me until I dismiss them."

"No," she said quietly, "I'm sure they don't, Your Highness." Her chin lifted. "How would they dare?"

"Watch what you say to me, woman."

"Why? What more could you do to me than you've already done?"

"You are in my country now. My word is—"

Karim fell silent.

Sweet heaven, what was he doing? Yes, she had lied to him. Made a fool of him. Now she was turning him into the very kind of man she'd accused him of being.

What kind of power did she have that she could reduce him to this? That she could make him lose his self-control not only in bed but out of it?

No.

He wasn't going to think about her in bed. Her seeming innocence at the start, her incredible abandon once she was in his arms.

Looking at her even now, knowing she had lied, that she had used him, he wanted her.

And she wanted him. She had to want him. She had to—

"I want to go back to the States."

"What if that isn't what I want?"

"Don't you get it? I don't give a damn what you—"

Karim pulled her into his arms. She struggled; he caught her hands, imprisoned them against his chest.

"Let go of me!"

"What happened in bed," he growled. "Was all that a lie, too?"

She struggled harder. He thrust one hand into her hair, held her to him.

"The sighs. The moans. The things you did, the things you begged me to do—"

"You're disgusting," Rachel said, her voice shaking. "And I hate you. I hate you—"

He kissed her. She fought and he caught her bottom lip

between his teeth, sucked on the sweet flesh, heard her whimper, felt her mouth soften under his—

"Stay in Alcantar," he said. "You can help care for the child during the day, and at night, whenever I'm here—"

She made a wild, terrible sound, pulled back in his arms and spat in his face.

"Stay away from me," she panted. "I swear, if you ever touch me again—"

Karim thrust her from him. The boiling rage within him—at her, at himself—terrified him.

"My pilot will fly you to New York first thing in the morning."

"Now," Rachel demanded.

"He cannot fly without sleep."

"That's your problem, not mine."

"My problem," Karim said coldly, "is making sure I don't have to set eyes on you again." He snapped his fingers; a servant came scurrying into the room, eyes averted. "Show Ms. Donnelly to her suite."

"I am not spending the night under the same roof as you!"

"If you prefer the desert sand to a bed, I can see to it that you are accommodated. I'm sure the snakes and the scorpions will appreciate the company."

He said something in his own tongue to the servant, then strode away, his very walk as supercilious as his attitude.

"Bastard," she hissed.

The look of shock on the servant's face made her feel better.

The thought of spending the night outdoors didn't.

"Where are the Sheikh's quarters?"

"In the north wing, madam."

"Fine," she said briskly. "In that case, please show me to a suite in the south wing."

The servant inclined his head and set off at a brisk pace, with Rachel following after him.

She was sure she wouldn't sleep.

She was too angry.

She'd made a fool of herself, thinking she loved the Sheikh—and thinking it was all she'd done.

Suki had always teased her.

"You're just not normal, Rachel," she'd say. "Not liking guys... What, are you frigid?"

Maybe she was. Or maybe she had been. Karim had changed that. She supposed she should be grateful to him for introducing her to the pleasures of lust, because what she'd felt for him was that.

Pure, basic lust.

Of course, being a strait-laced idiot, she'd had to give a purely primitive sexual need the trapping of romance.

"Stupid," she told herself, as she showered in a bathroom the size of a ballroom, then crept between the covers of a bed that could have slept a basketball team.

Stupid, indeed—and how could she ever expect to sleep, knowing that about herself?

And why was she remembering sleeping in his arms, his breath warm on the nape of her neck, his hand cupped over her breast...

The tears came as a surprise.

What was there to cry about?

Not him. Never him, she thought...

And buried her face in the pillow, to muffle her sobs.

Karim lay sleepless in his bed, arms folded under his head, staring at the dark ceiling.

He was still too angry to sleep.

Tomorrow loomed as a day filled with unpleasantries.

He had to talk with Suki Donnelly. The thought was distasteful. He'd disliked the woman on sight but he'd have to see if she was going to grant him custody of Ethan without a fight. She was the baby's mother, after all. Rachel, who was only his aunt, had flat-out refused.

He could not imagine the baby's mother would do any less.

If she did, he would sue for custody. And win. But it would be simpler if she agreed that letting him become Ethan's guardian would be the best thing for the child.

He'd also have to arrange for a nanny, since Roberta's foolish loyalty was surely to Rachel.

And he'd have to confront his father.

He knew exactly what the older man had done. The King had boasted of it.

"You gave me Rachel Donnelly's name. I arranged to have her investigated. It took very little time to find out that there was no record of her having given birth to a child—that there was, instead, a birth certificate issued to a *Suki* Donnelly. Locating her was even easier. She had no reason to hide. My people found her in Los Angeles in less than a day." His father's expression had hardened. "If you'd thought with your brain instead of your—"

"Watch what you say to me," Karim had growled.

But it was good that these things had been done. Otherwise he'd still be with Rachel, planning a life with her...

Karim pushed back the blankets, rose from his bed, pulled on a pair of jeans and paced from room to room in his suite.

It was a very large suite. Still, he felt trapped. Caged, like a captured wild beast.

How could he have made such a mess of things?

He never did anything before thinking it through to its logical conclusion. That was the code he demanded of himself. He never gave in to selfish wishes, or spoke without weighing every word.

Then he'd met Rachel.

He had wanted her, and he had taken her.

Not so terrible, really.

Sex was sex. You wanted a woman, she wanted you—there was no reason to hesitate.

It was what had come next that had been wrong.

When he'd felt himself falling in love with her he should not have let it happen.

Because it was true. He had fallen in love with her and it had been a terrible mistake.

He should have thought of the consequences, considered where undisciplined emotion might take him, remembered that he was a prince, not a man...

"Oh, God," he whispered as he sank into a chair and buried his face in his hands.

Bad enough he'd fallen in love with her, but he *still* loved her. He would never admit it to anyone but it was true.

He loved her.

He'd get over it, of course, but when? How long would it take before he stopped feeling empty without her beside him? How long would the pain of her deceit last?

This was impossible.

How could he think clearly? He had to get some sleep. Or do something useful.

Ethan.

How was the baby doing? The nanny was with him, but nothing else in the child's world was familiar. New surroundings, new faces.

No Rachel.

So what? His mother—his real mother—had him now. Surely there was something intrinsic in the bond between an infant and its mother...

Karim sprang from the chair, grabbed a shirt and left his rooms.

The palace corridors were long. It was a brisk few minutes' walk to the nursery where he and Rami and generations of royal children had been raised. When he reached it, he paused.

Then he knocked on the door.

Rachel's sister opened the door as quickly as if she'd been expecting him.

"Prince Karim," she purred. "How nice of you to pay me a visit."

She was wearing something long and pink and voluminous. Something that was also sheer enough so he could see glimpses of her body as she stepped back.

He thought of the first time he'd seen Rachel. She'd been wearing that foolish costume, her hair messy, her shoes kicked off. There'd been nothing sexy about her, but her beauty had stolen his breath.

And that first glimpse he'd had of her naked…how he'd deliberately parted the bath sheet she'd been wrapped in, her body lush and damp, her face scrubbed clean…

"Come in, Your Highness," Suki said. She smiled. "I've been hoping you'd come by."

Karim stayed in the doorway and cleared his throat.

"How is Ethan?"

"Huh?"

"Your son. How is he?"

"Oh. Oh, he's okay. Don't you want to come in and stay for a while?"

"I've told the kitchen staff to be sure his usual formula is available, as well as a supply of strained fruits and vegetables, but if you need anything else for him—"

"That girl—Rebecca, Roberta, whatever her name is—she's taking care of all that." Another smile, this time accompanied by a flutter of lashes. "This is really something. The palace, these rooms…" She fluttered her lashes again. "You."

"It must have been difficult for you, being away from Ethan for such a long time."

"Oh, sure. And there's a stocked bar here. I didn't know you people drank wine. I opened a bottle—there's some left. How about I pour us a drink? I don't know about you, but I could sure do with something relaxing after today."

"I don't want anything to drink."

"Uh…okay. You could still come in for a while and—"

"You said you sent Rachel money?"

"Right."

"Did you never phone her? To see how Ethan was?"

"Yes," she said quickly. Too quickly. "Sure I did."

"When?" He could hear the sudden hardness in his voice. "She and I were together for three weeks. Rachel has a cell phone but you never called her once during that time."

"Well, she wanted it that way."

"Rachel did?"

"Yeah. I, uh, I don't want to make her look bad—"

"She didn't want to hear from you?"

"See, she told me how she was doing me this big favor—telling me she didn't have time for taking care of the kid, all it was gonna involve, you know—and finally she said, 'Look, I know you'll be busy job-hunting, so if you send money I'll take care of the kid. Just don't drive me nuts checking up on me all the time.' You know?"

"The kid?" Karim said tonelessly.

"Right. Ethan."

Suki smiled. Licked her lips. The action was deliberate and diversionary; he knew he was supposed to notice it and he did—and thought how repellent her wet mouth looked, and how delicious Rachel's mouth looked when it was wet with his kisses.

"You positive you don't want to come in, Your Majesty?"

Karim didn't consider correcting her. "Majesty" wasn't an applicable title, but what difference would that make in what came next?

It was late, and he knew what he had to do if he was going to get any sleep at all.

He smiled. "On second thought…"

And he stepped inside the room, reached behind him, and closed the door.

CHAPTER THIRTEEN

EVENTUALLY weariness won out and Rachel fell into a troubled sleep.

She woke abruptly, alone in a strange room, with a ceiling fan turning high overhead, rain pounding against the arched windows.

Rain in the desert.

It seemed appropriate.

She sat up and pushed her hair from her face. She'd slept in a T-shirt and panties—not naked as she'd slept in Karim's arms...

She wasn't going to think about him. She'd cried over him last night but he was nothing to her now, just as she was nothing to him.

Her suitcase was on a low ebony bench. She opened it, her movements brisk, her head telling her that if she slowed down that brave thought of a moment ago would give way to despair.

Quickly, she dug out a bra and panties, a change of clothes. Five minutes in the bathroom—a fast shower, teeth brushed, wet hair drawn back in a low, no-nonsense ponytail—and she was dressed and ready.

The only thing she had to do, absolutely would do, was to see Ethan—no matter the objections she was sure Suki and Karim would make.

After that Karim's pilot would fly her home—and where, exactly, was that?

Home, people said, was where the heart was. Ethan was the reason Las Vegas had been home. Karim was what had made New York her safe haven.

Now what?

Rachel sank down on the edge of the bed.

This was foolish.

She was accustomed to being alone. She had been alone before Ethan, before Karim. So what if she was alone again?

She'd be fine.

Needing others was always a mistake. Surely life had taught her that.

If she'd just kept her emotional distance from the baby, if she hadn't let a man steal her heart…

No.

He hadn't stolen her heart. She'd served it up to him on a platter.

"Stop it," she whispered.

It was a waste of time to keep going over and over all this. The idea was to move on. She had to make plans, decide what town, what city she'd go to, then find a place to live, a job—

Someone knocked at the door.

It was probably one of the palace servants, come to tell her the plane was ready. Well, the pilot would just have to wait. She was not leaving here until she saw her baby…

The knock at the door came again.

Rachel ran her hands over her eyes and got to her feet. "I'm coming," she called as she hurried to the door, pulled it open…

Karim.

The sight of him, dressed as casually as she was, in a T-shirt and jeans, his jaw bristling with early-morning stubble, sent a wave of longing straight through her.

He still looked like the man she'd fallen in love with, but he wasn't.

She had to remember that.

"Good," she said coolly. "I thought I was going to have to waste time searching for you."

"May I come in?"

"I don't see any reason for it. What I have to say will only take a minute." She paused, told herself it was important to sound determined. "I want to see Ethan."

"He's asleep."

"I want to see him, Karim, and I'm not going to take no for an answer."

A wave of despair shot through him.

Despite everything, he knew he would miss Rachel. In his bed, yes. But this—this might be what he would miss the most. Her spirit. Her courage. Her determination.

Her eyes were red, as if she'd been weeping; she'd pulled her T on backwards—he could see the tip of the label peeking out of the neckline—so perhaps she wasn't quite as contained as she sounded.

He hoped so.

A woman who lied to a man, who let him think she was what she was not, should have at least some regrets...

His heart hardened.

And what kind of fool was he, to think he would miss *anything* about her?

As for regrets... Of course she had them. She'd lost a big ticket item when she lost him.

"Did you hear me? I want to see—"

"I heard you. The answer is no."

Rachel put her hands on her hips.

"I'm not leaving until I've seen him!"

Karim laughed. It was not a pleasant sound.

"You'll leave when I say—and that's twenty minutes from now."

"I demand—"

"Demand?" he said, his tone silken. "You're not in the position to 'demand' anything."

"Karim. If you ever—if you ever had any—any feelings for me—"

She cried out as he clasped her by the elbows and lifted her to her toes.

"Don't you speak to me about feelings," he growled. "You don't know the meaning of the word."

"I loved you." The words she'd promised herself she would never speak again tumbled from her lips. "I loved you so much—"

"I'm sick of your lies!"

"It isn't a lie. I loved you. I loved Ethan—"

"Yes," he said, letting go of her. "I believe that."

For a second Rachel's heart soared—but it didn't last.

"I believe that you do love Ethan, which is why I've come to talk to you." He paused. "He is going to need a nanny."

"Roberta will—"

"She won't. She'll stay the week but she's enrolled for summer classes in New York."

"Well, Suki will have to manage alone."

Karim's mouth twisted.

"Your sister and I had a talk last night. She's already gone."

"Suki? But—"

"Being given the choice between raising her son and granting me custody turned out to be no choice at all."

"You mean she's letting you keep Ethan?"

"She agreed to sign away her rights and let me adopt him."

Rachel stared at him. "Why would she agree to that?" Her eyes widened. "You paid her off."

He had. That was why he'd agreed to step into the spider's parlor. Suki had expected sex. What she'd gotten was a check for seven figures, an iron-clad document that bound her to silence about Rami, the baby, and anything pertaining to the matter, and a warning never to come anywhere near Ethan again. But he wasn't going to talk about that.

"Let's just say we reached a mutually beneficial arrangement."

"And—and the rest? Did she tell you that she'd lied about me?"

"We didn't discuss you, only Ethan."

Rachel nodded. She could feel the burn of tears behind her eyes. Why would they have talked about her when Karim had believed Suki's lies without hesitation?

"And?"

"And what?"

"And what are you doing here?"

"I thought you would want to know that I will raise Ethan. I assumed that would be important to you—that you'd be happy to know he will be safe."

Tears rose in Rachel's eyes.

"Thank you. That was—that was kind of you. To tell me, I mean."

Karim hesitated.

"You've done a fine job with him," he said softly.

She nodded. "I tried."

"I—I want you to know that I love him."

And me? she almost said. *Can't you love me?*

But he couldn't. She knew that.

He was a man to whom honor was everything, and by lying to him she had dishonored him.

"I know you do," she said. "And that's good." Her voice thickened. "Because he's going to need you, you know? He's only a baby, but—but this is going to be a hard transition for him."

Karim nodded. "I'll do everything I can to make it easier." He hesitated. "I regret the—the suggestion I made last night."

Rachel lifted her chin. "Is that an apology?"

"No. It's—it's..." He sighed. God, she was tough. "Yes. It is. But the fact remains, Ethan will need a nanny. I can find one, of course, but he cares for you, and you for him." Her eyes snapped and he held up his hand. "No. I'm not suggesting... I'm simply saying that if you wanted to be his nanny—only that, nothing more—" Dammit, this was not going well. "You'd have your own apartment in the palace, a significant salary and—"

"You mean, I would be your servant."

"I suppose that is one way to see it," he said stiffly.

"And," she said, her voice trembling, "how long would this arrangement last?"

"Until he is five, perhaps, or six. Until he no longer needs you."

Until he no longer needs you...

Rachel wanted to slap the Sheikh she'd been fool enough to love. That he could even think she'd accept being a temporary part of her baby's life told her everything she needed to know.

"Only a man with no heart would make such an offer," she said quietly. "And I pity you, Karim, for being such a man."

She brushed past him, half expecting him to come after her and stop her. But he didn't, and after a few minutes she found a servant and demanded to be taken to Ethan's room.

The servant said that was not possible. Rachel assured him it damned well was, and finally Karim strode toward them, barked out a command, and the servant bowed, then led her to the room where the baby was, as Karim had said, fast asleep.

She stood over his crib, wept silently, whispered to him

of how she loved him, how she knew he would grow up to be big and smart and strong, promised him that she would fight to get him back.

And then, before she could collapse with grief, she swung away from the child who held her heart in his tiny hands and ran through the palace, down what were surely a thousand steps, and out the front door into the rain.

A car was waiting.

The driver took her to the palace airport. Somehow she held herself together until she was on the plane and in a seat.

"Please fasten your seat belt," the still-polite flight attendant said. "We'll be taking off immediately."

Rachel nodded. She didn't trust herself to speak.

The jet's engines started up.

"We have direct clearance to New York, Ms. Donnelly," a tinny voice said from a speaker.

The attendant made her way up the aisle and vanished into the cockpit.

The jet began rolling along the taxiway.

I am not going to cry, Rachel thought, as she stared blindly out the window at the rain, *I am not...*

Sobs burst from her throat.

She leaned her forehead against the glass, let her tears spill down it.

The sky was weeping and so was she.

The plane moved faster and faster. Another few yards and it would reach the runway; the engines would race as it built up speed.

Then it would leap into the sky and all of this would be over.

Suddenly the pitch of the engines changed from a thunderous roar to a whine.

The plane began to slow.

A car, red and low and moving very, very fast, was racing along the rain-soaked taxiway toward them.

The jet rolled to a stop, engines idling. The co-pilot hurried into the cabin from the cockpit.

"What's happening?" Rachel said. Her voice rose. "I said, what's—?"

But she could see what was happening for herself. The co-pilot began opening the cabin door.

And as he did, the door of the red sports car flew open.

Karim jumped out.

Karim? Here? Rachel was baffled. Why?

The plane's door swung open. The staircase dropped into place.

Rachel fumbled with her seat belt.

She wasn't going to face Karim sitting down. She'd do it toe to toe, and if she had to fight him to leave this awful place—

Karim raced up the stairs, his face tight with anger.

"Damn you, Rachel," he said, and before she could say or do anything he hauled her into his arms and kissed her.

She twisted her head away. She didn't want his kisses, the feel of his arms, the strong, wonderful feel of his body against hers...

And then she sobbed his name, clasped his face and gave herself to him.

"I hate you," she whispered. "Do you understand me, Karim? I hate you, I hate you, I—"

"Don't leave me. I beg you, *habibi,* don't ever leave me."

"I can't stay. Not like this. I'm not going to be your mistress, and that's what I'd end up being because I can't keep away from you. I can't, I can't—"

"I love you."

"You want me. There's a difference."

"Damned right, I want you. I want you because I love you.

And you love me. Say the words, sweetheart. Tell me that you love me, too."

Rachel shook her head. He had broken her heart. All she had left was her pride.

"I don't," she said. "I don't love—"

Karim silenced her with another kiss.

"No more lies," he said fiercely. "Not between us." He clasped her face, lifted it to his. "I've been a fool, Rachel. Of *course* you lied about Ethan. I gave you no choice. I had come to take him from you, and you loved him too much to let that happen." He paused. "Rachel. We belong together. You. Me. Our child. Our Ethan."

"Don't," Rachel pleaded, "don't say things you don't mean!"

"I mean every word," Karim said. "Your sister brought Ethan into this world, but you—*you, habibi*—have been his true mother." He smiled. "As I will be his father." He paused and brushed his lips gently over Rachel's. "I love you," he said softly. "Marry me and be my wife."

"But you believed Suki…"

"I was in agony. I had given you my heart…" His voice cracked. "The heart you say I do not have."

"Karim. Please don't. I said it to—to hurt you…"

"I have a heart, *habibi*. But I learned early to guard it well. It is what happens when people see you only as a prince or a sheikh. They lie. They tell you what they think you want to hear. Even those I loved…" Karim cleared his throat. "Each time my mother came back from wherever she'd gone she promised she would not leave me again, but she always did. And Rami…we were different from each other, even as boys, but we loved each other. Then he turned into someone I didn't know and I—I let him go."

"We can't hold on to those who don't want us," Rachel said softly. "My mother. My sister—"

"Yes. I understand that now. But we—you and I—we want each other. We have each other." Karim smiled. "And we have Ethan. We can be a family, *habibi,* and we can be happy."

Rachel felt her heart swell with happiness. She stood on her toes and pressed a kiss to Karim's lips.

"I hated myself for lying to you, Karim. But I was so afraid I'd lose Ethan, lose you…"

"You'll never lose either of us, *habibi.* Not me, and not our son."

"Our son," Rachel said, and smiled.

Karim kissed her damp cheeks.

"This has been a long journey for me," he said quietly. "When it began, I thought I was learning about Rami. Now I know I was also learning about myself, and about what is important in this world."

"And what is?" Rachel asked softly, though by now she knew the answer.

"Love," Karim said. "Only love matters." He looked deep into her eyes. "Rachel. Will you marry me and be my love, forever?"

Rachel laughed.

"Yes," she said, "yes, yes, yes—"

Karim gathered her in his arms and kissed her, and as he did the rain stopped and the cabin of the plane filled with the brilliant golden light of the sun.

* * * * *

Heart of the Desert

CAROL MARINELLI

Carol Marinelli finds writing a bio rather like writing her New Year's resolutions. Oh, she'd love to say that since she wrote the last one, she now goes to the gym regularly and doesn't stop for coffee and cake and a gossip afterwards, that she's incredibly organised and writes for a few productive hours a day after tidying her immaculate house and taking a brisk walk with the dog.

The reality is, Carol spends an inordinate amount of time daydreaming about dark, brooding men and exotic places (research), which doesn't leave too much time for the gym, housework or anything that comes in between. And her most productive writing hours happen to be in the middle of the night, which leaves her in a constant state of bewildered exhaustion.

Originally from England, Carol now lives in Melbourne, Australia. She adores going back to the UK for a visit—actually, she adores going anywhere for a visit—and constantly (expensively) strives to overcome her fear of flying. She has three gorgeous children who are growing up so fast (too fast—they've just worked out that she lies about her age!) and keep her busy with a never-ending round of homework, sports and friends coming over.

CHAPTER ONE

'LET'S try somewhere else.'

Georgie had known that there was no chance of getting into the exclusive London club.

She hadn't even wanted to try.

If the truth be known, Georgie would far rather be home in bed, but it was Abby's birthday. The rest of their friends had drifted off and Abby didn't want her special day to end just yet. She seemed quite content to stand in the impossible queue, watching the rich and famous stroll in as the doorman kept them behind a thick red rope.

'Let's stay. It's fun just watching,' Abby said as a limousine pulled up and a young socialite stepped out. 'Oh, look at her dress! I'm going to take a photo.'

The paparazzi's cameras lit up the street as the young woman waited and a middle-aged actor joined her, both posing for the cameras. Georgie shivered in her strappy dress and high-heeled sandals, though she chatted away to her friend, determined *not* to be a party pooper, because Abby had been so looking forward to this night.

The doorman walked down the line, as he did

occasionally, and Georgie rather hoped he was going to tell them to all just give up and go home. Yet there was more purpose in his step this time and Georgie suddenly realised he was walking directly towards them.. Her hands moved to smooth her blonde hair in a nervous gesture as he approached, worried they had done something wrong, that perhaps photos weren't allowed.

'Come through, ladies.' He pulled open the rope and both women glanced at each other, unsure what was happening. 'I'm so sorry, we didn't realise you were in the queue.'

As she opened her mouth to speak, to ask just who he thought that they were, Georgie felt the nudge of Abby's fingers in her ribs. 'Just walk.'

The whole queue had turned and was now watching them, trying to guess who they were. A camera flashed and when one did, the rest followed, the photographers assuming that they must be *somebodies* as the heavy glass doors were opened and they entered the exclusive club.

'This is the best birthday ever!' Abby was beside herself with excitement but Georgie loathed the spotlight and the scrutiny it placed on her, though it wasn't only that that had her heart hammering in her chest as they were led through a dark room to a very prominent table. There was a tightening in her throat and a strange sinking feeling in her stomach as she fathomed that this might not be a mistake on the doorman's part.

Mistakes like this just did not happen.

And there was only one person in the world she could

think of who might be at this place. One person she knew who had the power to open impossible doors. The one person she had tried for months not to think of. One man she would do her utmost to avoid.

'Again—our apologies, Miss Anderson.' Her thoughts were confirmed as the waiter used what he thought was her name and a bottle of champagne appeared. Georgie sat down, her cheeks on fire, scared to look up, to look over to the man approaching, because she knew that when she did it would be to him. 'Ibrahim has asked that we take care of you.'

So now there was no avoiding him. She willed a bland reaction, told her heart to slow down, her body to calm—hoped against hope that she could deliver a cool greeting. Georgie lifted her eyes, and even as she managed a small smile, even if she did appear in control, inside every cell jolted, with nerves and unexpected relief.

Relief because, despite denial, despite insisting to herself otherwise, still she wanted him so.

'Georgie.' The sound of his voice after all this time, the hint of an accent despite his well-schooled intonation, made her stomach flip and fold as she stood to greet him—and for a moment she was back there, back in Zaraq, back in his arms. 'It has been a long time.' He was clearly just leaving. On his arm a woman as blonde as herself flashed a possessive warning with her eyes, which Georgie heeded.

'It has been a while.' Her voice was a touch higher

than the one she would have chosen had she had any say in it. 'How are you?'

'Well,' Ibrahim said, and he looked it. Despite all she had read about him, despite the excesses of his lifestyle. He was taller than she remembered, or was he just a touch thinner? His features a little more savage. His raven hair was longer than she remembered, but even at two a.m. it fell in perfect shape. His black eyes roamed in assessment, just as they had that day, and then he waited for her gaze to meet his and somehow he won the unvoiced race because, just as had happened on that first day, she could not stop looking.

His mouth had not changed. Had she had only one feature to identify him by, if the police somehow formed an identity parade of lips, she could, without hesitation, have walked up and chosen her culprit. For, in contrast to his sculpted features, his mouth was soft, with full lips that a long time ago had spread into a slow, lazy smile, revealing perfectly even teeth, but tonight there would be no smile. It was a mouth that evoked a strange response. As Georgie stood there, forced to maintain this awkward conversation as she met his gaze, it was his mouth that held her mind. As he spoke on, it was his mouth she wanted to watch, and after all this time, in a crowded club with a woman on his arm, it was those lips she wanted to kiss.

'How are you?' he asked politely. 'How is your new business? Are you getting a lot of clients?' And it told her he remembered, not just that night but the details she had so readily shared back then. She recalled all the excitement in her voice as she'd told him about her Reiki and healing oils venture, and how interested he had been, and she was glad of the darkness because maybe, just maybe, there were tears in her eyes.

'It's going very well, thank you.' Georgie said.

'And have you seen your niece recently?' How wooden and formal he sounded. How she wanted the real Ibrahim to come back, to take her by the hand and drag her out of there, to take her to his car, to his bed, to an alley, to anywhere where it could be just them. Instead he awaited her answer and Georgie shook her head. 'I haven't been back since…' And she stopped because she had to, because her world was divided into two—before and after.

Since a kiss that had changed her for ever.

Since harsh words had been exchanged.

'I—I haven't b-been back since the wedding.' Georgie stammered.

'I was there last month—Azizah is doing well.'

She knew he had been back, despite swearing she wouldn't try to find out. She delved just a little when she spoke with her sister, searched out his name in ways she wasn't proud of. His words were almost lost in the noise of the club, and the only way to continue the conversation would be to move her head just a fraction closer, but that, for her own reasons, Georgie could not do. As his date gave a pointed yawn and the hand on his arm tightened, Georgie thanked him for his help in getting them into the club and for the champagne, and in return Ibrahim wished her goodnight.

There was a hesitation, just the briefest hesitation, because the polite thing to do would be to kiss her on the cheek, to say farewell in the usual way—but as both heads moved a fraction for the familiar ritual, by mutual consent they halted, because even in this setting, even with the clash of perfumes and colognes in the air, the space between them had warmed with a scent that was a subtle combination of them, a sultry, intoxicating scent that was so potent, so thick, so heavy it should come with a government warning.

Georgie gave a wry smile.

It came with a royal warning!

'Goodnight,' she said, and as he headed out, she watched the people part, watched heads turn to this beautiful man and then back to her, curious eyes watching, because even that short contact with him, in this superficial setting, rendered her *someone*. Especially, when all of a sudden he changed his mind, when he left his date and strode back towards her. It was almost the same as it had once been, this charge, this pull, that propelled him to her, and she wanted to give in and run, to cross the club and just run to him, but instead she stood there, shivering inside as he came back to her, rare tears in her eyes as he bent his head and offered words she'd neither expected nor sought.

'I apologise.'

And she couldn't say anything, because she'd have wept or, worse, she'd have turned to him, to the mouth that she'd craved for so long now.

'Not for all of it, but for some if the things I said.

You're not…' His voice was husky. He did not have to repeat it, the word had been ringing in her ears for months now. 'I apologise.'

'Thank you.' Somehow she found her voice. 'I'm sorry too.'

She was.

Every day.

Every hour.

She was sorry.

And then he turned away and she could not stand to watch him leave a second time so she took her seat instead.

'Who,' Abby demanded as Georgie sat down, 'was that?'

Georgie didn't answer. Instead she took a sip of her champagne, except it didn't quench her thirst, so she took another and then looked over to the man who never usually looked back. But in the early hours of this morning he did—and so potent was his effect, so renewed was her longing that had he even crooked his finger, had he so much as beckoned with his head, she would have gone to him.

It was a relief when the door closed on him but it took a moment for normality to return—to be back in the world without him.

'Georgie?' Abby was growing impatient.

'You know my sister Felicity, who lives in Zaraq?' Georgie watched Abby's mouth gape. 'That's her husband's brother.'

'He's a prince?'

Georgie attempted nonchalant. 'Well, as Karim is, I guess he must be.'

'You never said he was so...' Abby's voice trailed off, but Georgie knew what she meant. Even though Georgie's sister had married into royalty, even though Felicity had gone to Zaraq as a nurse and married a prince, Georgie had played it down to her friends—as if Zaraq was some dot, as if royals were ten a penny there. She had not told them the details of this stunning land, the endless desert she had flown over, the markets and deep traditions in the countryside, contrasting with the glittering, luxurious city, with seven-star resorts and designer boutiques.

And certainly she had not told her friends about him.

'What happened when you were there?'

'What do you mean?'

'You were different when you got back. You hardly ever spoke about it.'

'It was just a wedding.'

'Oh, come on, Georgie—look at him, I've never see a more beautiful man. You didn't even show me the wedding photos...'

'Nothing happened,' Georgie answered, because what had happened between Ibrahim and herself had never been shared, even though she thought about it every day.

'Three times a bridesmaid!' Georgie could still hear her mother making the little joke as they stood waiting for the service to start. 'It's a saying we have. If you're a bridesmaid three times, then you'll never...' Her mother had given up trying to explain then. The Zaraquians were not interested in nervous chatter and they certainly did not make small talk—all they were focussed on was the wedding that was about to take place. Despite all the pomp and glamour, it wasn't even the real wedding—that had taken place a few weeks ago in front of a judge—but now that the king had recovered from a serious operation, and Felicity deemed a suitable bride for Karim, the official celebration was taking place before her pregnancy became too obvious. Still, even if no one was listening, Georgie's cheeks burnt as her mother chatted on, shame whooshing up inside her. She closed her eyes for a dizzy second, because if her mother only knew the truth... There was no reason for her to know, Georgie told herself, calmed herself, reassured herself, and then her mind was thrown into turmoil again because she opened her eyes to a long, appraising stare from an incredibly imposing man. He was dressed like his father and brothers in military uniform, but surely never had a man worn it so well. She swung between relief and regret because had they been in England she'd have got to dance with the best man.

She expected him to flick his eyes away, to be embarrassed at being caught staring, but, no, he continued to look on till it was Georgie who looked away, embarrassed. She'd had no say whatsoever in her bridesmaid outfit and stood, awkward in apricot, her thick blonde hair tightly braided so it hung over her shoulder and her make-up, which had been done for her, far too heavy for such pale skin. It was just so not how you wanted to first be seen by a man so divine. She felt his eyes on her all through the wedding and after, even when he wasn't looking, somehow she was aware of his warm attention.

She'd had no idea what to expect from this wedding and certainly it hadn't been to have fun, but after the speeches, the formalities, the endless photographs she began to glimpse the real people and place that her sister loved. There was a brief lull in proceedings when the king and the brothers disappeared and returned out of uniform: dark men in dark suits. There was the thud of music and stamping and clapping, a sexy parade dancing the bride and groom down palace stairs to a ballroom that was waiting, lit only by candles, and Georgie watched as Karim stood as his bride danced towards him. She saw her sister dancing, usually so rigid and uptight, now sensual and smiling, and it was a woman Georgie hardly recognised.

As the guests circled the couple the atmosphere was infectious but Georgie was nervous to join in. Then there was a warm hand on her back guiding her, and the scent of Ibrahim close up, his low voice in her ear. 'You must join in the zeffa.' She didn't know how to. Didn't know how to dance freely, even on the sidelines, but with him beside her, tentatively she tried.

She could feel the beat in her stomach and it moved through her thighs and to her toes, but more than that she could feel the moment, feel the rush and the energy, taste the love in the air—and it was potent. 'The zeffa usually takes place before the wedding, but we make our traditions to accommodate the needs of our people....' He did not leave her side, even when the music slowed and she found herself dancing with him. 'Today, yesterday, we do all the formalities expected of royals, but now, amongst friends and family, it is for the couple.'

They shared one dance and even if it was for duty, it felt like something else. To be held by someone so strong, so commanding, was confusing, and to be aware of his observation was dizzying by the end of the evening.

'Are you okay?' He must have followed her outside once they had bade farewell to the happy couple and she stood in the hallway, accepting a glass of water from a waitress.

'It was so...' She shook her head to clear it, the music still reaching them in the hall. 'I'm fine. I'm exhausted and not just from the wedding—it's been a busy few days. I never knew there would be so many things to get through before the wedding.' She gave a wry smile. 'I thought Felicity and I would be spending some time together, I was hoping to see the desert...'

'There are too many duties,' Ibrahim said. 'Come on. I'll show you the desert now.' He had nodded to the stairs and Georgie climbed them. They walked along the corridor, past her bedroom till they came to a balcony door, which Ibrahim opened—and there was the desert, spread out before them. 'There,' he drawled. 'Now you've seen it.'

Georgie laughed. She had heard about the rebel prince who loathed the endless desert plains, who would, Karim had said with an edge to his voice, rather sit in crowded bars than find the peace only isolation could bring.

'You prefer cities, then?' She had made light of it, but his dark eyes were black as they roamed the shadows and when he didn't answer, Georgie looked out again. 'It looks like the ocean,' she said, because it did in the moonlight.

'It once was the ocean,' Ibrahim said. 'And it will be again.' He glanced over at her. 'Or so they say.'

'They?'

'The tales we are told.' He gave a shrug. 'I prefer science. The desert is not for me.'

'But it's fascinating.' Georgie said, and they stood silent as she looked out some more. 'Daunting,' she said to the silence, and even if she shouldn't have said any more, after a while Georgie admitted a truth. 'I worry about Felicity.'

'Your sister is happy.'

Georgie said nothing. Felicity certainly seemed happy—she had fallen in love with a dashing surgeon, not knowing at the time he was a prince. They were clearly deeply in love and thrilled there was a baby soon on the way, but Felicity did still miss home and struggled sometimes to adjust to all her new family's ways.

'She wants me to come and live here—to help with the baby and things.'

'She can afford a nanny!' Ibrahim said, and Georgie

gave a tight smile, because she had privately thought the same. Still, in fairness to Felicity it wasn't the only reason that she wanted her sister close. 'She wants to…' Georgie swallowed. Even though conversation came easily there were certain things she did not want to admit—and that her sister wanted to take care of her was one of them.

'She wants to be able to look out for you,' Ibrahim said, because he had heard about the troubled sister. One who had often run away, her teen years spent in and out of rehab for an eating disorder. Georgie was trouble, Karim had sagely warned.

Ibrahim chose to decide things for himself.

And, anyway, he liked trouble.

'Felicity worries about you.'

'Well, she has no need to.' Georgie's cheeks burnt, wondering how much he knew.

'She had reason for a while, though. You were very sick. It's only natural she should be concerned.' He was direct and for a moment she was defensive, embarrassed, but there was no judgement in his voice, which was rare.

'I'm better now.' Georgie said. 'I can't get it through to her that she doesn't have to worry any more. You know, the problem with having once had a problem is everyone holding their breath, waiting for it resurface. Like that soup…' He laughed because he had seen her face when it had been served. 'It was cold.'

'*Jalik*,' Ibrahim said, 'cucumber. It is supposed to be served like that.'

'I'm sure it's lovely if you're used to it. And I tried,' Georgie said. 'I tried but I couldn't manage all of it, but even on her wedding day Felicity was watching every mouthful I took and so was Mum. It doesn't all go back to having an eating disorder—I just don't like cold cucumber soup.'

'Fair enough.' Ibrahim nodded.

'And as much as I can't wait for my sister to have the baby, as much as I'm looking forward to being an aunt, I do not want to be a nanny!' Georgie admitted. 'Which is what they would want me to be if I stayed on,' she added, feeling guilty for voicing her concerns but relieved all the same.

'You would,' he agreed. 'Which is fine if being a nanny is your career of choice. Is it, though?'

'No.'

'Can I ask what is?'

'I've been studying therapeutic massage and aromatherapy. I've got a couple more units to do and then I'm hoping to start my own business.

'As well as more study,' she went on. Told him so easily, told him in far more detail than she had ever told another, about the healing she wanted to do for other women, how massage and oils had helped her when nothing else had. Unlike many people he did not mock her because, even if he did not like its mysterious ways, he was from the desert and he understood something of such remedies.

And he told her things too, things he had never

thought he would tell another, as to the reason he didn't like the desert.

'It took my brother,' Ibrahim said, because when Hassan and Jamal had not produced an heir and a fragile Ahmed had been considered as king, rather than face it, Ahmed had gone deep into the desert and perished.

'Felicity told me.' Georgie swallowed. 'I'm so sorry for your loss.'

Such a loss. He could not begin to explore it and Ibrahim closed his eyes, but the wind blew the sand and the desert was still there and he hated it.

'It took my mother too.'

'Your mother left.'

Ibrahim shook his head. 'By the desert's rules.' He looked out to the land he loathed and he could scarcely believe his own words, the conversation he was having. These should be thoughts only, and he turned to Georgie to correct himself, to retract, to bid farewell, yet blue eyes were waiting and that smiling mouth was serious now and Ibrahim found himself able to go on.

'One day she was here, we were a family; the next she was gone and never allowed to return. Today is her son's wedding and she is in London.'

'That must be awful for her.'

'It pales in comparison to missing Ahmed's funeral, or so she told me when I rang this afternoon.' It had been a hell of a phone call but he had not backed down from it, had sat and listened and listened some more.

'I'm sorry.'

He wanted her to say she understood, so he could mock her.

He wanted her to say she knew how he felt, so he could scathingly refute it.

He did not want a hand that was surprisingly tender to reach out and brush his cheek. But on contact Ibrahim wanted to hold her hand and capture it, to rest his face in it, to accept the simple gesture.

And he could never know, only her therapist could know, how momentous that was, that her hand had, for the first time with a man, been instinctive. She felt the breeze carry the warm heat of the desert and it seemed to circle them and all she wanted to do was stay.

'You should go,' Ibrahim said, because Karim had warned him about this woman, warned him sternly to remember Zaraq's ways while he was here.

And she did that. She turned and left him staring out at the desert, and as she walked she was reeling, her fingers burning from the brief touch, her mind whirring at to the contact she had initiated.

'I thought you said they were stuffy.' Abby interrupted Georgie's memories, ones she had tried to quash. 'He doesn't look anything like I imagined.'

'It's different there,' Georgie said. 'There are different ways, different rules...' She didn't want champagne, she didn't want to dance with the man who was offering, but it was Abby's night and, yes, it was rather more fun being inside than in the queue outside. Not for a second did Georgie let on to her friend that her mind was elsewhere, but even Abby seemed more interested in Ibrahim than in the club itself, because in the early hours of the morning the conversation turned back to him again.

'You're going over there next week,' Abby reminded Georgie, and gave her a little nudge. 'Will he be there?'

Georgie shook her head. 'He goes as little as possible—he went for the wedding and again when Azizah was born, and he's just been recently. He'll be back in a few weeks when the future king is born, that's more than enough for him. I'll be long gone by then so I won't be seeing him for ages.' She took a gulp of champagne. 'Let's dance.'

And they did.

They danced, partied and Georgie was a good friend and stayed till 4 a.m., laughed and had fun.

Even though she'd rather be home.

Even though she'd rather be alone.

To think of his kiss.

To think of him.

It had never dawned on her that he too might be sorry.

CHAPTER TWO

SHE did leave the balcony, as he had told her to.

Georgie had left him staring out at the desert.

And he shouldn't have turned and neither should she.

He shouldn't have turned, for his mind was angry, damaged by the desert, because when he turned, when he saw her looking back over her shoulder, he saw a familiar escape.

And he should not walk to her, but instead go up to his suite, pick up the phone and summon safe pleasure— for there were women chosen to please a prince or king. They, his father had long ago warned, were his only option when here in Zaraq.

And they were beautiful women and had more than sufficed, he reminded himself, except there was grit in his eyes from the desert wind and there was darkness in his soul tonight. He could still feel the cool trace of her fingers on his cheek and he had never cared for rules and he chose not to now.

He walked to her.

She waited.

She had every opportunity to leave and yet she did not. Her room was behind her, but she chose not flee. She faced the terror and the beauty of the man who was striding to her and fought not to run to him. There was no logic. Only madness could explain it, a charge in the air, a line that connected, an inevitability she desired, because as he pulled her into him, as he lowered his head, she was waiting and willing, and wanted that surly, delicious mouth on hers.

And now it was.

A mouth that tasted not of smoke or whisky but the clean taste of man.

Until now she'd never enjoyed kissing just as she'd never really enjoyed sex. But held in the arms and caressed by the lips of a master, Georgie changed her mind. His mouth pressed into hers, his jaw harsh against her skin, but there was moist relief in the centre and his tongue was cool against hers and made her burn. His hands were as skilled as his lips, because her hair was freed from the braid, and she knew only by the weight of it tumbling. He caressed her long blonde hair as if he was confirming it was how he had pictured it. He smelt as he had on the dance floor, as if he had stepped out of the shower and splashed on cologne, and she wanted to kiss him for ever.

Her fingers felt the hair she had admired as his hands now roamed her waist and just when she thought nothing could be better, he pulled her hips into his, so purposefully, so specifically that for a second she thought she would topple, except he was holding her and the wall was behind her and her shoulders met it as he pulled her in.

She felt it then.

As his mouth savaged hers, as his erection pressed in, she felt all the promise in that lithe, toned body, glimpsed the delicious place to which they were leading. Always she had shied from that path, but she felt tonight as if she wanted to run down it. They could have been in Peru or at a bus stop, they could have been anywhere, and it didn't matter because she was absolutely lost in the moment he made.

It was Ibrahim who had control, because he stopped then, pulled that noble head back just a fraction and looked as no man, no person, no soul had ever looked. He looked so deeply into her eyes that she wanted to climb into him, to dive into the beauty they mirrored.

'Come…' He had her hot hand in his and he would take her to his bed, right now. He would lead her, and soon he would have her, but Georgie was greedy, she was hungry and she could not wait, could not climb a single stair if it kept her from the moment that was waiting to be made. She was out of control and for the first time she liked it, because somehow with him it felt safe.

'Here.' Her room was here behind her, her bed was here, and she wanted them both safe and unsafe behind closed doors, but Ibrahim was a prince and his seed so precious, the orders so ingrained, that he hesitated.

'We need…' His own room would be better. There were discreet drawers, regularly replenished for the women sent to entertain the young prince, but in the guest rooms there would be nothing,

And, yes, they did need. Her scrambled brain, her rushing thoughts were grateful for his care yet she raced to a speedier solution and her voice leapt in delight as she recalled.

'I've got some.' She thanked the gods watching over Heathrow Airport who'd taken the two pounds she'd put into a machine and delivered not the mouthwash she had selected but a little parcel she hadn't wanted, but she was very grateful for it now.

And worlds collided for Ibrahim.

That she came prepared was perhaps to be admired. In London he would not give it a thought, but here…

He did not belong here, he reminded himself.

The rules did not apply.

So why the pause?

Why did it matter?

It did not, he told himself as they moved into her suite, and then when he kissed her again, he didn't have to tell himself any more because it simply did not… matter.

It did.

For Georgie something else mattered.

She closed her eyes to his kiss and tried not to think about *it*, tried to forget and just be warmed by his tongue, which was hot now.

Hot and probing and done with her spent mouth. Now that he had kissed her onto the bed, he pulled the straps on her dress and licked down her chest, his hand pushing up the hem of that hateful dress, but not all the way, because her hips rose so high into him he was blocked. It was urgent, urgent and desperate and completely delicious, her body responding as if it had been waiting for ever to join him. She tore at his jacket, his shirt, her mouth in his hair, on his ear, her hands on his back, her stilettos tearing the silk of his trousers as their legs entwined, wishing the heat from their bodies would melt their clothes so they could connect with skin.

It mattered.

She could not ignore it—could not forgo her strange principle. As she knelt on the bed and lifted her hem as Ibrahim lowered his head, not knowing whether or not it would matter to him, Georgie said, 'We can't...'

He liked her game.

'We can.'

He liked her feigned reluctance.

Liked the sudden shyness as his mouth met her stomach.

'I can't.'

'You can,' he breathed as his hands pulled at her panties and brushed off the hands that sought to keep them on.

'Ibrahim, please...' And he realised then that it wasn't a game. Or rather that she'd been playing a very dangerous one, because he could not have been closer, could *not* have been closer. He was still hard and he was back to angry and for a moment there he did not like his own thoughts, but he hauled himself from her, looked down at his torn clothing, could feel the scratches from her nails in his back and shot daggers at her with his eyes.

'I'm sorry...' Georgie gulped, and wondered how could she explain *it* suddenly mattered.

'I'm not like that.'

'You pretending to be demure was lost in the hallway.'

'I haven't—'

'Don't try to tell me you're a virgin.' He gave a nasty smirk. 'A condom-carrying virgin.'

'I'm not.' She wasn't and she certainly wasn't about to explain to him in this mood about the Heathrow gods. 'I didn't mean to lead you on.'

'You meant it,' he said. 'You meant every second of it.' He wasn't hard any more, he was just pure angry. He'd been told she was trouble and he should have listened. 'What are you holding out for, Georgie?' It dawned on him then. 'Jealous of your big sister, are you? Want a rich husband of your own?' He mocked her with a black smile. 'Here's a tip for the future—men like a little or the lot.'

She was angry too. Angry at herself and now at him for not letting her explain. And she was embarrassed, which wasn't a great combination because she bit back with harsh words of her own.

'Oh, so you'd have loved me in the morning?' She answered her own question. 'As if.' He was a bastard, a playboy and she'd been playing with fire from the beginning, she just hadn't known it at the time.

But there was a beat, a tiny beat where their eyes met.

A glimpse of a tomorrow that might have been, which they'd lost now.

That made him even angrier, 'I wouldn't touch you again if you were on your knees, begging. I'll tell you what you are…' Ibrahim said, and he added an insult that needed no translation and it hurtled from his mouth as he walked from her room.

She pulled up her knees as he slammed closed her door and then pulled a shaking hand across her mouth because how could she tell him *what* had suddenly mattered?

Georgie wasn't looking for a husband.

She already had one.

CHAPTER THREE

I⊤ DID not abate.

Ibrahim Zaraq rode his horse at breakneck speed along the paths, across the fields and back along the paths, his breath white in the crisp morning air, and, despite the space, despite the miles available to him to exercise his passion, today, this morning, and not for the first time lately, Ibrahim felt confined.

London had been the place that had freed him, the place of escape, and yet as he pulled up his beast, as he patted the lathered neck, Ibrahim, though breathless, wanted to kick him on, wanted to gallop again, to go further, faster, not follow a track and turn around.

There, in the still, crisp morning, in the green belt of a city, the desert called him—just as his father had told him it would.

And though Ibrahim resisted, again he felt it.

This pull, this need for a land that supposedly owned him, and for just a moment he indulged himself.

'You would love it.' He climbed down and spoke in Arabic to his stallion, a beast who kicked and butted the walls of his luxurious stable, who paced the confines of his enclosure and bit any stranger who ignored his stable-door warning and was ignorant enough to approach. 'For there,' he said to the beast, stroking the rippling muscles, hearing the stamp and kick of his hooves, 'you would finally know and relish exhaustion.' Only the desert could sate. Again Ibrahim glimpsed it—the endless dunes, the fresh canvas the shifting desert provided each morning. He did not just glimpse it, he felt the sting of sand on his cheeks, the scarf around his mouth, the power of a horse unleashed between his thighs.

Yet his life was in London.

A life he had created, business and riches that came with no rules attached, because he had built them and they were his. His mother was here—forbidden to return to Zaraq because decades ago she had broken the rules.

'I'll take him, Ibrahim.' A young stablegirl he sometimes bedded made her way over and he handed her the reins. Ibrahim saw the invitation in her eyes, and perhaps that would help, he thought, as she unstrapped the saddle. Ibrahim took the weight of it from her, saw her hands soothe the angry beast, saw the stretch of her thighs as she put on the horse blanket. He waited and wanted to feel something, for it would have been easier, so much easier to soothe the burn of his body and the turmoil in his mind with his favourite solution. 'Is there anything I can do for you?' Hopeful, beautiful, available, she turned to him—and the answer on any other morning would have been yes.

It wasn't today.

Neither had it been the other night.

After seeing Georgie, he had directed his driver to his date's home instead of his and had declined her invitation to come in.

'Come to bed, Ibrahim.' Her mouth and her hands had moved to persuade but Ibrahim had brushed her off and when tears hadn't worked, she'd got angry. 'It's that tart from the nightclub that's changed things, isn't it?'

'No,' Ibrahim had said coolly. 'It's entirely you.'

'Ibrahim?' The stablegirl smiled and he looked down at her breasts, which were pert and pretty. He gauged the length of her hair and then walked away because, though her hair was dark, it was long and thick and her frame too was slender. Ibrahim knew he'd have only been thinking of her.

Of Georgie.

He did not want to think of her and his mind turned to the desert instead.

He picked up pace, his boots ringing across the yard. He would go to his property in the country this weekend, for he knew if he was in London he would end up calling Georgie. He did not like unfinished business, did not like to be told no, and seeing her again had inflamed things, but more trouble with his family was the last thing he needed now. The country was a good option—there he would find space, there he could ride for ever, except as he climbed into his sports car he glanced at the sat-nav and felt as if he were staring at an aerial map. He could see the fields, the houses, the hedges, the trees, the borders…

And his father had been right, and so too his brothers, who had told him that one day the desert would call him.

The king had let his son go with surprising ease when he had left to study engineering, confident that when the time was right he would return.

'Of course I will be back.' Surly, arrogant, back from his compulsory stint in the military, a young Ibrahim had been ready for London. 'I will visit.'

'You will be back as a royal prince to share your new knowledge, and your country will be waiting.'

'No.' Ibrahim had shaken his head. 'For formal functions occasionally I will return and, of course, to see my family…' His father did not seem to understand, so he had spelt it out. 'My life will be in London.'

But the king had just smiled. 'Ibrahim, you are going to study engineering. Remember as a child all the plans you had for this country of ours, all you could do for the people.'

'I was a child.'

'And now you are a man—you get to make real your dreams. When it is time, you will come back to where you belong.' Ibrahim had rolled his eyes but the king had just smiled. 'It is in your blood, in your DNA. You may not want to listen to your father, but the desert has its own call—one you cannot ignore.'

He wanted to ignore it.

For years now he had, but everything had changed when he'd returned for the wedding.

Ibrahim sped the car through the grey Sunday

morning, out of the city and into the country. He hugged tight bends and accelerated out of them. His father's patience was running out, his future awaited him and he raced from it till his tank was almost empty and again rules rushed in.

'Breathe till I tell you to stop,' the policeman ordered, and Ibrahim did. He even emptied out his pockets and let the man inspect his boot. He saw the suspicion in the officer's eyes when everything turned up clean.

'Where are you going in such a hurry?' the officer asked again. He had seen Ibrahim's driver's licence and was sick of the rich and the young royals who thought the laws did not apply to them. This man was both.

'I don't know,' Ibrahim answered again. Normally it would have incensed the policeman, normally he would have headed back to the car to perform another slow check just to make the prince wait because a fine would not trouble him, but there was something in Ibrahim's voice that made the policeman hesitate. There was a hint of confusion in this arrogant, aloof man's tone that halted him. 'I'm sorry.' The officer frowned at Ibrahim's apology. 'I apologise for not following your laws.'

'They're there for your own protection.' And Ibrahim closed his eyes because, albeit in English now, those were the words that had swaddled him through childhood, through teenage years and into adulthood.

'I appreciate that,' Ibrahim said, then opened his eyes to the concerned face of the policeman. 'Again I apologise.'

'Is everything okay, sir?'

'Everything is fine.'

'I'll let you go with a warning this time.'

He would rather have the ticket.

As he climbed back into the car, Ibrahim would far rather have paid his dues, accepted the punishment, and it had nothing at all to do with the fact he could afford to—he did not want favours.

Ibrahim drove sensibly, even when the police car left him as he turned into the petrol station. Ibrahim stayed within the speed limit all the way back to London, and as he turned into the smart West London street he did not look at the stylish three-storey house but at the railings in front of it, and the neatly trimmed hedge, to the houses either side and the next house and the next, and he couldn't bring himself to go in.

Had the policeman been behind him he would have pulled him over again, for Ibrahim executed a highly illegal U-turn and then reprogrammed his sat-nav. His decision was made.

He would get it out of his system once and for all.

The future king was due to be born in a few weeks' time and he certainly didn't want to get caught up in all that. He would ride his horses in the ocean and desert for a few days, hear what his father had to say and then he would return to London.

To home, Ibrahim corrected himself.

Despite what his father said, London *was* his home.

He just had to be sure of it.

His mind flicked to Georgie, to unfinished business,

to a woman who did not want the desert, who had been on his mind for far too long now, and another decision was made…he would visit the desert and return, and *then* he might call her.

CHAPTER FOUR

THERE was a new lightness to Georgie as she took out her blonde hair from its ponytail and combed it, and there was a smile on her lips as she applied lip balm. Not even the prospect of the long flight ahead could dim a world that suddenly felt just a little more right.

That her divorce had come through that morning might not seem to many something to be pleased about, and a marriage that had been a mistake might seem nothing to be grateful for, but it had taught her a lot.

Even though she had left him years ago—left a marriage of just a few weeks—the fact it was officially over brought her relief.

Now she was free.

Her only regret was that it hadn't come through sooner. That the morals that kept her from sleeping with anyone, even with her divorce pending, had kept her from Ibrahim that night.

Georgie closed her eyes for a moment, told herself not to go there—it was a path she had chosen. Her illness, her father's abuse, a marriage that had seemed an escape—it would be so easy to look back with regret, yet she had learnt so much from it all. She had grown into a strong woman, a confident woman who knew herself, because she had chosen to learn from, rather than rue, her mistakes. It was a hard path to follow but, for Georgie, the right one. Guilt and regret had led her to troubled places, but no more. She wanted to talk with Felicity, wanted to thank her for all her support through the difficult years. Georgie swallowed, because she was still undecided, but she wanted to tell Felicity about Mike, to clear the past and make way for a glorious future.

Ibrahim's apology had helped too.

It had been unsettling seeing him, of course, but she took his apology as a sign that the chapter was closed and that it was time to move on.

To have no regrets.

The air ticket her sister Felicity had sent meant she bypassed the nightmare queues at Heathrow. She sat, awkward at first, in a first-class departure lounge, but as she sipped champagne and checked her emails, it was soon easy to relax. She accepted the delicacies on offer without thought. A new smile spread across her face as she realised just how far she had come. The endless abacus was finally silent—no more calories versus tread-mill, no penance for pleasure, just the sweet taste of a pistachio macaroon dissolving on her tongue. She didn't need a plane to fly to Zaraq. Her mood was so buoyant as she boarded, her high so palpable, Georgie could have flown there on happiness alone. Finally, the dark days were over—the soul-searching, the introspection, the agony of healing was behind her. She was ready to move on, even if the plane wasn't.

Just a little nervous of flying, Georgie took a vial of melissa oil from her bag and massaged a drop into her temples. The attendant offered her another drink, but Georgie didn't want one. 'When are we taking off?' Used to economy class, Georgie half expected to be speaking to thin air by the time the words were out, or at best to receive a brusque answer, but she was reminded she was travelling first class when the attendant smiled and lingered. 'We're sorry for the delay but we have an unexpected passenger. He shouldn't be too much longer…' But even in first class there was a pecking order, because the attendant's voice trailed off and Georgie was no longer the focus of her attention. She watched as the woman's cheeks darkened. Curious, Georgie followed the woman's gaze and her heart seemed to stop as all efforts to move on were halted, any chance of forgetting lost.

'Your Highness.' The attendant curtsied as he strode past but even she couldn't halt the flicker of confusion on her smooth brow at their passenger's attire. He was dressed in mud-splattered white jodhpurs and black jumper, and there was a restlessness to him, a wild energy that seemed to have boarded the plane along with him. He didn't respond to the attendant, neither did he glance in Georgie's direction. There was such purpose to his stride it looked as if he was heading for the cockpit, prepared to fly the plane himself, but at the last minute he turned and, yes, there were levels of first class because it would appear Ibrahim had his own suite. The attendants fluttered away from their charges and gathered together to discuss the latest arrival, and just a moment or so later a steward slipped into the suite with a bottle of brandy as the others watched.

She wanted to stand, to stop the plane that was now taxiing along the runway, to get off, for she could not face being there with him.

She didn't even notice the plane rise off the ground, or dinner being served, her mind consumed by her fellow passenger. 'Is everything okay, Miss Anderson?' The flight attendant removed her plates untouched and Georgie just nodded, too stunned to answer, let alone eat. The thought of being back in the palace with him, of being in such close proximity to him, had her reeling.

She had done everything possible to ensure that he wouldn't be there—oh, so casually asking her sister about his movements—and even in the nightclub he had given no clue.

But, then, neither had she.

Maybe there had been an emergency. His father had recently been sick after all. Why else would he be boarding a plane dressed like that? Or maybe this was how the rich lived, Georgie pondered. Who flew long haul in riding boots? Maybe he was so laid-back about travelling that he didn't even give it a thought. He could step off a horse and onto a plane… But later, when she got up to go to the toilet, a steward was coming out of his suite carrying a laden tray and shaking her head. Georgie got a glimpse of Ibrahim before the doors to his suite were closed—he lay sprawled out on the bed. He hadn't bothered with the gold pyjamas Georgie had on. He was unshaven, boots off, sprawled out on a bed and fast asleep.

She got only the briefest look as the door was quickly closed, but it was an image that stayed with her through the flight.

Anguished.

Even in sleep his face wasn't relaxed. His full mouth was tense. Even at rest he somehow looked troubled— but more worrying than that was just how much Georgie wanted to know what was on his mind

She'd been looking forward to the luxurious bed the airline offered in first class, had been looking forward to stretching out and sleeping, but knowing he was so close she found she couldn't.

'Can I get you anything?' the attendant asked countless times through the flight, and each time Georgie bit her lip on her true answer.

Him, she wanted to respond. Can you take me to him? But instead she shook her head and tried to work out what she'd say when she saw him.

The flight was broken by a stop in Abu Dhabi and Georgie took the chance to stretch her legs. She braced herself to face him, but Ibrahim must have decided to stay on the plane so she amused herself watching the gorgeous attendants boarding with designer bags, one even carrying a large pink teddy. This time, when the plane took off, finally Georgie fell asleep, except there was no respite. Her dreams were flooded with thoughts of him.

'Miss Anderson, would you like some breakfast before we prepare for landing?' The attendant woke her. Georgie nodded, and felt just a slight wobble of guilt: she had always kept her name, though used Ms in London. Felicity had booked her ticket and, given she had no idea about the brief marriage, had naturally put Miss.

Georgie stared out of the window at the glorious blue waters and as the plane banked gently to the right she caught the first glimpses of Zaraq—the endless golden desert giving way to sandy-colored villages and domed buildings. The plane swept along the shoreline, the cabin lights dimming. The palace that would be her home for the next couple of weeks wasn't what grabbed her attention. Instead it was the mirrored skyscrapers of the capital Zaraqua that made her breath tight in her chest. There were pools and bridges seemingly suspended in mid-air and Georgie marvelled at their design rather than think of him. She tried not to guess his reaction when she exited the plane and they finally came face to face.

He didn't get off.

For a little while she wondered if somehow she'd imagined him, for not once during the flight had she seen him.

'Georgie!' Felicity looked great. Georgie had wondered how she'd be dressed, but as a married woman her sister did not need to wear a veil and looked stunning in a white linen trouser suit, her hair longer than Georgie had ever see it. Felicity oozed happiness and good health, but it was little Azizah who enthralled Georgie from the moment she landed—her niece, just a few months old and with the fascinating mix of her mother's blonde hair and her father's black eyes. Azizah had been just a couple of weeks old when Karim and Felicity had brought her to the UK for a brief visit, but she was her own little person now and, for Georgie, the love was instant.

'She's stunning.' Georgie said as she held her in the VIP lounge. 'I can't wait to get to know her. Where's Karim?'

'He's here. We had a call from the airline a couple of hours ago—it would seem his brother was on the same flight as you. He's gone to meet him.'

'I thought I saw him,' Georgie said carefully, 'though he didn't see me. Is everything okay?'

'Of course it is.' Felicity said. 'Why do you ask?'

'No real reason. I just wondered if he'd dashed back for an emergency. He looked...' Her voice trailed off and she chose not to tell her sister after all. Felicity would see for herself soon and could make up her own mind.

'Karim might have to dash off once we get home,' Felicity explained as Georgie fussed over her niece. 'There's a bit of health scare with the Bedouins. You know how much work he does for them.'

Georgie nodded. 'Is he still doing the mobile clinics?'

'Shh,' Felicity warned, because no one, not even the

king, knew the full extent of Karim's involvement with the local people. We'll talk about it later. I just want you to understand if he has to suddenly leave—I don't want you to think he's not thrilled that you're here.' She smiled suddenly. 'Here they are now!'

As Karim and Ibrahim entered the lounge, Georgie was glad she hadn't aired her concerns to her sister. She'd have looked like a liar because Ibrahim looked far from troubled and unkempt now—clean-shaven, dressed in linen trousers and jacket, sleek sunglasses on, he looked every bit a first-class passenger as he walked towards with his brother, carrying the large pink teddy Georgie had seen the attendants bring on the plane. He must have sent them shopping, Georgie realised, watching as his jaw tightened at the sight of her—not that Felicity noticed the tension.

'Thank you, Ibrahim.' Felicity took the huge teddy. 'Did you have to book another seat for her?'

'Georgie!' Karim kissed the cheek of his sister-in-law. 'You may remember Ibrahim from the wedding.'

'Of course.' Georgie gave a smile but he didn't immediately return it. All she could see was her reflection in his glasses. She couldn't read his eyes.

'I wasn't aware you were visiting.' Only then did he manage to force a smile. 'It is nice of you all to come and greet me,' Ibrahim said, 'but it was completely unnecessary. I didn't want a fuss, it's just a brief visit.'

'We're not here to fuss over you!' Felicity grinned. 'We're actually here to greet Georgie—she was on your flight.'

And Georgie was positive, completely positive that his dark skin paled, that behind those thick sunglasses, even if she couldn't see it, there was alarm in those dark eyes.

'Really?' Ibrahim responded. 'And you didn't say hello?' His question was polite and so too was her response, even if was a lie.

'I didn't actually see you.' She gave a vague wave of her hand as she lied. 'I just heard the steward saying that you were on board. I'm sorry if I was rude.'

'No need to apologise.' There was, Georgie was sure, a breath of relief in his voice. He even smiled again in her direction. 'Just make sure next time you say hello.'

The driver came up and had a brief word with Karim.

'What are we waiting for?' Felicity asked.

'Georgie's luggage has been loaded, but Ibrahim's is taking a while to come off.'

'*Lā Shy,*' Ibrahim said and Felicity, who must have picked up some of the language, frowned.

'You've got no luggage?'

'Just carry-on.' He held up a smart bag that Georgie was positive he hadn't been holding on boarding.

The car ride was short, the conversation seemingly pleasant, but it was mainly Georgie and Felicity speaking.

Back at the palace Ibrahim had an extremely cursory chat with his family, then excused himself with an outright lie.

'I couldn't sleep on the plane.'

When he left them, Georgie could relax a little and after Felicity had fed the baby, she was delighted to have a proper cuddle. 'She's stunning.' Georgie enthused again.

'Her lungs are!' Karim said. 'Half the palace was woken at four a.m. this morning.'

'I had the French windows open to let in some air.' Felicity grinned and Georgie could only marvel at the changes in her sister. She had always been so tense and uptight, but there was a lightness to her now. Her face glowed as she smiled up at her husband. 'Anyway, soon it won't just be Azizah disrupting the palace.'

'When is Jasmine's baby due?' Georgie asked.

'Jamal,' Felicity gently corrected her, because her sister found it impossible to keep up with all the names. 'She's got five weeks to go and I just can't wait.'

'Is that the aunt-to-be talking,' Georgie asked, 'or the midwife?'

'Both,' Felicity admitted. And as easily as that the conversation flowed.

Even if her sister was a princess now, even if she lived in a palace far away, she was still Felicity, still her big sister, still the person Georgie loved most in the world. Karim did have to dash off, but the girls hardly noticed, there was too much to catch up on. Long after they had eaten and late, late into the night, when everyone else was in bed, still the sisters sat talking in a sumptuous, surprisingly informal lounge at the front of the palace, the windows open and fragrant air drifting in. Felicity had the baby monitor by her side, and somehow Georgie found the words to tell her sister about a marriage that had happened more than three years ago, a marriage she had soon realised was a mistake.

'You're disappointed.' Georgie could tell.

'No.' Felicity shook her head. 'I don't know. I understand you felt you had to get away from home. I'm just sad you couldn't tell me.'

'I didn't feel I could tell anyone at the time.' Georgie admitted. 'I haven't told any of my friends. I just thought Mike... He seemed so solid, so mature...' She looked over at her sister. 'But it turned out he was a bully, like Dad—except he wore a suit and instead of beer it was expensive whisky. It only took a few weeks for me to come to my senses. I'm lucky...'

'Lucky?'

'A lot of women stay. I got out of it quickly. It just took a couple of years to face up to the paperwork and legalities and then another year of waiting. My divorce came through just as I was leaving for here. I'm finally free.'

'You've been free for ages,' Felicity said, but Georgie didn't try to explain her feelings to her sister. How some principle had held her back, how until her divorce was through she hadn't felt free to start dating, and in many ways it had been the healthiest thing for her—that time had taught her that she didn't need a man to escape to, or run to. Everything she needed, she possessed already.

'You won't tell Mum.'

'God, no!' Felicity's response was immediate. 'And

don't talk about it here, they just wouldn't understand at all.'

'Promise me that you won't tell anyone.' The intimate conversation was interrupted. Headlights flooded the lounge with light. The sound of a car unfamiliar to Georgie in the large grounds was followed by chatter and laughter and then the slam of a car door. There was the running of feet on the stone stairs and Felicity's lips tightened.

'He's so inconsiderate. It was the same last time he was here.' And when a wail came up over the intercom she pulled open the lounge door to address Ibrahim, who was talking loudly to a sleepy maid.

'You've woken Azizah.'

'Not necessarily.' So effortlessly he slipped from Arabic to English. 'I may be mistaken, but I'm sure I read somewhere that babies tend to wake in the night.'

Sarcasm suited him, it *so* suited him that Georgie let out a small giggle, but Ibrahim did not look at her. Instead he spoke to Felicity. 'I'm sorry if I woke her…I forgot there is now a baby in the palace.'

'There'll be two soon!' Felicity said. 'So you'd better start remembering.'

'No need. I'm flying back to London in a couple of days, before the palace turns into a crèche.' As Felicity headed off to tend to her baby, he acknowledged Georgie, his voice distinctly cool when he did. 'I was not expecting to see you here.' Ibrahim said. 'You never mentioned you were coming.'

'Neither did you,' Georgie pointed out.

'Your flight?' Ibrahim checked. 'How was it?' And something told her he was concerned that she *had* seen him, that she knew the sleek, poised man who had arrived in Zaraq had not been the man that left London, but Georgie chose not to tell.

'Wonderful.' Georgie said, but didn't elaborate, and Ibrahim said nothing to fill the stretch of silence, just walked across the lounge and sat on the sofa opposite as a maid brought in his drink. She didn't know what to say to him and he certainly wasn't giving her any help. Georgie was relieved when her sister called from the stairs. 'Georgie! Can you give me a hand with Azizah?'

'I'll say goodnight, then.' He didn't return the farewell, but she watched his jaw tighten when clearly she hadn't jumped quickly enough and Felicity called to her again. As she walked past, Ibrahim caught her wrist. 'That's what maids are for.' She looked down at his long fingers wrapped around her pale wrist and she wished he would drop the contact, wished he would not look up at her because her face was on fire. 'Tell her you are taking refreshments with me.'

'I'm happy to help my sister with Azizah.'

'At one in the morning?' Ibrahim said. 'Does she have you on call all night?' He watched her face burn, felt the hammer of her radial pulse beneath his fingers in response to his touch, and in that moment he could almost have forgiven her for rejecting him. He considered pulling her down onto his lap. 'Join me.' It wasn't a request, Georgie knew that—it was a challenge.

'I'm here to spend time with my sister and niece.' He dropped her wrist and without another word she left the room and walked through the maze of the palace to join Felicity in the nursery where she had settled down to feed.

'What kept you?' Felicity asked as Georgie closed the door.

'I was just talking to Ibrahim.' Georgie kept her voice light.

'Why?' And there was challenge too in Felicity's question, just a teeny call to arms, and Georgie refused to go there, choosing to tease instead.

'Why wouldn't I? It was either chat to a beautiful man or watch my sister breastfeed.'

To her credit, Felicity smiled.

'He asked about my flight. I just said goodnight.'

'Stay away from him,' Felicity warned. 'He's trouble. I've seen how he treats women—he'd eat you alive and then spit out the pips.'

'We were just saying goodnight!' Georgie laughed, but Felicity would not relent.

'He's so arrogant. Strolls back unannounced and expects everyone to jump to his whims, swans around the palace without a care in the world.' Georgie opened her mouth to interrupt because Ibrahim had looked far from carefree on the plane, but she decided against it, intuitively knowing Ibrahim wouldn't want that information shared. 'He's completely spoilt!' Felicity moaned on. 'Way too used to getting his own way, though not for much longer.'

'What do you mean?' Georgie asked, but Felicity shook her head.

'I've said too much.'

'It's me!' Georgie pointed out. 'And given what I told you earlier...'

'Okay,' Felicity relented, but, paranoid as ever, she had Georgie check and double-check that the intercom was turned off, then still spoke in a whisper. 'The king's had enough. Karim told me he's going to be talking to Ibrahim tomorrow. He wants him back in Zaraq, he's tired of his youngest son's ways. Ibrahim was supposed to go to London to study engineering and then come back, but he's finished his master's now and there's still no sign of him returning. Ibrahim's working mainly from there and saying that he wants to continue with his studies, but the king wants him here.'

'So, is he closing the open cheque book?' Georgie struggled to keep her voice light.

'He tried that a couple of years ago apparently.' Felicity sighed. 'And Ibrahim promptly went into business with one of Zaraq's leading architects. A lot of that dazzling skyline is thanks to my brother-in-law's brilliant brain. Ibrahim doesn't actually need royal financial support.'

'So how can he stop him?' Georgie asked. 'If Ibrahim doesn't want to be here, how can his father force him?'

'His father's king,' Felicity pointed out. 'And Ibrahim, at the end of the day, is a royal prince and privilege comes with responsibility.'

'You're starting to sound like them!' Georgie attempted a joke, but Felicity shook her head.

'Look at all the work Karim does for the people. He's out there now in the middle of the desert, working with sick people, while Ibrahim's working his way along the bar at the casino like a tourist. Well, Ibrahim's a prince and the king's tired of waiting for him to act like one.' Even though she was whispering, she still dropped her voice. 'He's going to be choosing a bride for him, whether he wants it or not. Soon Ibrahim's going to be coming home for good.'

CHAPTER FIVE

SHE'D slept too much on the plane and Georgie woke before sunrise, pulled the shutters open and properly surveyed her gorgeous room then climbed back into bed. After a moment's deliberation, she did what Felicity had told her to if she wanted anything, anything at all, and picked up the bedside phone. It didn't even ring once before it was answered, and in no time at all there was a tray laden with coffee and fruit and juices being delivered not just to her room but onto a bedside table. Her pillows were rearranged and Georgie cringed at the attention and wondered how Felicity could have so easily got used to it.

The coffee was too strong, too sweet and had an almost smoky flavour to it and she sipped it slowly, then chose to take her tray and enjoy the sight of the sun rising over the ocean.

Opening the French windows, she stepped out onto the balcony and watched the magical display—the sky lit up with pinks and oranges, the air warm on her skin. She was filled with a yearning to see a desert sunrise, to follow those warm fingers of light and see them awaken all that was behind. But as much as Georgie wanted to witness the splendour, she knew that again this trip it would be unlikely—Felicity was very busy and wouldn't want to leave little Azizah overnight.

One day she'd see it. Georgie told herself to be patient, but she was drawn to the magic Ibrahim had so readily dismissed, wanted to find out more for herself about the tales of the desert, to sample the food and inhale the oils, to see more of Zaraq than just the shops and the palace.

And then she saw him. A man on his horse. It could have been any of the brothers, from this distance it might even have been the king, but her heart told her it was Ibrahim. He certainly didn't look like a man who was recovering from the previous night's excess and not for the first time Georgie wondered if Felicity was mistaken about how Ibrahim spent his evenings. There was something about the speed of his riding, a combination of youth, vigor and power as he hurtled along the beach that told her it was him. He pulled up suddenly, patting the beast's neck and guiding him to a slow walk in the water, and then he looked up and saw the sun glisten on the palace and saw Georgie watching him.

He did not acknowledge her, did not lift a hand to wave. He just turned and kicked his horse back into a gallop, leaving a white streak of surf behind him, and she knew she'd just been snubbed. Still, you didn't say no to a man like Ibrahim and then expect a cheery wave the following morning.

Why was he here? Georgie wondered, as she showered

and dressed. What had suddenly prompted him to return unannounced? Oh, she'd seen him dashing and smiling, descending on Zaraq oozing charm and bearing gifts.

She'd seen the torment in his face too—only not even Ibrahim knew that.

The thought stayed with her as she showered and, dressed, joined her sister for breakfast.

'Is this okay?' she asked as she took her seat. It was a perpetual question for Georgie while in Zaraq. She was dressed in a loose-fitting cream shift dress with flat, strappy sandals and even though it was modest, she still felt as if she was showing way too much skin.

'Relax!' Felicity said. 'You look wonderful. It's only if you come out with me on official business, which you won't,' she hastily added when Georgie's eyes widened in horror, 'that you would have to cover up.' And then Felicity gave a wry laugh. 'Actually, technically you wouldn't. You're married after all.'

'Not any more.'

'Oh, but you are in Zaraq.' Felicity said, but didn't get to elaborate as the king came out to the courtyard where they were taking breakfast.

'Have you seen Ibrahim?' Felicity didn't turn a hair, but Georgie felt her heart pound because the king was a formidable man, especially close up, and he didn't look best pleased. 'No doubt he is still sleeping.' She wanted to correct him, to tell the king that Ibrahim was, in fact, out riding, but she knew it wasn't her place, even though the king sounded irritated. 'Where is everyone?'

'Karim left early to attend a meeting on the health

situation with the Bedouins,' Felicity answered calmly. 'I haven't seen anyone else.'

'Well, if you see Ibrahim, please remind him that I want him to come to my office before he no doubt disappears again.'

'Not likely.' Felicity said, once the King was safely out of earshot. 'I'm staying well out of their way today and so are you.' She smiled at her sister. 'We're off to the spa for the morning!'

It wasn't quite as simple as that. Felicity hadn't left Azizah for any length of time with Rina the nanny, and spent ages explaining to her about how her stored breast milk was to be used. She was still rather tense when she and Georgie climbed into the limousine.

'She'll be fine,' Georgie soothed. 'Rina seems wonderful with her.'

'I know.' Felicity admitted. 'I'm going to have to get used to leaving her—there are so many functions and I'm also thinking of going back to work! Just occasionally,' Felicity said, seeing Georgie's eyes widen. 'Midwifery is what I love, it's who I am, and I don't ever want to lose that. Rina is lovely and everything but Azizah doesn't seem to relax with her.' Georgie knew what was coming. They'd had this conversation so many times before and she tried to divert it.

'Maybe she needs a little more time—just her and Rina,' Georgie attempted. 'You do hover a bit. Rina seems wonderful, you just don't give her a chance. It's good you're out this morning.'

But Felicity would not relent. 'I want Azizah to grow

up with family.' She looked at Georgie. 'I want to be with my family too. Mum's considering it, but I know she'd jump if you were here too. Please, Georgie, say you'll seriously think about it.'

And it would be so easy to say yes, because she missed her sister and niece too. So very easy to give up trying to get her holistic healing business off the ground and just sink into the luxurious lifestyle her sister was offering.

Too easy.

Felicity had always looked out for her, had always looked after her through difficult times. The reason Felicity had first come to Zaraq had been to pay off the loan she had taken out to pay for Georgie's rehab, and though the offer was tempting, there was a need in Georgie to go it alone, to prove to herself she could get by without her big sister's help.

'Let's talk about it another time.' Georgie said as the car headed off and she craned her neck for a glimpse as the palace gates slid open.

'What are you looking at?'

'Just the view.' Georgie smiled. 'I can't believe I'm staying in a palace.'

'You could live in a palace.' Felicity pushed, but Georgie just gave a noncommittal smile, her mind elsewhere.

It wasn't the palace, she had been trying to get a glimpse of.

It had been Ibrahim.

It was always Ibrahim, not that she could admit it to

her sister. And he stayed on her mind as they arrived in Zaraqua and an external glass elevator propelled them to the forty-second floor of a skyscraper, and Georgie remembered that she didn't like heights.

'Ibrahim's work!' Felicity said to Georgie's pale face as they shot skyward. 'He designed this lift.'

'Then remind me to tell him I hate him!' Georgie shivered. 'And tell me when I can open my eyes.'

'Now.'

They stepped into spa heaven. The lights were dimmed and the air fragrant as they were led to a changing room that was twice the size of Georgie's small flat at home. 'I want to try everything…' Georgie said as she changed into a gown, her mind exploding with ideas for her fledgling business back home. 'Is there a menu?'

'It's all sorted,' Felicity said. 'We're here for the Hamman Ritual and there isn't a single decision you have to make. It's absolute bliss.'

It was.

Through dimmed rooms lit with candles they were led, and as Georgie's eyes adjusted she saw the tadelakt wall with its intricate tiling.

'It's so hot,' Georgie whispered.

'You'll get used to it.'

Oh, she'd love to get used to it. She was lowered into a sunken bath and her body washed with black soap and then, on emerging, she was led to another heated room where every inch of her skin was exfoliated, the bathing repeated and then every superfluous hair removed with sugar and honey. From heated room to heated room they were guided, every treatment skillfully applied, every scent thoughtfully chosen, and two hours later, wrapped in a robe, sipping at fragrant tea and enjoying the soft music, Georgie smiled back at her sister, who was watching her.

'I can't believe how far you've come.'

'I know.' Georgie admitted, closing her eyes and letting joy flood through her, because a couple of years ago today would have been impossible, the thought of a spa abhorrent, but now she could relax, could enjoy healing hands on her, and it was her dream to in some small way impart the same experience in her work. She wanted to help others as she had been helped.

'Your Highness!' Georgie had forgotten for a moment her sister was now a princess and she was jerked out of her introspection as a nervous receptionist approached. 'We would, of course, never normally disturb you, it is a strict rule of the spa, but the palace has called...'

'It's fine,' Felicity said, and took the phone and then spoke with a nail technician, who was standing by. 'Would you excuse us, please?' Only when they were alone did she take the call, a smile on her face as she listened, her voice reassuring when she spoke. 'No, you're not making a fuss...I'll come now.' She paused for a moment. 'You were right to call me.'

'What's going on?'

'Jamal,' Felicity said. 'She's done this a couple of times. Hassan's away and she's anxious, she's not sure whether or not she's having contractions.'

'Surely there are a million doctors on call for her?'

'Exactly.' Felicity rolled her eyes. 'The whole country is holding their breath about this baby and the palace doctor isn't taking a single chance—last week she ended up being taken to hospital and monitored. There were the press waiting before she even arrived at the hospital and it was only Braxton-Hicks' contractions. She probably doesn't want another repeat.'

'Poor thing.'

'You stay here and finish. If we both dash off, they'll suspect something,' Felicity said. 'I don't want to give anyone here a hint—I'll make out that Azizah's fretting for me or something.'

Georgie stayed for a little while, had her feet hennaed with pretty flowers and her toenails painted, but it wasn't as much fun without Felicity and after an hour or so Georgie chose to head for home, or rather the palace that she called home for now. Even as the car swept into the driveway, still she had trouble believing this was where her sister actually lived. It was just a world away from the small house in which they had grown up, in the North of England. A house Georgie had never considered home. A house she had run away from at every opportunity.

For the first time the palace doors didn't magically part as Georgie climbed the steps, but just as she was wondering if such a magnificent door even *had* a doorbell, it opened, and there, most unexpectedly, was Ibrahim.

'Where's Felicity?' She peered over his shoulder as he let her in.

'At the hospital,' he replied. As she stood in the hall-way two maids dashed up the stairs without stopping to greet her or bow their heads to Ibrahim. 'Jamal is having the baby, so things have been thrown into chaos here—they are trying to get hold of Hassan.'

'I thought it was a false alarm. It's too soon!' Georgie said, but Ibrahim seemed unperturbed.

'Your sister says it is a little early, but it will be just fine. My father just left for the hospital. Felicity explained you were at the spa. She was going to have a message sent for you but things started to move rather quickly, otherwise I'm sure we would not have been left alone.' And that small comment told her he had been warned about her, but he did not linger on the matter, just stood silently as a group of robed man swept past, all deep in urgent conversation.

'Where's Azizah?'

'With the nanny. She is getting her ready.' At first she assumed it was a slight slip in English, that the nanny was changing a nappy or getting her niece dressed, but Georgie soon realised there had been no miscommunication.

'She will bring her to the car. You need to get your things together too. We should leave soon,' he said, but Georgie just stood there.

'Leave?'

'We need to get to the hospital.'

'Me?'

'You're family,' Ibrahim said. 'And the future king

is about to be born. Why wouldn't you want to be there?'

'Because I've never spoken to my sister's sister-in-law before for starters!'

Felicity had warned her to hold her tongue, to think before she spoke, and Georgie wondered if she'd gone too far, but his mouth moved into a smile she hadn't been privy to in a very long time, a smile like no other because it told her that his question had been teasing, that he took no offence at her response. It was a smile that welcomed her to his world, that told her he understood how bizarre this all must seem. Then he must have remembered he was still sulking because his smile faded and his words were stern when they came.

'I am looking forward to this about as much as you are. There is no choice.'

Rina came down with little Azizah, who was wrapped in a delicate cream shawl ready to meet her new cousin, and the enormity of what lay ahead hit Georgie then.

'I really don't think anyone would notice if I didn't attend.'

'Oh, they'd notice.' Ibrahim said. 'You are to bring Azizah.'

'I'm not ready...' She gestured to her clothing. The loose white dress was crumpled from the oils, her hair heavy and greasy from her scalp massage, and she didn't have a scrap of make-up on. Worse was the thought of being amongst the royals. Being a part of such a prestigious event had her head in a spin—but a maid slithered a veil over her and Georgie was grateful in that moment for the robes, for the shield, for the anonymity it would afford her.

Without it, she would never have made it through the day.

As they all walked out to the waiting car and she saw the police motorbike escorts waiting for them, it was all too intense for Georgie. The silver limousine with blacked-out windows that had taken Felicity and herself to the day spa had been replaced by a black vehicle that was far more formal. There was even a flag at the front.

'It's like a royal parade,' Georgie attempted as the door opened, and then she swallowed at Ibrahim's response.

'That's exactly what it is.'

One minute she was enjoying a spa day with her sister, the next she was to be a visible member of Zaraq's most prominent family. One minute she was an occasional, albeit enthusiastic aunt. Now, though, when Rina handed her Azizah, she carried in her arms Zaraq's newest princess.

'Why aren't the windows blacked out?'

'We are on official duty!' Ibrahim informed her. 'The people of Zaraq want to see their royal family on a day like today.'

Perhaps he mistook her panicked eyes. 'We can go separately if you prefer,' Ibrahim offered, but it wasn't being with him that had Georgie nervous, it was the thought of doing this without her sister.

'No,' Georgie croaked. 'Stay.'

She was a complicated mix, Ibrahim thought as he climbed in beside her. So outwardly confident, so bold and assured, and yet… He looked over, but she stared ahead, her blue eyes unblinking, and he could hear her drawing in deep breaths. There was a fragility to her that his brother missed, that others missed, and he could not just abandon her on a day like today. As the car moved from the palace and into the streets, Ibrahim told her a little of what she could expect.

'Now that the king has arrived at the hospital, there will be great excitement, people gathering.'

It was all more than Georgie could immediately take in, though later she would surely go over it in her mind again and again, for as they approached the hospital, crowds of people were waving and cheering as the latest royal car arrived. It was the most bizarre moment of her life, and as she climbed out, holding Azizah, never had Georgie felt more responsible. She was filled with a need to take care of her niece as Felicity would want her to. She held Azizah close and pulled the shawl to shield the baby's eyes from the fierce afternoon sun. Ibrahim waited patiently and then walked beside her, greeting waiting staff members who briefed him as they went to join the rest of the royals.

'It won't be long apparently,' Ibrahim informed her. 'The birth is imminent, and Hassan has just arrived.'

They arrived at a waiting room like no other. There were staff on hand offering refreshments, and Rina, who had followed in another car, offered to take Azizah, but

Georgie declined. 'I'll hold her. Where's my sister?' she asked, and it was Ibrahim who found out.

'Felicity is staying with Jamal for the birth.' He saw her blue eyes shutter. 'I know it's a bit overwhelming.'

'A bit?'

'Very,' Ibrahim conceded. 'I will stay with you.' Even if it had been forbidden by his brother—in fact, just that morning, as Ibrahim had been heading out for a ride, Karim had issued an updated warning for him to stay away from Georgie—he did not care. The ways of his family overwhelmed even Ibrahim at times, so how much harder must it be for Georgie? And without the help of her sister too. 'You don't have to worry about anything.'

Georgie blew out a breath. 'I don't know how Felicity copes…'

'It's the life she has chosen, though it's not like this all the time' He watched as she held little Azizah closer, more, he guessed, for her own sake than the baby's.

'Well, I couldn't do it.'

'She does very well.'

She frowned as she turned to him, surprised by the genuine admiration in his voice when he referred to Felicity. 'I thought you didn't like her.'

'I like her a lot,' Ibrahim said. 'My concern is for you.' And then he gave a wry smile. 'Not that you want it.'

'She's not using me.'

'Of course she is,' Ibrahim said. 'And I don't blame her a bit for it. She is here alone in a foreign country, she wants her family close—and she wants you to use her too.' He'd voiced every one of her thoughts. 'She wants you, the sister she loves, to share in the riches, but you feel beholden.'

And she closed her eyes, so raw was that nerve.

'Look after yourself, Georgie.'

'Like you do?'

He was about to say, yes, give his usual arrogant reply, yet she made him think, made him pause, and rather than answer her question, he looked at his niece, sleeping the sleep of the innocent. He ran a finger down the baby's cheek and his reply was honest.

'Like I try to.' Ibrahim said, 'but we are all beholden.'

For now, circumstance dictated he be here for the royal birth. It was his duty to see it through, yet he was surprised at his building anticipation. He had been touched by the people's joy as they had driven through the streets. He was relieved perhaps because, when his father had been ill, when Hassan and Jamal had failed to produce a baby, there had been talk of Hassan renouncing his birthright, which would have bought Ibrahim one step closer to the unthinkable—that he might one day be king.

He was relieved, that was all, Ibrahim told himself as the lusty cries of a newborn assured Zaraq's future.

'A son!' The king beamed. 'Our future king has been born. A little small, a little weak, but the doctor assures us he is healthy, that he will grow and be strong.' He looked over at his errant youngest son and in a rare tactile moment embraced him. 'It is good you are here to share in this day.'

It felt good.

The unvoiced admission surprised him.

'Come,' the king ordered. 'We move to the balcony to share the joyous news with our people.'

It was a good day, an exciting day, a miraculous day. Ibrahim looked at Georgie, who was completely out of her depth and more than a little lost, and as he went to her side he could see the terror in her eyes. As promised, he stood by her as they moved to the balcony.

'This,' he explained, 'is the announcement. This tells our people all is well. When Hassan and Jamal's first son, Kaliq, was born and we knew he would not survive, there was a small press release and no further comment. Today the people of Zaraq will know all is well.'

She stepped onto the balcony, holding her tiny niece, and heard the screams and cheers from the streets below.

'You're doing great.' He was being incredibly nice.

'Thanks.' Georgie shivered through her teeth. 'The thing is I have no idea what it is I'm doing.' Still, the excitement was palpable and Georgie joined in, even waved to the people below and had an 'if only they knew' moment when she thought of her friends back home. 'Luckily it's just for today.'

But it wasn't just one day for Ibrahim. This was what he was being asked to return to, he thought as he stared out at the crowd. This might be his future.

CHAPTER SIX

'Do I have to wear this?' This was so not what Georgie had come to Zaraq for. It was a trip to see her sister, to spend time with her niece, but now she was to dine tonight with the princes and the king, and it seemed there was no getting around it.

'The heir was born today.' She could hear the exasperation and guilt in her sister's voice. 'Georgie, we will have time together, it's just with Jamal's baby coming early... Please, just go with things for a couple of days.'

It was arguably worse than the wedding. To ensure she was fit for the king's table, maids had braided her long blonde hair and kohled her eyes, and now a garment had been laid out on her bed—a long lemon dress with beading and patterns down two front panels. It wasn't even close to anything she would have chosen.

'You look gorgeous,' Felicity lied, because the lemon would have looked stunning with olive skin and a coil of dark hair, but it clashed with blonde and both sisters knew it.

'I look like a lemon meringue pie.' Georgie responded,

but she didn't want to add to her sister's guilt. She actually managed a laugh as she peered in the mirror. 'And why is my rouge orange? Anyway, it doesn't matter, it's just dinner…I'll be fine. You will be sitting next to me?' Georgie checked, but her heart tripped to a race when Felicity grimaced.

'I will, but I might have to pop up and feed Azizah. She fell asleep straight after her bath so I don't think she's going to last the whole meal.'

'You can't leave me with them.'

'I wouldn't normally—who could know Jamal was going to have the baby early? And I didn't know there'd be a formal function the day he was born.'

'Formal!' Georgie gulped.

'Well, not formal exactly,' Felicity quickly backtracked. 'I mean, it's family but Jamal's family are coming too and they're very traditional…Georgie, I don't want Rina to feed Azizah unless I really can't be there. I have had to stand my ground with this—it's the height of bad manners here to excuse yourself during a meal, but Karim's spoken to his father…'

'You've got an exemption.'

'I can't back down.' Felicity was torn. 'But if it is too much for you… If it's going to set you back…'

'Felicity.' Georgie was firm. 'Not everything goes back to my eating disorder. Any person would be nervous at having to attend a formal dinner with a king.'

'I know. I'm just so sorry that it's on your second night. It won't happen again. We don't usually dine with the king—normally it's Karim and me in our suite.'

'So who's going to be there?'

'The king, and Hassan will be there with Jamal's parents and family. Ibrahim, I hope.'

'Hope?' Georgie closed her eyes for a moment. She really did not want to face him looking like this.

'That's all you can do when he's around.' Felicity gave a wry smile. 'How was he today?'

'He seemed to enjoy the celebration—he was thrilled for his brother.'

'Karim said you two spent a lot of time together.'

'He speaks English,' Georgie said tersely. She did not have to explain herself, they had done nothing wrong, but she quickly changed the subject. 'What about the queen?'

'You know she doesn't live here.'

'So when will she get to see her grandson?'

'When Hassan and Jamal take him to see her—like I did when Azizah was born. Mind you, with him being a little bit premature, it might not be for a while.'

'So she won't get to see him?'

'Georgie, please…' Her sister was nervous and it irritated Georgie.

'We're not allowed to talk about it even in the privacy of my bedroom?' Georgie shook her head in disbelief. 'I don't know how you live like this, Felicity.'

'I have a wonderful life,' Felicity said, 'and of course we can talk about things. It's just…' Felicity screwed her eyes closed for a second. 'Just not at dinner. Georgie, I'm asking you to be discreet. There are things that aren't to be discussed.' She tried for the umpteenth time to explain to her younger sister the strange ways of Zaraq. 'It's a very delicate subject, The king misses her terribly, he mourns for her.'

'She's not dead,' Georgie pointed out. 'All he has to do is pick up the phone.' She rolled her eyes. 'Don't worry, I'm not going to say anything to embarrass you— I'll be suitably demure.'

She was, and it had nothing to do with Felicity's warning. The vast table, the company, the introductions, the surroundings had Georgie overwhelmed.

There was no sign of Ibrahim and she heard the king say his name a couple of times to Karim.

'When do we eat?' Georgie asked her sister, when they had been sitting for what seemed ages.

'When the prodigal son appears.' Felicity answered, and Georgie felt nervous on his behalf. 'Are you okay?'

'I'm fine.' But even if she appeared calm, inwardly she was dreading that her sister might have to leave. Especially as Felicity had told her that though they usually did their best to converse in English when she was around, it wasn't possible tonight as Jamal's family spoke only Arabic. 'They are discussing when a photo of the new heir will be released.' Felicity did her best to keep up with the conversation, but even that lifeline was lost when a maid whispered in her ear and Felicity, with a rather terse nod from the king, excused herself.

It was interminable, smiling and laughing and nodding when the others did, though Georgie had no idea what was being said. She actually found herself wishing they'd bring the food out, just to give her something to do. But then, like a summer shower on a stifling day, Ibrahim strolled in and all Georgie could wonder was how he got away with wearing Western clothes—he was in black dinner trousers and a slim-fitting white shirt and she wondered if he'd been out riding and had just pulled some clothes on, because his hair was tousled and he hadn't bothered with shaving.

'You are late.' The king was less than impressed. The conversation was in English now, no doubt to avoid any embarrassment in front of the esteemed guests.

'I had to make a phone call,' Ibrahim said without apology.

'It is dinner,' the king said.

'With family.' Ibrahim's smile was black as he made his point. 'Surely we can relax and share in such a fine occasion.' He slid into the empty seat beside Georgie.

'Felicity is sitting there.' Karim's response was immediate.

'Where is she, then?'

'Feeding Azizah.'

'She left you to deal with this lot?' Ibrahim looked less than impressed and just shrugged as Karim frowned at him. 'I'll sit with you till she gets back.' He switched back to Arabic then and spoke for a moment or two with the guests and then turned his attention back to Georgie.

'You look…' His eyes drifted down and then back to her face, and there was a hint of a tease in his smile. 'Like you did the day I met you.'

'Ah, yes,' Georgie said, remembering the apricot bridesmaid's dress. 'I don't think the maids are used to dressing blondes.' She winked. 'I'll have to have a little word.'

He was wonderful company. She even forgot to be nervous for a little while, forgot, if it was possible to, just how attracted she was to him. She was just herself with him that night, and that was all she needed to be.

'I thought they'd be serving now that you are here,' Georgie commented when, despite Felicity's prediction, it seemed that the dreaded meal was taking for ever to come out.

'It shouldn't be too much longer,' Ibrahim explained, 'Most of the socialising is done before dinner. Once it gets to coffee, the evening is over.'

'Really?' Georgie gave a tight smile in Karim's direction. 'My sister never said.'

Still, when the first course was finally served, somehow he must have sensed the small lick of hers lips wasn't borne of anticipation as a stream of maids approached with dishes.

'You'll be fine.' He watched as she politely nodded, but he could see the nervousness in her eyes. 'You really will.'

'I read that it's rude not to clear your plate.' Georgie was almost breathless at the admission, but without Felicity beside her, the prospect of dining in such plush surroundings with food she was unfamiliar with was becoming increasingly daunting.

'It's mezze,' he said, 'just the starter—dips, pastries

and pickles...' He explained the lavish spread. 'Just take a little and if you like it, go back for more. Excuse me a moment,' he said, and turned his attention to his father. '*Bekra*,' came his brief response, then he turned back to Felicity. 'My father is asking when I am going to the hospital again. I said tomorrow.'

Somehow she relaxed, so much so she barely noticed when Felicity returned and after a brief awkward moment Ibrahim moved to the other side of the table.

'I'm so sorry.' Felicity said in a low voice. 'Georgie, I really am—'

'It's fine,' Georgie said. 'Honestly. Ibrahim's been wonderful.' She saw her sister's lips tighten, saw Felicity's worried blink as she glanced briefly at her brother-in-law and then back to Georgie.

'What?' Georgie frowned.

'Nothing,' Felicity said, but Georgie could tell she was rattled.

Ibrahim's behavior was impeccable. As the endless courses were served he spoke with the guests but he still carried on talking to Georgie, guiding her through the courses whenever Felicity was drawn into the main conversation.

As they ate their dessert—*mahlabia*, Ibrahim informed her from across the table, a creamy pudding layered with rose water—again she felt Felicity tense. Her sister's reaction incensed Georgie. Admittedly, thorough no fault of her own, Felicity had left her to her own devices all day, and Georgie shuddered to think how the day would have been without Ibrahim's guidance. Now

Felicity seemed annoyed that the two of them seemed to be getting on, even nudging Georgie when she laughed at something Ibrahim said.

'What?' Georgie asked. 'What have I done wrong now?'

'I'll talk to you later.'

She would be talking too.

Oh, yes, she'd say something, but later and when they were alone.

Coffee was served and, as Ibrahim had predicted, the evening ended. As farewells were said to Jamal's family, Hassan declared he would now return to the hospital to spend the first night with his wife and new son. But it would seem the evening was not quite over, for the king accepted another coffee and small biscuits were served. Just when everyone should be able to relax a touch more, the king frowned in annoyance as Ibrahim's phone rang loudly.

'Excuse me.' He stood as he answered it. 'I have to take this call.'

It was clearly the height of rudeness, and the conversation was strained as Ibrahim took his time. The king's face was like thunder as the minutes stretched on, and even Georgie was nervous as to what might happen when almost half an hour later an unrepentant Ibrahim returned to the room.

'What?' He glanced up at the silence and boldly addressed it.

'I will speak with you later.'

'Speak with me now,' Ibrahim said.

'You have kept the table waiting for the second time in one meal.'

'I told you to carry on.'

'We celebrate *as* a family.'

'Not quite.'

It wasn't indiscretions from Georgie they had to worry about. There was a dangerous edge to Ibrahim, a challenge in his stance as he took his place at the table and clicked his fingers. 'I would like champagne...' he glanced at his father '...to celebrate the birth of Zaraq's future king.'

There had been champagne at her sister's wedding, but only for visitors, and clearly it was not expected tonight, for the servant hesitated until a tense nod came from the king. 'Will anyone join me?' Ibrahim asked. Gorgeous black eyes swept the table and then met hers.

'No, thank you.' She could almost hear the sigh of relief from her sister as she declined his offer and everyone else at the table did the same.

'Not *quite* a family celebration.' Ibrahim picked up the conversation once his champagne was poured, and Georgie realised he wasn't just ignoring his father's anger, he was provoking it. 'Did not one of you think to call her?' Ibrahim's eyes roamed to his brother and then to his father. 'That is why I was late for dinner. I called my mother, naturally expecting her to already know the news...that this morning she became a grandmother.'

'Ibrahim,' Karim broke in. 'Not here.'

'Where, then?' Ibrahim said. 'This is family, is it not? Where do we discuss such things if not at dinner?'

'Tonight is a celebration,' the king said, though a muscle flickered in his cheek. 'I was going to have my secretary ring—'

'Your secretary?' Ibrahim sneered. 'Is that the same one who rang her when her son died? The same one who rang her when Hassan and Jamal's firstborn died? You know how her heart broke.'

'I had not spoken to your mother in years then.'

'But you're talking to her now,' Ibrahim said. 'You're more than talking with her, you're...' He stopped and collected himself then carried on. 'Could you not have rung today to make her heart soar?' His disgust was evident.

'You did not ring,' the king said.

'I thought you had!' Ibrahim would not back down. 'I assumed her husband had, given you are talking now, and that you were in London two weeks ago on *business*.'

'Silence.'

'That call I just took was from your wife,' Ibrahim sneered, 'my mother, our queen. The news I gave to her before dinner has just sunk in, now she is crying, sobbing, that she cannot see the future heir till Hassan can fit in a visit. She begs me to celebrate for her, to give him a kiss from the grandmother who cannot be here. She has poured champagne back in London and is raising a glass—I told her that I would do the same.'

His eyes scanned the table. 'Will anyone join my mother and me?'

There were no takers.

Karim shook his head, as did Felicity, and Georgie wanted to shake her.

'Georgie?' he offered, and she was beyond tempted to say yes this time, not for the drink but for the point he was making. But she refused to partake in a battle that was not hers, to play a game when she was not privy to the rules. She could hear the pain behind his statements, feel the injustice on his mother's behalf, but she was here with her sister, here to support her, not make trouble for her. Still, there was regret in her heart when again she declined.

'No, thank you.' She licked suddenly dry lips and dropped her gaze, but not before she saw a flash of disappointment in his eyes.

The king was not about to bend to his son.

'Tomorrow.' He rose from the table and immediately Karim stood and so too did Felicity. At her sister's nudge, Georgie followed. Only Ibrahim sat, not for long but there was reluctance, insolence even as rather too slowly he also stood. It did not go unnoticed. 'You will be in my study at eight a.m. Tomorrow, Ibrahim, you will listen to what I have to say.'

The door closed behind him but the tension did not leave the room.

'Why tonight, Ibrahim?' Karim challenged. 'Why did you have to spoil it?'

'Spoil it?' Ibrahim did not understand his brother,

his brother who would have been the king's choice as heir, a brother who had not even cried when his mother had left them. 'You mean voice it.'

'I mean, you make trouble whenever you return. There was no reason for this display.'

'No reason?' Ibrahim looked at his brother and then at Felicity. 'Imagine, years from now, Felicity, if it was Azizah who had delivered a child while you were on the other side of the world and Karim did not think even to call you.' He picked up the bottle and left them alone and Georgie fought the urge to follow him.

'He has a point.' Felicity turned to her husband. 'A very good one, in fact. You should have called her.' When Karim didn't answer, Felicity pushed on. 'We need to arrange a trip home.'

'We've been,' Karim said. 'We took Azizah home to meet your family and my mother when she was born.'

'Well, arrange another one,' Felicity said. 'I want Azizah to know all her family.'

'I'll sort it.' Karim stood. 'I'll go and speak to my father now. See how he is.'

But any magnanimous feelings Felicity had towards her brother-in-law were fleeting. 'Bloody Ibrahim,' Felicity shrilled when they were safe in her suite. 'He does this every time he's home.'

'As you said, he had a good point.'

'Well, of course you'd jump in on his side.' Felicity was pacing. 'Will you just stay away from him?'

'Why should I?' Georgie challenged. 'When he's the

only person whose been there for me all day. Am I not supposed to speak to him?'

'Of course you can speak to people—it's the little private conversations, the laughing at each other's jokes...' Felicity was having difficulty keeping her voice even and then she said it, just came right out and said what had been obvious to everyone. 'You two were flirting all night.'

'No!' Adamantly Georgie shook her head. 'We were talking. We were just talking...' Except that wasn't true. It had been his black eyes she had sought, his smile, his voice that had summoned her senses, and she couldn't blame her sister for noticing. 'I wasn't deliberately flirting.'

'You were the same at the wedding,' Felicity said. 'I know he's attractive and I know women don't stand a chance when he turns on the charm, but not here, Georgie, not in Zaraq, not with my husband's family. You can do what you like in London.'

'What's that supposed to mean?' Felicity always did this—made out she was some wild child, some perpetual problem to be dealt with.

'Just...' Felicity ran a hand thorough her hair. 'Let's just leave it, please, Georgie.'

'Leave what?' Georgie said.

'Nothing.' Felicity shook her head. 'I don't want to argue.' She gave a weak smile. 'I'm overreacting. It's been a long day and not just with Jamal. Karim's worried about the Bedouins, he's speaking with his father to try and sort out what to do. I've felt guilty all day for leaving you and it *was* good of Ibrahim to take you under his wing. I'm just tired, overreacting.'

'Go to bed,' Georgie said. 'You'll be up for Azizah in a couple of hours.' She saw Felicity's face pale just at the thought of it. 'Why don't you let Rina get up to her tonight?'

'Not you too!' Felicity was close to tears. 'I don't want Rina.'

'I can get up if you want,' Georgie said. 'You look exhausted.'

'You don't have to.'

'I want to,' Georgie said, and before Felicity could jump in, she did. 'I know she's to have your milk, but there's a whole freezer full. I'll take the intercom and you get some sleep and we'll have a nice day tomorrow.' She watched as Felicity nibbled on her lip. Clearly there were more duties she had to perform. 'Or the next day. It's not your fault the future king was born the day after I arrived.'

'You do understand?'

'I do,' Georgie lied, because she couldn't really believe everything her sister had married into. There were unspoken rules everywhere and no matter how she tried she seemed to put a foot wrong.

As she walked back to her bedroom she saw him standing on the balcony, looking out to the desert he loathed. He didn't turn round but she knew he had heard her because she saw his shoulders stiffen. She stood for a moment, wondering if he'd acknowledge her, wondering what she'd do if he did, but Ibrahim just poured another drink and deliberately ignored her.

'I can manage, thanks.' Felicity smiled at the maid in her bedroom, who was there to help her undress, and she blew out a breath when finally she was alone.

She should have said yes to him tonight.

There were a thousand ways she could justify not doing so. As she pulled out her hair, she thought of a few—she was here for her sister after all, it would have been disrespectful to the king...Georgie slipped off her shoes, undid the buttons on her dress and then took off the horrible rouge and kohl, slathered on some face cream and rubbed more melissa on her temples, telling herself she'd done the right thing, but her heart wasn't in it.

After brushing her teeth, she rinsed her mouth then poured the water down the sink. She looked into the mirror and could justify no more.

Taking the glass, she picked up the intercom and walked out through her suite and into the hallway to where he stood on the balcony. He didn't turn to greet her and she hadn't expected him to.

'I'm sorry.' But Ibrahim shook his head. 'I'm trying to apologise.'

'Well, you don't have to.' Finally he turned and filled her glass. 'I should not have put you in that situation.' The most difficult, complicated man she had ever met looked into her eyes and she wished that she could read what was in his. 'You are not beholden to me.' Always he surprised her. 'But, Georgie…' he glanced down at the intercom '…neither are you to your sister.'

'I'm just looking after my niece for the night.'

'I'm not just talking about that—there is tension between the two of you.'

'We love each other.'

'I know you do,' Ibrahim said. 'But there is…' He could not quite identify it. 'You hold back and so does she.'

'You're wrong.'

'Maybe,' Ibrahim admitted. 'But sometimes a row can be good. Sometimes the air needs to be cleared. You feel you are beholden?' he asked. 'That you owe something to her?' And his voice for the first time ever was tender, and there was both guilt and relief as she nodded, being more honest with another person than she had been in her life. Georgie rarely cried, and only really for physical pain but she hadn't fallen over in a long time. But just as he had at the nightclub, Ibrahim brought her near tears with just a few words.

'That's not good, Georgie.' He knew her from the inside; he pulled out her demons and told her to banish them. For a moment she wanted to run.

'She's helped me so much, though.'

'Have you thanked her?'

'Of course.'

'Did you mean it?'

She nodded.

'Then you're done,' Ibrahim said, except it surely

wasn't that simple. 'Lose the guilt, Georgie...' he smiled '...and come to bed with me instead.

'That last bit was a joke,' he added, then it wasn't his smile but the swallow beneath that told her something else—that he was remembering. For the first time in months he moved closer into her space and there was an almost imperceptible tightening to his nostrils, but to Georgie it was magnified tenfold, for she knew he was drawing in her scent as he lowered his head.

'*Bal-smin.*' He inhaled the fragrant air that swirled between them and she wondered if he would kiss her, could hardly hold onto her breath as she tried to keep speaking normally.

'We call it melissa...' And then there was no hope of speaking because his breath was on her cheek.

She thought he might kiss her, so badly she wanted to taste him again, she thought he might pull her just a little further in, but all he did was torment her with a slow appraisal that made her feel faint. He breathed in her scent, though he did not touch her physically, but to have him so close made her feel weak and, whatever his assessment, he was right to assume he could kiss her; he could touch her; he could have her right here on the balcony, and that, Georgie thought in a brief moment of clarity, was a very good reason to say goodnight.

'I've got to go,' she croaked.

'Then go now,' Ibrahim warned, which was wise.

She took the baby monitor from the ledge, walked to her room and made herself, forced herself, not to turn round, but there was little sanctuary in her bedroom.

She took off her dress and lay naked between cool sheets, knowing there was just one door between them and wondering if he'd pursue her—already she knew what her response would be.

But he didn't.

He left her burning, aroused and inflamed as once she had left him, as perhaps was his intention, Georgie realised. Maybe he did want her on her knees, begging, just so he could decline.

Thank God for the baby monitor.

An electronic chastity belt that blinked through the night and made lots of noise, and, far from resent it, Georgie was grateful to have it by her side.

For without it she'd have roamed the palace, looking for his door.

CHAPTER SEVEN

'You wanted to see me.' Ibrahim strode into the king's plush office ten minutes early. Yesterday's reprieve from his father had come more as an irritation than a relief to Ibrahim. He did not avoid things and though he wasn't looking forward to this conversation, he would rather it was over.

That he state his case and move on.

'Have a seat.' The king's voice was tired rather than assertive, which was unusual, but what came next was a complete surprise. He had expected to be met with a tirade, a challenge, but it was the father, not the ruler who met his eyes. 'You were right.'

'I'm always right.' Ibrahim smiled, perhaps the only one of the sons who dared and sometimes could get away with cheeking his father. 'Can I ask about what?'

'I should have informed your mother.' The smile faded from Ibrahim's face as his father continued. 'She deserved better than to hear it from her son, or the news, or my secretary.'

She deserved better, full stop, Ibrahim wanted to add, but knew better than to push it.

'She would not come to the phone this morning to accept my apology, so I am heading there to deliver it in person.'

'You are leaving Zaraq now?' It was almost unthinkable. The streets were awash with celebration, this was Zaraq's greatest day, and his father was leaving?

'I will be home in time for his discharge from hospital and I will visit the baby this morning. The people do not necessarily have to know. And if they do find out…' The king gave a dismissive shrug. 'I am visiting my wife to share in person the joyous news.' He looked at his son, at the youngest but the deepest, the one, out of all of them, he could read the least. 'You don't look pleased.'

'Why would I be?'

'Since my illness I have been going to London more often. Your brothers are pleased to see your mother and I getting on…but not you.'

'No.' Ibrahim was honest, to his detriment at times, but he was always honest. 'I don't like my mother being treated as a tart.'

'Ibrahim.' There was a roar that would surely have woken Azizah, but Ibrahim didn't even flinch. 'Never speak of her like that.'

'That is what you make her,' Ibrahim said. 'For years you ignored her.'

'I housed her, she had an allowance.'

'Now you lavish her with gifts, fly over there when you are able…' He lifted his hands and danced them like a puppeteer and just sat as his father came round the table and raised his fist to him. 'Go ahead,' Ibrahim said, 'but it won't silence me—it never has before.' As his father dropped his fist, Ibrahim continued his tirade. 'You expect her to be home, to drop everything when you deign to come over, yet at important times, at family times, she cannot be present—what would you call her then?'

'I don't need your approval.'

'That is good,' Ibrahim said, 'because you will never get it.' He stood and his father ordered him to sit.

'I would prefer to stand.'

'I did not dismiss you. There is more to discuss.'

'As I said, I would prefer to stand.'

'Then so too will I,' the king said, and he stood and faced his youngest. There was challenge in the air and neither would back away from it. 'I have been patient,' the king said. 'More than patient. But that patience is now running out. You are needed here.'

'I am needed there,' Ibrahim retorted. 'Or will you only be happy when she is completely alone—will her punishment be sufficient when all her children are here in Zaraq?'

'This isn't about your mother. This is about you and your duty to Zaraq.' Ibrahim refused to listen. He turned to go but his father's words followed him. 'Your place is here—you can run, but the desert will call you, I know that it *is* calling you.'

Ibrahim laughed in his face. 'I cannot stand the desert.'

'You fear it,' his father taunted. 'I see you ride along

the beaches and along the outskirts, but this time home you have not been in. If you choose not to listen to that call, then you will listen to me. I am selecting a bride—'

'I can make my own choices.'

'You never make wise ones, though,' the king said to his son's departing back.

He wanted to leave and he would, Ibrahim decided, just as soon as his father had gone—he did not care to share a flight with his father. He wanted no more of this land, of its rules, and he would not have his wife chosen for him.

He had been right to come back, Ibrahim realised. It reminded him how he could not bear it.

And then he saw her.

A very unwise choice.

Sitting on the sofa, her laptop on her knee, her blonde hair high in a ponytail and with credit card in hand. He saw her blush as he entered, though she didn't look at him.

He didn't have to even be there to make her blush this morning.

Just her thought process last night made her burn with shame.

He could have taken her on the balcony, had he chosen to. He could have come to her room and taken her then—what sort of babysitter was she? She wanted to get away from the palace today, wanted to clear her mind before it went back to thinking of him. She'd expected his talk with his father to take for ever, that by the time they were finished she'd be long gone, but instead he walked up behind her.

'What are you doing?' he asked as she tapped on her computer. Most people wouldn't look, Georgie thought. Most people wouldn't come up behind you and stare over your shoulder at the page you were on, and even if they did, most people would pretend not to be taking an interest.

Ibrahim, though, wasn't like most people. Georgie was scared to turn, her skin prickling at his closeness, the air between them crackling with energy.

'I'm booking a tour.'

'A tour?'

'Of the desert.'

'Scroll down.'

She really couldn't believe his audacity.

'Are you always this…?' She couldn't even sum it up in one word—rude, nosy? And then when clearly she hadn't followed his command quickly enough, when clearly she hadn't jumped to his bidding in time, he leant over her shoulder, moved her hand to the side and scrolled down for himself. In that second Georgie found her word—invasive.

'An authentic desert experience…' Every word was mocking. 'You are staying at the palace, your sister is a princess and you are considering a guided tour?'

'Felicity is busy,' Georgie sighed.

'With Jamal?'

'No. Karim is heading out to the west today to assess

the situation with the Bedouins—he wanted her to go with him, and she agreed. She won't be back till late.'

'So why aren't you auditioning for the part of nanny? Didn't she ask you to watch Azizah today?'

'She did.' Georgie gave a guilty blush. 'But I said no. I said that I'd seen she was busy and had already made plans for the next couple of days.'

'Bad Aunty.'

'Good Aunty,' Georgie said, because she had given this a lot of thought when feeding Azizah overnight. 'I want to be her aunt, not her nanny. So when Felicity asked this morning if I could watch her, I told her I had plans.' She rolled her eyes. 'Now I just have to make them.'

'You can't go on a tour.' He shook his head. 'That is like asking me to dinner and then I have to ring for a take-away.'

He was angry after his talk with his father; restless and confined, and in a moment his mind was made up. 'I will take you.'

'I don't think that's the best idea.' Georgie swallowed, imagining Felicity's reaction.

'It's a very good idea.' Ibrahim said, because two days in, his homesickness had gone. Two days in Zaraq and he remembered why he'd left in the first place. 'You should see the desert—and I would like to go there too.' He would face his demons head on. The desert did not call him—the desert was not a person or a thing. Yes, maybe he had taken his horse only to the edge this visit or had ridden it on the beach, but he would go to the desert today because he refused to fear it. He would give Georgie her day and then he would leave. 'I'll tell them to prepare the horses.'

'I had one riding lesson nearly a decade ago.' Georgie said. 'I'll stick with my air-conditioned bus.'

'Then I'll drive you.'

Insane, probably.

'Look, I don't think my sister would approve and it has nothing to do with...' Her voice trailed off. After all, why shouldn't she go out with Ibrahim? Especially with what he said next.

'You have to promise to keep your hands off me, though.' He said it with a smile. 'Or our souls will be bound for ever.' He rolled his eyes as he said it. 'It's a load of rubbish, of course—I mean, look at my mother and father. Still we'd better not take that chance.'

'I'm sure I can restrain myself.' Georgie smiled back. 'You're not that irresistible.'

'Liar.' He gave her a very nice smile. 'I'm saving you for London.'

His presumption did not irritate, instead it warmed. That she might see him again without all the confines brought hope without compromise.

'Ring Felicity now, tell her you have booked a tour,' Ibrahim said, 'with an experienced guide...'

Blushing even though she was on the phone, Georgie did that, but instead of questions and a demand for details from Felicity all she got was guilty relief.

'What if she finds out?'

'How would she?'

'Won't the staff say something?'

'I'll smuggle you out,' Ibrahim said. 'I'll have them pack me lunch. They always pack enough for ten—they are used to me heading out.'

'Are you sure?'

He wasn't.

Not sure of anything, and least of all her.

A woman who changed her mind at less than a moment's notice, a woman his brother had warned him against yet again just this very morning, was serious trouble.

And there was unfinished business, which did not sit well with Ibrahim.

Still, where they were heading, there could be no conclusion, for the desert had rules of it own.

'I would like to spend the day with you.'

It was the only thing he knew.

CHAPTER EIGHT

HE FROWNED at her carefully planned desert wardrobe when she climbed into his Jeep.

Cool capri pants, a T-shirt and flat pumps were clearly not what he had been expecting her to change into.

'See if your sister has robes.'

'I'm not wearing them!' Georgie said. 'Anyway, on the tour guidelines it said—'

'That was for a play date. This is the real thing,' Ibrahim interrupted. 'You'll get burnt.'

'I've got sunblock on.'

'Don't come crying to me then at 3 a.m.,' Ibrahim said, and then he changed his mind, gave her a flash of that dangerous smile. 'Well, you are welcome to— just don't expect sympathy.' And Georgie swallowed, because they *were* flirting and a day in the desert, a whole day alone with him, was something she hadn't dared dream of and certainly not with him looking like *that*.

He *was* dressed for the desert and it was an Ibrahim she had not once glimpsed or envisaged. The sight made her toes curl in her unsuitable pumps, for if her mind could have conjured it up, this was how she'd have envisioned him. A man of the desert in white robes, his feet encased in leather straps and a black and white kafeya that hid his hair from sight and allowed more focus on his face.

'What?' Ibrahim asked, as he often did to silence.

'Bring it back,' Georgie said, and they were definitely flirting because he smiled as he registered what she meant.

'Consider it packed.'

They drove for miles, until the road ran out. Then Ibrahim hurtled the Jeep over the dunes, accelerating and braking, riding the dunes like a surfer on a wave. He had been wrong to fear it, Ibrahim decided, because all it was was fairy-tales and sand.

He parked near a vast canyon, with a few clusters of shrubs and not much else.

'Is this it?' Georgie asked, curious at her own disappointment.

'This is it,' Ibrahim said. 'You take the rug and I'll bring the food over.'

'Where?'

'To the picnic table,' he teased.

'Ha, ha,' she said as she stepped out. She knew she was being a bit precious, or just plain shallow—she didn't want belly dancers or for Ibrahim to produce a hookah. She'd just dreamt of it so, built it up to something majestic in her mind, and all there was…was nothing. She felt the blistering heat on her head and she scanned the horizon, trying to get her bearings, to see the city and the palace behind, or the blue of the ocean that circled the island, but there was nothing but endless sand.

'What direction is the palace?'

'That way,' Ibrahim said, spreading a blanket at the side of the Jeep for shade. She sat down and accepted some iced mint and lemon tea, but her eyes could not accept the nothingness.

'You want camels?' He grinned.

'I guess,' she admitted. 'And I'd love to see the desert people.'

'We might come across some. But most are deeper in the desert.'

'What is this illness that the Bedouins are suffering from?' Georgie asked.

'A virus,' Ibrahim explained. 'It is not serious with treatment, and most have been vaccinated. Most in Zaraqua anyway, but out of the city...' He looked out to the horizon. 'Beyond the royal tent there is nothing to the west. It is accessible only by helicopter. There is no refuelling point, no roads...'

'What if they need help?'

'It is how they choose to live.' Ibrahim repeated his father's words, though today they did not sit well in his gut. 'Ten years ago there was talk, contractors were bought in, proposals made, but the elders protested they did not want change and so, instead we concentrated on the town, the hospital and university.'

He watched her wriggle on the blanket, her capri pants and linen shirt uncomfortable now and her cheeks pink. Instead of saying 'I told you so', he headed to the vehicle and retrieved a scarf, which he tied for her, and it was bliss to have relief.

'Here.' As he sat down he pulled something from the sand and he handed her a shell. 'You are protected—that is what they mean.'

'There really are shells? From when it was ocean?'

'Maybe,' Ibrahim said. 'Or maybe a small animal. There are more questions than answers.' He smeared some thick white cheese on bread and offered it to her, but Georgie took a sniff and shook her head.

'I don't like goat's cheese.'

'Neither do I,' Ibrahim said, 'when it is from a high-street store. Try it.' He held it to her mouth and it was a gesture Georgie usually could not tolerate. Despite her healing, still there were boundaries and unwittingly he had crossed one. He held the morsel to her lips, told her what she should eat, only his black eyes caressed her as they did so, and there was, for the first time in this situation, the absence of fear. 'Try,' he teased, 'and my apologies if it is not to your taste.'

It was to her taste; there was a note to it that she could not detect and he watched as those blue eyes tried to work it out.

'The goats graze only on thyme,' Ibrahim explained. 'It makes this a rare delicacy.'

And she tasted other things.

Fruits she had never heard of that had been dried by the desert sun. She felt cool beneath the scarf. She felt brave in his company and not scared of the silence when they lay back on the rug for a while—and she knew he would not kiss her, knew, despite the energy that thrummed between them, that their day must end soon. They had driven for hours and there was only half a tank of fuel, but she wanted something else from the desert.

She wanted more.

'You would get a greater sense of it if I left you alone.' He spoke to her as he looked at the sky.

She smiled at him. 'I'd be bored out of my skull.'

'No,' Ibrahim said. 'That is how they make you fear it.' His face turned to hers and they lay on the rug, just talking, sure that they would play by the rules. 'When I was four or five, my father brought me. I was the same as you. Bored with the picnic...'

'I'm not bored.' Georgie corrected. 'I'm not bored with you.'

'Bored,' he said. 'That was how I felt, and unimpressed really, and then my father climbed into the Jeep and his aide drove off. I thought they had forgotten me, that it was a mistake, but, no, it was done to all of us.'

'They left you here.' She was appalled.

'They watch you apparently from a distance, but you don't know that. It is to make you strong. When it is just you, when you are alone, then you are in awe of it.'

'And did it make you strong?'

'No.' Ibrahim grinned. 'I cried and I sat down and I cried some more, I cried till I vomited and then I cried some more when my father whipped me for being weak, which I was.' He shrugged. He told the truth because he would never let them shame him for how he had felt, and that was what had angered his father most. 'I wanted my mother.'

'That's so cruel.' Georgie couldn't believe it. 'That won't happen to Azizah.'

'No.'

'What if they have a son?'

'Could you imagine Felicity?' He laughed at that thought and so too did Georgie. 'I think we can safely say any future nephew will be spared that particular induction. Do you want me to drive off now?' he asked. 'To leave you alone with it for a while?'

'No,' Georgie said, because the thought made her shiver, but she did still want more from the desert. 'Can we wait for the sunset?'

He turned his face skywards.

'Sunset is hours away.'

'Can we stay?'

And, no, they could not sit in the desert for hours— he could, for he had done his time in the land, but she was fair underneath the scarf and not used to the heat. He was about to tell her so but then something more fleeting than a thought changed his mind.

'We can go to the tent,' he offered. 'We can wait there for sunset. There are horses we can ride if you wish. I will find you a docile one. I can refuel. Bedra, the housekeeper, will be there with her husband. It is a royal tent, it is ready always for the princes or the king.' And he sounded very confident, as if he were suggesting they stop off at a café for coffee on the way home. Yet he had not been back to the tent in years and it was not a prospect he usually relished—but for reasons unknown even to himself he wanted to show her.

'What if Felicity—?'

'Why do you need her permission?' Ibrahim asked, a bit irritated now, but not at her, more at himself for his stupid offer. He had no desire to go to the tent and was rather hoping she would refuse. 'You are your own person. Do you want to come or not?'

'Please.'

She did not really understand the change in him, for he whipped up the blanket and threw it in the vehicle, threw the remains of their food for the unseen wildlife and Georgie took off her scarf. They drove in tense silence and maybe it was because of too much sun because she certainly wasn't relaxed in his company now. Still, she must have nodded off because she woke up with her head against the window to find his mood not improved by his unresponsive passenger or the increasing winds that threw sand against the windscreen and screamed around the vehicle. Inside the car it was almost dark, the sky bathed in browns and gold, and he had the sat-nav on. Ibrahim glanced over briefly as she stirred beside him.

'We're in a sandstorm?'

'We have been for the last hour,' Ibrahim said. 'We will just refuel and then leave. You wouldn't be able to see the sunset anyway. I will have Bedra prepare us some refreshments and then we will head back to the palace.'

'Isn't it dangerous?'

'If you don't know what you are doing,' Ibrahim said. 'We'll be fine.' Even though he sounded confident, he wasn't so sure. Visibility was extremely low and worsening and could change to zero in a matter of seconds. Really, unless the storm passed they would have to wait it out at the tent. He had even considered halting the Jeep but if the storm worsened they could find themselves buried, so he had decided to head for the tent and assess things then.

Ibrahim had listened to the warnings before they'd left, would never have brought her out here had he known a storm was building, but even listening to the radio now, tuning in for updates, still there was no mention of this storm. He glanced as her hand fiddled with an air vent. 'Leave it closed,' Ibrahim barked, and then checked himself. She really had no idea just how dangerous this was.

'Why have we stopped?'

'Because we are here.'

They were. Beyond the curtain of sand Georgie could just make out material billowing a few metres away.

'Wait there,' Ibrahim said. 'I will come and get you.'

She didn't need him to open her door and ignoring him Georgie climbed out herself and immediately realised Ibrahim hadn't been being chivalrous. The sand tore at her hands as she moved to cover her eyes, the scream of the wind shrilled in her ears, filled her mouth and nose and in a moment, in less than a moment, she was lost, completely and utterly lost. The vehicle was surely just a step or two behind her, the tent somewhere in front, but it was like being spun around in blind man's buff. Completely disorientated, she felt something akin to panic as she glimpsed for the very first time the might of the desert, and then she felt a wedge of muscle, felt Ibrahim's thick white robe and his arm pulling her, smothering her face and eyes with his kafeya. He guided her from the screaming wind, every step an effort, until she felt the wall of the tent in front of her and then the bliss of relative peace as he pushed her inside.

The peace didn't last long.

She coughed out sand. He lit an oil lamp and his expression was less than impressed when it came into view in the flare of the flame. Her coughing died down.

'When I tell you to wait—you wait.'

'I was trying to...' To what? Her voice trailed off. To show him she didn't need her door opened? To show her independence in the middle of a storm? There wasn't a single appropriate response.

'I'm not sure if you're naïve or ignorant.' Ibrahim was furious. 'You could have died.' He showed no mercy and neither did he exaggerate. 'In the time it took me to get around that vehicle, you could have been lost. *Listen to me!*' he roared. 'In a storm, and one as severe as this one is becoming, you can be lost in a moment—or choked by the sand. It is that simple.'

'I'm sorry...' she said, but Ibrahim wasn't listening.

'Bedra!' He shouted. 'Where is everyone?'

He strode into the darkness, lighting lamps as he

went, revealing more and more beauty with each flare
of light. The floor a scatter of rugs, the tent walls hung
with them too, and there were ornaments, instruments
she didn't recognise. It was the desert she'd dreamt of
and she wandered in quiet appreciation as Ibrahim grew
more irate, walking down white corridors that led to
separate areas. He called down them all.

'There's a note.' Georgie found it as Ibrahim searched
for the staff. 'At least, I think it's a note.'

She handed it to him and watched his expression turn
to one of incredulity as he read it. 'Why would Bedra
and her husband be out helping with the sick? Their job
is to tend to the desert palace—they should be here at
all times.'

'Well, given that she is a doctor, maybe her skills
were better needed elsewhere,' Georgie responded, and
then instantly regretted it, because from the frown on his
proud features she realized, he didn't know. Felicity had
told her about the secret desert work that she and Karim
did for the Bedouins, the mobile clinic they ran, how
Bedra was so much more than a maid. She had assumed
that even if the king didn't know, Ibrahim would—he
was Karim's brother after all—but clearly he hadn't
been told.

'She's not a doctor,' Ibrahim said derisively. 'She's a
housekeeper. She should be here.'

But as they explored the empty tent, clearly there
were things that Ibrahim did not know, because beyond
the servants' quarters, where royals would never ven-

ture, was a treatment area as well stocked as any modern doctor's surgery.

'I'm not sure,' Georgie could not resist as Ibrahim surveyed it, 'if you're naïve or just ignorant.'

She wondered if she had pushed him too far, but he conceded with a slight shrug and a shake of the head. 'Clearly I'm ignorant,' he said. 'She's really a doctor?'

'I shouldn't have said anything. I hope I haven't got Karim into trouble.'

'As if I'm going to tell on him. So that's why he was always out in the desert? I was wondering what his problem was—how much contemplation one man needed?'

He did make her laugh, but it changed into a cough and Ibrahim was still cross with himself for placing her in danger. 'I checked before we came out…there was no indication of a storm as big as this one. It seems to have come from nowhere.'

'Are there lots of them?'

Ibrahim nodded. 'But this is severe.'

'Could the tent blow away?'

Ibrahim just laughed. 'They are designed for these conditions.' And then he went into engineer mode, talking about vents and rigging, but Georgie had other things on her mind.

'Will Felicity and Karim be all right?' She thought of them out there and her heart started racing.

'They will be fine,' he assured her. 'Karim will know exactly what to do. They will be waiting it out like us. They just won't be able to fly back.'

'Felicity will be frantic.' Georgie closed her eyes. 'I should have stayed at the palace and looked after Azizah.'

'In case her mother got caught in a storm?' Ibrahim shook his head. 'You can't think like that.' The wind screeched a warning and Ibrahim knew when he was beaten. 'We will stay till it passes, but I think we are here for the night.' They headed back out to the lounge area and he stood as she roamed, watched her expression as she looked at the wall hangings and her nosy little fingers picked up priceless heirlooms and weighed them. He would never have planned this. Would never have bought her here if he'd know they would be alone.

Her cheeks were pink from the sun and her arms just a little bit sunburnt. Her clothes were grubby and her hair wild from the sand and the wind. And how he wanted her. Though he would not blatantly defy the desert, he would follow the rules while he was here, but his way.

Ibrahim did not have to chase, all he had was the thrill of the catch. He had never had to want or wait or been said no to—except once.

And here she was.

With him tonight, and now he didn't want to wait till London.

Tonight he would sample the thrill of the chase; tonight he would make certain that she would not refuse him again. He would romance her, feed her, turn on every ounce of his undeniable charm—he would ripen her with his mind and let her simmer overnight. They would rise early, Ibrahim decided, she could see the sunrise and then he would take her to a hotel and bed her, take her ripe and ready and plump and delicious. And he wouldn't even need to reach out. She would fall into his hands without plucking.

In fact, he decided with a smile, she would beg.

'What?' Georgie asked, seeing a smile pass over his face.

'I was just thinking. You will have your authentic desert experience. Bedra will have left food, the table is set, we can feast tonight, and tomorrow, and when the storm is past you can rise early and see the sunrise.' He saw a flicker of a frown on her face, but he moved to relax her. 'We must have separate rooms. Come, I'll show you the guest quarters.'

They walked through the lounge, the air thick and warm, and she glimpsed a large curtained area with a bed so high and deep you would almost need stairs and a springboard to dive into it. The room was heavy with scent—musky, exotic oils that aroused, to ensure future generations, and the bed throbbed with colour, drapes and cushions. He let her eyes linger for more than a moment, made sure she had seen it, and then gently he took her elbow.

'That is mine. Your room is over here.'

It was thirty-four steps away, she knew because she counted the distance between their rooms. Ibrahim knew she would be counting them again in her head later, for though hers was absolutely beautiful, for royal guest, not a princess, and just that tiny bat of her eyelashes told him she knew.

'It's lovely,' Georgie said, because it was.

It was!

Apart from the palace, it was absolutely the nicest room she had ever been a guest in, and she told herself that again as she enthused and thanked him, but her mind was somehow in his room, with heavy silk spreads and a bed you could drown in. 'Here.' Ibrahim was supremely polite. 'Make use of the guest quarters as you please.' He pulled back a drape and the space pulsed with colour and rich fabrics.

'I can't just wear someone's things.'

'These are for guests who arrive unprepared.' He slowly looked around the room. 'Nothing changes...' There was a pensive note to his voice, but he didn't elaborate. 'I will leave you to bathe, just help yourself to anything. Perhaps dress for dinner?'

'Dress?'

'You wanted an authentic desert experience, well, let me give you one.' He watched her swallow. 'I'll prepare the lounge.'

Despite the ancient ornaments and artefacts, there was every modern convenience and Georgie filled the heavy bath with steaming water and chose from the array of fragrant oils. After several hours in the Jeep and the grit and the sand she had accumulated, it was bliss to stretch out in the warm, scented water. She could have lain for ages, except she really was hungry.

Georgie had had no intention of selecting clothing from the guests' wardrobe.

A charity cupboard stocked for inappropriate guests she did not need, and she wasn't keen on the idea of playing dress up. Except maybe she was, because she thought of Ibrahim in his robes in London and there were still angry red marks on her waist where her capri pants had cut into her, and the pale fabric that had looked so cool and elegant on the hanger in the high-street store was now crumpled and rather grubby.

Georgie flicked through the wardrobe: vast kaftans that would swamp her delicate frame. And what was it with Zaqar and shades of yellow? Yet her first brisk hand movements grew slower, her eyes drawn to the intricate beading and embroidery, every piece a work of art. They were in decreasing sizes too, she realised, for there near the end was a slim robe in a dark blood red with small glass beads on the front and a dance of gold leaves around the hem—it was nothing like something she would ever choose for herself, but was perhaps the most beautiful article of clothing she had ever seen.

The fabric slid coolly beneath her fingers, the finest of silks. It beckoned, and she closed her eyes in bliss as she gave in and slid it over her head. It skimmed her body. As she looked in the mirror and saw a different Georgie, her stomach tightened in strange recognition at the woman who met her gaze. Not a girl or a young woman but a woman with all awkwardness gone, and it bewildered her. It was as if the fragrant bath had surgically removed that awkwardness, because

she liked what she saw and wanted to enhance it. Her
eyes glanced down to the heavy brushes and flat glass
containers filled with rich colours to perfume bottles,
and she pulled the stopper from one and inhaled the
musky scent, she wanted to dress for him. She wanted
her night in the desert.

Ibrahim's catering skills ran to ringing his favourite restaurant and telling them the number of guests.
His kitchen in London was stocked and maintained by
his housekeeper. At the palace, occasionally at night
he wandered in and chatted to the overnight chef, who
would prepare Ibrahim a late-night or rather pre-dawn
snack, but here in the desert things were different—here,
a young prince was left for a period to fend for himself.
Not that he had to this evening, for Bedra *was* both
a doctor and royal housekeeper. When he opened the
third fridge, there were platters fit for a king, or should
a reprobate prince happen by, and there were jugs too,
all lined up and ready, that had herbs measured and
prepared. All Ibrahim had to do was add water and carry
trays through, but he was pleased with his handiwork.
He even lit some candles and incense and turned on
some music to soften the noise of the wind. Then he
headed to his quarters to bath and change.

Ibrahim shaved, which he did not normally do in the
desert, but his face was rough and as watched the blade
slice over his chin, he thought of Georgie's cheeks, of
her mouth and her face and, yes, deny it as he may, he
was preparing himself for her.

Preparing himself for tomorrow, Ibrahim warned himself, because this tent was a place you brought your bride. This was a place where the union was sealed and even if he didn't strictly believe in the tradition, tonight he would respect it.

He headed out to the lounge area. He wanted to eat and wondered what was taking her so long, because he was ready and had *prepared* dinner too. But every moment of waiting was worth it as, looking just a little bit shy but definitely not awkward, she came to him.

'You look…' He did not finish, he could not finish, because not only did she look beautiful as she stood with her long blonde hair coiling as it dried, her skin flushed from the warm water, somehow she looked as if she came from the desert. Somehow, despite her pale features, despite it all, she looked as if she belonged here, and Ibrahim wondered if this night, together but apart, was more than he should have taken on.

Wondered how far he should tease her.

Her eyes were very blue in her pale face. She had none of that kohl that sharpened them, just a shimmer of silver on her lids that glittered each time she blinked. It was her mouth that had been painted, in the same blood red as her dress, and it trembled a little as his eyes fell on it, and it killed him that he must wait till tomorrow to kiss it.

She sat on the floor at the low table and Ibrahim did the same. He had seen her a little nervous around food, but now her eyes were just curious. The nerves, he knew, were for another reason, for long before she had sat down he had seen the leaping pulse in her throat, the glitter not just on her eyelids but in eyes that shone with arousal.

'Here.' He handed her a heavy fruit, which looked like a cross between a peach and an apple, and selected one for himself. As she went to take a tentative bite he shook his head. 'It is marula, you drink it.' He squeezed the heavy fruit between his fingers and she watched as sticky goo ran between them. He selected a straw and plunged it into the fruit and he took her mind to mad places, because the fruit was her flesh and she held her breath as he pierced it.

'You,' he said, and she broke the skin of her fruit, not as easily as him but it worked and she drank from it. Though the fluid was sweet and warm and delicious, somehow she wanted to lean and lick the moisture still damp on his fingers.

She ate, and it was different, because she was thinking about food again, about every morsel that slid down her throat, but it was far from with loathing, because each swallow of her throat was watched by him—and she wanted his mouth there.

She wanted their tongues to meet in one half of the pomegranate, but he offered her only her share and then ate his.

'No spoons.' Ibrahim said, and made eating seem debauched, but in the most thrilling of ways, and for the first time there was regret that a meal was over. As they moved to the couches, she wanted back at his table.

And Ibrahim knew.

But it was safer on the sofa and she sipped sweet coffee gratefully and had another cup to help her sober up, because that was how he sometimes made her feel.

'The trouble with antiques,' Ibrahim drawled, filling her cup with the jug that had been used since his childhood, 'is that nothing gets thrown out. Nothing changes. Always it is the same.'

'You hate it here?'

'No.' Ibrahim said, and then went on, 'Not always.' He saw her confusion. 'I know every corner of this tent. We came as children—it was good then.' He didn't want to talk, he wanted to slowly seduce, he wanted her wanting him in the morning, but somehow she demanded, without him always realising, more from him.

Sometimes he found himself talking with her, not about things that teased but things that tortured. He heard his voice saying things he had never said before, and she didn't just listen, as others would have, she did not agree but partook.

'When your mother was here? Was it after she left when it changed?' she probed, and he closed his eyes, but her question remained and he thought about it, because when his mother had been here, it had been different. Then his father would laugh and the children would play and spend a whole day searching for one rare wild flower for the maid to put on their mother's breakfast tray. He and Ahmed would play in a cave a morning's walk from here and the servants would find them at dusk, but the scolding had always been worth it.

Then there had been no fear when he had been with Ahmed, just the arrogance of youth, for surely nothing could harm the young princes.

'It just changed,' Ibrahim said.

'After Ahmed died?'

She had gone where no one should, where not even he dared.

'For him I would have been king.' He was beyond angry, his voice was raw. 'Had he just asked me, had he even bothered to tell me his fears. Instead…' He could not forgive his brother, and that killed a part of Ibrahim too, and he could not linger on it either, so he spoke of other things instead. 'It changed for many reasons. For a while it was a playground, but at seventeen you spend a month alone before you go to the military. It is a time of transition. For a month you wander and then return to the tent.'

'No staff?'

'None,' Ibrahim said. 'You remember the fear when you were left as a child, but there is no one watching this time. So slowly you build up for the walk home.'

'You walk home?' She could not keep the shock from her voice—that a teenager would be left to fend for himself then walk for miles. 'And then you get to join the army—some reward!'

'No.' Ibrahim shook his head. 'First you become a man. There is a very good reason to find your bearings and keep walking back to the palace. There, waiting, is your reward.'

Georgie blinked and as his eyes never left her face, as realisation slowly dawned, her pale skin darkened. 'That's disgusting,' Georgie spluttered.

'Why?' He was genuinely bemused. 'I am a royal prince—the woman I marry must be a virgin. It is my duty to be a skilled lover.'

'To teach her!' Georgie spat.

'Of course.' Ibrahim said. 'But even a teacher first has to be taught.'

'You make it sound so clinical.'

'When?' He challenged. 'You interpret it as clinical—I assure you it was not.'

'You can't *teach* it…' she flared but right there her argument started to weaken, because in his arms she had learnt so much. 'It isn't just…' she tried again, but words failed her. 'Some things,' she attempted, and then closed her eyes in defeat, because how could she admit that it wasn't just his skill that brought her to frenzy, it was him.

That just the curve of his arrogant mouth and the scent of his skin prompted vigilance, that if he sat there now and did not move, if all he did was stay still as she leant over and kissed him, if all he did was lie there as her hands roamed his body, it would be every bit as good as her recall. It wasn't Ibrahim's skill her body craved— it was him. 'When we…' Georgie swallowed. There was something she needed to say. 'When I stopped you, it wasn't because—'

'I don't want to discuss it,' Ibrahim said, because it would be too dangerous here to recall that night. Going into the details of their time together would not help.

'Please. I want—'

'You heard what I said.'

He could be so rude. Annoyed at him, angry at how he just closed off whenever it suited him. She refused to drag conversation out of him. She wandered around the lounge and there was much to amuse and interest her. She ran her fingers along one instrument and another and for the first time in her life she actually wanted to dance. She wanted to turn up the music and turn to him, and she felt as if she was fighting insanity, wondered just what it was in the fruit, because the desert made her dizzy with freedom from inhibition. She forced herself to explore rather than linger, picked up a heavy glass bottle and pulled out the stopper, but Ibrahim came over.

'They are not for cosmetic…' Ibrahim shook his head, took the glass jar and replaced the stopper. 'They are medicinal.'

'I know,' Georgie answered, irritated. 'This is what I study.'

'These are potent.'

'I do know!' She saw the dismissal in his single blink. It was a reaction she was used to, yet from Ibrahim it annoyed her. 'Just because you don't believe in my work…'

'But I do.'

'So why are you so scorning?'

'I am not...' His voice trailed off, because in truth he was. 'There are thousands of years of learning, of wisdom in these oils, our ways—'

'That can't be learnt in a four-week course!' Stupidly she felt like crying, not at his scorn, not at his derision, but because she felt there was truth in what he was saying. It was a question she had asked herself. She had sat in a classroom and later with clients wondering if she was worthy of imparting such ancient knowledge.

'Do you believe in what you do?' Ibrahim asked.

'Of course,' Georgie said. 'Well, I do, but I know there is more, much more to learn.'

'Always there is more to learn, for ever there will be more to learn,' Ibrahim said.

'So you don't think I should practise.'

'I did not say that. I go for my massage in London. There are practitioners like you...' He said it without scorn. 'They work with the oils, but their minds are not present.' How could he explain something he did not fully understand himself? But Georgie understood.

'Mine is,' she said, and took the bottle back from him. She held it a moment then took off the stopper, placed a drop of oil on her finger and moved it to his throat. He stood rigid as her finger slid down to his throat and in tiny circular motions massaged over his thymus—that area held past issues and his was full. She could smell the frankincense, the bergamot and a note she couldn't identify, and still her finger circled and her mind was present. It was Ibrahim who pulled back.

'This is what you do for a living?' He captured her hand.

'You make it sound like I'm running some seedy massage parlour. It's about energy and healing and relaxation.' She gave an impatient shake of her head. 'I don't have to explain to you what I do.'

He dropped his grip and still her finger circled. 'Show me,' Ibrahim said, which normally would have been a dangerous tease, an extension of his game, but it was more than that. He could feel the tiny flickers of her pulse in the pads of her fingers, and he also wanted some of this peace she talked about. 'Show me,' he said again.

He was used to massage—a keen horseman, there was all too often a hip or a shoulder that had taken a beating. He used massage just for physical ailments but wanted more. Often in London he found himself face down on a table, but no matter how skilled the hands, no matter how they relaxed his body, his mind did not quieten, and it was that he craved—some peace and clarity, for conflicting thoughts to still so he could assess them. For a second she had given him that quietness and he wanted more.

He pulled off his robes and lay on the cushioned floor. Just a sash covered him and it was Georgie who was awkward as she prepared her oils from the vast selection. It was she who was facing the biggest test, she wondering how to remain professional because he was utterly and completely exquisite. She was used to shy, fragile women, and there could be no greater contrast.

His back gleamed with muscle and awaited her touch, but there was a pertinent problem and as she prepared her dishes and vials she tried to keep her voice matter-of-fact.

'You need to lie on your back.'

She watched his shoulders stiffen, watched his expanded chest still as he held air in, then he turned round and she covered him, because this was not about sex, this was about something more.

But for Ibrahim any hope of relaxing, of merely enjoying a feminine touch, was dashed then, because lying like this with her kneeling next to him, it would take every ounce of concentration he possessed to ignore her, not to give in to the natural response of his body. He must lie there now and think of things, anything other than the woman who was moving down to his feet. He must not think of the hands she rubbed together to warm in preparation and he was about to roll over, to tell her not to bother, but as she captured a foot her fingers were so silky and oiled he lingered.

She had felt him resist, felt him fight, but as her hands slid to his feet and she stroked his sole, there was a tentative surrender that she recognised, a shift when a mind handed itself over to you. She wasn't sure if that trust was merited. Just a ping of doubt went through her as she thought of a four-week course versus the arts of the desert, then she knew what to do, and there was no more trepidation. She felt as if the roof had lifted from the tent, felt as if it was daylight again and the wind was gone, that the sun was beating directly into her head, spreading through her body and warming her fingers. Her hands knew what to do, and Georgie gave in to the healing along with Ibrahim and did what the desert told her.

She oiled his feet with lavender and spruce, worked slowly up past his calves, and when his legs were oiled and his body relaxed, her mind with his, she oiled her fingers and moved to his navel. There was a brief hesitation as her fingers hovered, and then it was only about him and she worked gently there with jasmine and neroli. She moved to his chest, small clockwise motions around his heart, and she couldn't hear the wind, just its message, and she worked on forgiveness with geranium and other drops of different oils, but she still felt resistance, his urge for her to move on. She moved to his stomach again. She worked on release, with ylang ylang and blue tansy, but he would not give in to it.

She added melissa, the fragrance he had smelt on her that night on the balcony, or as he called it—Bal-smin. It was the chief of oils and Ibrahim met his match in it. She saw his eyes close tighter, and if it had not been Ibrahim, so proud and removed, she would have sworn it was a man fighting back tears. Then she felt the release, felt the pain slide out beneath her fingers as he freed Ahmed. And then she went to his heart again, which didn't need her hand now because he had forgiven, and her hand slid down his body, down his legs, then to his feet to finish.

And it was more than intimate, it was more than sex, it was the closest he had ever been to another person, and when she had finished, when he opened his eyes, he willed her to go on. But she could hear the music and see the man before her now, and it wasn't her vocation that led her—it was instinct. She watched her own fingers as they dripped oil low on his stomach, and it was the woman she had only today first seen in the mirror that peeled back the sash. Her warm hands slipped around him, stroked him while she looked at him, slid both palms around in a skilled motion she had never so much as attempted before, and he looked into eyes that were wanton and a red mouth that in moment would take him—and how he wanted it to.

'We cannot be together here.'

She could feel him sliding through her fingers, could feel the beat of her heart in her throat, and it was him and only him that made her bold.

'No one would have to know.' He watched her lips part in a smile. 'What happens in the desert stays in the desert.'

Ibrahim's fingers moved up her chin and slid into her hair and how he wanted to guide her head down, rather than wait till the morning. He wanted to break a rule, but he was stronger than that, or was he weak, because he could not defy the desert.

'This is how you work?'

He watched colour flood her face, ached unfulfilled as her hands released him.

'Of course not.'

'Go to bed.' he stood and pulled her from her knees to her feet and felt guilty for shaming her. He fought a rare need to explain himself, that it was safer if they were apart. 'Anyway, you might change your mind again at the last minute. Just go to bed, Georgie.'

CHAPTER NINE

I<small>T WAS</small> the longest night and she lay there both embarrassed and wanting.

The air was thick and warm and soon her jug of water was empty. Georgie wanted to go to the kitchen to replenish it, but was scared to move.

She had tried to seduce him. She closed her eyes in mortification—with all her banging on about being professional, she could hardly believe what she'd done, what the desert had made her do.

Georgie. She could hear him calling her.

Georgie. She heard it again and stood.

Georgie. It was his voice, she was sure of it, and she padded across the room, parting the drape, ready for his summons, but then she heard the shriek of laughter from the wind that taunted her and she ran back to bed and curled up, wondering if she was going mad.

Ibrahim. He heard it too, but he was prepared for it. He heard the desert tease, heard the wind drop into a low seductive voice that danced around his bed, saw her face in his dream and when he awoke, when he could not sleep, when his teeth gritted and his head thrashed with insomnia, his hand stalled on its way down to private solace, for even that release was denied him by the laws that bound him tonight, because he would have been thinking of her.

And sunrise should have brought relief, but there was none. Still the winds blacked it out as they screamed, still it was dark, and she heard his chant of prayer and finally she completely agreed with Ibrahim, for Georgie now hated the desert.

'Can we go?' she asked, when his prayers were completed and she padded out of her room.

'The winds are still heavy,' Ibrahim said but he did not look at her. 'Get dressed and we will have breakfast.'

'I'm not hungry.'

'Then go back to bed and rest,' he ordered. 'I will do the same. As soon as it is safe to do so, we will leave.'

'I'm scared,' Georgie admitted 'I'm scared of the noises…'

'It's just wind.'

'I feel like…' It sounded madder in words than in her head. 'I feel like it knows I mocked it last night.'

'Don't.' He loathed what he had said to her in an urgent attempt to halt what they had been doing. 'You did nothing wrong. I should not have spoken to you like that. Georgie…it's just tales I was telling.'

'You believe them.'

'No.' He shook his head. 'Yes. I don't know.' He didn't know. He could see her outline in the lamplight, he could hear the fear in her voice, and tales of old were illogical.

'Come here.'

She stood, scared to do as he said, scared to return to her own bed.

'Come on.'

His voice was real, the wind was not, and as the wind let out a screech, she ran those thirty-four steps to him, to the solid warmth of his arms. He could feel her heart hammering in her chest as he held her close, because she really was terrified.

'It's just…' He struggled for the words. 'Old wives' tales.'

'So they're not true?'

'No.' he started, but he could not quite deny them. 'I don't think so. Come…' His bed was warm and her skin was cold and he pulled her in.

'Did your parents not tell you tales when you were younger?'

'No.' She gave a cynical snort. 'We weren't exactly tucked in with a bedside story each night.'

'Is that why you ran away?' He felt her tense. 'Karim told me,' he admitted. 'Not everything, he was talking more about Felicity, about her childhood, how mistrusting it made her. Your father—'

'Was a drunken brute,' Georgie finished for him. 'My mother was terrified of him. Even after he died, he still left his mark on her. She's still taking tablets to calm her nerves, still scared of her own shadow.'

'What about you?'

'I wasn't scared of him—I just wanted to get away from him.'

'Which was why you ran?'

'I was always sent back.' She was angry at the memory, angry at the injustice. 'He never hit us—which made it fine, apparently. We were living in chaos, dancing to his temper, but...' She didn't want to talk about it, didn't want to relive those times again—times when the only thing she had been able to control had been the food that had gone into her mouth, but Ibrahim seemed to understand without her saying it. She felt his hand dust her arm and slip to her waist, to the slender frame that was softened now with slight curves. As her hands had helped him, his hands did their work now, each touch, each stroke assuring her somehow that he knew how hard fought each gain had been, how fiercely she had fought for survival.

He could not *not* kiss her.

Just a kiss, and as he moved to her mouth for a moment he fought it.

'What would happen?' Georgie whispered, and he could taste her sweet breath.

'Nothing probably.' With her next to him, he could rationalise it. 'As I said, look at my parents...'

'But they still love each other,' Georgie said. 'They're still bound. Felicity told me—' she did not know if she was betraying a secret '—that Karim wouldn't let her leave the desert till—'

'It's old wives' tales.' He was sure of it now. 'After

all, I can bring a mistress from the palace to the desert and I am not bound to her. It's just superstition.'

'Why doesn't she come to you?' Georgie asked. 'I mean, when you're younger. Why do you have to walk to the palace?' She liked the tales, liked hearing the stories.

'It would be different.' Ibrahim said. 'Your first time, at such a young age, you would not be able to separate the two—and if you love her in the desert...' It was too illogical to even try to explain it, so he smiled instead and felt her calm beside him. There was peace in his heart this morning that had been absent for ages, forgiveness in his soul, and he would be forever grateful to her for that, and he really could not not kiss her.

And that had caused trouble before, but this was a different kiss: this was slow and non-urgent and, a first for Ibrahim, it was a kiss that was purely tender.

And a kiss couldn't hurt when it felt so nice, and she was content with his kiss, because she'd craved it for months. The taste of his tongue and the weight of his lips. For a while Ibrahim too was content, to feel her breast through the fabric as his mouth explored hers, but then a kiss did not quite suffice, and he opened the buttons as far as they would go. 'Did your sister design this gown for you?' he teased, because even with all the buttons undone, he still couldn't get to her breast and his hand slid to her waist to pursue from a different angle, but that would not be wise so, just a little disgruntled, he pulled back.

His eyes asked permission, for what she didn't know,

but she licked her lips in consent and he tore the fabric and went back to kissing her. She felt his sigh of satisfaction in her mouth as his hand, unhindered now, met her breast, and she kissed him and felt the satin of his skin beneath her fingers. It was still just a kiss, though her hands roamed. They felt the chest she'd once touched and explored it again, felt the dark, flat nipple beneath the pads of her fingers. It remained at a kiss even as her hands slid down.

And then, recalling last night, there was hesitation, but his apology came by way of his hands that led her to him and he moaned in her mouth as she held him.

Still just a kiss as she touched and explored what all night she had thought of, then it was far more than a kiss because his mouth would not suffice and her lips trailed down his torso, tasting the salt of his skin till Ibrahim halted her, because he wanted more of her, wanted longer with her, than her mouth would allow.

'We mustn't.' Georgie said, as he pulled her body over his, because she was starting to understand there were rules.

'We won't,' Ibrahim said, because he had more control than anyone, that much he knew.

He liked living on the edge, the brink, and this morning he did just that. 'We can do this.' Ibrahim said, and he pulled her till her legs were astride him. He took a breast in his mouth and his hands slid over her bottom, and she steadied herself with her hands and thought she would die because it felt like heaven.

'We can't,' she said, which was different from the *I can't* she had once halted him with.

'We won't,' he insisted, as the tip of his thick length stroked her clitoris and he waited for the wind to warn him, or for a sign to halt him, or for Georgie to again recant. Except the desert was silent and there was nothing to halt him, and Georgie bit down on her lip to stop herself begging him to enter her.

She didn't need to.

He slipped in just a little way and she could never again say no to him, because he felt sublime.

And there was only one law that they followed, and that was nature's. He inched into her and then lifted her just a little further each time. He wanted the stupid nightdress off, but he did not want to stop touching her for a second. It was Georgie who lifted the fabric over her head and at the sight of her arms upstretched and her body above him he could no longer tease and cared nothing for rules, and he pulled her full down onto him.

The force of full entry had her cry in surprise, so purposefully and assuredly, he filled her, and though she tried to stretch for more of him, her body clamped down in possession, as if to assure herself she wouldn't flee from him again. He watched, he slid up on the cushions so he could watch them, and she saw more than passion in his eyes. She saw something else too and she wanted to share it, so he pushed her head down a little, so she could share in the dark and light they made. She loved the rules as she watched them unite, she wanted to be bound for ever. Then he guided her head to his and his cool tongue met hers—every beat of her orgasm matched his, every finger knotted in his hair met by the tug on her own scalp. Then, afterwards, their eyes were mirrors both searching for regret or dread at dues now to be paid, and both finding none.

She lay beside him, knew he was thinking and so too was she. 'Later today…' he kissed her shoulder, as if confirming a thought '…I will take you back to the palace and then I must leave for London.'

'You're leaving?'

'I have to go.'

She looked up at him.

'I need to speak properly with my father. I need to think about…' He didn't say 'us', but she was sure that he almost did. 'He has flown there today to visit my mother.'

'Because of what you said to him?'

'In spite of what I said to him.' The loathing in his voice did not match their tender mood.

'Is it always like this between you?'

'Always,' Ibrahim said. 'He demands I respect him—but how? Why can't he just let her go?'

'Let her go?' Georgie didn't understand. After all, his mother had her own life in London.

'She is still his wife.' Ibrahim looked down at her, took in the flushed cheeks and rumpled hair, and it felt so good to share his thoughts with her. 'She regrets her indiscretion—so much so that all this time she has stayed loyal.'

'But it's been years.'

'And there will be many more years. After all this time ignoring her, now he drops in at will. Who's to say next month, next year he will be too busy? And she is expected to wait.'

'Can't she divorce him?'

'There is no divorce in Zaraq. It is so forbidden that there is not even a word for it. A lacuna, there is no concept, no precedence. My mother knows that even if legally it is taken care of overseas, still always, to him, to the people of Zaraq, she is his wife and nothing can change it.'

He did not notice her flushed cheeks pale suddenly.

'There's nothing that can change it?'

'Nothing,' Ibrahim confirmed, and she felt her heart still. 'You cannot undo what is done—that is the rule of Zaraq.'

CHAPTER TEN

HAPPY its work had been done, the desert was silent and finally Ibrahim slept. Unlike on the plane, now, for the first time, he looked relaxed, and as she watched him, it was Georgie who was tense. She was starting to make sense of the strange rules, could see now what Felicity had been saying—that to the people of Zaraq she was still married.

Ibrahim would not mind, she tried to console herself. He would understand, she tried to convince herself, but wrapped in his arms she was unable to face him, felt like a liar, and she rolled over in shame.

At what point should she have said it?

Yesterday, or at the wedding? Was she supposed to walk up to someone and give them so much of herself on contact? But there had been opportunities, her conscience reminded her.

She had tried to tell him last night, but he had halted her, Georgie told herself, then guiltily admitted she had been relieved when he had stopped her, more than pleased to avoid seeing his face when she revealed the truth.

Georgie closed her eyes, and his arm wrapped around her, his warm, sleek body spooned in from behind. There was a possessiveness there that felt tender. There was a beauty in his embrace and a promise in his words that told her this had meant something to Ibrahim, that again they had glimpsed a future, but with what she knew now it was a future that again she might have to deny him. It was an uneasy sleep she fell into, filled with dreams of sacred oils and laughing winds, man-made structures and the sound of an engine.

'Get dressed.' His voice was urgent and jolted her awake. 'Someone is coming. I heard a helicopter.' The noise hadn't been a dream. She could hear the whir of the blades slowing. Surely there was time to race back to her room. All she had was a torn nightgown. He threw her a sash of cloth as he pulled on his clothes and she went to dash to her own quarters, but even as she stepped outside, she knew she had left it too late. She stood, shivering and embarrassed in the lounge area, and she couldn't look at Karim so she turned pleading eyes to Felicity, whose face was as white as chalk.

'Enjoying your tour?' Felicity sneered. 'So where's your *expert* guide?' Georgie was incredibly grateful when Ibrahim, dressed, thoroughly together and not remotely embarrassed, appeared from his chamber and took control.

'Your sister and I intended to return last night. There was a storm…'

'Enough!' Karim's shout was to silence his younger brother, but Ibrahim refused.

'Georgie, go and get dressed,' Ibrahim said, his voice supremely calm, 'and I will take you back to the palace.'

'Ibrahim,' Karim warned, but it fell on deaf ears.

'Go,' he said to Georgie. 'I will speak with my brother.' He eyed him darkly. 'We have done nothing wrong.'

'I warned you!' Karim shouted. 'I warned you to stay away from her.'

'And I chose not to listen. How dare you both walk in here with rage in your eyes and shame her? Have you forgotten how you met your wife?'

Georgie watched colour flood Felicity's cheeks—for their one night of passion had resulted in Azizah. But her sister seemed to have forgotten that fact as she followed Georgie to her room because Felicity was incensed. 'How could you, Georgie? This is my husband's family. You've been here a few days and you tumble into bed with him.'

'It wasn't like that.'

'Oh, please.'

'As Ibrahim said, you hardly waited before you jumped into bed with Karim,' Georgie retaliated.

'We weren't in Zaraq!' Felicity said. 'Here you play by the rules.'

'You know what?' Georgie had had enough. 'You really are starting to sound like them. What happened to my sister?'

'She grew up,' Felicity shouted. 'She behaved responsibly—but you were never very good at that were you, Georgie? Bunking off school, running away from home…' And Georgie could see the years of hurt she had caused in her sister's eyes, the hurt she had apologised for over and over again.

'I've done everything I can to help you and now you do this.' Felicity had tears streaming down her cheeks. 'I paid for your rehab when I couldn't afford it. Karim has helped too.'

'And I'm very grateful,' Georgie said, but she recalled Ibrahim's words and would not feel beholden.

'So this is how you show it!' Felicity shrilled.

Georgie did not break and she did not crumple, because all it was was a row, a confrontation that needed to be had, and no longer was she scared of it. 'I don't have to show anything.' Georgie said, her voice calm. 'I'm a different woman now; I'm a different person from who I was all those years ago. Ibrahim and I weren't just having a bit of fun.' She was sure of that, quite sure.

'It is fun to Ibrahim! Don't you get it? All this is to him is a diversion, a bit of fun to pass the time while he's here.'

'I don't have to prove him to you,' Georgie said.

I haven't got time for this.' Felicity shook her head. 'I have to wash and get changed and get back out there. They're loading the helicopter.'

'Can we just talk?' Georgie begged, because things needed to be said, the air needed to be cleared so they could both move on fully. 'Felicity please, I really need—'

'You always *need* something from me, Georgie, yet

you give nothing back.' Felicity shouted. 'Right now, I don't have time for it. There are people who are sick, you selfish cow, and Karim and I need to get back out to them. For once it isn't all about you!'

And she swept out and left Georgie reeling but angry. How dared her sister dash in and pass judgment? She was sick of them, sick of Zaraq and its so-called mysterious ways that only applied when was convenient.

And Ibrahim was sick of it too.

'They are the rules!' Karim roared. 'Only a king can change them. If you love her, then you stay in London. You have the rest of the world to be the prince of your choice, but here, in this land, you abide—'

Ibrahim could not stand to hear it said again and he interrupted with a shout of his own. 'Then I leave the land behind.'

'Ibrahim.' Karim wished it was that easy. He ached for his brother, physically. 'You are a royal prince of *this* land—our people are sick. Hassan is with his new baby, he has a fever...' He saw his brother's appalled expression. 'He will be okay, but he was a little premature. Hassan should be there for him. The king is in England, I am needed in the desert. Can you really walk away now we need you to be the ruler you were born to be?'

'I am not walking away.' Ibrahim's voice was hoarse, realisation hitting him. He was being asked to step in and he met that challenge. 'Of course I will stay while I am needed, and our father will return when he hears the news.'

'That may not be possible. I have spoken with advisors—they suggest closing the airports.'

'Fine,' Ibrahim said. 'I will step in as leader.' But as leader Ibrahim had rules of his own and spelt them out. 'Georgie will be by my side.'

'No,' Karim said, for it was impossible.

'She is mine now,' Ibrahim said, because for once the rules worked for him. After all, he had slept with her in the desert.

'She can never be yours.' Karim took no pleasure in delivering the news, no relish in revealing the secret his wife had shared with him the other night. 'She is married.' He watched darkness descend on his brother.

'No.'

'She is divorced, but….' Ibrahim closed his eyes as his brother continued. 'You know that does not count here. She cannot live with you here—she cannot be your bride.' Every word was like a hammer on his flesh but still Ibrahim stood. He sought a solution.

'She can wait for me in London.'

'As our mother waits for our father?' Karim asked. 'Would you really do that to Georgie?'

Ibrahim shook his head. 'Then do the right thing by her.' Karim suppressed a roar. 'End it with her properly—end it now so there can be no doubt in her mind.'

CHAPTER ELEVEN

'WILL you take care of Azizah for me?' Felicity asked when Karim said it was time for them to leave.

'Are you sure I'm responsible enough?' Georgie responded tartly, but she could not sustain her anger, for she knew how much being apart from Azizah would hurt Felicity. 'She'll be fine.' Georgie said and she took her sister in her arms and gave her a cuddle. For the first time she felt like the older one. 'She'll be completely fine.'

'I'm sorry.' Felicity was, but Georgie didn't need her to be.

'I hurt you,' Georgie said. 'All those years I was sick, I know how much it hurt you, and I was too weak then and too fragile for you to say how you felt. I'm not now.' She gave her sister a smile. 'Better out than in, so they say.'

'Felicity,' Karim called, and as together as Georgie felt, she didn't go out and face her brother-in-law just yet.

'You'd better go.'

'There's my milk…'

'I know,' Georgie soothed. 'You just head out there and do what you have to do without worrying.'

'I really am sorry...' Felicity shivered '...for all the things I said.'

'They've no doubt been building for a long time,' Georgie said. 'We're fine now and you don't have to worry about Azizah and neither do you have to worry about me any more.'

Except Felicity knew that she did have to worry, at least for a little while longer. She could see her husband's clenched jaw and Ibrahim's stern features and knew that Ibrahim had been told.

A fully dressed, blushing Georgie forced herself out of her room to say farewell to Karim and Felicity and she and Ibrahim stood in silence as they watched the helicopter leave.

'I must get back to Azizah,' Georgie said. 'How long will the drive take?'

'A helicopter is being sent.' He did not, could not, look at her. 'I need to get back to the people as soon as possible.' He felt it descend then, the weight of responsibility. 'I am to stand in as ruler. Decisions need to be made swiftly. There will be a lot of anxiety, a lot of unrest.'

'You'll be wonderful,' Georgie said, and went to touch his arm, but he moved it away. 'I'll help in any way I can.'

'You?' He could not keep the mirth from his voice.

'Yes, me.'

'A four-week course and you're an expert suddenly in the ways of the desert?'

She couldn't understand the change in him. 'I wasn't applying for the job of your advisor!' Georgie snapped back at him. 'So I'm good enough to sleep with, but not good enough to stand by your side.'

'The people would never accept it.'

'Oh, please.' Georgie was sick of it. 'The people don't mind Felicity.' She let out a mocking laugh. 'Oh, yes, but she was pregnant with a possible heir.' She watched as Ibrahim briefly closed his eyes, his strong features paling a touch at how very careless they had been. 'I'm not going to fall pregnant. Don't panic. I'm on the Pill.'

'Of course you are.' And that was the bit for Ibrahim that hurt, really hurt. This was a girl who carried condoms in her make-up bag for just in case, who waited on the street outside nightclubs. This was the divorced woman who could not be his princess, and he was angry, and it showed. 'Don't tell me—you're on the Pill for medical reasons.'

She could have slapped him.

Gone was the tender man who had held her. Back now was the scathing one and she didn't understand why. As the helicopter hovered, as she turned her head and covered her eyes with a scarf, as they ran beneath the blades and climbed inside and Georgie put on her headphones, she watched the tent where they had found each other disappear in the distance, and all too soon she saw the palace come into view, but not once did he look at her, not once did he attempt conversation.

As they stepped out and walked to the palace, he still refused to communicate. Elders and advisors were waiting for him and Georgie stood in the hallway a moment as Rina spoke in rapid Arabic, unsure how to behave without Ibrahim or Felicity to guide her. Briefly he glanced in her direction and only then did he speak.

'She asks if you want a room next to Azizah. If they should move your things?'

'Please.' Georgie nodded. 'Can you tell her for me?'

'Of course.' He spoke to Rina and to another maid for a brief moment, and then he turned back to her.

'All is taken care of. I have asked that they move *Ms* Anderson's things.' He hissed the word so savagely that there could be no mistake. He had been told that she had been married, and for a second she was angry at her sister for telling Karim, but she knew the fury was misdirected.

She was angry at herself.

As for Ibrahim, he still hoped his brother was mistaken, wanted her to tell him he was wrong. 'Is it Miss or Ms?'

'*Ms.*' She croaked the word out, then tore her eyes away, but not quickly enough to miss his look of disgust.

It should have been she who told him first. At least she could have explained things better. Now, looking at his cold black eyes, Georgie wondered if she'd ever get that chance. 'Ibrahim…' There were people everywhere, there was nothing she could say, but she willed him to give her one moment of his time, willed him to pull her aside, for a chance to explain, but he gave her nothing. 'Can we talk? Just for a moment.'

'Talk?' Ibrahim sneered. 'I have nothing to talk about with you—there is nothing to discuss.

'And never can there be.'

CHAPTER TWELVE

IT WAS the longest day.

All Georgie wanted to do was throw herself on the bed, curl up into a ball, hide and grieve and cry and mourn, but there was Azizah to think of.

Azizah, who hated the bottle that wasn't her mum, who wasn't used to the bonier arms of her aunt and cried through the afternoon and long, long into the evening.

Georgie had been pacing the floor with her and had finally sat in the family lounge, where Felicity often did, and Azizah had at last given in, taking the bottle she hated and almost, *almost* falling asleep, until Ibrahim returned from a visit to the army barracks. It wasn't just her heart that leapt at the sound of him. Hassan, the prince first in line, did too. He came pounding down the corridor to greet his brother.

'You should have consulted me!' Hassan was furious. Georgie could hear them arguing as she sat in the lounge. When Ibrahim had returned she had wanted to flee, but the baby had just been settling and she'd sat as the argument had spilled into the living room.

'You should have spoken with me before closing the airports.'

'You were with your wife and son,' Ibrahim pointed out. 'You are needed there. I am more than capable of dealing with this.'

'You have closed the airports, cancelled surgery.'

'Excuse me,' Georgie said, and perhaps it was poor form to interrupt two princes when the country was in crisis, but the palace was big enough for them to take their argument elsewhere and a restless Azizah was just closing her eyes. 'She's almost asleep.'

'Then take her to the nursery,' Ibrahim snapped, and it was face him or flee. As Hassan took the phone from a worried maid, Georgie chose to face him, turned her blue eyes on him and refused not to meet his gaze.

'Hard day at the office, darling?' she said in a voice that was sweet but laced with acid. 'Should I make the children disappear?'

'Just you,' Ibrahim hissed, because it was hell seeing her and not being able to have her, hell having dared to almost love her and then to find out what she had done. 'I wish *you* would disappear.'

'It is our father.' Hassan handed him the phone. 'It is you he wishes to speak to.'

And now would have been an ideal time to leave, to slip away, as Ibrahim wished she would, except Georgie wanted to hear, wanted to be there, even if he'd rather she wasn't.

She could hear the king's angry voice even from across the lounge, and though Hassan was pacing,

Ibrahim was calm, his voice firm when he responded to his father.

'I took advice,' was his curt response, but when that clearly didn't appease his father, he elaborated. 'I took advice from experts. You have known about this for days apparently and did little.' She could see a pulse leaping in his neck. It was the only indication of his inner turmoil as he stood up to the king. 'The priority is the people,' he interrupted, 'not your flight schedule and certainly not Hassan's ego. His mind is on his newborn son, where it should be, where it can be, because there is another prince more than capable of stepping in. I have spoken with our soldiers, and the army is to open a field hospital to the west. Flights will remain grounded till we are happy this virus is contained. If you move for an exemption from the flight ban, if you feel I am not capable, then of course you must return,' Ibrahim said, and then his voice rose slightly in warning. 'And if you do, I will hand the reins back to you.' For a second his eyes flicked to Georgie. 'And I will leave Zaraq on your incoming plane.'

'You—' he spoke to Hassan when the call had concluded '—either take over completely or leave it to me. I am not ringing the hospital and waiting while they pull you from the nursery to make my decisions.' He eyed his brother. 'What is it to be?'

'The people need—'

'The people need strong leadership,' Ibrahim said. 'Which I am more than capable of providing. If you think otherwise, I suggest you ring Jamal and tell her a helicopter is taking you out to the west tomorrow, as is my schedule, to see first hand how this illness has affected our people.' He did not relent, he did not appease, he was direct and he was brutal. 'And perhaps you should check with the pediatrician. We have all been immunized, of course, and if that proves ineffective there are anti-virals, but I would check if they want you in contact with a premature newborn.'

Georgie watched as Hassan paled.

'So what is it to be?' Ibrahim pushed. 'Because if I'm not needed I'm heading for the casino.' And he would, Georgie knew. He'd head too to another woman, any woman. He was angry and she had provoked it.

'You have my full support,' Hassan said. 'And I thank you for stepping in. I am going to visit my wife and son.'

He nodded goodnight to Georgie and a now sleeping Azizah and finally they were alone.

'That was low,' Georgie said.

'That was common sense.' Ibrahim snapped. 'I don't care how safe it is, how effective the immunisation is, if it were my newborn…' And he looked at where Georgie sat holding a baby, and he was black with anger, because that morning he had almost envisaged it, not a wife and a baby but a future with someone who was not a stranger to his heart. The role of prince and a return to the desert had seemed manageable with her by his side. 'I have to work.' He turned to go, but she called him.

'Can we please talk, Ibrahim?

'I don't wish to talk to you.'

'Please.' Georgie said. 'It was something that happened a long time ago, something—'

'That cannot be undone,' Ibrahim interrupted.

'When did you become so perfect?' Georgie asked. 'I don't get why everything has to change.'

'Because it has.'

'It was a few weeks,' Georgie said. 'I was nineteen. It was hell at home and I'd lost my job when I got sick again…' She tumbled out words when he didn't respond immediately, argued her case while she still had a chance. 'I thought he was nice.'

'So you married him because he was *nice*.'

'There are worse reasons. He was older, he seemed safe, but I see now that he was a drunk like my father. I see now I just ran straight to the same thing.'

'You think that makes it better. That you tossed everything away for some middle-aged drunk.'

'It was ages ago,' Georgie said. 'I know it's frowned on here but in London—'

'I am a royal prince!' Ibrahim struggled to keep his voice down, for the sake of the baby.

'Not when you're there.' And she watched lines mar his forehead, his hand going up to his face in a gesture of frustration. He was saving her from herself and that she didn't understand. He thought of his mother, sitting by the phone, waiting. Of a life married to a man who could not always be there, who had children scattered by both geography and allegiance, and he must not, Ibrahim told himself, do that to Georgie. So instead he did as his brother had suggested, said words that would leave her in no doubt.

'I'm a royal prince,' Ibrahim said again. 'Which means...' He swallowed before continuing, but she didn't see it, just heard his low, even voice as he very clearly stated his case. 'I don't have to deal in damaged goods.' If she hadn't been holding Azizah Georgie would have stood and slapped him, but instead her eyes left his face and she sat holding the baby for comfort, holding her sweet, warm body as she chilled inside. 'The bride that will be chosen for me will know what is expected. A bride fit for my side is not found outside nightclubs with a smorgasbord of contraception and her divorce papers in her bedside drawer. If you want me to look you up in London, if you're bored one night—'

'Never!'

'Then...' Ibrahim shrugged '...we're done.'

'You're a bastard.'

'When I choose to be.' Ibrahim shrugged again. He heard her shocked silence and little Azizah start to whimper.

'Would you do as you suggested earlier and disappear with the baby?' Ibrahim said. 'I've got a country to run.'

CHAPTER THIRTEEN

IT DID not abate.

Not for a single minute.

There were demands and there were questions and he dealt with each and every one.

He flew deep into the desert and witnessed the suffering, then returned to have his competence questioned by a hungry press.

He did not care about tourism was his surly response at the conference.

And anyway, he questioned the questioners, did the tourists want to visit an empty desert—a ghost town of what once was?

He silenced his critics with his performance, yet for Ibrahim there was no respite, for each night he slept alone.

He went for the phone on several occasions, but it wasn't just sex he wanted. For the first time it was someone else's opinion he craved.

One other person's opinion.

'I tell him he does well.' Home from the hospital before her baby, Jamal sat at breakfast and spoke in broken English to Georgie, when Ibrahim made a surprise appearance one morning. She spoke for a little while longer to Ibrahim then turned and smiled at Georgie. 'Soon Felicity back.'

'How soon?' Georgie asked, her eyes jerking to Ibrahim, because she wanted to leave so badly, because even if she hardly saw him, just the occasional passing on the stairs, where the greeting was polite and cool had been hard enough. Now that he was sitting at the table, it was almost more than she could bear.

'Karim called and said the situation is much improved—he wants her to come home, though he will stay out there.'

'And the airports?' Georgie asked.

'I'm meeting with the doctors today. They are proposing that all visitors be vaccinated…but…' He paused, waited for her to fill in, to offer her thoughts, but Georgie didn't. 'Once the new guidelines are in place, there seems no reason not to reopen them.'

'How soon?' Georgie asked, because she did not want a debate, just answers.

'Perhaps as early as tomorrow.' Ibrahim selected a fruit from the platter, then changed his mind and Georgie looked down and saw the pomegranate. She could have picked it up herself, could have taunted him a little, but she was too bruised and raw to play games: she just wanted to go home.

'You stay till I bring the baby home,' Jamal said—the future king would not be named for some time yet. 'It will be a good day.'

Georgie gave a noncommittal smile and when the maid came to tell Hassan and Jamal that the car was ready to take them to the hospital, Georgie stood to leave too, but Ibrahim halted her.

'Will you stay when Felicity gets here?'

'Why?'

'As Jamal said, the baby will be home soon and with the illness receding, there will be much celebration.'

'I don't really feel like celebrating.'

'You could have time with your sister.'

'Not this visit.' Georgie gave a shrug and went to leave.

'Georgie.'

'What?'

'Maybe we should talk…'

'About what?'

He didn't know, but he was aching for her.

'Maybe tonight, when the palace is quiet, you could come—'

'As I said,' Georgie hissed, 'never.' And she went to walk out but he called her back and she was more angry than she had ever been in her life, because he thought he could summon her, that sex might soothe the heartache; angry too, that she was considering it.

'Georgie, you do not walk out—'

'Am I supposed to curtsey?' she hurled back at him.

'You do not leave till you're excused.'

'Oh, I've already been excused,' Georgie responded.

'When you called me damaged goods, Ibrahim, you excused me for life.'

'Like it or not, we are here together.' He just wanted to talk, but she was too angry to see that.

'Not for much longer,' Georgie snarled. 'Felicity's back tomorrow.'

'We still don't know about the airports.'

'I'll swim home if I have to.' Georgie said, and she meant it, absolutely she meant it. At the very least she would check into a hotel.

She spent the day packing, in-between looking after Azizah. She did everything she could to keep him from her mind, but as night crept in, she gave in a little and fed her craving—watched the news reports, flicking channels, because sometimes there were subtitles, and even if she didn't understand completely, there was no denying that the young prince had stepped in and brought calm. His deep voice soothed the troubled nation. Difficult decisions, it seemed, were effortlessly made, but they had taken their toll.

She could see that.

Did everyone notice the clench of his jaw as he listened to questions, or the tiny fan of new lines around those dark Zaraq eyes? Did they see that those magnificent cheekbones had become more accentuated in these past days, or the taut lines of his shoulders?

Or did only love make those details visible?

And she changed channel and changed it again, but it made no difference, because even if she closed her eyes, his face was still there and, yes, very unfortunately for Georgie, she loved him.

'Oh!' She jumped as he walked into the lounge. It was close to ten but still early for Ibrahim to be back and she had wrongly assumed the interview she was watching was live. 'I thought you were...' She gestured to the television. 'I'll say goodnight.'

'You don't have to hide in your room.'

She felt safer there, but didn't say that. She simply didn't answer, just walked past the sofa, but he caught her wrist.

'Did you understand what was being said?' He glanced over at his own image on the screen.

'Not really.'

'Things are improving.'

'That's good.' She could feel his fingers on her skin, feel the pull to join him, to sit, but she stood. 'I saw the news earlier.' She still couldn't look at him. 'There were subtitles...they were talking about the young prince, what a magnificent job you were doing...' She watched her tears fall on his fingers. 'There was talk of a bride...'

'There is always talk of marriage,' Ibrahim started, but the plight was real, he could not lie. 'If I am here as a prince, if I stay...'

'There's no if.' Georgie was angry. 'You've had your taste of power and now you want more.'

'No.' He wished it was that simple. 'It is not about power, it is not about want. I am *their* prince. The people have been patient while I grew up, but now it is time to accept the responsibility, all of it…' He looked at the television screen, the arguments, the raised voices. 'Do you understand what is being said?'

'No.'

'That is one of the elders. He asks if our rulers do care, why is there no hospital on the west side? Why does it take five days to get aid? Zaraq is rich, yet its people suffer.'

'It's changing, though.' Georgie swallowed. 'There are outreach programmes, there is a hospital—'

'That they cannot access.' Ibrahim looked at her. 'They choose to be isolated—that is what the journalist is saying now. They make us promise not to invade their desert, not to take away their ways… It is complicated.'

'There's no easy solution,' Georgie attempted, and then she saw his face, saw the worry and the lines and the pressure on him. 'Is there?'

'No easy one,' Ibrahim said. 'There is a need for more infrastructure. I told you my father tried once. He brought in experts but they do not understand our people's ways. There was a road planned, just in from the coastline, but it meant bridges. There were arguments…' And she started to understand. She felt it in her stomach, in her throat.

'You do, though?'

He nodded.

'I sit in London and I design elevators and pools that stretch from high-rise to high-rise and I focus on the skyline, but I have not forgotten the ground. I understand some of the magic and the science. I can see bridges that can negotiate the canyons. I can see how it can be done, in ways the people would allow, ways that would benefit them yet uphold their desire to live freely...' She watched as his analytical mind started to dream, then she turned her attention back to the screen, listened and read the subtitles as the interviewer asked if the prince would oversee the changes.

'For now,' Ibrahim had answered, 'we deal with the current issue. Then we move to ensure it never happens again.'

She looked at him, at a face that she could read, an expression that was suddenly familiar—even though he wasn't asleep, it was the face she had seen on the plane, a troubled face that spoke of inner torment.

'What's wrong, Ibrahim?' He closed his eyes to her question. 'I did see you when you stepped on the plane and you were nothing like the man that stepped off. Is this where you want to be?'

'Honestly?' Ibrahim said, and she nodded. 'I don't know. This is where I am needed.' He opened his eyes and looked to her and he was grateful that she stayed silent, that she didn't point out that she needed him too, didn't fight for her corner of his torn heart.

'When this is over,' Ibrahim said, 'when I get back...'

'You belong here.' Georgie said, because over the last days it had become clear that he did. He stood up and headed out, but as he got to the door he changed his mind. As he had in the club, he turned round and walked back to where she was still standing.

'What I said, about damaged goods…'

'Please don't say sorry,' Georgie said. 'Because I'd hate myself if I forgave you.'

'I don't expect you to forgive me and I don't expect you to understand—just know that by saying what I did, I had hoped to hurt you less in the long term.'

'Well, it didn't work,' Georgie said. 'It can never work.'

And somehow, to live the rest of her life, she had to accept that.

CHAPTER FOURTEEN

'It's not long now.' Georgie tried to soothe the little girl, but she missed her mother. 'Mummy will be home soon,' Georgie said, and instantly regretted it, because just the mention of her mother and Azizah's screams seemed to quadruple. 'Come on,' Georgie said, tired of pacing the luxurious nursery. Feeling the heat from her niece's cheeks, she unlocked the French windows and stepped out onto the balcony. The cool night air surprised Azizah into silence. 'I'll take you down to the beach tomorrow,' Georgie promised and stared into the black eyes of her niece for a moment, but she tore her gaze away, because Azizah had inherited Zaraq eyes.

Georgie felt the air still in her chest as she caught sight of Ibrahim walking on the beach, and when he looked up this time he did not dismiss her; this time he did not look away. She just stood and stared down at him. She could not see for sure, but thought he was looking right at her, unashamedly staring, as was she. She stared, not just at him but at a memory, and she knew they were both reliving the desert.

She did not move, tasted his lips in her mind as he walked slowly on, and she knew what to do.

Georgie put the sleeping babe in her cot, locked the French windows and headed back to her own room.

She did not need to turn the key in the lock—she knew he would never come to her. He had ended it, and would not be so cruel as to revoke it, no matter how much he wanted her this night.

This long night, before tomorrow, before normality returned.

Georgie knew it was their last chance to be alone, their last chance for a goodbye, but not in words.

Her last chance to thank him because, despite his cruel words, he had changed her, had shown her the beauty of her body, had taken her to a very different place.

He would be prince, so she must kiss him goodbye.

He found her in his bed and didn't humble her with questions.

He kissed her warmly along her neck down to her shoulder and then back to her neck. Then he spoke about that which was so painful they hadn't been able to speak of it before. 'I wish you had told me.'

'Why?' Georgie asked. He had thought it obvious, but as he went to answer he checked himself and Georgie answered for him. 'So you could have avoided me, so that it would never have happened.' And she felt his lips back on her neck and his strong body pressing into hers and she understood why she had chosen to keep quiet. 'So we could never have known this.'

'How do we go on now?' He turned her onto her back, made her look at him. 'Next time you are here visiting your sister and I am with my bride...' He was so cross with her, so cross because accepting his father's choice of bride might not have been great but it would have been bearable. Now, though, it would kill him.

'We'll come separately,' Georgie replied.

'Weddings, births and funerals generally only have one sitting, which means we will both be there, but separate and somehow denying this.' He could feel every inch of her skin beneath his, feel the body that belonged to him in every way but by law, and even if he wanted her, he was still angry. 'Am I to shake hands with your future husband, admire you children?' He could not, just could not envision it. 'Or are the next fifty years to be spent slipping out after the meal, hoping we meet in the gardens...' She shook her head.

'No.' Georgie said, because she couldn't live like that. And Ibrahim recalled something then. 'Was that why you stopped me? Not guilt about your sister?'

'My divorce wasn't through then. It just seemed wrong.'

'She's got a conscience too.' He spoke to the devil on his shoulder with a mixture of regret and wry humour. 'So that rules out a mistress.'

So, this was the last time. He climbed off her and then walked over and turned on every light, and she lay there as he walked back to the bed and pulled off the heavy silk sheet. Her hand moved to grab it, but then she let it go. She lay silent as his eyes roamed her body and she was shaking on the bed as she let him look, but she was shaking with desire rather than shame.

He looked at her toes and the fading henna flowers that climbed up her feet. He looked at knees and thighs till they felt like water, to her place that tomorrow would become private, to her stomach and then breasts he had tasted. Without him voicing his request, she heard it and turned round, and she felt like crying as his eyes swept her. Then she let healing tears come as he loved every fault, every bit that made Georgie.

She felt the heat from his gaze linger on her spine, then find a birthmark beneath her ribcage, and the little cluster of faded stretch marks on her hips. He etched his memories in his mind and then climbed into bed and made them with his mouth—touching her everywhere his eyes had been. She could feel his lips on her skin, her calves, her toes and back up again. He turned her over and she felt them rest on her stomach, where she had stopped him once. He took for ever, which was what they didn't have, but his mouth worked down and he explored her very slowly, till she pleaded with him to stop. She pulsed in his mouth and couldn't give any more, but still he would not relent, coaxing an orgasm so deep and intense she was scared to go there, and she knew what he was doing. Heard her voice shouting his name, as was his intention—a subliminal branding as he married her with his mouth, because as he took her over the edge, as she sobbed his name, Georgie knew she could never now go there again and not think of him.

She would always hold back for fear of calling out the wrong name.

He was so good it made her angry, so perfect and so exactly her size, yet she could never own him—would forever have to look through the windows of her mind to glimpse this.

Only now, when there was nothing left to give, did he take a whole lot more. He moved up her body and for the first time since the desert he kissed her mouth, and his eyes were open as he entered her and so too were Georgie's, scared even to blink. To remember this was her priority—because she never wanted to forget how his eyes adored hers so much as he moved deep within her. How pale her arm looked against his dark shoulders, and she tried to imprint in her mind the scent of him when aroused.

The hardest week was wiped from his mind. If he could just have her, then anything would be easy. He wanted to come, but he didn't want it to be over, so he resisted his body, and it hurt not to give in to it, because his body wanted the release she could give.

'Please,' Georgie said, because she was almost there and she wanted him with her. 'Please,' she said again, and then pressed her mouth in his shoulder because she didn't want to beg.

She felt like they were lying on quicksand and being drawn down into it, or sucked back into the vortex the desert had made them create, the world that they had when there was no one around. She would not, could not wait for him a second longer. She would not beg, but her body demanded on her behalf, for it rose beneath him and tightened around him; it beat a tune that he could never deny. And he gave in so that he could join her. Each urgent thrust took her further, not just to the edge but away from him, and both knew it. They both fanned the last flickers of orgasm from a fire that must die.

His hand moved down to her stomach and rested there and his mind lingered there and so too did Georgie's.

Hopefully it would hurt less when she was out of his arms, but she lay and tortured herself for a little while longer and Ibrahim did the same.

'What would happen if you don't take your Pill?'

'Nothing, probably.'

'But perhaps?'

'We won't find out,' Georgie said, her face burning because, yes, she had considered it. 'Because I took my Pill this morning and I'll take it tomorrow. I will not force you into a decision.' She was fragile in his arms but strong in her mind, and he loved her for it.

'If it was just for a few weeks…' Her skin was against his and he let his mind wander, explored options that would have once been unthinkable, except her body dared him to dream. 'Could there be annulment?'

'It happened.' Georgie's voice was hollow. 'You yourself said it cannot be undone.'

'But it was such a short time, there are no children… If it was a mistake, something you regret…' And then she was the bravest she had ever been, the clearest in her mind she had ever been, because even if she loved him, she was still herself.

'I don't regret it, though.' She watched his face darken.

'How can you say you don't regret it? That a marriage to some drunk, a marriage you admit was a mistake, a marriage that has cost us each other, is not something you regret?'

But she would not back down. 'I don't regret it because I've learnt from it.' Georgie's voice was a touch shaky as she struggled to hold onto her convictions. 'I've learnt from my mistakes. And once I would have said I regret it, because it's what you wanted to hear...I would have done anything to please you.'

'Because of your past we have no future...'

'Because of my past I'm a better person,' she interrupted. 'Because it taught me to say no, to walk away, to accept nothing but the best... So don't try to make me say I regret it. I'm not ashamed of my past, Ibrahim. If you are...' She rose from his bed and put on her gown. She walked when she didn't want to, because otherwise she might lie there, might bend herself into the woman he needed her to be, instead of the woman she was. 'That's your issue.'

'You'll come back soon?' Felicity asked as they sat in the car that was waiting to take them to the airport. Her sister had been shocked when, almost the second Felicity returned from the desert, Georgie said that she wanted to leave. But Georgie had stood her ground.

She needed to get away or she'd be back in his bed that very night, would be back in his bed till his virgin was found for him, and she was worth more than that, and so was his bride.

They needed to be apart to heal.

'Of course I'll be back,' Georgie said, though in her heart she didn't know how. How could she ever be here and be without him?

'And I'll be home in a few weeks.' Felicity tried to keep her voice light as the car drove away from the palace and Georgie deliberately didn't turn round.

But she couldn't stay brave at the airport when she hugged her sister.

'You'll get over him,' Felicity said when Georgie crumpled. 'You will.'

'I know I will,' Georgie said, but her heart wasn't sure.

The captain told them to look to the right after take-off for a spectacular view of the sun setting over the desert , but Georgie refused to turn her head because she didn't want to see a sunset without Ibrahim.

'Is everything okay, Miss Anderson?' the steward asked.

'Ms,' Felicity corrected him, because it was who she was, whether Ibrahim could accept it or not.

CHAPTER FIFTEEN

HE WAS in London.

Since their last night together, as surely as Georgie checked her horoscope in the morning, so too she typed 'Zaraq' into her search engine.

Clicked 'News'.

And just as she had so often, she scrolled through the latest offerings.

The illness that had crippled the country was all but over.

Hassan and Jamal had brought their baby home.

The king was pleased with his youngest son, so pleased that after a brief return home the king had again headed for the UK to resume *business*. Her eyes scanned faster than her fingers could click and though Ibrahim was often mentioned, today was not one of those days.

For four days now there had been no mention of him, but he was in London Georgie was sure, because Felicity had been vague when Georgie had tried to find out, and though there was no way she could properly explain it, her body told her so.

It was the hardest thing to continue working.

As much as her medically minded sister raised an eyebrow, as much as it didn't make logical sense, Georgie's work was more than touch, more than scent. To be effective it required a piece of herself, and as Georgie greeted her clients throughout the week, there weren't many pieces left to give.

Between each one she checked her phone, her messages, her emails.

She fed the craving that would not abate then forced herself to go on.

'I had booked a scalp massage, but tonight I have to go out.' Sophia Porter was a new client and Georgie checked carefully through the questionnaire she had filled in. 'Perhaps I should rebook, though I was hoping I could purchase something...' The woman closed her blue eyes and pressed her middle finger to her forehead. 'I suffer with migraines. I've tried so many medicines, so many different treatments.'

'Why don't you let me give you a hand massage?' Georgie offered, because it was her favourite initial contact. It was so non-invasive. It was often all her young clients would allow, but as the woman wavered, perhaps thinking Georgie was being pushy, she offered, 'Complimentary, and you can see if it helps before you buy anything.'

Sophia rested back in the chair, and Georgie prepared her oils. She had no ready-made blends, preferring to assess the client first and make her choices instinctively.

Lavender was a favourite for migraines, but sensing Sophia's anxiety she added clary sage and then a drop of marjoram, then Georgie moistened her hands with the fragrant brew and took her patient's hands.

Like a kitten who had never been let out, the woman's hands were soft, quite beautiful in fact, long fingered and exquisitely manicured, but despite Georgie's best efforts her client would not relax, asking Georgie questions. Sometimes talking relaxed people, so Georgie told Sophia she'd just got back from holiday.

'Anywhere nice?'

'My elder sister lives in Zaraq. It's an island—'

'I have heard of it.' Sophia smiled.

Georgie opened another vial and took out the dropper. Some melissa might help to help relax her client, and with scent being a key to memory, in that moment she was back in the desert. Her hands stopped working as well as they had, because they were shaking a little as she recalled him. As she paused to regroup, Sophia closed her eyes and inhaled.

'Ah, Bal-samin...' Sophia relaxed back in the chair. 'Tell me about Zaraq. Is it very beautiful?'

'Very,' Georgie admitted, and she felt the woman's hand relax as she talked and so she talked some more, told her about the endless sands and the miracle of finding a shell in the middle of a desert. She pulled gently on each finger in turn till the tension seeped out; she told her of the sky that went on for ever and the sun that beat down, feeling like a skullcap on your head, of the mad winds and strange rules, and when it hurt to recall it, when she could not speak of it and not weep, she looked up and saw her client asleep.

'My headache is gone,' Sophia said when Georgie woke her gently. Despite Georgie's protests, she insisted on paying and also purchased some melissa oil, and she gave the most enormous tip. 'You have a gift.'

'Thank you.'

'Could I book again?'

'Of course.' Georgie opened up her calendar on screen, and went to type in details from the form Sophia had filled in.

'Mrs?' Georgie checked. 'Or Ms? You didn't put your title.'

'There wasn't a box for "Queen".' Sophia said, and Georgie felt her heart still, felt as if she had been lied to. 'Put Ms. That is what I go by here—it is far easier than trying to explain.'

'You weren't here for a massage?'

'No,' Sophia admitted, 'but I will be back again—if you will have me. I really have had the most terrible headache. I never thought a massage could clear it but I was wrong.' She gave Georgie a tired smile. 'I worry about my son.'

'Have you spoken to him?'

'I have. He is here in London.' Georgie's heart leapt but only for a moment because now it was confirmed he was here, it hurt that he hadn't made any attempt to call. 'And you are every bit as beautiful as he describes, every bit as warm and as loving.'

'He's spoken about me?'

'Ibrahim is not one for confiding but, yes, finally he admitted what was on his mind. He misses you.'

'He hasn't called.'

'He worries about you,' Sophia said. 'Worries at the cruel press you will receive in Zaraq and what it will do to you.' She gave Georgie a smile. 'He saw what it did to me. I left, and for two years the press went wild about me. My husband forgave my indiscretion, the people of Zaraq did not. But I do not need their forgiveness. I have a wonderful life here, and my husband comes often.'

'But you miss it?'

Sophia gave a nonchalant shrug, 'Sometimes—but I am happy here, where I can be myself. I have told Ibrahim the same.' Sophia denied the pain in her soul and looked Georgie in the eye as she did so. Not for a second did she feel guilty for lying. All she saw was the chance to keep her son.

To avoid losing the last of her family to the desert.

For years she had pleaded with Ibrahim not to return and for many of those she had never thought he would. Yet since the wedding there had been a restlessness to him that at first she had tried to ignore, but seeing him from afar lead a county in crisis, hearing him talk about building a future for the people of Zaraq, she had been sure she had lost him—that again the desert had won.

Then he had told her about Georgie, about a woman who could never live there, a woman that he loved, and finally Sophia saw a way into the future, with a family to grow old with, with grandchildren who weren't strangers and Christmas and birthdays not taken alone.

'You can have both worlds,' she had told him. 'Don't turn your back on love. You will find a way, Ibrahim. Together you can work it out.'

And she told Georgie the same thing.

'He told me you were fragile, and of all you have been through.' And that confused Georgie, because she thought Ibrahim saw her differently. 'But you are not ill now. I can see for myself that you are strong. If the papers in Zaraq speak badly of you, you will not crumple. Anyway, as I pointed out to my son, you will be here. He can protect you, defend you... He should not let your past affect your future.'

'I don't think we've got a future.'

'I wouldn't be so sure.' Sophia smiled. 'I know how you feel, Georgie. I understand your fears, and if you need someone to talk to, if you want to talk to someone who can relate, you have my details.'

CHAPTER SIXTEEN

IT DID not abate.

There was a constant call and he tried to ignore it.

There was blackness in his heart and restlessness in his soul.

His tie choked every morning.

The city streets were crowded, the rain was filthy, but home could be here.

He had listened to his brothers, to the king, but he did not agree with them. He had listened to his mother too as she urged him not to close that door to his heart.

That he did have choices.

And he would exercise them, Ibrahim had finally decided. Home *would* be here and he could still help the people of Zaraq.

He climbed the stairs to Georgie's small office in long, deliberate strides, his mind made up and nothing could change it.

'I've got a client due any moment...' She recognised his footsteps on the stairs and did not look up because she didn't want to look at him—didn't want to see his face, didn't want another image added to what she must somehow one day erase.

'I am your appointment. I had my PA make it in her name.' The details did not matter. 'I need to see you...'

'It's better if we don't.'

'Better for who?' Ibrahim demanded. 'Do you feel better, not seeing me?' He saw her pale face, worried about her slender figure. 'We need to talk.'

'I'm not ready to talk.' She wasn't. The sight of him, the scent of him, to have him in her space, was overwhelming. She wanted to touch him, to fall in his arms, but she was scared to have to lose him all over again.

'Then don't talk, just listen.' He swallowed. 'I would be proud to have you as my wife.'

'But?' Georgie questioned.

'There is no but.'

She was quite sure there was and she didn't want to hear it, was scared to look at him and ask the question that she knew she must. So she forced her eyes upwards, saw the pain in his eyes and knew how badly she'd been missed. She made herself ask the question.

'What about my work?' She danced around the issue and yet subtly she broached it—so subtly, even Ibrahim did not realise it.

'I'm not asking you to give anything up.'

'You love that land, Ibrahim. You want to be there, I can see it, I can feel it, I know it...'

'No.'

'Yes.'

And it was true.

A curse that attached to him, that lived within him, but he could have both, of that he was sure.

'We will live here. I can return for work, to see my family, but our home will be here.'

And she wanted to say yes, she wanted so much to say yes, to fall into his arms, to accept his offer, to be his wife. Every beat of her heart propelled her to say yes, to give in to the throb of her body, but she was less impulsive now than she had once been, stronger now, and would first take care of herself.

'And I will return with you?'

He hesitated a moment before he shook his head. 'When the news comes out about your past, there will be outrage—but you will be here, I will protect you from that.'

'I don't need your protection,' Georgie said. 'Because it's not going to happen.'

'I'm offering you—'

'Half a princess, that's what you're offering me,' Georgie sneered, surprising herself at the bitterness in her own voice, but it was there, right there beneath the surface, black and angry, just like the truth beneath his shiny offer. 'Well, I'm worth more than that.'

'I will give you everything you need here.'

'But you cannot take me to your home. I cannot live there like my sister...'

'So you want a palace?' He too was bitter. 'You want all the finery?'

'Yes,' Georgie said. 'If I marry you, I want all of it.'

'You're not who I thought I knew,' Ibrahim said, but she was ready for him.

'I'm better than her,' Georgie said. 'And every day I get better. You know I'd have taken it a few months ago, hell, I'd have taken it last week. I'd have taken any crumb you offered just to be with you, but not now…'

'Hardly crumbs.' He was offering her everything he possibly could and then some—half his life spent in a plane just to be with her at night.

'I don't just want birthdays and Christmas and a husband at weekends. I don't want access arrangements with a family that hates me. I won't be an army wife to a country that won't even acknowledge me.' And she met his eyes with another demand. 'And don't ever describe me as fragile again.'

'I never have.'

But she didn't believe him.

'You don't have to protect me, or hide me from my past. I'm glad for every last mistake I've ever made because six months ago, six days ago, had you come and offered me this, I'd have taken it.

'I would have been your bride without question but not any more.

'I want you in my bed each night.

'I want the palace and the desert and sometimes I want to come back home to London,' she told him, each sentence delivered more strongly than the last.

'I want it all and I deserve it, and if you can't give it to me, if you can't share all of you, then I won't take the half that you're offering. I'm better off single, better off being able to go freely to Zaraq and see my sister and niece, better off being my own person than an exiled wife.'

'You're saying no?'

'Absolutely,' Georgie said.

'All that I can give you…'

'Save it for the wife your father picks for you, Ibrahim,' Georgie said. 'Save it for your virgin.' She almost spat at the thought of it, but she contained herself with words. 'No matter how well you *teach* her, she'll never be as good as me.'

CHAPTER SEVENTEEN

THE trouble with angry words, Georgie thought, as he stormed from her office, was that you didn't get to rehearse them.

She wanted to run after him, to reframe her words, to explain better—that she wasn't talking about sex, wasn't declaring herself as the world's best lover. Well, she was, but only to him.

And it wasn't just about sex. It was the conversations, the thoughts shared that he could surely never repeat so easily with another.

But she would not run after him, she was stronger than that.

Fragile indeed!

How dared he?

So she took to her oils and inhaled melissa, then hurled the bottle against the wall when she smelt Balsmin, just as Sophia had, because now it would always take her back to the desert.

Always.

How could Sophia stand there and tell her she was happy when her son and her grandson lay buried in the desert, when she had heard Ibrahim tell his father how she had wept at the birth of Hassan's son.

Sophia had lied and Georgie didn't blame her a bit for it.

Maybe she should go and talk to her, but honestly this time. Perhaps it might help to hear her true pain, to confirm how it felt to be half a wife, to seal the decision she had made.

CHAPTER EIGHTEEN

'You fool!' Ibrahim strode in, straight past his mother, to where his father sat. He left a trail of black energy that had his mother standing at the door fearful to go in, for, try as she might, she could no longer halt them. She could not contain the conflict between the two men she loved most.

'You dare to speak to me like that.' The king rose to defend himself. 'I am your father, I am your king.'

'You are not my king,' Ibrahim said. 'You will no longer be my king, for I am done. The knife of the family should not cut—and yet you have cut my mother out.'

'There was no choice.'

'You are king,' Ibrahim sneered. 'You get to choose. You make the rules.'

He could hear his mother crying in the hallway, but he would not stop. 'She deserves to be at home with you, not holed up in another country as some secret. She is the mother of your sons.'

'She cheated.'

'As did you!' Ibrahim challenged what no man

should. He stood and questioned the ways of old, the ways that chained him, his father, his family from a future. 'You had mistresses, many, even when you were with her...'

'I am king!' Indignant, he roared. 'Your mother had four young children. I was helping her so she could focus on the children, not have to worry herself attending to my needs...'

'What about her needs?' Ibrahim roared. 'Clearly she had them, but you were too blind to see.'

'Ibrahim, please,' Sophia begged from the hallway. 'Please, stop.'

As Georgie pulled up at Sophia's house she could see her at the door, bent over and crying, and as she climbed out, she heard raised voices and Sophia ran to her. 'He will kill him for how he is speaking. Stop him, Georgie. You must.'

But he would not stop and Georgie knew it. As with Felicity, there were too many words left unsaid, a confrontation that needed to be had, so she held Sophia's hand and listened as Ibrahim roared. 'You didn't even give her the dignity of ending it.' He shook his head in disgust at his father. 'You need to bring her home.'

'My people will not accept her and they will not respect me if I am seen to forgive her.'

'Some won't!' Ibrahim challenged. 'But there are many who will respect you a whole lot more—your son included.'

And the king looked at his youngest son, the one he could not read, the one he had accused of being the weakest when he had wept in the desert and just would not stop. The child that wept till it choked him, till he vomited, when his body should have been spent, when he should have curled up and accepted his lesson. Still Ibrahim had not, because he would not give up on what he believed in, and the king saw then the strength in his son.

'I love Georgie,' Ibrahim said. 'She will be my wife, and without her by my side, I will not return to Zaraq. I will never return and neither will our children.' He meant it. The king knew his son meant it. 'If I am to be a prince, she is to be royal—as my mother should be.'

'You can't just give it all away.'

'I just have.' There wasn't a trace of regret in his voice and Georgie closed her eyes as she listened and learnt just how much he loved her.

'You cannot just turn your back—the desert calls...'

'There is no call from the desert. The call was from my heart.'

'Don't mock the ways of old.'

'But I'm not,' Ibrahim said. 'The desert knows what it is doing, because it brought us together. It's the ruler who is blind.' He was done with his father. Now he just had to find Georgie, but even before he turned round she was there beside him and she took his hand, not just for him but because she was still intimidated by a king.

'Is this what you want for him?' the king challenged, and Georgie wasn't so strong.

'You don't have to give it up, Ibrahim. We can work something out. I know how much you love it.'

'They have to love me too,' he said, and it sounded a lot like her. 'I would be a good prince, a loyal prince. I can help them move forward and bring much-needed change, but only if they want all of me, and a part of me will always be with you.' He meant it, Georgie realised, he truly meant it. Gone was the tension and doubt. There was no fight inside him, no wrestling with himself, and without a glance backwards he walked from the house, taking Georgie with him.

'Do you realise what you've done?' Georgie asked.

'Do you?' Ibrahim checked, for the first time in his life bordering on embarrassed, because all that she wanted he could not now give her. 'You won't even be half a princess.'

'Am I yours?' Georgie asked, and he nodded. 'Are you mine?' she checked, and he closed his eyes and nodded again.

'Then I have everything.'

She looked down at his fingers coiled around hers, to the darkness and light that they made, then up to his eyes and the talent behind them—and there was her palace.

She had her prince.

EPILOGUE

'THE hard part will soon be over.'

Ibrahim meant the formal part of the wedding, but as she smiled back at him, it meant something more too.

The hard part was long over, but if it reared up again, she could face it.

Could face anything with Ibrahim by her side.

'Soon,' Ibrahim said, 'we can go to the desert.' Now he looked forward to his time there. Now he understood that it was wiser than anyone could begin to understand.

But his mind did not linger there. This night his attention was on Georgie. She didn't like the spotlight, the limelight, and he shielded her from it as best he could, and thankfully, though it was their wedding, there was another couple that dimmed the glare just a touch.

Zaraq was celebrating two happy couples today, Georgie and Ibrahim and also their king with his queen.

The people had always loved her, had mourned her son on her behalf, and now she was back, glowing and radiant. She sat at the table by his side as the king read his speech.

He was proud of his country and people and he thanked them for sharing this day, and he was thankful to his wife too, especially, he added on a whim, for her patience. Even Ibrahim managed a wry laugh and then his father looked right at him and he was proud as he thanked both his youngest and the wildest, even for rebellion, because challenge was good, the king said, it was how we learned. And he smiled at Georgie and thanked her too—because she had taught him so much.

Then the hard part was over and seemingly now they could enjoy.

Except Georgie couldn't.

She stood at the stop of the stairs, heard the beat of the music and the crowd urge them on, the procession that danced them, and his hand in hers.

'I can't do this.'

'You are doing it,' Ibrahim said, because she could walk if she wanted to and that would be enough, but he knew she was capable of much more. 'You're doing it now.'

Had the king been so jubilant at Felicity's wedding, so happy and proud?

She could see her mother, smiling, and the radiant face of Sophia, who was home now, and her sister glowing.

But more than that there was Ibrahim beside her and halfway down the steps, with him beside her, Georgie found her rhythm, found she could dance, even terribly, and still he adored her.

She was as she was, perfect to him.

Which gave her courage she had never imagined she could have.

To dance those last steps and accept the love that surrounded her and not care if she stumbled or fell, because Ibrahim was there to catch her. And she was there too for him.

She danced the zeffa, moved toward him and away from him, danced around him and beside him, felt the beat in her stomach that spread down her thighs to her toes, and now she could give in to it and then there was contact and she rested in his arms.

'Take me to the desert.'

'Soon,' Ibrahim said, because still there was duty, so they danced one more dance then two and then headed to a loaded table, where Georgie took her time to select from the lavish spread.

He watched nosy, bony fingers pick up a pomegranate, he saw the servant move in with a knife, but he took over and tore the fruit in two.

'Take me to the desert,' Georgie said, because she hadn't been there since that night and her womb ached for him.

And Ibrahim was about to remind her, but he checked himself. Yes, there was duty, except he had other priorities today. They had posed for the photos, had waved to the crowds, had feasted and danced—had done every last thing Georgie hated—and his duty was now to her.

'You can't just leave,' her mother chided, as Ibrahim spoke with the king. 'You can't leave midway through your own wedding.'

'Yes, she can.' Felicity hugged her sister as Ibrahim returned.

'What did he say?' Georgie asked, but it was too noisy for him to answer. They were supposed to dance again, and with the end in sight, she did. Out of the palace and to a waiting helicopter, and they flew into a desert that looked like an ocean and for a while there were no words, just his kisses as they flew over it.

'What did he say?' Georgie asked, when finally they were alone in the desert and she still worried that they'd caused trouble. 'What did the king say when you told him we were leaving?'

'To look after you.' Ibrahim replied. 'Which, I told him, goes without saying.'

She stepped into his tent and braced herself for servants, for Bedra, for bathing and petals and all the drama that was a royal wedding, consoling herself that in an hour or so they could escape to bed, but it was Ibrahim lighting the lanterns that led them.

'Where is everyone?'

'Gone,' Ibrahim answered. 'It's just you and me and no one waiting, no one watching to make sure we're safe…' He looked at his bride, at the broken mould that was Georgie, and he wouldn't change a single thing just to have this moment. 'Which you are.'

Safe in the desert, alone with him.

The Sheikh's Destiny

MELISSA JAMES

Melissa James is a born and bred Sydney-sider who swapped the beaches of the New South Wales Central Coast for the Alps of Switzerland a few years ago. Wife and mother of three, a former nurse, she fell into writing when her husband brought home an article about romance writers and suggested she should try it—and she became hooked. Switching from romantic espionage to the family stories of Mills & Boon was the best move she ever made. Melissa loves to hear from readers—you can e-mail her at authormelissajames@yahoo.com.

This book is dedicated to Vicky, my beloved sister-in-law, who never once denigrated this job I love and, despite dyslexia, bought and read every book I've had released. To a wonderful sister and dearly beloved aunt to my kids, thank you for showing us what true courage under fire means. We think of you and miss you every day. 2nd December 1963–9th October 2009

To Michelle, Donna and Lisa, the 'angels' who nursed Vicky through her illness, giving her last months dignity and love despite work and family commitments. Thank you from the bottom of my heart. I can only invent heroines—but each of you is one in the eyes of our family and all the many who loved Vicky.

The road to Shellah-Akbar, Northern Africa

THEY were closing in on him. Time to open throttle.

Alim El-Kanar shifted down into low-gear sports mode, in the truck he'd modified specially for this purpose. He wasn't letting the men of the warlord Sh'ellah—after whose family this region had been named—take the medical supplies and food meant for those the man made suffer, so he could keep control and live in luxury. Alim wasn't going to be caught, either—that would be disaster, but for the people of this region, not him. As soon as Sh'ellah saw the face of the man he'd taken hostage, he'd hold Alim for a fabulous ransom that would keep them in funds for new weapons for years.

When he had the ransom, *then* he'd kill him—if he could get away with it.

But Sh'ellah hadn't yet discovered who Alim was, and he gambled his life on the hope the warlord never would. Even the director of Doctors for Africa didn't know the true identity of the near-silent truck driver who pulled off what he called miracles on a regular basis, reaching remote villages held by warlords with medicine, food and water-purifying tablets.

With a top-class fake ID and always wearing the male headscarf he could twist over his famous features whenever he chose, he was invisible to the world. Just the way he liked it.

Who he was—or what he'd been once—mattered far less than what he did.

He always gave enough medicine to each village to last six to eight hours. Then, when Sh'ellah's men came for their 'share', most of it was gone; they took a few needles, some out-of-date antibiotics, and strutted out again.

The villagers never told Alim where they hid the supplies, and he didn't want to know. They kept just enough bread, rice and grain out for Sh'ellah's men to feel smug about their theft. To Sh'ellah, such petty control made him feel like a man, a lion among mice.

Even Alim, flawed as he was, would be a better leader—*Don't go there.* Grimly he shifted down gear, following the indented tracks in the scrubby grass on what was loosely called a road to the village of Shellah-Akbar. He'd had tyres put on this truck like the ones used in outback and desert rallies so he could fly over rocks and sudden holes the wind made in the dusty ground. He also had a padded protective cage put inside the cab, much like the one he'd had in his cars when he was still The Racing Sheikh.

He'd once been so ridiculously proud of the nickname—now he wanted to hit something every time he thought of it. His fame and life in the fast lane had died the same day as his brother. The only racing he did now was with trucks with much needed supplies to war-torn villages. And if the term 'sheikh' was technically correct, it was a privilege he'd forfeited after Fadi's death. It was an honour he'd never deserve. His younger brother Harun had taken on the honour in his absence, marrying the princess Fadi had been contracted to marry. Harun had been ruling the people of his principality, Abbas al-Din—*the lion of the faith*—for three years, and was doing a brilliant job.

Thinking of home set off the familiar ache. He used to love coming home. *Habib Abbas*, the people would chant. *Beloved lion*. They'd been so proud of his achievements.

If the people wanted him to come home, to take his place among his people, he knew an accident of birth, finding some oil or minerals, or the ability to race a car around a track didn't make a true leader. Strength, good sense and courage did—and Alim had lost the best of those qualities with Fadi's death, along with his heart and a lot of his skin. He had just enough strength and courage left to risk his neck for a few villagers in Africa. The fanfare for what he did was silent, and that was the way he liked it.

He growled as his usual stress-trigger, the puckered scars that covered more than half his torso, began the painful itching that scratching only made worse. He'd have to use the last of his silica-based cream on the pain as soon as he had a minute, as soon as he lost these jokers—and he would. He wasn't Habib Abbas, or The Racing Sheikh, any more—but he still had the skills.

Stop it! Thinking only made the itch worse—and the heart-pain that was his night-and-day companion. *Fadi, I'm so sorry!*

Grimly he turned his mind to the job at hand, or he'd crash in seconds. The protective roll cage inside his truck might be heavily padded with lamb's wool so if the truck rolled, he could use his modified low centre of gravity shift and oddly placed air bags to flip back right way up—but it wouldn't help if he was too busted up to keep going.

He checked the mirror. They were still the same distance behind him, forty men packing weaponry suitable for taking far more than a truck. They were too far away from him to shoot accurately, but still too close to shake. He couldn't do anything clever on this rugged, roadless terrain, like spilling oil to make them slide: it would sink straight into the dirt before the enemy reached the slick, and he'd risk his engine for nothing.

But he had to do something, or they'd follow him right to Shellah-Akbar and take the supplies. He had to find a way to beat the odds currently stacked against him like the Spartans at Thermopylae thousands of years ago.

If he could rig something with the emergency flare…could he make it work?

Alim's mind raced. Yes, if he added the tar-based chemical powder he kept to help the tyres move over the sand without sliding to the volatile formula inside the flare, and tossed it back, it might work—

He was used to driving one-handed, or steering the wheel with both feet. He shoved a stone on the accelerator, angling it so it kept going steady, and drove with his feet while pulling the flare apart with as much care as he could, given his situation.

He was nearing the four-way junction ten miles from the village, where he must turn one way or another. He had to stop them now or, no matter what clever methods he employed to evade them, they'd know where he was going. They'd use their satellite phones, and another hundred thugs would be at the village before sunset, demanding their 'rightful' share of the supplies proven by their assault rifles.

He poured the powder in with shaking hands. He had to be careful or he'd kill them; and, murderers though most of the men undoubtedly were, it wasn't his place to judge who had done what or why. He'd had a childhood of extreme privilege, the best education in the world. Most of the men behind him had been born in horrendous poverty, abducted when they were small children and taught to play with AK-47s instead of bats and balls.

He'd leave enough food and supplies behind so their warlord didn't kill them for their failure. Part of the solution or perpetuating the problem, he didn't know; but in this continent where human life was cheaper than clean water, everyone only had one shot at living, and he refused to carry any more regrets in his personal backpack.

He grabbed the wheel as he neared the far-leaning sign showing the way to the villages, and slanted the truck extreme left, away from all of them. Good, the wind was shifting again: it was time for a good old-fashioned wild goose chase.

He put the flare together, closing it tight with electrical tape, shook it and opened the sunroof. He lit the flare, counted one-hundred-and-one to one-hundred-and-seven, shoved his foot hard over the stone covering the accelerator as he tossed the lit flare up and backward, and pulled the sunroof shut.

The truck shot forward and left, when the *boom* and flash came. The air behind him turned a dazzling bluish-white, then thick and black, filled with choking, temporarily blinding chemicals. Screams came to his ears, the screeches of tyres as their Jeeps came to simultaneous halts. He'd done it... Alim arced the truck hard right, back to the crossroads. He didn't wind down the window to check. He'd either blinded them all, or he'd be dead inside a minute.

Half a kilometre before the junction, he threw out the half-dozen boxes of second-rate supplies he'd been keeping for the warlord's pleasure. They'd find them when the chemical reaction from their tears would neutralise the blindness. There was no permanent damage to their retinas, only to their pride and their ability to follow him for about half an hour. Factoring in the wind shift, all traces of his tyre tracks should have vanished by then, covered with red earth and falling leaves and branches from the low, thin trees. They'd have to split up to find him, and by the time they reached the village he'd be long gone.

Then a whining sound came; air whooshed, a loud *bang*

filled the cab, and the truck leaped forward as if propelled before it teetered and fell to the left.

Alim's head struck the side window with stunning force. Blood filled his eye; he felt his mind reeling. One of his specially made, ultra-wide and thick desert tyres had blown. One of the warlord's men was either not blinded in the explosion, or he'd made the luckiest shot in the world, and blown his back tyre. The only drawback to his special, extra-tough tyres was their need for perfect balance. If one tyre went, so did the truck.

He couldn't black out now, or he'd die—and so would the people of Shellah-Akbar. He fought passing out with everything in him. He stopped the truck and pulled on the air-bag lever. As the truck tipped, the four-foot-thick pillows that flew to position outside the doors bounced it back up. As the truck righted itself he took his rifle and blew the tyres, the two on the passenger side quickly, but he had to wait until the truck was up and keeling back over to the right before he could balance it by blowing the driver's side.

The truck landed hard down on the ground as the blackness took over. Alim shoved the truck in first and took off. The rocks and sand would destroy the thick rubber coating with which he'd covered his rims in case of emergency, but he could make far more than the remaining six miles, and there were spare tyres in the back. The tyres weren't modified, and it'd be a miracle if he made it back to the Human Compassion Refugee camp two hundred and sixty kilometres south-west, but it would get him to where the food-aid pilots could pick him up.

He had to reach the village; he was going to pass out any moment. Blood gushed from his temple wound, and his blood pressure was falling by the second. If he could put the truck in the right direction, and set the cruise control…the compass and GPS system both said he only needed a straight line now to make it.

He pressed the emergency direction finder on his satellite phone; his only hope now was that the nurse he knew lived in Shellah-Akbar had her receiver switched on.

Holding the wheel like grim death, he put the truck in second, made sure the stone was still in place over the accelerator, and fell forward.

The truck came into the village of Shellah-Akbar seventeen minutes later.

A woman was at the wheel. She'd run from her bunk in the medical tent as soon as the emergency signal reached the village. The only one with full medical experience, she'd ridden an old bike as fast as she could while Abdel, the village Olympic marathon hopeful, followed, to ride the pushbike back to the village. While the truck was still moving she'd stopped just in front of the driver's door, tossed the bike down for Abdel to find, yanked open the door and jumped inside. Sprawled beside her, his head in her lap, was one unconscious driver, who had risked his life so that others may live.

'In-sh'allah,' she whispered, and recited the words of a prayer taught her from infancy: a prayer that hadn't kept her own life intact, but might help God smile upon this courageous man.

He wasn't going to die. Not today. Not if she could help it.

CHAPTER ONE

'GET the driver into my hut, and get rid of the truck,' Hana al-Sud yelled to two villagers in Swahili when she pulled the truck up outside the medical tent. 'Don't cook the food. Feed plain bread to those who need it most. Bury the rest in Saliya's grave.'

'The fruit will lose its vitamins, Hana,' her assistant protested.

'One seed or core can be found in seconds,' she replied calmly enough, given the urgency of their situation and the rapid pounding of her heart. She ran around the truck to the driver. 'We can get it back out tonight to feed the children, without losing nutritional value. Just do it, please, Malika! And sweep away any traces of tyre marks!'

An older man ran to the passenger side to take the driver as the fittest young man in the village jumped into Hana's place in the driver's seat. The other villagers opened the back of the truck to unload it. Two women ran over with the vital tarpaulins, snatched medical kits and ampoules of antibiotics and insulin to bury it. The future of the entire village depended on everyone working together, and working fast. They'd be here in minutes. The warlord's satellite phones were the best money could buy. Any sniff of betrayal meant unbearable consequences for them all.

'Take the driver to my hut. He's Arabic,' Hana said tensely in Swahili. 'I'll patch him up. When they ask I'll say my husband came for me.'

The men took the unconscious man to Hana's small hut beside the medical tent.

Within fifteen minutes it was as if the truck had never been there. Abdel would leave it somewhere in the desert, take the exact coordinates and return on foot. He was the only one with the perfect cover. As he was a long-distance runner aiming for the Olympics, no one thought it strange if he wasn't in the village at all times.

In the hut, Hana had the injured man laid on an old sheet. 'Wound and suture kit—an old resterilised set.' This brave man deserved better, but if she used the new kits he'd brought today and didn't dispose of them in time, the warlord's men would know the truth. They had to get every detail right.

There was blood on his face and shirt. 'Haytham, I need a clean shirt!' Haytham was her friend Malika's husband, and approximately the same size as this man. She stripped off the bloodied shirt and tossed it in her cooking fire, noting the angry, inflamed mass of burns scars criss-crossing his chest, shoulder and stomach on the left side. She'd treat them later. Right now she had to save his life.

She checked her watch. From experience, she knew she had five minutes to get it all done. She cleaned his face of the blood, and prepared to suture the wound. She'd wash his hair after, to remove the last traces of his identity as the driver.

She stitched his wound as fast as she could, grateful it was close to his hair; she'd cover it with his fringe, and would have to risk infection by using cover-stick around the reddened skin. There was no way she could risk a bandage, but she'd use one vital ampoule of antibiotic, needle and syringe; the wound could turn septic with hair and make-up on it.

She injected him between his toes, as if he were a junkie with collapsed veins. It was a place Sh'ellah's men wouldn't think to look for signs of injury and medical attention. 'Bury these fast,' she ordered Malika, who took the precious supplies and ran.

Hana washed the worst of the dirt and blood from his hair with a damp washer, coated with some of her precious essential oils, and covered the wound with the cleaned hair and make-up. Then she rolled the man off the sheet, bundled it up and tossed it in the roaring fire. She put the clean shirt on him—he'd been through several operations for those burns, by the patches of grafted skin over the worst of it—buttoned up the shirt, and checked her watch. Four minutes thirty-eight. Not bad, really. She checked over the hut for any signs of wound treatment.

Nothing, thank God. Hana dragged in a deep sigh of relief, and finally allowed herself a moment to look at her patient's face.

'No, no,' she whispered, horrified.

She'd known as she ran to save this man's life that he'd pulled off the impossible today—but the feat suddenly didn't seem quite so impossible, if he was who she thought he was.

*Please, God, just make it a freak physical resemblance…*because if it was him, then by his mere presence he'd brought far more danger to the village than by any supplies he'd brought.

Even Sh'ellah's followers would know him. Most men loved fast sports and money, and this man combined both. Just put a helmet on him and it was the former face of the world's most expensive racing-car team. He'd won the World Championship twice—and brought both riches and research to a once-struggling nation. He'd found oil and natural gas reserves in a place few had thought to look, with his chemical background and analytical racing driver's mind.

'*La!*' he muttered, in either fever or concussed confusion. '*La, la, akh! Fadi, la!*'

No, no, brother! Fadi, no!

In dread, Hana heard the words in the Arabic native to her childhood home country, begging his beloved brother Fadi to live. It broke her heart—she knew how it felt to lose those she loved—and then she listened in horror as he relived the drive to the village in graphic detail, including the complex mixture of chemicals he'd used to blind Sh'ellah's men.

The fine-chiselled, handsome face—the faint scars of burns on his cheek, the horrific wounds on his body…even his miraculous escape today made perfect sense. He'd obviously had extensive training in the creation of compounds, and how much of each to add to make something new—such as a flare that could blind the men chasing him.

'This is all I need,' she muttered in frustration to the delirious face of Alim El-Kanar, the missing sheikh of Abbas al-Din. 'Why couldn't you be anywhere but here?'

The former racing-car champion kept muttering, describing the flare-bomb he'd made.

At the worst possible moment, the sound of a dozen all-terrain vehicles bumping hard and fast over the non-existent road reached her. Sh'ellah's men all spoke Arabic similar to that of the man lying in front of her. They'd identify him in moments, take him for enormous ransom…and destroy any evidence of their abduction. Within ten minutes she and all her friends would be blown to bits: another statistic to a world so inured to violence that they'd be lucky to make it to page twenty of a newspaper, or on the TV behind some Hollywood star's latest drunken tantrum.

'Fadi—Fadi, please, stay with me, brother! Stay!'

She had to do it. With a silent apology to the hero of her village, she heated a wet cloth over the fire and shoved it over his famous features to accelerate the fever already beginning to burn under his skin; she rubbed him down with a dry towel to make the temperature of his arms and legs rise. Her only chance lay with scaring the men into staying away from him...

And by shutting him up. She put her fingers to his throat and pushed down on his carotid artery, counting a slow, agonising one to twenty, until he collapsed into unconsciousness.

He had to be dreaming, but it was the sweetest dream of angel eyes.

Alim felt the fever creating needle-pricks of pain beneath his skin, the throbbing pain at his temple...but as he opened his eyes the confusion grew. Surely he was in Africa still? The hut looked African enough with its unglazed windows, and the cooking fire in the centre of the single room; the heat and dust, red dirt not sand, told him he was still in the Dark Continent.

'Where am I?' he asked the veiled woman bending over the cooking fire.

When she turned and limped towards him, he recognised the vortex of his centrifugal confusion: his angel-eyed goddess wasn't African. The face bending to his was half covered with a veil, but the green-brown eyes that weren't quite looking in his, gently slanted and surrounded by glowing olive skin, were definitely Arabic. They were so beautiful, and reminded him so much of home, he ached in places she hadn't disinfected or stitched up.

Perhaps it was the limp—anyone who climbed into a moving truck would have to hurt themselves; or maybe it was her voice he'd heard in fevered sleep, begging him to be quiet—but he was certain she'd been the one to save his life.

'You're in the village of Shellah-Akbar. How are you feeling?' she asked in Maghreb Arabic, a North African dialect related to his native tongue—haunting him with the familiarity. She was from his region—though she had the strangest accent, an unusual twang. He couldn't place it.

Intrigued, he said, 'I'm well, thank you,' in Gulf Arabic. His voice was rough against the symphony of hers, like a tiger sitting at the feet of a nightingale.

Her lashes fluttered down, but not in a flirtatious way; she acted like the shyest virgin in his home city. But she was veiled as a married woman, and working here as the nurse. He remembered her rapping out orders to others in several languages, including Swahili.

His saviour with the angel eyes was a modern woman, too confident in her orders and sure of her place to be single. Yet she chose to remain veiled, and she wouldn't meet his eyes.

She must be married to a doctor here. That had to be it.

It had been so long since he'd seen a woman behave in this manner he'd almost forgotten its tender reassurance: faithful women did exist. It had been a rare commodity in the racing world, and he'd seen few women that intrigued him in any manner since the accident.

'Now could you please tell me the truth?'

The semi-stringent demand made his dreams of gentle, angel-eyed maidens drop and quietly shatter. He looked up, saw her frowning as she inspected his wound. 'It's infected,' she muttered, probing with butterfly fingers. He breathed in the scent of woman and lavender, a combination that somehow touched him deep inside. 'I'm sorry. I had to cover the sutures with make-up and your hair, and increase your fever so Sh'ellah's men would believe you had the flu.'

'I've had far worse.' He saw the self-recrimination in those lovely eyes, heard it in the soft music of her voice. Wanting to see her shine again, he murmured, 'You were the one who came to the truck. That's why you're limping.'

Slowly she nodded, but the shadows remained.

'Did you stitch me up?'

Another nod, curt and filled with self-anger. Strange, but he could almost hear her thoughts, the emotions she tried to hide. It was as if something inside her were singing to him in silence, crying out to be understood.

Perhaps she was as isolated, as lonely for her people as he was. Why was she here?

'May I know my saviour's name?' he asked, his tone neutral, holding none of the strange tenderness she evoked in him.

The hesitation was palpable, the indecision. He took pity on her. 'If your husband...'

'I have no husband.' Her words had lost their music; they were curt and cold. She turned from him; moments later he heard the tearing sound of a medical pack opening.

He closed his eyes, cursing himself for not understanding in the first place. It had been so long since he'd dealt with a woman of his faith he'd almost forgotten: only a widow would come here, and one without a family to protect her. So young for such a loss. 'I'm sorry.'

With a little half-shrug, she leaned down to his wound. 'Please lie still. If your wound is to heal—and it has to do that, fast, before Sh'ellah's men return—I have to clean it again.'

He should have known she wouldn't be working on a man in this manner if she was married, unless she'd been married to a Westerner, and then she wouldn't be veiled.

The veil suited her, though. The seductive sweep of the sand-hued material over her face and body covered her form in comfort but protected her skin from the stinging dirt and winds without binding her. And the soft swish of the hand-stitched material as she walked—how she moved so beautifully with a limp was unfathomable, but he knew his angel was also his saviour.

She walks in beauty like the night. Or like a star of the sunrise...

'Thank you for saving my worthless life, Sahar Thurayya,' he said, with a bowing motion of his hands, since he couldn't move his head without ruining her work.

A brow lifted at the title he'd given her, *dawn star*, a courtesy name since she refused to give him her true name, but she continued her work without speaking.

'My name is Alim.'

To give her that much truth was safe. There were many men named Alim in his country, and courtesy demanded she introduce herself in return.

'Though dawn star is prettier,' she said quietly, 'my name is Hana.'

Hana meant *happiness*. 'I think *dawn star* is more suited to the woman you've become.'

She didn't look up from the intricate task of cleaning hair and packed-on make-up from his wound. 'You've known me all of ten minutes, yet you feel qualified to make such a judgement?'

She was right. Just because she was here, cut off from her own people, and was radiant with all forms of beauty *but* happiness—she seemed haunted somehow—gave him no right to judge her. 'I beg your pardon,' he said gravely in the dialect of his homeland.

'Please stop talking,' she whispered.

It was only then that he noticed the fine tremors in her hand. So his mere presence, their shared language, hurt her heart as much as hers did him. He closed his eyes and let her work in peace, breathing in the clean warm air and scent of lavender, a natural disinfectant.

She still wasn't risking using the medicines he'd brought, then.

When she seemed to be almost done with his wound, he murmured, 'Where's my truck?'

'Abdel drove it out to a remote part of the area. The villagers wiped all traces of the tyre tracks from the way in and out of the village. Don't worry, he'll hide it well, and will give you exact coordinates so you can get to it when you're feeling better.'

'Who am I?' When she frowned at him, obviously wondering if concussion had given him temporary amnesia, he added, 'To Sh'ellah's men, when they came? Who did you say I was?'

The fingers placing Steri-Strips over his wound trembled for a moment; again her agony of indecision felt like shimmering heat rising in waves from her skin.

He waited in silence. It seemed the last thing she needed was his voice, his language and accent reminding her of what she no longer had—though he wondered why she wasn't home with their people. Why his presence hurt her so.

She put the last Steri-Strip over his wound, and stepped back. 'When they came, I wore a full burq'a so they'd assume I was married. If they can't see, there's less for them to be tempted. You know how life is here.'

Intrigued again by this woman and the most prosaic acceptance of the ugly side of life, he nodded.

'When they came in here, they assumed you were my husband. Even unconscious, your presence as my man inspired respect for me, and protected me from abduction and rape—for now at least,' she finished bluntly. 'Sh'ellah still wants us to believe he's our saviour, and we're not giving him any reason to think otherwise.'

Alim saw the bubbling mass of emotion inside her pull apart into distinct, jagged pieces. Memory began returning to him like little shards of glass. She'd risked her life to come to him in the truck; she'd done so again by treating him in her hut, and claiming him as her man. He owed this woman his life at least twice over.

Slowly, as delicately as if he were creating an explosive cocktail of chemicals, he said, 'I'm privileged to be your husband in name, Sahar Thurayya. I'd be more honoured still if you would trust me while I'm here. It won't be long.'

She returned to his bedside with a cup of water. She took a sip first, then handed it to him and he drank in turn, his eyes on hers. The cup of agreement and peace: a traditional sign of mutual respect. A tradition he'd once given and accepted with so little thought—but now, looking in those brave, sad eyes, he felt the full honour of her offer.

It told him far more about this woman than anything that had come from her mouth. She was from Abbas al-Din, no matter what language she spoke.

Her eyes smiled, but her hand didn't touch his as she gave him the cup. 'Thank you.'

He noted she didn't use his name; she still kept her distance. In Hana's eyes, obviously trust was something earned, not given. He wondered how high the cost had been for misplaced trust in the past. Why did a woman with such pain beneath her smile risk her life and virtue in a place where nobody would live, if they had a choice?

'I'm afraid you can't leave yet. They know the supplies went somewhere, and you're the only stranger in the district,' she said as he filled his parched throat with cool water. 'Sh'ellah will have placed a dozen men on every way out of the village. They've been here several times in past months, collecting more than half our millet and corn harvest to feed his soldiers,' she said, bitterness threading through her voice. 'With a stranger in the village, they'll be watching all of us for weeks to come.' She sounded strained as she added, 'So I'm glad of your promise, since we will have to share my hut as husband and wife. There's only one bed here.'

He choked on the final gulp of liquid. Coughing, he turned his gaze to her. Strange that, with a throbbing headache and eyes stinging, he knew where she was at all times. His ears strained for the swish of her burq'a. She made a sound he'd heard all his life so alluring, so incredibly feminine. She seemed to infuse her every movement with life, light and beauty.

She made a sound of distress as she went on, 'I'm sorry, but we can't afford to bring in a spare bed in case Sh'ellah's men raid during the night, or lead a sneak attack. We have to sleep in one bed or risk suspicion—and out here suspicion is explained with an assault rifle.'

Alim stared at her back, so unyielding, refusing to face him. He thought of every day of his adult life spent avoiding this kind of intimacy, using the death of his young wife ten years before— the wife he'd liked but had never loved—as his excuse not to fulfil his duty and remarry. He thought of his adopted career of car racing, travelling from place to place, never settling down— holding himself off from living. Even now, wasn't he in hiding?

And he smiled; he grinned, and then burst out laughing.

'What's so funny?' Hana turned on him at the first sound of the chuckle bursting from his lips. Her veil fell from her lower face, showing lush dusky lips pursed with indignation. Her eyes flashed; even in the midst of angry demand, her voice was like the music of a waterfall. Her face, now revealed for a moment in all its glory, was harmony to its symphony.

And he was a complete idiot to think of her that way.

But it was the first time he'd truly laughed in three years, and he found that once he started again, he couldn't stop. 'It's—it's so absurd,' he gasped between fresh gusts of mirth.

Hana straightened her shoulders and looked him right in the eyes for the first time—and hers were contemptuous. Every feature of that lovely face showed disdain. 'Maybe it's ridiculous to you, but if it saves the lives of a hundred people— and I presume you care about their lives, since you risked your life to come here with food and medicines for them—I'll put up with the absurdity. The question is, will you?'

CHAPTER TWO

'WHAT's the unusual note in your accent?' the sheikh asked her, his tone abrupt at the subject change, but his dark green eyes were curious. Assessing her beyond the questions his simple words spoke. 'You haven't lived in the emirates all your life.'

Hana felt as if he were dissecting her without a scalpel. So he hadn't been fooled by her use of Maghreb, nor put off by her unaccustomed abruptness.

Not in the six months she'd been here in the village had simple conversation been fraught with such danger. If he knew the truth about his so-called saviour, he could take her freedom away with a snap of his fingers.

Her heart beat faster at the thought of saying anything—but thousands of Arabic girls grew up in Australia. Not so many people from Abbas al-Din had lived in Perth, of course, but enough that she wouldn't be easily traced.

Then she laughed at herself. What a ridiculous thought—as if Alim El-Kanar would care enough to trace her past! This wasn't the kind of information she needed to hide; it wasn't the reason she'd been shunned by her people. 'I was born in the emirates, but raised in Australia from the age of seven,' she answered, realising that a few minutes had passed while she'd been lost in thought—and that he'd allowed her to think without interruption.

'Ah.' He relaxed back on his pillows; she'd barely noticed his tension until then. 'I couldn't place the twang. Are you fluent in English?' he asked, changing languages without a break in speaking.

She nodded, answering in English. 'I lived there from the ages of seven to twenty-one, and went to state-run English schools.'

He grinned. 'You sound totally Aussie now you're speaking English.'

She laughed. 'I guess that's how I consider myself, mostly. My dad—' she'd practised so long, she could say 'dad' without choking up any more '—was offered an opportunity in the mining industry. He was a miner, but saved enough to go to university, and became an engineer. So he was rather unique in that he knew both sides...' *And that was way too much information!* She clamped her lips shut.

'I can see why any big mining corporation would want him,' he said, sounding thoughtful.

She'd started this, she had to finish or the sheikh would remember the conversation long after he was gone. She forced a smile through the lump in her throat, 'Yes, the money he was offered was so large he felt it would be irresponsible to the family to not take it. When we'd been there a little while, he and Mum felt it would be best for us if we retained our culture, but understood and respected the one we lived in. We lived not far from other Arabic families—but while we attended Islamic lessons, we also attended local schools.' And she'd just said more words together about herself than she had in years. She closed her mouth.

After a slow, thoughtful pause, the sheikh—she couldn't help but think of him as that—said, 'So if your father was in the mining industry, you lived in the outback? Kalgoorlie or Tom Price, or maybe the Kimberley Ranges?'

Her pulse pounded in her throat until her breath laboured. 'No, we didn't, but he did. We—my mother, my sisters and brother and I—lived in a suburb of Perth, and Dad lived in Kalgoorlie and came home Fridays. He wanted us to live close to...amenities.'

The sheikh nodded. She saw it in his eyes: he'd noticed the omission of the word *mosque*.

Even thinking the word was painful. She couldn't enter a mosque without people wanting to know who she was and where she was from; and she couldn't lie. Not in a holy place.

So she didn't go any more.

'Did you always wear the burq'a?' he asked, with a gentle politeness that told her he respected her secrets, her right to not answer.

'No. I'm from a moderate Sunni family. I wear it for protection.' She shrugged. 'Sh'ellah's very sweet to us—most of the time. But he could turn without warning.'

He's already sent men to ask if I have a man, or whether they can see whether I am young and pretty enough for his tastes.

She kept the shudder inside. Sh'ellah might be sixty-two, but he was a man of strong passions. Though he kept two wives, he had concubines in droves—and those were the women who pleased him. The others he discarded...and none of them ever came home.

Since she'd had the first warning of Sh'ellah's tastes, she'd kept the burq'a on as a knight's armour, wore her fake wedding ring like a talisman. She'd claimed her husband was travelling, and he'd soon be on his way here.

Her time here was over. Now she'd claimed the sheikh as her husband, Sh'ellah would expect her to leave with the sheikh when he went. Otherwise she'd become fair game.

She had two backpacks packed and ready, hidden in the dirt beneath her hut, ready to disappear at a moment's notice, to head by foot to the nearest refugee camp if need be. It was two hundred and sixty kilometres away, but she knew how to find edible plants filled with juice, and collect dew from upturned leaves. With two or three canteens of water, some purification tablets, three dozen long-hidden energy bars and a compass, she could travel at night and make it in fourteen days.

She'd been used for a man's purposes once. She'd rather die than be used that way again.

The sheikh nodded, as if he understood what she'd left unsaid. Maybe he did, if he'd been in the Sahel long enough.

'Were you brought up in the emirates?' She turned to the pit fire as she asked, making an infusion of her precious stores of willow bark for his fever in a tiny hanging pot. If people were seen to be carrying things into this hut, Sh'ellah's men would be searching here in minutes. She'd give them no excuse to pay attention to her.

She didn't have to wonder if he noticed she'd lapsed into their native language; she saw the flickering of those dark eyes, and knew he was sizing her up like one of his chemical equations. He took long moments to answer. 'Yes.'

That was it. Flat and unemotional-sounding, a mirror-world of unhealed pain behind the thin wall of glass, ready to shatter at a touch. She spooned some of her infusion into a cracked plastic mug. 'I'm sorry I have no honey to sweeten this, but it will lessen your pain.'

She saw the surprise come and go in his face. He wasn't going to ask, and she wasn't going to volunteer why she minded her own business; but she knew he'd think about it. Why she asked nothing more, demanded no answers in return for hers. 'Drink it all.'

He nodded, and took the cup from her. His fingers brushed

hers, and she felt a tiny shiver run through her. 'You don't call me by my name.'

She drew a breath to conquer the tiny tremors in her hands. What was wrong with her? 'You're a stranger, older than me, and risked a lot to help our village. I was taught respect.'

'I'm barely ten years your senior. I gave you my name,' he said, and drained the cup. He held it back out to her with a face devoid of expression, but she sensed the challenge within. The dominant male used to winning with open weapons…and beneath lurked a hint of irritation. He didn't like her calling him older. She hid the smile.

'You gave your name, but it's my choice to use it or not.' She took the cup back, neither seeking nor avoiding the touch. Just as she neither sought nor avoided his eyes. It was a trick her mother had taught her. *Everything you give to a man he can refuse to return, Hana. So give as little as possible, even a glance, until you are certain what kind of man you face.*

It had been good advice—until she'd met Mukhtar.

'You don't like my name, Sahar Thurayya?'

She washed the cup and returned it to its hook on the wall. Since she had no bench or cupboard, all things were either stacked on a box or hung on walls. 'I'm waiting to see if you live up to it.' She didn't comment on his poetic name for her, but a faint thrill ran through her every time she heard it. Just as she caught her breath when he smiled with his eyes, or laughed. And when he touched her… She closed her eyes and uttered a silent prayer. Four hours in this man's company, three of them when he'd been unconscious, and she was already in danger.

'So I must live up to my name?' Again she heard that rich chuckle in his voice. Without even turning around, she could see his face in her mind's eye, beautiful even in its damaged state, alight with the mirth that made him look as he had four years ago, and she knew she was standing in emotional quicksand. 'My brother always said I was misnamed.'

Alim: wise, learned.

She didn't ask in what ways he was unwise. He'd risked his life over and over for the thrill of racing and winning...

'It seems we were both misnamed,' he added, the laughter in his tone asking her to see the joke, as he had.

Hana: happiness.

I used to live up to my name, she thought wistfully. *When I was engaged to Latif, about to become his wife, then I was a happy woman.*

Then Latif's younger brother Mukhtar came into her life—and Latif showed her what her dreams of love and happiness were worth.

'I need to check on my other patients,' she said quietly. Checking to be certain her veil fully covered her, she walked with an unhurried step towards the medical tent—it hurt to rush since she had twisted her knee climbing into his truck—feeling his gaze follow her for as long as she was in sight.

Alim watched the doorway with views to the medical hut long after he could no longer see her. He still watched while the setting sun flooded the open door, long after his eyes hurt with the brightness and his head began knocking with the pain that would soon upgrade as the foul stuff she'd given him wore off.

She didn't draw attention to herself in any way—quite the opposite, including the burq'a the colour of sand, obviously handmade. She moved as little as possible, said nothing of consequence. She certainly wasn't trying to seem mysterious. Yet he sensed the emotion beneath each carefully chosen word; he saw the pain he'd caused her by saying her name didn't suit her.

She'd been a happy woman once—that much was obvious.

Something had happened to turn her into a woman who no longer saw happiness in her life or future.

There was a vivid *life* inside her, yet she lived in dangerous isolation in an arid war zone, in a hut with no amenities, far from family and friends. She was like a sparkling fountain stoppered without reason, a dawn star sucked down into a black hole.

He wanted to know why.

What would she look like if she truly smiled or laughed? To see her hair loose, wearing whatever she had on beneath the soft-swishing burq'a...

The last rays of the setting sun painted the ochre sand a violent scarlet. He blinked—and then it was blocked as her silhouetted form filled the doorway. She took on its hues, softened and irradiated them until she looked ethereal, celestial, a timeless beauty from a thousand Arabian nights, trapped in a labyrinth, needing a prince to save her.

'Do you need more pain relief yet?' A prosaic enough question, but in her voice, gentle and musical, it turned their native language into harps and waterfalls.

Alim blinked again. Stupid, stupid! He'd obviously knocked the part of his brain that created poetry or something. He'd never thought of any woman this way before, and he knew next to nothing about this one. Perhaps that was the fascination: she didn't rush into telling him about herself, didn't try to impress or please him. He was no Aladdin. If she needed a prince, he wasn't one any more, and never would be again. Then he would become a thief: of his brother's rightful position, stolen by a death he'd caused.

And if he kept thinking about it, he'd explode. Time to do what she was doing: make his thoughts as well as their conversation ordinary. 'Yes, please, Hana.'

The shock of sudden pain hit his eyes when she left the

doorway and the west-facing door took back the mystical shades of sunset, vicious to his head. It felt like a punishment for turning his saviour into an angel.

He'd obviously been alone too long—but after three years he still wasn't ready to show any woman his body. If he couldn't even look at himself without revulsion, he couldn't expect anyone else to manage it, let alone find him remotely attractive. Yet there was something about Hana that pulled at him, tugging at his soul—her beautiful eyes, the haunted, hunted look in them...

Hana's unveiled face suddenly filled his vision, and he blinked a third time, feeling blinded, not by the sun, but by her. Catching his breath seemed too hard; speech, impossible.

She didn't seem affected in any way by his closeness. 'Let this swill under your tongue a few moments; it'll work faster that way. You'll feel better soon, and tonight we can sneak in some paracetamol. I'm sorry we have no codeine, it's better for concussion, but stores are limited, as you know.'

Though her words were plain, it felt as if she was doing that thing again, saying too much and not enough. Talking about codeine to hide what she was really feeling.

Had he given himself away, shown that, despite his best attempt at will power, he couldn't stop thinking of her? The internal war raging in him, desire, fascination and self-hate, was so strong it was no wonder she saw it.

Then he realised something. He wasn't itching. He hadn't had the stress-trigger since he'd woken. And the scent of lavender and something else rose gently from his body. She'd rubbed something into his skin while he slept. She'd not only seen the patchwork mess that was his scars, but treated them.

The permanent reminder that he'd killed his brother, his best friend...

Grimly he swallowed the foul brew she handed him,

wishing he could ask for something to knock him out again. He handed it back with no attempt to touch her. She didn't want him, and touching her threatened to turn swirling winds of attraction into gale-force winds of unleashed desire that could make him start wanting things he didn't deserve.

'Thanks,' he said briefly, keeping his words and thoughts in prosaic English. Arabic had too many musical cadences, too much poetry for him to hear her speak it, see her lovely form and not be moved to his soul. But she couldn't possibly feel the same after seeing him. He revolted himself, and for more reasons than the physical.

'I'm fine if you need to see to your other patients. I'll sleep now.' He turned from her.

'You should eat first. You don't want to wake up hungry at midnight.'

Irritated beyond measure by her good sense, by her care for what he'd most wanted to hide, he rolled over and snapped, 'If I want food I'll ask for it, *Hana*.' He used cold, deliberate English, to remind her of the danger if she kept distancing herself from him.

In return she made a mocking bow, a liquid movement like the night gathering around her. 'Of course, my lord. I'll bring your food at midnight after caring for you and my patients all day, if such is your wish.' She wasn't smiling, but there was a lurking imp in her eyes…and she still hadn't said his name.

She'd left the hut before he recovered from the surprise that she was making fun of him. Putting him in his place with a few words… He watched her walk away, her body shimmering beneath her shifting burq'a like a fluid dance. 'Hana!' he yelled before he could hold it back.

She turned only her head, but he felt the smile she held inside. 'Yes, my lord?'

Though the term could be a continuation of her teasing, it

made him frown. What did she know about him? 'I'm sorry,' he growled. 'I'll eat whenever you think is best.'

She inclined her head. 'Concussion makes the best of us irritable.' Then she was gone.

It was forgiveness, he supposed, or understanding. He didn't particularly like either—or himself at this moment. He'd lost his inborn arrogance the day Fadi died, or so he'd thought.

Never had he acted with such arrogance with the lowest pit worker, and he'd *never* lost it over a woman's disinterest before. Yet within two hours of meeting Hana he'd become a cliché—a guy in lust with his nurse, cheated because she wasn't entertaining him with flirtation, or distracting him from his pain and lack of control over his body by touching him.

Cheated because she'd touched his body as a nurse, not a woman…by seeing him as a patient—a scarred, angry patient she needed to heal—and not a man.

Growling again, he rolled over and punched the thin pillow, folding it to make it thicker. But rest was impossible while he knew she'd be back.

It was deep in the night when he came awake with a smothered exclamation—smothered because a hand covered his mouth. 'Not a word,' an urgent voice whispered. The bed dipped and sagged as a soft, rounded backside snuggled into the cradle of his hips. Strange back-and-forth motions made the rusted bed squeak.

The hut was a gentle combination of silvery light and shadow. The tender lavender she wore ignited his senses; the feel of her against his body instantly aroused him. Did she taste as sweet and silky as she smelled and felt on his skin? And her hair was loose, reaching her waist in thick waves, falling over his bare arm in butterfly kisses. Like a paradox, the hand reaching backward, covering his mouth, held him silent in ruthless suppression.

'What are you doing?' It came out as muffled grunts.

'Sweeping my body indents from the ground,' she replied in a fierce whisper. 'I told you to be quiet. Now they'll know we're awake, and will want to know why. Take off your shirt.' She stood, and as he stripped off his shirt her burq'a fluttered to the ground, leaving her only in cami-knickers and a thin cotton vest top. 'Lie on me, and pretend to enjoy it,' she mouthed.

Pretend? The moment he was on her she'd know just how far from a game this was. He thanked Allah that though she'd seen and treated his scars, she couldn't see them in the dark.

Moments later she gasped softly and closed her eyes. Lying stiff and cold beneath him, she managed to whisper, 'Make sounds of pleasure.'

He groaned. Moving against her softness, his body realised how long it had been since he'd loved a woman. It was screaming to him to take this pretence to a perfect conclusion. Yet there'd been an odd note of intensity in her whisper. It went beyond what he would have expected in this situation, and from a widow.

Frowning, he looked down at her, moved by the incandescent beauty of her uncovered face, by the glossy waves of hair shimmering across his pillow and over her shoulders in the moonlight. 'It's all right, Hana, I've done this before.'

'What, you've faked it for killers before? What an adventurous life you've led,' she murmured mockingly in his ear; yet her teeth were gritted, her body so taut with rejection of his touch he thought if he moved at all, he might bounce right off her.

Lifting his face to see her more clearly in the glowing half-light, he saw her eyes were still closed, and there was a sheen of sweat on her brow. She was terrified and trying her best to hide it, but of what was she more frightened: the danger all around them, or the fact that the scarred, ugly stranger lying on her body was obviously ready for action?

Working on the instincts that had saved his life several times, he murmured in a croon he kept for intimate situations, but in English so the men outside wouldn't understand, 'Hana, this goes only as far as it needs to for Sh'ellah's men. You saved my life—you're saving my life again right now. I'd never hurt you or impose my will on you.'

She made a moaning sound that wouldn't fool Sh'ellah's men if they were in the radius of hearing. Her eyes remained squeezed tight shut. 'Thank you.' She arched her body up to his and made a more convincing noise of passion.

Feeling her sweet-scented, fluid body against him, he almost forgot his good resolutions.

Then she stiffened and made a muffled noise, as if finding release. 'Alim,' she cried, using his name for the first time. 'Alim, my love, I've missed you so much!'

Moments later a face appeared at the window; its shadow blocked the moonlight. 'Who is there?' Alim demanded harshly in Maghreb. 'Leave us to our privacy!'

The light reappeared as the head disappeared. He heard a whisper in a mixture of English and another language, but was unable to make it out. He spoke all forms of Arabic, French, German and English, but the African cadences were beyond him.

'Swahili,' she whispered, as tense as her body, though her voice had returned to the voice of a stranger, keeping him at a distance. 'They're saying that Sh'ellah—the local warlord—won't be pleased at this. He had plans for me.'

'I know who Sh'ellah is.' Anyone who'd worked more than a year in the Sahel knew the names of local warlords and what boundaries were where. A wise man also made certain he knew when and where the borders shifted, or he ended up carrion feed. 'He wants you?' he almost groaned in despair. 'That complicates matters.'

'He wants me because I'm young and different to most women in the region. He knows nothing of me. I've always been heavily veiled when his men come. All they or he ever see is my eyes.' She shrugged, in a fatalistic gesture. 'I'm packed and ready to leave. I can go tonight—but you won't make it. We have to wait another day.'

'No.' He knew what she hadn't said: Sh'ellah would think nothing of killing him to have Hana once or twice, before dumping her body in the shifting sands. 'I've worked through injury before. We should get out of here tonight.'

Worried eyes searched his. 'We have to be several kilometres away before they find we're missing, and you were unconscious only hours ago. Fever and concussion aren't conditions to play with.'

Touched by her concern, he whispered, 'I'll be all right.'

She made an impatient gesture. 'No, you won't—but there's no choice. We need to head to the refugee camp. A plane arrives on Wednesdays. It's Thursday now—it will take almost two weeks by foot. With your injuries, we'll need an extra day, travelling by night. We'll take pain-relief tablets with us, a suture kit and extra water.'

'If we head for the truck we don't need to take more than four days. We can drive the rest of the way.'

She frowned. 'That's sixty kilometres away.'

Teeth gritted now, he muttered, 'I'll make it.'

'All right, if you say so.' Those lovely, slanted eyes stared in open doubt. 'I think you can roll off me now. It's customary.'

He wanted so badly to laugh, he did, but made it low and rippling, like a lover's laugh.

He was stunned by her quick thinking and thorough planning. His respect for her grew by the minute. Yet Alim was acutely aware of her near-nude body beneath him, her braless state, the sweetness of her skin and her gentle scent. It was almost a relief to move away, to gain distance—but she snuggled into his arms, making sure the sheet covered the clothes they still wore.

'My love,' she murmured in Maghreb. 'We'll have to take an old suture kit, and bring only the willow-bark infusion,' she whispered, making it seem intimate. 'I'm sorry, but we buried all the new medications. We can't afford to dig them up now.'

'It's okay.' He gathered her against him, kissing her hair—and the lavender filled his head. 'I love your scent.'

Her mouth tightened. She stiffened in his arms, and the budding trust vanished. 'It's not meant to entice. It's to keep off fleas, mosquitoes and bed bugs. Scorpions don't like it, either.'

She sounded frozen. Given the stiff revulsion she'd exhibited only moments before, Alim wanted to kick himself for being so stupid as to think she could want him. Right now, he could think of no reassurance that she'd believe, so he drawled, 'Bed bugs and scorpions…oh, baby, nobody does pillow talk the way you do.'

After a stunned few seconds, she burst out laughing.

Relief washed through him, and he grinned—but the way her face came alive with the smile, the harplike sound of her laughter, made him ache. Now he could see how well her name suited her—or it had once.

Then she whispered, 'I have an aloe and lavender cream for your scars, as well. It looks as though you need pain relief for it. You never finished the plastic surgery you needed, did you?'

She'd ruined their connection by the question, by mentioning his deformity and all its reminders. He moved away from her, trying not to show how hard it was not to fling her away. It was all he could do to ground out a single word. 'No.'

As if she heard his thoughts, she backed off. 'We need to be gone in an hour. There's only one way from the village they won't be covering—where the wild dogs are. It'll be dangerous, but they usually sleep until dawn. We have to be past their territory by then. There's a small track, an old dried stream we can take, which has some shade for sleeping by day.'

'Right,' he replied, wondering if the feel of his skin against her had done anything but revolt her, having seen him unclothed...having treated his burns as no one had done since he left the private facility in Bern three years ago.

He closed his eyes, squeezing them tight. No wonder she'd been so stiff and cold with him. No wonder she'd turned aside when he'd called her his dawn star. He was a poet from the slag heaps, a monster daring to look upon beauty and hunger for what he couldn't have.

Hana wasn't the kind of woman who'd welcome his touch for his wealth, and he was fiercely glad of that—of course he was. He wasn't that desperate.

'I'll ask one of the men here to pack you a change of clothes. We can only take one each; we need the room for water and medicine. I have dried fruits and energy bars stored in my backpack. We'll fill one canteen with willow-bark infusion for your pain. You'll have to be sparing with it.'

He kept his voice brisk and practical, hiding his turmoil of desire and sickening acceptance of her rejection. 'Travelling at night should help. I have some ibuprofen in my pack I can use. Only a dozen tablets, but—'

She rolled up and sat at the edge of the bed. 'Excellent.' She actually smiled at him. His heart flipped over at the look in her eyes, holding no pity, just approval; and even if she only smiled in relief that he wouldn't be moaning and groaning all the way to the refugee camp, he'd take it. He'd take any piece of happiness she doled out to him, because it felt as if she hoarded it like miser's gold. And it might just mean she wasn't totally revolted by him.

What had happened to her to change her from the happy woman she'd been once, he didn't know—but he had at least a week to find out.

CHAPTER THREE

IT WAS close to three a.m. before they left the hut. Flickering lights a short distance away showed Alim how closely the village was being watched.

'We'll need to commando crawl,' he whispered as they watched another cigarette being lit, another flashlight sweep a slow arc. 'These packs are bulky.'

She nodded. 'And we have to move in silence. They have to believe the villagers know nothing except my husband showed up without warning yesterday, and we disappeared at night.' She handed him a bundle of clothes. 'Put these on. You need to blend into the environment.'

He looked at the clothes, some kind of dun colour, smeared with mud and dirt, and felt intense admiration for her yet again. She thought of everything. 'Can you turn your back?' he asked gruffly, unable to stand that she'd be revolted by his body again.

She nodded and turned away. He felt pity radiating from her, but her practical words made him wonder if the compassion he'd sensed had been the workings of his paranoid imagination. 'You won't be able to wear your clothes until we're out of Sh'ellah's reach.'

As he turned to answer she slipped out of her burq'a with

a swift movement, and his breath caught in his throat, remembering her lovely curved body in the knickers and camisole…

He swallowed the ridiculous disappointment. Of course she wore jeans and a long-sleeved shirt with running shoes beneath! What colour he couldn't make out in the murky darkness, but probably brown, like his; her hair looked plaited. She rolled the garment up and stored it in her backpack, and shoved her plait beneath a brown cap.

She shouldered her pack and dropped to the ground, and began belly-crawling. 'Let's go.'

Ignoring the severe pounding inside his head, the light fever that still hadn't abated, he lay down flat and followed her.

It took a gruelling half-hour to make it past the village boundaries to the territory of the wild dogs. Now the moon had set past the village, the delicate filigree beauty around him had faded to a grim, dusty night as thick as the dirt coating them further with every movement.

Alim followed Hana around the hut to the fields, heading towards the only path out, his concentration on two things—being quiet, and trying with all his might not to cough or sneeze. The neckerchief she'd given him to cover his nose and throat was so thickly coated in dirt it was hard to breathe. His scarred skin began to pull and itch in moments.

At the head of the path, she thrust a canteen in his hands. 'Wet the bandanna using as little water as possible, and wring it out,' she whispered in his ear. 'We have to stay flat until we reach the stream bed. Our last opportunity to fill the canteens for fifty kilometres will be there. Move slowly, and try not to let your sweat touch ground. We can't afford to make a sound, or give off any scent. The dogs don't have assault rifles, but they can tear you apart in seconds.'

So that was why she'd only brought dried, wrapped food, and double-wrapped everything in tight-tied bags. Fighting

the unwanted arousal her lips against his ear had given him—
damn his body for all the stupid ideas it had—he nodded and
kept following her. Elbows thrust forward and sideways, then
a knee, one side then the other, measuring every movement
in case it was too big or would dislodge a pebble and make a
noise to alert the dogs.

The next hour was excruciating. *Breathing through a wet
bandanna, don't move too fast, don't cough or sneeze, don't
itch, don't break into a sweat, don't make a noise or you'll
become dog meat.* He was forced to follow her, his head
pounding with concussion and the stress of aching to go
forward, to take the lead and somehow protect her, but this
was her turf. She alone knew the way out of danger.

For the first time in his life he had to trust a woman in a life
and death situation—but from everything she'd already done,
all without flinching or complaint, he knew if there was one woman
on earth he could hand control to without fear, it was Hana.

Finally, as he knew he had to breathe clean air or pass out,
the flat ground gave way, and they slithered slow and quiet
down a little slope; the dust became hard, crusty earth, the
cracked mud of a dead stream, and when he heard Hana give
a soft sigh he sensed they'd passed at least the first of the
current menace facing them.

He slipped the bandanna from his nose and mouth, and
dragged in a breath of fresh air without a word. Never had
breathing felt so luxurious.

'No water here.' She sighed. 'Our task just got harder, and
you're still concussed. Are you sure you're up to this? Once
they know we're gone there's no turning back.'

'I can do it,' he reiterated through a clenched jaw. Did she
think he couldn't take a little hardship just because of a bump
on the head, a touch of fever?

'We have to turn north as soon as we can.' The words

breathed in his ear, softer than a whisper, slow and clear, making him shiver in sensuous reaction. 'We still have fifty kilometres to the truck.' The second zephyr of sound stirred his hair and left a small trail of goose bumps.

'Maybe we should leave it where it is and travel south toward the refugee camp by night,' he whispered, as soft as he could. 'If they've found the truck they'll expect us to come for it.'

'You'll never make it to the camp by foot with concussion—it will only worsen without rest. And the boundaries for the warlords change almost daily. If we cross one unseen line, you're dead, and I soon will be, once Sh'ellah finishes with me.'

He shuddered with the force of the flat whisper. 'It'll take three more days to reach the truck, and then we have to backtrack. A hundred and sixty kilometres through enemy lines in a truck so noticeable it practically screams *foreigners*.'

She looked at him, her eyes cool, calm—and how she made him ache with her beauty when she was coated in dust and clumps of mud, wearing a baseball cap and a shirt that looked like charity would reject it, he had no clue. 'Let's go.'

The utter relief to be upright, enjoying the luxury of walking again, flooded him until the headache grew to severe proportions. He said nothing to her until she called for another halt.

After he'd taken some tablets with water, she said, 'We've gone almost as far as we can before sunrise.' She saw him rubbing at his underarm with his arm, trying to scratch unobtrusively. 'How's your skin? Is it itching with all the dirt?'

His jaw tightened and he stopped moving. Yet another reminder: Beauty was letting the Beast know just who he was to her, reminding him what he was to himself. 'I'm fine.'

'I don't want to embarrass you. You won't be able to travel at night if the grafted skin or the burns rip, bleed or itch. We just crawled more than five kilometres. There has to be damage.'

'I said I'm fine.' He sounded curt with rejection she didn't deserve, but he couldn't help it. 'Give me the cream and I'll do it when I need it.'

Hana sighed. 'There are ways to rub the cream in that optimise stretching and physical comfort for you while we're travelling. It will also give you better sleep. I can see you're uncomfortable with my doing it, but we have four days of hard walking to go, sleeping in dirt and mud that could irritate your skin, and—'

Alim heard his teeth grind before he spoke. 'You're not going to stop arguing until you get your way, are you?'

'Probably not,' she conceded with a gentle laugh.

His head felt like a light and sound show, brilliant stabs of pain shooting from his neck to his eyes. He couldn't manage rubbing the entire length of his scars now if he tried. 'Do it, then.'

The words had been clipped, order from master to servant, but she didn't argue. 'Stay still, and close your eyes.' Her voice was gentle, soothing, stealing into his battleground mind with tender healing.

He felt her undoing the buttons of his shirt…oh, God help him for the male reaction to her touch she'd be bound to see. The sun was beginning to rise.

'Your tension won't help, you know. Breathe deeply, relax and let me make it better.'

She might have been speaking to a child, but her warm, wet hands against his itching, burning scars, filled with beautiful, scented oils, took away any power to speak. He breathed, and felt the irritable tension leaving him, leaving him only aroused.

'That's it, much better. I'm sorry I can't use any water to wash away the dirt, but the olive oil is helping.' Her hands were tender magic, kneading softly, moving in slow, deep circles. Her fingers rotated over his skin, deep then soft; her palms pushed up and around, spreading more oil. 'This solution is fifty per cent cold-pressed olive oil, forty per cent pure aloe juice and ten per cent essential oils of lavender, rosemary and neroli. I make ten litres a month for burns victims or scarring from rifle wounds. A village about forty kilometres from the refugee camp is a Free Trade village, and orders everything I need.'

'Hmm.' She could be reciting the alphabet or the phone book for all he cared. Her voice was a siren's call, an angel's song; her touch was sweet relief, *bliss*, releasing him from the burning ropes of limited movement, giving him freedom to lift his arm as she moved it to massage where the scar tissue was worst. Though she said and did nothing a nurse wouldn't do for any patient, she made him feel like a man again, because she'd treated him like a man.

'It's feeling better?' she asked softly. She sounded—odd.

'Oh, yeah,' he mumbled. Feeling as if he were floating, he opened his eyes to a slit—and if he weren't so utterly relaxed he'd have started. Hana was looking at his body as she massaged, and it held no revulsion, no clinical detachment. Her eyes in the soft rose light of the sunrise looked deeper, softer…her breathing had quickened…she wet her lips…

Then she looked at his face, her cheeks flushed and her lips parted in innocent, lush surprise, and in her expression was something he'd *never* seen from any nurse.

It was something he'd never seen from any *woman*. Those lovely, slanted almond eyes held something like innocent languor…beautiful, breathtaking, aching *desire*. Good, old-fashioned, honest wanting, woman to man.

Then she saw his eyes open, and the look vanished as if it had never been there. 'Good. I'm glad it helped,' she said, her tone aiming for crisp, but it wobbled a touch. 'Get dressed. If

I remember rightly, there's a good overhang a few kilometres away, where we can sleep.'

Was he possibly grinning as widely as he wanted to? 'Why don't we sleep here? You look so tired, and it's been a long, hard day for us both.'

'It isn't far enough from the village.' She was the one now speaking through gritted teeth. 'When we reach the truck, you call the shots. Right now, this is my territory. If you want to live, you're doing things my way.'

Unable to muster up an argument when she'd saved his life again tonight, he shrugged; but he hated that she was right and he couldn't argue, couldn't take charge and protect her somehow. 'Three days,' he said softly. 'Then you'd better believe I'm calling the shots. I'll get you to the refugee camp safely, Hana, that I swear—but you'll obey me, no questions asked.' *And we're going to explore that look you gave me just now,* the man in him vowed, exultant.

She nodded; far from pushing back, there was a suspicious twinkle in her eyes. 'I will obey you joyfully, my lord, for I am a weak woman in need of your strength.' She mock-genuflected before him, touching her forehead to the ground as she spoke. 'It must be the reason why I never left the village before. I was waiting for you to guide and direct me.'

He had to choke down laughter at her unexpected sense of humour. 'Can it, Hana,' he said, using a phrase from one of his former pit crew, 'and let's get going.'

She grinned and bowed again; then, with a grin that held more than a touch of the imp—pretty, so damned *pretty*—she said, 'We should crawl again for a while. It's getting light.'

The prospect made him forget temptation for the present. Alim groaned and dropped to his stomach, but Hana was ahead of him, already wriggling down the hill.

He'd been too busy trying to breathe before to notice how

enticing that wriggle was. No—he'd ignored it, thinking it was useless. But after that *look*…

If they'd been anywhere else, had she been another woman…but they were crawling through mud in wild dogs' territory with a warlord's men with assault rifles in every other direction; and this was Hana, who'd frozen beneath him. She deserved his respect, not the burden of unwanted fascination from a man who looked like a damned monster—and he had no magical spell she could reverse with her kiss. The way he looked now was how he'd look for life.

The look had to have been a mistake. He was a nowhere man with no home, no position. He had nothing to offer any woman but ugliness, emotional baggage and a cartload of regrets—and he suspected she had more than enough of her own without taking his on board. Whatever that look had been, she didn't, couldn't want him. He could take that. Just keep commando crawling *and don't look*.

'The creek bed's lined with stones for the next few kilometres. Take these,' she murmured tersely a few minutes later, flipping some leather gloves back at him. 'You'll sweat, but it's better than leaving a blood trail behind for jackals and dogs to find.'

'Thanks,' he muttered back, pulling them on. The skin of his hands had begun to rip, and his clothes were well on their way to becoming shreds, but his hands were the worst. He pulled out a plastic bag from his pack, and shoved it between his T-shirt and the dying jacket to keep his scars from bleeding. If nothing else, it would stop the blood from touching the ground for a few more minutes.

'Come on,' she whispered in clear impatience as she crawled on.

That was the only conversation they had in two hours.

The sun had risen above the eastern rim of the creek wall

before she called a halt. 'We're only seven or eight kilometres from the village, but this overhang's the best shelter we'll find for hours. Let's eat and get some sleep.' She leaned against the overhang wall and stretched her back and shoulder muscles with a decadent sigh before rummaging in her backpack.

Refusing to watch—she was killing him with every shimmering movement of her sweetly curved body, her pretty face—Alim sat beside her and stretched too, over and over to work out the kinks—and he was surprised to find the concussion hadn't left him revolted by the thought of food as it always had before when he had concussion, after hitting his head in a race. Despite that his brain was banging against his skull and his eyes ached and burned, his stomach welcomed the thought with rumbling growls.

So he stared when all she handed him was a raisin-nut energy bar.

'Eat it slowly. It's all we can afford to use. I'd only saved enough for me to escape with, so half-rations are all we have.' She surveyed his face, his eyes. 'You're in pain. Take a few sips of the willow bark before you sleep.'

Irritated by her constantly ordering him around, by seeing him as a *patient* after their gruelling trek, he flipped his hand in a dismissive gesture. 'I'll sleep it off.'

'Don't be stubborn. You'll be no use tonight if the pain gets worse. You're less than twenty-four hours from concussion. Take the willow bark, and some ibuprofen with it.'

She was really beginning to annoy him with her imperious, *'don't be stupid'* tone. No woman apart from his mother had ever spoken to him this way. But she was right, so he obeyed the directive, drinking a long swig of the foul medicine with one precious tablet.

'Go ahead and say it.' She sounded amused.

He turned to her, saw the lurking twinkle in her eyes. There were smile-creases in her face through the caked-on dirt. And no poetry came to his mind. No woman had ever laughed at him, either, unless he'd made a joke. 'What?'

She waved a hand as scratched and cut as his. 'You know, the whole "don't boss me around, I'm the man and in control" routine. You're the big, strong man, and dying to put me in my place. Go on, I can handle it.' Her teeth flashed in a cracked-mud smile.

With her words, his ire withered and died. 'Did it show that much?' he asked ruefully.

She nodded, laughing softly, and he was fascinated anew with the rippling sound. If he closed his eyes, he didn't see the maiden from the bowels of the worst pig-pits, torn and bleeding and coated in mud. She stank; they both did—but he'd rather be here smelling vile beside Hana than in a palace with a princess, because Hana was real, her emotions honest, not hidden because of his station in life. She laughed at him and teased him for his commanding personality, and once the initial annoyance wore off he rather liked it.

'I have no right to assert my authority over you.' Stiff words from a man unused to apologising for anything—but it felt surprisingly good when it was out there.

Flakes of dried mud fell from her forehead as her brows lifted. 'Did that hurt?'

He sighed. 'You really are Australian in your outlook, aren't you? You bow to no man. Your father must have had a really hard time if he was the traditional kind—'

He closed his mouth when he saw the look in her eyes. Devastated. Betrayed. A world of pain unhealed. And hidden deep beneath the pain was defiance. She was fighting against odds he couldn't see, and he sensed she'd refuse to show him if he asked.